A Lady's Guide to Marvels and Misadventure

A Lady's Guide to Marvels and Misadventure

A NOVEL

ANGELA BELL

BETHANY HOUSE

a division of Baker Publishing Group

Minneapolis, Minnesota

© 2024 by Angela Bell

Published by Bethany House Publishers
Minneapolis, Minnesota
www.bethanyhouse.com

Bethany House Publishers is a division of
Baker Publishing Group, Grand Rapids, Michigan

Printed in the United States of America

Library of Congress Cataloging-in-Publication Data
Names: Bell, Angela, author.
Title: A lady's guide to marvels and misadventure / Angela Bell.
Description: Minneapolis, Minnesota : Bethany House, a division of Baker
    Publishing Group, 2024.
Identifiers: LCCN 2023040917 | ISBN 9780764242137 (paperback) | ISBN
    9780764242717 (casebound) | ISBN 9781493445110 (ebook)
Subjects: LCGFT: Christian fiction. | Romance fiction. | Novels.
Classification: LCC PS3602.E4477 L34 2024 | DDC 813/.6—dc23/eng/20231003
LC record available at https://lccn.loc.gov/2023040917

The author is represented by MacGregor Literary.

Baker Publishing Group publications use paper produced from sustainable forestry
practices and post-consumer waste whenever possible.

24 25 26 27 28 29 30   7 6 5 4 3 2 1

This book is dedicated
to the woman who taught me to read and write.
The woman who taught me to offer hospitality
in a teacup and embrace my inner hat lady.
The woman who, through example, taught me
to love when it's hard, hope when it hurts,
and cling to Emmanuel even when He feels far away.

This one's for you, Mama.

I love you more!

FEBRUARY 1860
LONDON, ENGLAND

For Miss Clara Marie Stanton, the task of preventing her family from being committed to an asylum had become as commonplace as it was exhausting.

Ever since word of her broken engagement had gotten out three months prior, rumors had flown about town like a colony of bats, screeching allegations of hereditary insanity and a contaminated bloodline. Unfortunately, her ever-amused family found their new title of "dangerous loons" quite hilarious and saw no reason to temper their eccentric habits.

Which is why, on this late-February day, Clara found herself dashing across London to stop her dear mother from protesting outside yet another millinery shop that trimmed their wares with avian plumes.

Clara worried her hands, aggravating the frayed seams of her gray gloves as she navigated one of the West End's popular shopping districts that teemed with parasols and pretension. Why must Mum go sneaking off like this? Why couldn't she have ignored the advertisement for Petite Paris' new stock of feathered fans? If she would simply bide her time, Mum could resume her unconventional cause as soon as they were out of danger. Not today, when the slightest bizarre incident might bring ruin to those she loved most.

"Is that the Stanton girl? Mr. Forrester's fiancée?"

A mother and daughter strolled arm in arm as they blatantly gawked in her direction.

The mother smirked. "Former fiancée. Lucky bloke missed the noose on that one."

Clara's jaw clenched. Gossiping gnats always turned things the wrong way round, biting the wounded who dared to bleed. She averted her gaze and used the brim of her bonnet as blinders. Would she ever cease to be shocked by London's insatiable desire for gossip? By mouths eager to spew ash and soot, like so many factory chimneys, with little regard for those who suffocated in the process? By Rupert's lack of remorse for igniting the rumor mill's blaze?

No, not Rupert. Mr. Forrester. The man forfeited the right to such familiarity months ago, so she'd not grant it to him now, even in thought.

A sign hanging above the crowded street caught her eye. The wood, carved to resemble a globe, was emblazoned with the initials J. W., backed by a crown. Ah yes, it was Mr. James Wyld's distinguished cartography shop, favored by the queen herself. She used to love perusing that establishment with Papa. They'd go in to acquire up-to-date maps for his fleet of merchant ships, and inevitably, after much oohing and aahing from Clara, she'd walk out with a new map all her own.

She paused before the familiar storefront. A pair of globes stood in the window display. One terrestrial and one celestial, both accented with gold leaf and perched upon bases of mahogany. Betwixt them, resting open-faced upon a blanket of velvet, lay a map of Italy. Elegant in its exactness. Pristine in its design. She traced a finger across the glass separating her from the Mediterranean Sea. Beautiful waters she'd only ever read about.

The waters she'd planned to sail across on her wedding journey.

Clara's fingers curled into a fist upon the glass. All her maps had been packed in trunks and entombed in the attic for a reason. She'd not the time to entertain foolish dreams. She had responsibilities. A family counting on her to be their level head and steady shoulders now that Granny was no longer here to do so.

Prying herself away, Clara turned onto the next street, where the fashion industry ruled, and passed fortunate mercers and milliners currently not blockaded by her mother.

Minutes later, a strident voice with the authority of a general and the sweetness of a sugarplum assured Clara her quarry was near. Standing on tiptoe to gain perspective over the throng, she spotted Mum chanting and marching in a one-woman military formation. *Caught you, Mummy dearest.*

She hastened toward Petite Paris Millinery, where the object of Mum's fury was displayed with a sign reading, *The finest fashions direct from France.* The finest, apparently, were white satin bonnets paired with ivory-handled fans and parasols— all trimmed with fluttering plumes. Mum wouldn't be easily averted from this affront to her principles.

Mum turned on her heel and discovered she'd been caught, which only enhanced the impish twinkle in her blue eyes. "Excellent timing, ducky. I was about to begin a dramatic reading of 'Maker of Heaven and Earth.' When I reach the stanza 'Each little bird that sings,' why don't you pipe in with a convicting chant such as 'They sing no more, dead in your store'? That will ruffle some feathers of conscience."

The stares of passersby branded *dangerous loons* on the back of Clara's neck. "Mum, I can't—"

"Of course you can. Resist the treacherous tentacles of timidity." Mum dragged Clara into the conspicuous demonstration. "Let's march a bit to build your confidence."

"Mum. We've discussed this. We agreed to abstain from protests until—" A gasp seized Clara's throat. "Tell me my sight is failing and you are not wearing Fred about your neck. Please. Tell me I need spectacles. Tell me I'm hallucinating."

"Your sight is as keen as a hawk's."

Perfect. Fred, the very alive ermine, lounged about Mum's neck like an expensive stole. "Mum, you promised."

"I promised to do what was best, and taking a stand against cruelty is the best thing to be done. Those feathers belong on birds, amongst the clouds, not plucked and pinned to a matron's coif. And don't even get me started on the ivory." Tears puddled in Mum's eyes as her pinched lips fanned out in a manner tragically comical. "When I think of what is done to those precious elephants . . . those majestic, God-formed pachyderms . . . I-I-I—"

Oh dear. Here it comes.

Clara grasped the silver vial of smelling salts hanging from the chatelaine pinned to her skirt and shoved it under Mum's nose before a fit of vapors could draw an audience. "Breathe. Come now, Mum. Inhale gently . . . now exhale. Good. Once more, inhale."

"Gah, I've snorted one!" Mum's face contorted as she sneezed and sputtered. Sputtered and sneezed. "Owww! Mercy, but those salts burn something fierce."

"Perhaps you'll remember that fact and not inhale so aggressively in the future." Clara reattached the vial to her chatelaine and opened a small pouch hanging from a different chain, soon producing a clean handkerchief. "Here you are."

Mum accepted the handkerchief, dabbing stray tears, before giving her nose a sound blow. "Thanks, ducky. I don't know what I would do without you."

"Get arrested, I expect, which is why I must insist we go home. Making your stand amid speculation of insanity is hardly beneficial to your cause." She stepped closer to whisper, "And what of Fred?"

Clara met the spoiled ermine eye-to-eye, attempting to glower in censure, but the endeavor was undermined when his whiskers tickled her nose. She suppressed a grin. This adorable rascal, with his lame legs that trailed behind him when he scuttled about the house, was her favorite of all Mum's disabled rescues. And the one that caused the most trouble. "Oh, Fred . . . you don't exactly defend Mum's soundness of mind, you know."

Vocalizing his pleasure with a soft *took-took-took*, Fred tilted his furry brown head and begged to have his chin scratched.

Clara obliged his request, scratching his tiny jaw . . . until pedestrians with more perfume than politeness began to stare. She withdrew her hand from the "stole" and straightened her shoulders. "Please, listen to reason. We cannot afford for Fred to indulge in excursions at present."

"Horsefeathers." Puckering her lips to Fred, Mum stroked the top of his brow. "You needed fresh air, did you not, Freddy? Poor little dear. Besides, he's a champion reformer. Nothing makes a lady reconsider the violent tendencies of fashion like admiring a beautiful stole only to have it nibble her hand."

"Mother!" Clara glanced at a giggling party of shoppers. *Please, God, let it be that no one heard that remark.*

With a gentle yet determined grip, Clara guided Mum away from Petite Paris and endeavored to conceal them behind a lamppost. She took a breath to rid her voice of the fear and irritation churning in her stomach. "Mum, you know I love and support you, always. However, in our current circumstances, we must be cautious. If Fred nips one more hand—just one—

the constable warned you could be brought up on charges. Even arrested. Like it or not, you can't help a single creature if our good name is reduced to refuse in the gutter, so please, promise me—no more protests or outings with Fred until our current predicament has been resolved."

With a huff, Mum crossed her arms. "Such vain imaginings are absolute balderdash. But I shall agree for your sake. On one condition."

Thank heavens. "Anything."

"Get yourself out of the house more often."

"Why . . . I leave the house every day."

"Popping into the clock shop to check on your grandfather hardly qualifies. Much of your time is spent stuffed up in the house, working. You work as your grandfather's nurse. You work as your papa's secretary. You work as our housekeeper and my very right hand. So much labor without any amusement is not healthy. You need to have fun, ducky. Attend the ballet. Meet people. Take a trip to the seaside. Have an adventure like you always planned."

Like Rupert—Mr. Forrester—and I had always planned.

When they'd first met, she'd been a starry-eyed dreamer of twelve, and he'd been a furrow-browed planner of fifteen. Spending their time tucked away in the library with a stack of travel guides, an open map, and voracious wanderlust. Growing, planning, and dreaming together. Little Atlas and Buccaneer Bill off to tour the world . . . until they weren't. Until she'd discovered his duplicitous reasons for matrimony. Until she had given up the ring and any desire for adventure.

Pollutants in London's atmosphere triggered a fine, stinging mist in Clara's eyes. "If I attend a ballet with Papa's escort, may we call a truce?"

"Very well." Mum gave Clara's arm a tender pat. "I probably ought to return home in any case. In my haste this morning,

I neglected to give Cook instructions regarding tonight's dinner party."

Clara's heart tilted on its axis. Society had been turned against them—spies had been sent amongst them—and Mum wished to host a dinner party? "W-with humans?" *Please let the guests consist of feathered friends.*

"Only a few of your father's business associates. And some neighbors. And a couple ladies from my whist consortium. And a couple more from the Charitable Ladies League. I invited Emily and Bridgette, but they've yet to send a response, so I don't know whether to expect them."

Of course, her would-have-been bridesmaids hadn't bothered to reply. Like the rest of her friends, they'd severed all ties once the rumors began and the scandal broke, lest they become tainted by association. Just last week, on her way to Grand's shop, Emily and Bridgette had spotted her and promptly crossed to the other side of the street in a choreographed *cut*, as if they'd never known her and didn't wish to suffer the misfortune. Only kindhearted Mum would take such a slight to be accidental and invite them to dinner in good faith.

"If the girls don't pop by, we should only have sixteen guests, all told."

A vein in Clara's temple twitched. Sixteen people in the house, and any number of them might well be informants for Mr. Forrester. Lured by his coin. Armed by his spite. Dispatched by his command to scour their home for the leverage he sought to validate his claims and cement his revenge.

"How can you welcome outsiders into the house after all that transpired? After what happened just yesterday? Your room is still in shambles." Drawers overturned. Chair cushions sliced. At least this latest spy, a chimney sweep who'd charmed Mum into giving him work, had been decent enough to look shamefaced when caught and confess by whom he'd been paid—a dapper bloke by the name of Forrester. A revelation that confirmed her mounting suspicions and worst fears.

Mum gave Clara's cheek a gentle pat meant to reassure. "Things can be replaced, and the room can be set to rights soon enough. No real harm was done."

But the potential for harm was all too real. She shuddered to think how differently things might have ended yesterday. "What if that man had taken his knife to you or Papa instead of the furnishings?"

"The man was a dishonest and destructive thief, I admit, but I can't believe he'd have gone so far as to hurt anyone. People with dimples are rarely given to violence."

Oh, Mum. How could she still be so naïve? "Call off the dinner party, please. Inviting people into the house poses too great a risk. As long as Mr. Forrester persists in his search, we should operate under the assumption that all outsiders are spies and we can trust no one."

"Fiddle-faddle and twaddle. What did your Granny always say? 'Don't let the bite of one grass snake . . .'"

"'. . . prevent you from enjoying the garden.'"

"That's right, and my mama was the smartest woman to grace God's good earth."

Blinking away a sudden blur of tears, Clara nodded, conceding that irrefutable point. If only the serpent who'd bitten them had been a harmless grass snake rather than a venomous adder.

"There now, that's settled. We shall have our party, and a marvelous time shall be had by all. Dinner, laughter, good conversation. Perhaps an impromptu dance or two. It will be splendid, won't it, Fred?" Mum leaned an ear to the ermine's snout and nodded. "Fred concurs. Now let's be off before those horrible French fashions change my mind."

Clara hastened to match Mum's gait, twitching temple now

a pounding migraine in the making. Somehow, she must prevent this dinner party from ending in disaster. Somehow, she must corral Mum's menagerie of rescued animals, make the house appear as normal as possible, and keep a wary eye on their sixteen guests. If she spotted any evidence of a wolf in sheep's clothing—so much as one wolf hair on a guest's woolen coat—out the door they'd go! She refused to lower her guard and let her family be put in greater peril because of her misplaced trust.

She set her jaw. By might and main, this day would not end with the remaining pieces of her heart being carted off to a madhouse and locked away forever. She'd already lost two people she loved to the horrors of an asylum.

She'd not lose another.

Years ago, she'd been too young and powerless to save her family from that pain. Now she had the advantage of years and wisdom. She was a strong, independent woman, after all. She could take care of her own. On her own.

Clara pulled back her knotted shoulders. Of course she could. For she would not let down her family and her God a second time.

Now. Wherever was she to hide the infernal talking parrot?

Hello again, London, old girl."

Theodore planted his crutch on the street, absorbing the rattling, growling city that thrummed beneath his single worn boot. He inhaled the city's unique stench—burning coal, horse manure, sewage from the Thames, and a hint of pretentious cologne. Just like he remembered.

By George, how he'd missed this place. Countless times, he'd wanted to return. Longed to return. How excruciating it had been to wait for the haggard years and hard miles to form a rusted patina on his polished appearance and thus eliminate the risk of being recognized. Now, finally, that day had come. All that remained was to find some tucked-away spot where he could settle down, tinker for his supper, and forget why he'd been forced to become a vagabond in the first place.

A peddler woman trudged by with a basket of posies clutched in her arthritic hands. Theodore acknowledged her with the tip of an imaginary hat. Her wrinkled grin set him off with a jaunty air to his one-legged, crutch-aided gait. Right-oh. Everything was going to be all right. The sun had risen in the east, constant and reliable as a finely crafted clock. Life carried on with a chorus of clomping horse hooves, shouting costermongers, and laughing street urchins celebrating the spoils of a successfully picked pocket. And now it was his turn to—

"Oi, get back here!"

A ragamuffin barreled into Theodore and knocked him off-kilter. Reeling, he braced against his prop and tensed every muscle, somehow managing not to hit the ground as a ruddy constable dashed by in pursuit. The crutch dug into Theodore's armpit as he breathed through clenched teeth, clinging to the names he'd carved deep in the woodgrain. The names of the men he'd lost at the Charge. A tribute to the fallen, and a tangible reminder that he was just like them. Forgotten in death.

Father had made sure of that.

Quickly, Theodore shoved the memories back in the clock casing that kept his pain hidden. Contained. Without that mental encasement . . . without Arthur . . . he wouldn't have been able to carry on all those years ago. Only when the case door was shut tight and his broken pieces locked away was he able to find his bearings. Right-oh. Everything was going to be all right . . . so long as he could keep up the pretense that nothing was wrong.

After trekking along for an hour or so, he reached the tick-tocking heartbeat of London's timepiece trade, where entire streets were lined with clockmakers' shops. Ones that hopefully needed an extra pair of hands. Question was, which one would be willing to hire a drifter off the street?

All the shops appeared to have been designed by one architect with traditional tastes and a limited imagination. Wrought-iron hooks held glossy signs overhead that the elements were forbidden to touch. Marble columns framed every doorway like pairs of footmen in livery, afraid to so much as sneeze. Immaculate window displays boasted refinement and perfection, luring full purses with ornate clocks that varied from porcelain mantelpiece numbers to longcase clocks inlaid with gold. Fine goods that indicated a chap wouldn't get far without a smart suit and impressive references.

Yet one establishment at the end of the lane stood out like a hearty smile amid upturned noses. An older building ambushed by progress and surrounded by new construction. No fewer than six paint colors flaked off the speckled storefront, each shade representing a different season—long ago—when the owner had still bothered to keep up appearances. The windows were devoid of wares for sale. Devoid of anything apart from dusty curtains that veiled the interior in mystery. There wasn't even a sign over the door, just a pair of rusted chains robbed of purpose. Surely this place wouldn't snub a man who blended so well into its façade?

Leaning on his crutch, Theodore limped toward the anomaly. Nails pinned a torn sheet of parchment to the sun-bleached door, bearing seven words clumsily scrawled in black ink.

Drosselmeyer and Son, Unique Clocks and Dreams.

Theodore traced his finger across the last word. Dreams too often darkened to nightmares. Why, then, was this shop's name so appealing? Probably because this ramshackle place was likely the only one to give him a chance to make some sort of life for himself.

With his free hand, Theodore swung open the door and hobbled inside, trading brilliant sunshine for the homey glow of gaslight. A ragtag army of clocks pitched camp on every square inch of space, tick-tick-tocking in uniform rhythm. He stopped in the middle of the uninhabited room, mouth agape. The clockwork regiment heralded the new hour with an enthusiastic hurrah of gongs, chimes, dings, and cuckoos, as if to extend him a friendly welcome. A greeting that stirred the very windings of his soul.

One wounded soldier limped to join its brothers, sounding a metallic ping at two minutes past. Hmmm . . . the regulation needed adjusting. If he could regulate the clock's movement, it might induce the proprietor to consider him for hire. Theodore approached the east wall's cluttered shelves in search of the tardy timepiece, only to be distracted by a captivating cuckoo. A graceful ballerina twirled in place of the expected bird. Never in all his days had he beheld finer craftsmanship. Not even amongst the timepieces he'd taken apart as a boy and reassembled gear by gear at Kingsley Court.

His mind recoiled too late. The jaws of wretched memory clamped down hard and fast, piercing him once more with Father's words. *"If you were going to besmirch the family honor so spectacularly, you might've at least had the decency to die."*

The memory spit Theodore from its maw, and he caved upon his crutch, trembling inside and out. Coming here was a mistake. A shop of dreams was no place to escape one's nightmares.

As he turned to make his escape, an insect landed on his shoulder. He brushed it off, but the persistent pest buzzed round and settled on his crutch hand. *Bothersome gnats.* Ready with a well-aimed smack, his free hand stilled over a tiny butterfly. Switching the prop to his unoccupied hand, he raised the bug to eye level. By jove, it was a machine!

Superbly crafted from tarnished brass, the automaton resembled a life-size speckled wooden butterfly, complete with white enamel spots inlaid along the edge of each delicate wing. The butterfly's antennae twitched and wings undulated, readying to take flight with the aid of an intricate clockwork movement, the likes of which he'd never seen.

"My inventions have always been able to recognize other

clockmakers." A male voice chuckled behind him, and the butterfly alighted, as if beckoned by the sound.

Theodore whirled round to find an elderly man with bright eyes topped by feathery brows of wizened white. The clockwork butterfly joined a flutter of others nestled in the man's receding hair and unkempt mustache. A bemused grin creased the fellow's face as he studied Theodore. "Who'd you apprentice for, lad?"

Tremors be hanged. He couldn't afford to pass up interest from a potential employer. "I've trained under clockmakers in Switzerland, Austria, Germany, France, Italy, and even as far off as Egypt and India. None of my previous employers are notable beyond the borders of their respective countries, but each are skilled and talented craftsmen. I learned a great deal from them, one and all. Although I didn't stay in any one place long enough to receive proper references, I give you my word that I'm a hard worker. Knowledgeable and willing to learn more still. I can prove as much, if you're willing to give me a chance, sir."

The man shuffled over, leaving open the door to what must be his workshop. He extended a hand, weathered but steady. "C. E. Drosselmeyer at your service."

Accepting the handshake, Theodore smiled. "What's the C. E. stand for?"

"An old family name with more letters than is decent. Folks just call me Drosselmeyer. Much simpler. Rolls off the tongue like that drivel called poetry. And you are?"

"Name's Arthur." He'd said it often enough, it almost felt true.

"Arthur . . . what?"

"Just Arthur." A name chosen at random, a name without shame or shadows. "Much simpler." Theodore winked. Respond with minimal information and misdirection. Worked like a debutante's charm . . . if only it weren't becoming so dratted hard to pull off. Five long years of stuffing traumatic memories and overwhelming emotion deep inside had stressed the hinges of the casing he'd built to confine them.

Drosselmeyer twirled his downy mustache. "From where do you hail, young man?"

"As my unwritten reference suggests, I've lived here, there, and everywhere in between."

"No, son. I mean, where are you from? Where is home?"

Where, indeed. After years of searching, he'd yet to find such a thing. Theodore mustered a hearty chuckle that, on a good day, would've come naturally. "I don't have any property to my name. Houses and land aren't for the likes of me. Roads and rails, that's where I live."

"Again, you mistake my meaning. Home is neither house nor land." Reaching into his wild mane, Drosselmeyer gathered three of the butterflies and arranged them in a row on one finger. "Home is your people. Generations, roots, family."

"Family?" Pain snapped in Theodore's chest, paralyzing breath like a broken rib.

"Aye, the ones you miss. The ones who miss you."

The one I disappointed from birth.

The one who'd rather throw dirt on my grave than claim a broken failure as his son.

Theodore tightened the grip on his crutch to keep from swaying and fought to prevent his grin from slipping. Of all the questions to ask, why must the bloke fire off one that struck his weakest point? If he told the truth of his origins, the strained casing that held him together would crack wide open and scatter his broken movement across the floor for all to see. No, he couldn't afford to fall apart when he was unworthy of seeking repair from the only Maker capable of reassembling a shattered soul.

"Dear, dear. Have you lost your family, lad?"

Breath resumed with laborious agony. One might say that

. . . but he couldn't. Theodore pointed to the walls of clocks as if noticing them for the first time. "Incredible work you've done here. Do you tinker alone, or is the son of Drosselmeyer and Son off in the backroom? 'Twould be an honor to shake his hand."

The sunny glint in Drosselmeyer's eyes faded as though obscured by a passing cloud. Gaze unblinking, he grasped the pocket of his waistcoat and stared at the wall of clocks, seeming to see straight through them.

Theodore knew that vacant look. Had felt the grief that dwelt within that void. This man was bereft of a son as surely as he was bereft of a father. Blast his idiot mouth! He'd never meant the diversion from his pain to awaken pain in another soul. He needed to fix this. Now.

He searched the room for possible sources of distraction and spotted the tardy clock, a wall-mounted mahogany lyre clock. That would have to do. "Mr. Drosselmeyer, I'd like to demonstrate my proficiency in clock repair in hopes that you might better consider making a place for me here." He removed the clock from its nail. "If you'd be so kind as to indulge my forwardness?"

Drosselmeyer blinked into coherency, though his countenance remained shadowed. "Certainly, certainly. My tools are in the backroom."

"Thank you, sir. But I won't be needing them." Setting the lyre clock on the sales counter, Theodore shed his overcoat and spread it beside the timepiece, revealing the hidden lining covered from seam to seam in mismatched, handsewn pockets weighted with the whole of his worldly goods and various bits, bobs, and tools he'd collected over the years. "As you can see, I'm equipped to tinker in a pinch." He tossed the old chap a wink and was rewarded with a feeble smile.

Right-oh, now he was getting somewhere. "Are you prepared to time me, sir? For my aim is to disassemble and reassemble this clock in just five minutes, beating my previous record of six minutes, five and forty seconds."

Eyebrows hoisting his wrinkled forehead in astonishment, Drosselmeyer produced a gold pocket watch from his waistcoat. "Ready, lad. On your mark. Go."

Theodore's hands took flight, alighting to the work that challenged mind and thrilled heart. Going beyond an artistically designed casement to the intricate workings within, where every cog and gear served a purpose, every pendulum and spring had a place to belong. Where brokenness that haunted with silence and stillness could always be mended and revived to tick-tick-tock once again. "Done!"

"Time." Drosselmeyer gawked at his pocket watch, the glint restored to his eyes. "Remarkable, remarkable. Five minutes, squarely on the dot." He hunched to inspect the clock. "And you've managed to fix the regularity problem and eliminate the two-minute delay. Remarkable. With skills such as this, and a quick visit to a tailor, you could get hired at any shop in London. Are you certain you wish to settle for an apprenticeship here, lad? I can't offer much."

A chance to settle was all he asked for. "Absolutely, sir. But only if you're certain I can be of service." He'd not take advantage of this kind man's grief-induced vulnerability. Not for anything. "Perhaps a trial period would be wise? To ensure you're pleased with my work."

"Nonsense, nonsense. I've seen enough to be pleased, and I've orders enough to make use of an extra pair of hands. If you agree to lighten my workload, I can provide you with an apprenticeship that includes your food and lodging. No salary, I'm afraid. However, I could build you a mechanical leg to rid you of that confounded crutch."

Food and lodging with clocks to tinker on. Perhaps this was a shop of dreams after all. A place he could belong . . . at least for now. "How long would this apprenticeship last?"

"Why, for as long as you care to stay, of course. I much prefer when friendships last indefinitely, don't you?" Drosselmeyer extended a hand. "So what say you, lad?"

A permanent apprenticeship? The offer was unusual, unorthodox, and unquestionably just what he needed. Theodore shook Drosselmeyer's hand. "When do I start, sir?"

"This very minute. First order of the day is to get your new leg sorted out, and then we're off to my daughter's house for a dinner party. Come along." Drosselmeyer scuttled off to his workshop.

"D-dinner party?" Theodore gulped. Either he was soon to enjoy a splendid evening of good food and jolly conversation . . . or he was about to face a firing squad of inquiring minds.

CHAPTER

3

"Call me a tart one more time, and I shall formally take offense. Are we quite clear, Mr. Fowler?" Clara glared at the Timneh parrot perched on her fingers, her thumb firmly clamped over black talons to prevent the cheeky bird from alighting to the crystal chandelier hanging above the foyer of the Stanton Zoological Society or, as she called it, home.

Pale yellow eyes unrepentant, Mr. Fowler fanned his mottled gray feathers and squawked. "Quite clear. A right pretty tart, pretty tart."

Insufferable. "This is why you're not permitted to converse with genteel company. Those sailors taught you to spit vulgarities like chewing tobacco."

Clara ascended the broad oak staircase, free hand gliding over the ornamental railing carved with climbing vines. She really must speak with Mum about this latest act of charity. It was one thing to care for animals with physical wounds, restoring the ones that healed to their natural habitat and sheltering those with disabilities that prohibited such restoration. But to rescue delinquent animals in an attempt to reform their character went a step too far. Mum was neither a vicar nor a practitioner of psychology. Her methods might be inspired by love, but that didn't make them effective. Calling a parrot Mr. Fowler didn't make him a gentleman any more than reading the Gospels to him would sanctify his lewd beak. Mum must be made to see that before Mr. Fowler insulted a humorless constable.

The longcase clock on the second-floor landing met her with a face dear and familiar. Out of habit, Clara traced a finger along the beloved name Grand had carved into the mahogany case. *Norma*. Grief sliced through her with the force of a gravedigger's shovel. How she wished Granny Drosselmeyer were here to help with tonight's slapdash dinner. She'd have brought flowers to dress the table and a sunny outlook that could brighten even the darkest of days. Her peaceful spirit, words of wisdom, and steadfast love had been the family's anchor—until her sudden passing had set them adrift. Preventing shipwreck had become Clara's responsibility, one that allowed no time to sort through her own grief. Even now the clock's brass hands tick-tick-tocked away minutes that ought to be spent preparing for their guests' arrival, not fighting back tears.

Stiff upper lip, girl. And be quick about it. To compose herself, Clara reexamined her mental list of tasks. She'd outlined a three-course menu and received assurance from their capable cook, Mrs. Collins, that dinner would be served on time despite the short notice and short-staffed kitchen now running without the scullery and kitchen maids who'd quit them rather than work for a "mad" mistress. Clara had hidden evidence of their private zoo, dusting feather and fur off the furnishings and draping doilies over claw-marked varnish. Mudgett, their fastidious butler, had polished the silver and arranged the table. All that remained was corralling Mum's menagerie upstairs, and the guise of normalcy would be complete.

"Pretty tart."

"Oh, do shut up!"

Clara stomped across the landing and swung open the door to her parents' bedchamber, where three geese and one duck that thought itself a goose roosted on a nest of shredded pillows amid the general chaos left behind by the chimney sweep. She hadn't the time to tackle that mess, or the lingering fear it incited. Depositing Mr. Fowler amongst the avians, she shut the door and locked it from the outside, using the master key on her chatelaine.

Heaving a sigh, she plucked stray feathers off her dinner dress of plum taffeta and hid them in a pocket. Let's see . . . had she missed anyone? The twelve feline apostles were sunning in her room's bay window. The canine quartet was lounging in Papa's office. The rabbit and goat kid were feasting on vegetable scraps in the kitchen. Who was she forgetting? Perhaps she ought to scour downstairs a tenth time.

Clara made for the stairs, only to halt before the library door, now ajar despite her having closed it minutes prior. Aha, that's who she'd forgotten. A breeze fluttered the library's gold damask curtains hanging over the double doors, now open to the balcony, where a Pygmy marmoset scampered along the precarious marble ledge. Mercy, not again! Dashing onto the balcony, she snatched up the oblivious monkey just before his paws met open air.

Clutching the wee dear to her chest, Clara stroked his soft brown fur to calm her racing heart. "Really, Bartimaeus. How could you give me such a fright? Blind you may be, but your sense of smell ought to have deduced that Mum's pocket of treats isn't on the balcony. She detests heights, you know."

Bartimaeus trilled, as if to say he'd forgotten, then reached tiny paws in the general direction of her pockets.

She smirked. "You are a determined scamp, but I'm afraid your candied orange craving will have to wait."

After locking the balcony doors, Clara placed Bartimaeus on the tufted sofa between Fred, the living stole, and Beatrix, the perpetually napping hedgehog. She patted each creature in turn. "You're in charge, Fred. Keep a sharp eye on the monkey."

As she walked back onto the landing, the longcase clock harkened the top of a new hour with a single gong that harmonized with the doorbell's metallic pring. Clara smiled. Grand, precisely on time, as always.

Mum's voice leapt from downstairs. "Hurry along, ducky. Your grandfather's arrived, and he's brought a friend."

Unease pricked gooseflesh along Clara's nape. All of Grand's friends had long since passed into eternity. Had Mr. Forrester hired a new spy so soon after the last? She leaned against the banister, craning her neck in hopes of appraising the stranger below unobserved.

In the foyer, her parents exchanged pleasantries with the "friend" at Grand's side. A young man with hair so fair as to seem white. Beard scruff of the same fairness contrasted against a tan complexion that indicated he spent a great deal of time outdoors. Not a gentleman, then. His well-worn coat and oft-patched trousers suggested he possessed little to no income. He held a crutch like a walking stick. An old battle injury, perhaps, for he stood with militaristic perfection. In short, the outsider presented the optimum sympathetic figure for Grand's emotions—a penniless, crippled, veteran-turned-vagrant.

How convenient. Clara pursed her lips, disgusted by the acidic churn of cynicism in her gut. If this man had arrived at their door last year, she'd have smiled as Mum served him a hot meal, Grand offered the coat off his back, and Papa slipped a few pound notes into his pocket. But she couldn't afford to hazard smiles now. Not when the last man she'd let near her family had proven to be a viper. One determined to slither his way back into their lives.

She needed to ascertain whether this stranger was, in fact, a spy for Mr. Forrester before her tenderhearted family was robbed, gutted, or conned. Taking the stairs two at a time, Clara raced toward the foyer and landed upon the newly polished hardwood with significant momentum, skidding straight across the vast entry into Mum's plush posterior.

"Gracious!" Mum grasped Clara's hand in time to prevent an unfortunate topple as boisterous laughter set her blue eyes twinkling. "What a theatrical entrance, ducky. I shall have to remember that one for our next social gathering."

With her luck, Mum would too. Embarrassment singed Clara's cheeks as she feigned a chuckle. "Forgive my tardiness, Grand. I was seeing to last-minute preparations."

"Of course, of course." Grand wrapped her in a warm hug, squeezing ever too tightly as his customary kaleidoscope of clockwork butterflies danced about their heads. With a loud clap on her back, he pulled away and motioned to the stranger in their midst. "Clara, this is Arthur. My new apprentice."

Clara bit her lip. Her tongue. Her cheek. Anything to keep the panic from escaping. This was of more concern than a spy dispatched with the pretext of a single errand like cleaning the chimneys. By insinuating himself into Grand's workshop, this outsider was positioned to witness all manner of oddities that could be twisted to support the rumors of hereditary insanity.

More dangerous still, he'd be in proximity to the letter that gave those rumors the ring of truth.

Had Mr. Forrester altered his tactics?

Apprentice Arthur dared to grin in the face of her fears.

"Pleasure to make your acquaintance, Miss Stanton." Hand outstretched in greeting, he stepped forward and crushed her slipper with the full weight of Buckingham Palace.

Clara's scream startled man and metal alike, scattering automaton butterflies hither and yon as her nails dug into Grand's jacket.

"Rusted cogs!" The man recoiled, liberating her wounded foot.

Pain surged through Clara's toes. Whimpering, she choked back a few of Mr. Fowler's favorite words.

"Do forgive me, Miss Stanton. I'm still getting used to this contraption." He gestured toward the floor.

Breathing through gritted teeth, Clara glowered at the man's offending boots—one crafted of cognac-hued leather and the other composed of shining brass and bronze. Her jaw slackened. "You're an automaton."

Apprentice Arthur dared to chuckle in the face of her pain. "Not quite, but Drosselmeyer was kind enough to fit me with a custom prosthetic boot."

A blasted heavy boot. Waves of pain, pulsing from toes to ankle, segmented Clara's breath. Salted paper cuts, it smarted! "Grand, would you . . . help me to the parlor? I think . . . I need to sit down." *And get away from this maladroit man.*

Grand assisted her into the adjacent parlor, wherein she lowered herself with a stifled moan upon a chaise lounge and carefully elevated her throbbing foot upon a pillow embroidered with leaping gazelles. Remain. Calm. No matter how much she wished to drop a bronze paperweight of a dunce cap on Apprentice Arthur's skull, she must remain calm and gather more information on this potential spy. "Grand, tell me, where did you find that man?"

Reclining on the nearby sofa, Grand tucked a thumb under his collar. "He found me, actually."

Of course he did. The previous spies in Mr. Forrester's

employ had found her family easily enough. The merry ship captain she'd discovered rummaging through papers in Papa's office. The elderly charwoman she'd caught at the parlor desk reading Mum's correspondence. The darling little boy who'd delivered a box of groceries, only to wind up in the library, leafing through books as if hoping a letter would fall out. Not to mention the charming, dimpled, knife-wielding chimney sweep who'd torn her parents' chamber apart just last night.

Mr. Forrester must've deduced that the proof he needed to gain leverage over her wasn't to be found in the Stanton home and had shifted his attention to Grand's shop.

Clara worried her hands. "Grand, what do you really know of this person? What is his surname? Are we acquainted with his family? Do they live in Greater London?" And had they any connection to her determined ex-fiancé?

"No surname or family to speak of, poor chap. He's alone in the world. Sort of a wayfaring traveler, I gathered, but he's an excellent clockmaker."

Another enticing lure to draw Grand into a snare. "Who has Mr. . . . erm . . . bother. What am I to call the man if he has no surname?"

"Simply call him Arthur, my dear."

Her mouth threatened to fall agape, but Clara snapped it shut before making herself a codfish. Call a single man—a stranger and a probable spy, no less!—by his Christian name? Out of the question.

She clasped her hands upon her lap. "Who has Mr. Arthur apprenticed for previously?"

"I'm not sure. He didn't provide a reference, but knock me down, that boy is as skilled a clockmaker as I've ever seen." Grand leaned forward, brass butterflies aflutter. "Not only did my inventions seek him out, but earlier today, while I was constructing his prosthetic, he had a marvelous idea for improving the knee joint's flexibility. Mark my words, Little

Atlas. Now that Arthur has agreed to make himself a permanent place in the shop, brilliant innovations are bound to shine forth from every loose board and windowpane."

A twitch toyed with Clara's right eyelid. "Did you say . . . p-permanent?"

"Aye. I saw no reason to limit Arthur's apprenticeship to a set number of years. As long as he's keen to learn, it will be my pleasure and honor to teach such a capable student."

Fabulous. Grand had picked up a no-name drifter who "just so happened" to be without relations or past employers who could vouch for his character—a well-suited pawn for Mr. Forrester to buy off with the meager enticement of a five-pound note. And to make matters worse, Grand had all but adopted the rogue. She sighed. How was she to protect her family from spies and swindlers when they insisted on trusting anyone and everyone on sight?

"Grand, don't you think it's the least bit suspicious—"

The doorbell rang, and the foyer echoed with chatter and merriment.

Grand rose with the ease of rusted hinges. "Come along, Little Atlas. I want to introduce everyone to Fritz."

Clara's breath snagged in her chest. Oh dear. She snatched the cuff of Grand's jacket and pulled him close so she might hold his hand. Hold him steady. "Grand, Uncle Fritz isn't here. He ran off fifteen years ago." With that meddlesome general who'd promised the impressionable youth a shining military career in exchange for seven years' service as his valet, and in so doing, yoked her family with a burden of heartache that had never lifted. "Uncle Fritz . . ." Her throat closed over the truth. Her uncle had died. Not on the battlefields of Crimea, but off the southern coast of England.

In an insane asylum.

Clara would never forget the day the letter came. They'd waited months for news, knowing only that Uncle Fritz was considered missing. Grand had finally written to a friend of Fritz's, a soldier in the general's command, begging for help in locating his son. The response not only confirmed their worst fears—it revealed horrors they'd never thought to contemplate.

Uncle Fritz had been injured in battle, and while he'd recovered physically, his mental faculties were deemed damaged beyond hope. Unbeknownst to his own family, he'd been conveyed to a government institution, along with other soldiers who'd succumbed to lunacy. The day Lieutenant Harbinger had arrived at the asylum was the day Uncle Fritz had breathed his last.

The lieutenant's letter contained this news, along with an outraged account of the conditions in which he'd found her uncle. An account so horrific it had attacked Granny's heart and left them with two funerals to plan instead of one.

Clara closed her eyes. If only Mr. Forrester hadn't been present when the letter was delivered—hadn't seen the information it contained with his own eyes—how very different life might be now.

Taking a breath to gather herself, she once more met Grand's twinkling gaze. "Uncle Fritz never came back, Grand."

His eyes slowly dimmed. "Of course, of course. Just a slip of the tongue, that." Grand brushed her hand away and clutched at his waistcoat pocket, where the letter was interred with honor, preserving his son's final words—*I want to go home.*

Clearing his throat, Grand shuffled toward the foyer. "The others are going in for dinner. We mustn't tarry."

Clara moved to follow, but nerve-pinching pain stilled her instantly, drawing her attention back to her swollen foot. She clenched her jaw. The outsider must be to blame for Grand's "slip of the tongue." A young man moving into Fritz's old room could certainly dredge up memories. As soon as dinner was over, she must speak with her parents. That man had to be sent packing. And Grand must be convinced to heed her pleas and burn that cursed letter.

After testing the stability of her foot, Clara limped to join the party gathered in the dining room. Her parents anchored either end of the long table Mudgett had arranged for sixteen—an arrangement now thrown off balance by the unexpected absence of Mum's companions from the Charitable Ladies League. A sinking feeling weighed on Clara as she sat, staring at the empty chairs and polished silver that would go unused. The desertion of her own friends she could endure, but to see Mum shunned on account of vicious gossip broke her fractured heart.

As the dinner commenced and Mudgett served the vegetarian courses, conversation at the table revolved around Mr. Arthur as if he were the sun. He charmed their party with charismatic repartee. Laughing and winking and regaling them with what had to be highly exaggerated tales of his travels abroad. Did he seriously expect them to believe he'd broken the nose off the Great Sphinx or that he'd almost been arrested at the Taj Mahal for defending himself against a troop of vicious macaques? The concoction of such outlandish stories made one wonder what he was trying to hide. Like, perhaps, a covert mission to steal a certain letter for a certain snake?

When the second course had been cleared, Mudgett brought in Mrs. Collins' crowning achievement—a three-tiered citrus custard arranged to perfection on a cobalt blue glass pedestal cake stand and decorated with candied orange peels and blossoms. Applause rippled through the room, and Clara allowed herself to partially relax against her chair as Mudgett served the dessert. The dinner would conclude soon. If she could only draw their suspicious guest away from the company, she might be able to interrogate and extricate him from their lives before the first dance.

A rustle in the folds of Clara's skirt set her every nerve on edge. For *she* had not stirred.

Swallowing a squeal, she constructed a framework of calm and looked down. A tiny tail, striped with black and gold fur, dangled out of her pocket. Her mouth went arid. Stars above. Amid the commotion of Mr. Arthur's arrival, she must've forgotten to lock the library door. Perspiration beaded on her brow as the revelers conversed over custard. *Steady, Clara. No need to panic.* She could handle this. All she had to do was secure Bartimaeus in her pocket and excuse herself. No one would be the wiser about the monkey, and all would be well.

While everyone's attention was fixed on Mr. Arthur as he waxed eloquent about the Pyrenees, Clara discreetly plucked the pieces of candied orange off her custard, slipped them to the stowaway, and then clasped her pocket closed with a determined grip. She exhaled. There. That was easily done. Now to make a quick getaway.

Clara faced Mum, seated on her right, but a collective gasp silenced her excuse. She turned in time to witness Fred scaling the side of Papa's chair. The ermine reached the top of an acorn-shaped finial and stretched his neck to survey the stunned humans. Clara held her breath. Dash it all, the little imp was looking for Mum! Ever so slowly, she rose from her chair. She had to get him before—

Fred leapt from chair to table, catapulting silverware to the floor with a clatter. Lame legs trailing behind, the ermine scurried across the entire length of the table amid a cacophony of gasps and shrieks and "By Joves." Scuttling up Mum's arm, Fred draped himself about her neck and took to cleaning his front paws.

In utter silence, the visitors gawked at the plates of custard now marred with paw prints.

Clara pursed her lips. How was she to salvage this?

Mr. Arthur's laughter broke the silence for her with a

baritone rumble. "Thank God above, 'tis only an ermine! For a moment there, I thought the macaques had come for their revenge."

The table erupted in hearty guffaws.

Taking advantage of the distraction, Clara snatched Fred and escorted him upstairs, along with the monkey. After depositing the troublesome pair in the library with the still-snoozing hedgehog and triple-checking the lock, she hobbled downstairs. Come morning, the ermine-in-the-custard story was bound to make its way about town, but there was little she could do to mitigate the damage. No amount of diplomacy could make an ermine frolicking through dessert sound normal. Her energy would be better spent in securing Mr. Arthur for questioning.

Alas, in her absence, the party had adjourned to the ballroom, thwarting her best chance of whisking Grand's apprentice away discreetly. Across the floor of black-and-white checkered marble, couples paired off for the first of many reels to come from Papa's fiddle. For now, there seemed nothing for her to do but remain alert and bide her time. And hope the canine quartet upstairs didn't take to howling, as they were accustomed to doing when Papa played in the evenings.

"Care to dance, Miss Stanton?" Mr. Arthur's voice startled her, grating on her last frayed nerve. Standing before her, crutch in hand, the man offered a sweeping bow and paired it with a lopsided grin, as if they were old chums. "Seeing as I've yet to break in this clanker of a boot, I'm sure to make a fool of myself, but that's a paltry sum, I say, for a diverting lark about the dance floor." With a downward tilt of his head, he placed hand over heart. "Upon my honor, I promise not to trample your other foot."

If the man thought he could win her over with a wink and a smile, like all the others, he was sorely mistaken. "Your honor is of no assurance to me, Mr. Arthur, as it is yet unsubstantiated. Moreover, at present, your questionable origins and serendipitous arrival are of more concern to me than your clumsiness."

Her frankness rendered Mr. Arthur a wide-eyed mute.

Seeing as the man was rarely silent, she might as well seize the opportunity to verify her suspicions here and now. Clara arched an eyebrow and lowered her voice. "Tell me, Mr. Arthur, exactly how much is he paying you?"

"Is that what you're worried about?" Mr. Arthur sighed as though relieved. "Rest assured, Miss Stanton, I've no intention of taking any money from your grandfather. Drosselmeyer made it clear that my apprenticeship would be without salary. He's offered me room and board in exchange for honest work, and for that, I'm grateful."

How could he claim to provide honest work when he refused to be forthright about anything? With such a man, there was no use beating about the bush. It was time to call Mr. Arthur No Name's bluff. Clara crossed her arms. "I wasn't referring to Grandfather. I was referring to your *actual* employer."

Mr. Arthur was proving himself adept at looking oblivious. "I'm afraid I don't know what you're talking about, Miss Stanton. Drosselmeyer is my sole employer, and my only wish is to be of service to him."

"Is that so?" A twitching vein plucked at Clara's temple. The man *might be* telling the truth, but seeing as she was still living with the consequences of having been fooled by a skillful liar, *might be* wasn't sufficient assurance. "Well, Mr. Arthur. If you wish to be of service to Grandfather, then I suggest you pack your things and leave. I'll double whatever price Mr. Forrester's suborned you with to spy on us and steal what's ours. Just be gone by morning."

If Mr. Arthur's eyebrows migrated any farther north, they'd cross the border into his hairline. "What in the blazes are you talking about? I don't know this Forrester bloke, and nobody's paid me a shilling to do anything. Give me a chance, Miss Stanton. How can I convince you I'm not an enemy informant?"

"You want a chance, Mr. Arthur? Fine. You shall have this one. Answer me plainly. What is your full name, and from where do you hail?"

Mr. Arthur's gaze tripped. Jaw clenched.

"Do you refuse to answer me, sir?"

His fair brows lowered into an entrenched furrow, and his bronzed knuckles whitened in their grip on his crutch. "Every man has the right to leave the past behind and make a new life for himself, Miss Stanton."

"That may be so, Mr. Arthur. But every woman has the right to protect her family from dubious vagabonds who crush unsuspecting toes. Whether or not you're associated with Mr. Forrester, you are not family, and you've given me no cause to trust you with mine. I must insist that you be on your way. Wherever you came from, you certainly don't belong here."

For the first time that evening, somberness weighed Mr. Arthur's voice. "Of that I am well aware, Miss Stanton. Vagabonds don't belong much of anywhere. Nevertheless, I was invited."

With that, the man strode off and planted himself at Grand's side, making it quite clear he had no intention of leaving.

Clara and Grand stood on the banks of the Nile River, admiring golden stalks of papyrus as they bowed to the wind like servants paying homage to the mighty Pharaoh. Grass clung to the river's edge, drawing life from waters more precious than lapis lazuli. Emboldened by worship, the sun oppressed man and beast. Raising her parasol, she led Grand along the undulating sands and sought shade beneath the fronds of a palm tree. Then a stranger's sneeze sprayed her cheek and broke the fourth wall of imagination with the unpleasantness of reality.

Clara grimaced before the magnificent Nile, now reduced to a winding line upon the enormous relief map of Africa on the third story of Wyld's Great Globe. The domed building's inverted model of the Earth had opened nine years ago to promote Mr. Wyld's maps to the untold masses who'd flocked to the Great Exhibition, but she was now of the opinion that certain members of the public ought to be barred entrance.

Specifically, those who coughed and sneezed without regard for their fellow man.

Nose scrunched, Clara glared at the portly fellow who'd dared to invade her haven of solitude. "Excuse me, sir, are you in possession of a handkerchief?"

The man raised his unified eyebrow. "Aye, miss." A quick rummage through his pockets produced a clean linen cloth. "Here you are, miss. Always glad to assist a lady."

Ah, such luck had she, to encounter a gallant knight with a cold. Clara accepted the proffered handkerchief, wiped the sneeze residue from her face, and then returned the cloth. "Thank you, sir. Might I suggest that in future you assist the ladies of London by making use of your own handkerchief or, better yet, by putting yourself under quarantine until such time as you are no longer a walking contagion."

The man's eyebrow lowered, and he stormed off with a huff, mumbling under his breath about the fickleness of women.

"Your mother can chastise me about prejudice all she wants, but I still don't think I should care to meet a Nile crocodile." Grand's contemplative remark evoked a smile from Clara. Travel guide tucked under his left arm, he remained transfixed by the deserts of Africa, head quite bare without its usual crown of automaton butterflies. He was a dear to leave them at home for her peace of mind.

"Don't fret, Grand. Mum might have stalwart opinions, but she'd never force you to socialize with a crocodile, I'm sure." Clara rested her head upon the well-worn shoulder of his jacket. The soft tweed against her cheek and the aroma of peppermints stored in a waistcoat pocket presented all the comforts of home. "Should we explore the pyramids next?"

"Oh, for sure. For sure. After traveling so far on those malodorous camels, we mustn't forget to survey one of this land's most impressive marvels. 'Twould be a shame." Grand lowered wire-rimmed spectacles from the top of his head to the end of his nose and took out the crimson copy of *A Gentleman's Guide to Ancient Egypt*, proceeding to read the chapter on the pyramids. His relaxing timbre painted exotic imagery across the canvas of imagination, whisking them away on yet another adventure.

Contentment eased the tension that perpetually resided in Clara's shoulders. If she ever chanced to meet Mr. Wyld, she must thank him for constructing his Great Globe. For this place had brought Grand back to them. In the bleak days after Granny and Uncle Fritz died, Grand had boarded up his warehouse at the docks, closed the clock shop, and entombed himself in the upstairs apartment. One by one, the clocks in the shop had fallen silent, and as days of sorrow turned into months of neglect, Drosselmeyer and Son had fallen into disrepair. She'd feared Grand would never emerge from its faded walls.

Until, at last, she'd roused his curiosity enough to visit the "Monster Globe" in Leicester Square. That first visit had turned into weekly outings, then a beloved tradition. As public interest had waned and visitors diminished, the all-but-abandoned globe had become a refuge from society. One she treasured more by the day.

Clearing his throat, Grand turned the page. "'Egyptologist Karl Richard Lepsius wrote the first modern list of the pyramids in 1842, counting their number at sixty-seven.' Most interesting, that. Most interesting. Don't know if these old knees will get us to all sixty-seven today, Little Atlas. Might have to set up camp early and take in the other tombs come sunrise." Tilting his head, Grand tossed her a wink that she pocketed with glee.

"That's quite all right with me, Grand. Extending our stay another night will allow us a chance to study the constellations with your telescope."

"Capital idea. Arthur told me a remarkable thing the other

day that he observed while in Egypt. Apparently, the belt stars of Orion align with the three pyramids on the Giza Plateau. I should like to see that myself."

As Grand resumed their tour of the pyramids, Clara picked at the frayed seams of her gloves. *Arthur. Arthur. Arthur.* She was sick of hearing that man's name elevated with praise every other minute. Grand's willingness to believe anything his apprentice said had robbed days of peace and nights of sleep for the past two weeks. She didn't like how much time this stranger was spending alone with Grand. Not one bit. However, she couldn't exactly move in with Grand and become his shadow. Mum had forbidden it.

In addition, Clara had no evidence to substantiate her nagging qualms. Since Mr. Arthur's arrival, none of their possessions had been destroyed, nor had any private details of their life appeared in the newspapers. Even Fred's romp through the custard was conspicuously absent from parlor gossip. Despite several unannounced visits to the shop, at various times of day, Clara had yet to catch the man in the act of spying, and despite her persistent pleas for the letter to be burned, it remained safely in Grand's pocket. He could not bear to let it go, and she could not bear to ask it of him anymore. As long as her family disregarded her fears about Mr. Arthur, there was nothing more she could do. Except, once again, remain alert and bide her time.

A prospect frustrating and frightening in equal measure.

The travel guide shut with a thwump, and Grand tucked it under his arm. "I've had enough of this desert heat. What say you to pursuing a cooler climate up north?"

Clara nodded. She needed to stop fretting and enjoy this moment. "Lead on, Grand."

Leaving Africa behind, they strolled through the gallery's Moorish interior and started up the next staircase within the Globe. Due to the dome's poor ventilation system, the stale air thickened as they ascended to the next viewing platform. Clara smirked as perspiration glued her lavender dress of lightweight organdy to her skin. Cooler climate, indeed. Grand's powers of imagination must be particularly heightened this day.

When they arrived at the next gallery, Grand guided Clara to the expected portion of the colossal map. She smiled. A trip to the Great Globe would not be complete without a visit to Bern, Switzerland. The city of Granny's birth. The city where she and Grand had spent their wedding tour. Plaster models of the Bernese Alps rose from the map and jutted toward them and the globe's core as sunshine streaming through the glazed skylight glittered off the white crystals dusting every snow-capped peak.

A wistful smile settled on Grand's face. "One morning, I snuck out while Norma slept and hid an automaton on the bear fountain that was just outside our window. When we left later in search of food, my pocket watch struck the hour as we passed the fountain and activated the automaton. Norma nearly jumped out of her skin when one of the bear cubs came to life and began dancing around its bronze mother's claws. My, how she laughed." He reached out to touch the River Aare's azure waters as though to recapture the memory, but his hand fell short to his side. "Have I ever told you that story?"

Hundreds of times, but it could never be repeated too often. For every time it was told, she could hear Granny's contagious laughter once again. A single tear navigated the wrinkles of Grand's face, and Clara caught it on his cheek with a kiss. Perhaps they'd explored enough for today. "Shall we go, Grand?"

"Go." Grand echoed the word and seemed to watch it hang in the air. A light flickered in his blue eyes. "Why don't we, Little Atlas? Why don't we go this very week and explore the real city of Bern together? I could leave the shop with Arthur, and we could set off on a genuine adventure."

Clara's mouth hung agape. Leave the shop? With a complete stranger? She needed to nip this notion in the bud before it blossomed into trouble. "As wonderful as that sounds, I couldn't possibly think of traveling at present. I have too many pressing responsibilities at home."

"Your responsibilities could be delegated to someone else for a few weeks."

Delegated? Clara bit back the scoff. To whom, exactly, would she delegate? The one person who had promised to care for her and her family—the one person she had dared to depend on—had tried to rob them blind the moment her back was turned. No. The idea was ludicrous. Only she could understand the needs of her unique family.

Papa had said as much, just days after the dual funeral, when Mum began increasing her demonstrations to escape her grief and Grand had taken to bed with his. *"My dear, capable Clara Marie, you're the only one of us who's managed to keep a stiff upper lip through all this. It comforts me to know that while I'm tending the business, you've got things well in hand at home."*

Home, that was her place. Taking care of the family, that was her duty.

And that left no time for a personal holiday.

Clara offered Grand the most lighthearted smile she could muster and softened her tone. "My responsibilities are my own. I would never shirk them. Besides, if I left town, who would take care of the family?" Who would guard them against Mr. Forrester and keep an eye on Mr. Arthur?

Shadows gathered in the creases of Grand's face. "Taking care of this family is not your responsibility to bear alone, Clara."

She chuckled, shaking her head at the absurdity of that statement. "Of course it is, Grand. I'm Little Atlas, remember? Balancing our world on my shoulders is my purpose. Speaking of which . . ." Scooping up the silver pocket watch on her chatelaine, she confirmed the lateness of the hour. "We really must be heading home. I have to help Papa organize and tidy his disaster of an office because he's lost an important shipping manifest, and this evening, I must accompany Mum to her whist consortium's biweekly meeting. Otherwise, she's sure to take Fred along and get herself into some sort of scrape."

Snapping her pocket watch shut, Clara turned her back on Switzerland, and in so doing, noted a glare of brashest yellow amid the gallery's neutral surroundings. Her stomach turned. Half-obscured by the farthest column to her left, Mr. Forrester sported his favorite waistcoat of paisley silk in that distinctively hideous shade of yellow she'd once referred to as garish canary.

She pressed a quaking fist against her bodice, willing her roiling stomach to still. In a blink, her ex-fiancé had turned her haven of seclusion into a menacing trap. She needed to get Grand and the letter away from here. If she distracted Mr. Forrester, perhaps she could buy Grand time to traverse all the stairs and reach the Globe's custodians in the lobby. "S-stars. I almost forgot. Last week, I left one of my travel guides on the uppermost floor. Why don't you head downstairs, Grand, whilst I dash up and see if it's still there? Save your knees the trouble."

Grand eyed her askance, but even so, he gave her shoulder a firm squeeze and then shuffled in the direction of the downward stairs.

Once Grand was beyond her sights, Clara wheeled about with a furious swooshing of skirts and confronted her former betrothed. Unaffected and unabashed, Mr. Forrester looked the same as ever, his customary air of suave assurance as heady as his sandalwood cologne. Just the right amount of pomade smoothed the sides of his brown hair into place with shining precision, and he wore a bowler hat. Every stitch of his ostentatious suit was expertly tailored, every hair of his thick chin whiskers neatly groomed, and his silk cravat was tied with the sort of finesse that could only be achieved by a dedicated dandy.

Or a garish canary.

The whole of Clara's self-restraint had to be mustered to keep her voice at a respectable volume, but not even that could prevent her gloved hands from balling into fists. "Do you presume to stalk me, Mr. Forrester?"

Mr. Forrester's grin broadened, uncovering the schoolboy dimple at the corner of his mouth that had once thimblerigged her into believing him guileless. "Stalking is reserved for strangers. We have too much history for that, you and I. *Watching out for you* would be a more accurate turn of phrase." He leaned against the nearby pillar with the relaxed ease of a Sunday afternoon and spun a golden band around his left ring finger.

The one bearing an inscription that bound their names in noose-like scroll.

Clara's mouth went dry. For what purpose had he resurrected that cursed ring from the grave?

"Though we've been parted these long months, I *have* been watching out for you, my dear, and it has grieved me to see you suffer. Shunned and stigmatized. Lacerated unjustly day in and day out by the cruel tongues of idle gossips."

Tongues he'd set to wagging the day he sauntered into Mum's birthday party, uninvited, to accuse her family of lunacy. Brandishing his knowledge of Lieutenant Harbinger's letter, he'd announced to all their friends that Uncle Fritz had died in an asylum—a "kindhearted warning" for them to mind the company they kept. Poor Grand, honest man that he was, had refused to deny it, and overnight, Uncle Fritz had gone from a war hero to a madman. Her family's desire to keep their heartbreak private twisted into deliberate intent to conceal their inborn insanity.

Was the man so daft as to think she'd forgotten what he'd done?

Apparently so, for Mr. Forrester moved to her side now, brows knit together and hazel eyes agleam with the appearance of concern. "Won't you reconsider my offer of marriage? Coming under the protection of my good name would surely snuff the flame of scandal surrounding your family."

Frigid waters seemed to pour over the length of Clara's body. She'd been expecting him to play his hand but not so soon. Had he grown tired of his fruitless search, or was he simply running out of time? Regardless, he must be quite desperate to risk a renewal of his troth now. Without the letter's compelling leverage, Mr. Forrester was betting everything that slander and spies had been sufficient to back her into a corner, one tight enough to make her renege. Accept his offer of rescue from the perils he'd created.

Grant him access to the Stanton coffers he needed to save himself.

"Say you'll accept my offer, darling, and let me set everything right. Say you'll become my bride, and let me care for you as I promised."

The cold settled into her bones with a sobering numbness. Mr. Forrester's appearance was not the only thing unchanged—his candied promises still concealed arsenic-filled centers. "You're not capable of caring for anyone other than yourself, Mr. Forrester. Never have been. Never shall be."

"Come now, pet. You must know that I care. That I've missed you terribly. Let us put these wretched months of separation behind us and be as we were before." Mr. Forrester reduced the space between them to a mere breath, his dimpled grin extending an invitation. "Marry me, Clara. I assure you, becoming my wife would have numerous benefits." His right hand glided across her cheek in a scalding caress.

A single slap to that insolent dimple freed Clara from his touch.

A well-aimed kneecap to the loins vented a measure of her fury.

Cheek burning and fists poised to fly at the slightest provocation, Clara glowered at Mr. Forrester, now leveled to his knees upon the floor and moaning in insufficient agony. "Understand this, Rupert Forrester. You may as well choke on that forked tongue of yours, for I won't be taken in by your snake-charmer act a second time. I will never pledge myself to be your wife, and no amount of scheming, seducing, or groveling will change my mind. Not now. Not ever. I'd sooner drink from the putrid Thames than marry you!"

Her emphatic declaration reverberated through the still and silent hall. Clara swallowed, covering her mouth. When had she taken to shouting? Stars, if the gossips caught sight of her now . . . What a pitiful spectacle she must be. A wobble unsettled her knees.

Home. She needed to go home this very moment before her stupidity caused the family more irrevocable harm.

Clara fled across the gallery toward the winding staircase that would take her to fresh air and the comfort of peppermint-filled pockets.

"Don't go! Clara . . . I need you."

The angst-ridden plea grated on the back of her taut neck, and she gripped the rail at the top of the stairwell. Of course he needed her. Everyone always needed her. "After all the havoc you've wrought . . . tell me, Mr. Forrester. Why, exactly, am I supposed to care any longer?"

A growl infused his voice with menace. "Because the bloodletting creditors latched to my back are devoid of patience or scruples. Without your family's money, I'll be dragged back to—" Mr. Forrester bit off his own words with a curse. "Blast! You love me, woman. Shouldn't that be reason enough?"

Clara sighed. No, it wasn't. The naïve love she'd once felt for a lad she'd called Buccaneer Bill could never be reason enough to shackle herself in matrimony to the heartless man he'd become. "Stay away from us, Mr. Forrester. Stay far, far away."

The spring catapulted from the clock with a metallic snap, nearly taking out Theodore's eye as it soared across the workshop and landed . . . somewhere.

It was hard to locate anything amid the scattered heaps of tools and dismantled clock parts tossed onto dusty shelves, tucked into sticky drawers, and strewn across the battered desk. Drosselmeyer assured him there was an organizational system in place, but Theodore was beginning to question said system's efficiency. And soundness. Just when he'd committed the whereabouts of an item to memory, he'd find it replaced with a long-cold cup of tea or a rosy-eyed automaton rabbit.

Either the system was a bad fit for the shop . . . or he was.

"Wherever you came from, you certainly don't belong here."

Seated on a wooden bench before the creaky desk that nigh rested upon his knees, Theodore caved into a slouch. A month later and Miss Stanton's words still needled. Still raised doubts like drops of blood upon pricked flesh. Why did the woman distrust him with such vehemence? She'd acted as though he were the worst of criminals. Interrogating, charging, and passing judgment within minutes. He couldn't fault her for being protective of her grandfather or for eyeing him with caution.

But to accuse him of acting as a spy for some chap he didn't even know was frustrating. And odd. There had to be a story there. A reason for Miss Stanton's behavior. Something had wound her suspicions so tightly that she'd been poised to snap like yonder spring. When he'd ventured to ask Drosselmeyer about it the morning after the dinner party, the old man had said only that it was *her* story to tell.

Not that she was likely to ever tell it to him, the *dubious vagabond*.

He rubbed a hand over his beard and round to the back of his taut neck. What was he doing—allowing criticism from a fair face to distract him as though he were a gangly besotted boy? He was no boy.

And he abso-bloomin-lutely was not besotted.

Theodore pried his knees out from under the blighted dollhouse furnishing and strode across the workshop in search of the flying spring. He turned up the flame on the nearest wall-mounted gaslight and rummaged through an open drawer in the speculated landing area, clanking cogs against brass clock hands of varying sizes. Miss Stanton could fire bullet-force glares all she liked. He'd not be scared off or shamed into running. Not anymore. Not from this place. Nor from these people. Drosselmeyer and the Stantons were too kind and generous to consider parting from them. He'd never find a better benefactor, not if he searched a month of Sundays. And he had, by jove! For five exhausting years.

Theodore shoved the drawer closed with a thud that rattled the whole bureau. Hang his doubts and the lady's censure! He was staying on and would enjoy himself, at that. If Miss Stanton was determined not to like him, then he'd be equally dogged in convincing her of his good intentions and somehow win over the pretty little grump.

Drosselmeyer's warbling whistle emanated from the upstairs apartment, increasing in volume as he flew down the stairwell and entered the workshop. Brass-rimmed goggles inset with amber glass encircled his head. He didn't alight at his desk but rather winged his way toward the door, a knapsack slung over one shoulder. "Fair morning and fair thee well, Arthur. I am off to see the world."

A grin quirked the side of Theodore's mouth. He snatched up his crutch and followed Drosselmeyer into the vacant storefront. For all her glares, he had to respect the way Miss Stanton looked in on her grandfather and accompanied him to the Great Globe for adventures of imagination. This week's choice to aid imagination with fancy dress felt strange, though. Even for them. He'd not have pegged Miss Stanton as the type. What sort of costume might the pretty grump choose . . . and why was her grandfather leaving without her?

Theodore slipped through the shop door just as it closed in Drosselmeyer's wake. He shielded his eyes from the morning sun's fresh-out-of-bed exuberance. Just ahead, Drosselmeyer strode down the pavement with a purposeful gait. Whatever was the old man about today? Theodore gave chase and soon reached Drosselmeyer's side. "Shouldn't you wait for Miss Stanton, sir? You might get lost without your navigator."

Drosselmeyer neither slowed nor averted his sights. "I can't be waiting today. The wind is just right, just right."

Had Drosselmeyer and Miss Stanton instituted a new means of amusement? "Right for what, exactly?"

The man's gaze remained fixed on the blue horizon. A March breeze skipped botanical debris along the street. Perhaps the wind impaired Drosselmeyer's hearing?

Clearing his throat, Theodore spoke up. "I say, Drosselmeyer, right for what?"

The old fellow startled and, at last, stopped to face Theodore. The fine lines around his eyes deepened as his fluttery brows of white knit together. With a gnarled finger, he indicated the crutch beneath Theodore's arm. "You know . . . you no longer need carry that thing about, son."

A lump, cold as a headstone, formed in Theodore's throat. He tried to swallow the thing, but it would not be moved. Instead, he talked round it, his voice grating against the unpolished rock. "Perhaps . . . but all the same . . . it is mine to carry." His thumb found the oft-visited graves of every name memorialized in its grain, letter by hand-carved letter.

GORDON.

DENIS.

THEO—

"Good thing you caught me, lad. I almost forgot to give you this." Drosselmeyer placed a pocket watch in the palm of Theodore's free hand. "This heirloom was meant for my son, Fritz, but since he's long been walking the streets of gold, I should like you to have it now, Arthur."

The lump fell to the pit of Theodore's stomach with a sickening plunk. He held the watch at a distance, its gleaming gold case with matching chain and fob seeming to sear his work-soiled hand. The gift was too much. Too fine. Worse, it was given under false pretenses. For though he tried to pretend otherwise, he was no more worthy of a son's inheritance than his name was Arthur.

"I cannot accept . . . surely, your granddaughter ought to—"

"Keep it on your person at all times, Arthur. At all times. That pocket watch is the second-most important thing you shall ever have in your care."

Of all the bizarre riddles. "And what would be the first, sir?"

A grin twitched Drosselmeyer's mustache as he consulted

a pocket watch that he'd attached to his wrist with a leather strap. "I must be off, or I shall fall behind schedule."

Ah, so the pretty little grump *had* made alternate plans with her grandfather today. "I take it Miss Stanton will be following along later, then?"

Drosselmeyer lowered his goggles over twinkling eyes. Without a word, he resumed a resolute march down the streets of London.

Right-ooooh. Biting back the questions that quarreled in his mind, Theodore tucked the important watch into a waistcoat pocket and secured the fob to a nearby button. The gold chain draped across his faded waistcoat with an air of elegance lacking in the rest of his person. He'd wear the watch for safekeeping until Drosselmeyer returned this afternoon, but as soon as that dear old codger set foot through the door, the costly heirloom was going right back where it belonged—in Drosselmeyer's family line.

A brief jaunt returned Theodore to the workshop, and a lengthy search through its nooks and crannies produced, at last, the runaway spring. And an aching lumbar. As he wedged under the dollhouse desk to carry on with his work, there arose a such clatter, he stilled. Listened. Exactly how long had he left the shop unattended? A thud reverberated through the ceiling. Apparently, long enough for someone to slip into the apartment unseen. He extricated himself from the desk and rushed upstairs. Drosselmeyer was not getting robbed while he was in charge!

On the second floor, two bedchambers faced each other in a narrow corridor. The doors, normally kept closed, were wide open, and muffled sounds came from Drosselmeyer's room. Theodore charged inside and found a thin boy, no more than thirteen, rifling through the contents of a dresser. The lad whirled around and lunged, headbutting Theodore in the gut.

Theodore staggered backward with a grunt as the boy slipped by him like a greased eel. He snatched at the boy's collar, but it tore off in his hand.

The scamp disappeared down the stairwell like a flash.

Theodore regained his footing and gave chase, but encumbered as he was by his prosthetic on the stairs, he was no match for an agile boy, so nimble and quick.

When he finally reached the storefront, the thief was long gone.

Leaning against the sales counter, Theodore took a minute to catch his breath. He checked the money box, stored in the false bottom of a hidden drawer behind the counter. It remained locked and untouched. He took stock of the clocks. None were missing. He examined the rooms upstairs, but again, nothing seemed to be missing. He returned to the workshop, where the usual disorder remained in perfect order. He scratched his beard, equal parts confused and concerned. When Drosselmeyer returned this afternoon, they would have a talk about their slippery thief. In the meantime, he needed to be more vigilant.

The front door whooshed open and thudded shut. Good, a customer. Perhaps he could turn this day around and make a sale. If he proved himself capable of handling the shop on his own, Drosselmeyer was sure to be pleased. Might even be the first step toward securing the good graces of Miss Stanton. Assuming she had any good graces.

Theodore combed fingers through his rumpled hair, grabbed his crutch, and hastened to attend the waiting customer. Palm outstretched, he shoved open the swinging door and froze in the middle of the room before a pair of slate gray eyes, hard as steel and twice as sharp. He gulped. "Good day, Miss Stanton."

The store's brigade of clocks returned his greeting with a merry tick-tick-tock that amplified Miss Stanton's vociferous silence. Assuming the most unwelcome of stances—arms crossed, spine rigid, lips pinched—she stared him down and denied him the courtesy of a response. Pitch-black ringlets peeked from her bonnet and framed her ghostly white face. The woman spent far too much time indoors with the family's menagerie of animals. Probably training a raven to peck out his eyes. *Stand your ground, man, and stick to the plan. Win the grump over.* "May I be of service, Miss Stanton?"

By some means unknown to science, Miss Stanton's eyes conveyed the disdain of a raised brow without troubling her face to move a muscle. "I mean to take Grand on our weekly visit to the Globe, as you well know, so save the delusive pleasantries for some ninnyhammer who'll believe them. If you wish to make yourself useful, tell Grand I've come."

"Tell him?" The familiar sensation of a sinking ship in Theodore's gut indicated that he'd once again made a terrible error. "Aren't you meeting Drosselmeyer at the Globe today?"

Her disdain intensified, curiously enough, still without eyebrow assistance. "I always collect Grand here, every Thursday, at exactly half past eleven. Why should you think I would stray from that routine?"

"Because your grandfather left here not half an hour ago."

At last, one of the dark eyebrows showed signs of movement in the form of a twitch on the right-hand quadrant. "Nonsense. Grand always awaits my arrival. Therefore, he must still be here."

If he wasn't in perilous waters before, he sure as blazes was now. For Miss Stanton had just set his sinking ship aflame and left him with two equally dangerous courses of action. One, to agree with the woman by voicing a lie. Two, to contradict the woman by speaking the truth. Theodore ran a hand over his beard. Gah . . . there was no way to get out of this unscathed. Leastways, none that he could see. He'd best take the route of complete honesty. That way he'd at least be on the high ground when Miss Stanton buried him.

"As much as I loathe to contradict a lady, the facts force me to reiterate that Drosselmeyer is not here. See for yourself, if you must."

With a scowl, Miss Stanton barreled through the workshop door, leaving the poor scrap of wood swinging wildly in her wake. "Grand?" Stomping boots punctuated her unanswered call and tracked her progression up to the second-floor apartment. Another helpless door slammed against a wall. More stomping of boots, more abusive slamming of doors. "Grand?"

Stomp, stomp, slam. Stomp, stomp, slam.

A wince pinched the corners of Theodore's eyes. How many times would she pace betwixt the two empty rooms before—

Boots pelted stairs like a hailstorm. Theodore tightened his grip upon the crutch.

The still-swinging door fled before Miss Stanton. He expected the woman to yell. Scream. Plant fists on her shapely hips as she summoned a murder of ravens to make good on their name. Instead, Miss Stanton's gloved hands remained at her sides and an intense focus anchored her tone. "Tell me—exactly—what Grandfather said."

Tread carefully, man. Don't make this worse. "He said something about seeing the world and not being able to wait and the wind being just right."

"The wind . . ." Miss Stanton's face drained of the meager color it possessed. "He wouldn't. Surely, he wouldn't."

What the deuce was the woman so afraid of? "I apologize, Miss Stanton, for this communication failure on my part. When Drosselmeyer departed this morning, I assumed you'd meet him at the Globe in coordinating fancy dress."

"Fancy dress? Dear heavens . . . tell me Grand wasn't wearing goggles. Tell me he was dressed as Wellington or—or a wastepaper basket—anything other than those blighted goggles."

He swallowed. "As much as I loathe to contradict a lady—"

Miss Stanton fled. Bounded out the door before he could so much as turn round. What was it with this family and mysterious departures?

Giving chase for the third time that morning, Theodore locked the shop door and hurried after Miss Stanton, who was dashing toward a hansom cab parked down the street. What reason could she have for such haste? Drosselmeyer couldn't run into any real danger between here and the Globe . . . could he? Breaking into a stilted and uncomfortable run, he managed to gain ground and blocked her path with his crutch.

Miss Stanton stabbed a finger at his chest. "Get out of my—"

"You can disregard me all you like, Miss Stanton. Hate me till your blood boils and steam curls out your ears. But I am accompanying you on this errand, so don't waste time arguing the point. If Drosselmeyer has run into trouble on my account, I aim to set things right."

Lightning cracked in Miss Stanton's glare, but she allowed him into the cab without protest. Then she ordered the driver to head for the docks.

Though the cab navigated London's streets at a teeth-clacking pace, Miss Stanton's demeanor accused the driver of being a cautious governess afraid to jar her young charge's pram. Posture steeled and gaze fixed straight ahead, her boot tapped incessantly. She remained thus for the whole drive, despite being jostled and jarred. Even the noxious stench of the nearing Thames failed to make her sway.

The moment the driver brought his horse to a stop, Miss Stanton was off. Theodore asked the driver to await their return and then dashed off in pursuit, crutch tucked under his arm. Even with the improved mobility provided by his prosthetic boot, he struggled to keep Miss Stanton in his sights. Dodging wooden crates, murky puddles, and sweat-drenched longshoremen, she cut a winding path across the wharf that she seemed to have traversed many times before.

At last, Miss Stanton came to a stop, riveted by a vast warehouse that, by all outward appearances, didn't warrant such rapt fascination. She heaved a ragged sigh, a hand to her chest. "Thank God, the roof is yet in place."

Theodore leaned on his crutch and raised an eyebrow. "Does it have a habit of flying—"

A metallic screech rent the air, and Theodore grimaced. Ripping his attention away from the wide-eyed Miss Stanton, he gawked at the warehouse from whence emanated the sounds of machinery. A metallic moan, like rusted gears being forced to turn. A clanking, clinking, creaking racket, like a dilapidated pulley system whose unoiled chains were now on the move, grating against one another as they hoisted a load. But what the deuce was their load?

The roof stirred, or rather hefted, its flat metal surface toward the sky as old hinges accustomed to their rest shrieked in protest.

"No, no, no!" In a flutter of skirts Miss Stanton disappeared into the warehouse before Theodore could so much as blink.

Dash it all! Would the woman ever elucidate? Theodore readied to give chase for the fourth time in one very long morning, only to have a mighty burst of wind set him down with a shove. Careening backward, he landed with a thwunk on his posterior.

In a puddle of rancid Thames.

A groan rattled through his clenched teeth, and for the first time since his army days, Theodore was tempted to swear. Loudly. Until another slap of wind caused him to look up.

A giant automaton owl hovered in flight above the warehouse, creating gusts of wind with every flap of its broad wings.

Theodore's jaw dropped to join him in the puddle. He blinked, but the marvel did not disappear. He'd hit his head. Cracked his skull wide open and lost his mind. That was the only explanation for the sight before him . . . or was it?

The mechanical wonder turned, catching the sunlight with its gleaming brass feathers and transforming the world below into a swirling kaleidoscope of shadow and light. He'd never seen a machine constructed on such a scale! The owl's outstretched wings could span the width of Kingsley Court's immense ballroom, and standing at full height, its ear tufts must surely graze the vaulted ceiling.

In graceful silence, the owl winged its way his direction, drawing closer and closer until the delicate ticking heartbeat of a clockwork movement set his own heart to sprinting. Two round eyes, crafted of amber glass, set their gaze upon him. Behind those vast windows to the soul, at the helm of a refashioned ship steering wheel, sat C. E. Drosselmeyer.

The marvel *was* real! And judging by the murmur and shuffle of feet behind him, it was beginning to draw attention. Theodore glanced left and right. Uniformed ship captains. Disheveled longshoremen. A few three-piece-suit merchants. All dredged their courage with a net of curiosity and inched closer, pointing and gawking at Drosselmeyer's triumph of engineering.

Unpredictable things, crowds. One moment awestruck and curious, the next panic-stricken and furious. Theodore willed the old codger to perceive the warning in his furrowed brows and in his mouthing of the words *Be careful*.

Outfitted with goggles and a pair of leather gloves, Drosselmeyer responded with a smile. Then he turned the steering wheel to the right. Without a sound, the clockwork owl rotated one hundred and eighty degrees and vaulted into the clouds, soaring off with the agility of its avian inspiration as it made for the clear blue horizon.

When the last glimmer of brass dimmed from sight, Theodore came to himself. He lumbered to his feet, avoiding eye contact with the blokes still standing about as he wrung fetid water from his trousers. Like a tot who'd wet his clout, that's how he must look. And smell. The pretty little grump might deign to laugh when—

Rusted cogs! He'd forgotten Miss Stanton!

How could Grand be gone? Just . . . gone.

Clara stood in the middle of a considerable concrete floor, surrounded by four clapboard walls that had once housed the only invention Grand ever kept secret. His wonderous flying machine. The great owl that just moments ago had winged away with a third of her heart.

Surveying the open roof, she blinked at the daylight pouring in from the azure sky, an unpredictable expanse that could alter its mood from cloudless contentment to raging gale in the mere second it took for lightning to flash its jagged blade. Even now, Grand was facing those erratic elements. Without her to navigate . . . to remind him to eat . . . to make sure he was safe.

Imagined thunder rumbled through her as a shudder that buckled her knees. No. She would not give in to futile hysterics. She wrung her hands of their traitorous tremors. By might and main, she must gather her fragmenting wits and devise a course of action. Inhaling, she steadied herself with a deep breath and then scurried to check the flight log.

Grand's long-neglected second desk stood like an old draft horse. Stout and sturdy. Four deep drawers contained tools and parts for tinkering, but the narrowest one, located middle top, housed the owl's flight log. At least it had years ago. Before grief clipped Grand's wings.

With a gloved hand, Clara yanked open the slim drawer and exhaled. Bound in leather the color of freshly brewed tea, the flight log lay just where she'd hoped. She removed her gloves and tucked them into her pocket before picking up the ledger, softened and creased from use. Laden with memories that wafted on the faint aroma of peppermint. She'd forgotten how much she missed this place. Missed the time spent here with Grand before the warehouse had been left to rust. Back when the roof opened without a sound, its mechanism regularly oiled and maintained, and Grand took off on clandestine excursions made under the cover of moonless nights that she'd help record pre- and postflight. Wind speeds, machine performance, and flight patterns to aid recovery in the event of a crash.

"Just in case, just in case," he'd said. "Never know when I might need you to find me."

Clara swallowed. *Please, Grand, help me find you now.* Cracking open the ledger, she flipped through entry after entry written in the naïve flowery hand of her youth. Near the back cover, she at last spotted Grand's familiar scrawl. Not in the form of a flight itinerary, but in a page-long letter marked with the day's date.

March 29, 1860

Dearest Little Atlas,

Please do not fret upon finding this note. Though you may feel otherwise, I assure you, I have not acted rashly.

What I've done today, I've done in complete possession of my faculties after days of serious thought and nights of sincere prayer. My leaving in this way, I believe, is necessary for both our sakes. We've pretended, you and I, for far too long.

The time has come for us to embark on a true adventure and experience the sights we've beheld only in imagination. I had wished you to join me in the sky like you once did, but I doubted you might be convinced to relive those joyous times. Therefore, I've opted to entice you to follow my trail with the allure of a merry scavenger hunt. You shall find my next clue in the capital city where your mythical namesake holds the firmament upon his shoulders within a mapped marble hall.

Please join me on this journey, Clara, bringing along the gift I've left for your use. The time has come for you to dream again and finally write your own story.

Your devoted,
Grand

A twitch tugged the corner of her right eye. This was too much. Too much information to absorb. Too many emotions to squelch. If only Grand had spoken to her about all this . . . if only she had believed him in earnest when he'd tried to at the Globe. If some horrible accident befell Grand . . . A rogue tremor shook the ledger from her grasp, and it fell into the open drawer.

Steady, Clara. Refortifying her emotional barricades with a deep breath, she retrieved the little book, and in so doing, uncovered a parcel wrapped in brown paper that she'd failed to notice before. Was this the gift Grand mentioned? She set the ledger aside and made quick work of the wrapping to reveal a journal and a pen. Crafted of weighty silver, the pen was outfitted with a lid, hook, and chain for attaching to a chatelaine, while the pocket-size journal, bound in crimson leather, was embossed with the words *An Adventurous Lady's Guide to Travel*. She shook her head. If Grand wished her story to be written, he should've chosen a more fitting title.

Tucking Grand's gifts away in a skirt pocket, she flipped through the ledger's pages once again. There had to be more information hidden in here somewhere. Something besides a vague clue and an "alluring" scavenger hunt. She read Grand's note again and then turned the page over, revealing a single sentence scrawled on the backside, as though written in a hurry.

P. S. Be sure to invite Arthur along, for you shall require his assistance.

Clara's posture deflated along with her lungs. Did Grand really think her so inept? After years of caring for him and her parents unaided, had she not proven herself capable? How could he even insinuate that she required help from—

"Does it say where he's gone, Miss Stanton?"

Knuckles blanching in their grasp, Clara faced the automaton apprentice, who didn't deserve to set foot in this special place any more than young Rupert had all those years ago. "Your assistance is not required in this matter, sir. Therefore, I suggest you shove off."

Clara set off at a brisk clip, wanting nothing more than to leave Mr. Arthur and the stench of the Thames behind. Clutching the ledger, she stomped out of the warehouse and wove through the dock's maze of cargo and longshoremen. The cab she'd hired was nowhere to be found. She shook her head. If she'd been thinking clearly, she would've withheld payment till her return, rather than leaving it on her seat for him to pocket. Now, as it was, she'd just have to make do. Though it might defy convention, she was perfectly capable of walking home unescorted. Perfectly capable of walking the world over if that's what it took to bring Grand home.

"Wait up, will you?"

The clank of a metal boot and tap of a wooden crutch set Clara's eye to twitching once again. "In case it failed to register in your dense masculine skull, the term *shove off* infers that you go elsewhere. Preferably in search of a steep precipice."

"Come now, Miss Stanton. At least tell me what the deuce is going on. Let me fix this somehow."

The man had nerve. First, he took advantage of Grand, and now he wished to ride in like some hero? As if she'd be fool enough to trust him. She squared her shoulders. Perhaps ignoring the man would get her point across.

Hastening to her swiftest speed short of a run, she put distance between herself and the docks. Warehouses and shipping crates soon gave way to run-down tenement buildings. Haggard women leaned out of windows, stringing faded laundry on ropes between the apartments whilst gangly youngsters played in the road.

A little girl with unkempt curls and a threadbare dress stood apart from the other children, excluded from a game she watched with teary brown eyes. Being ostracized by one's peers as an adult was bad enough. Teaching little ones to discriminate with the prejudices held by their parents . . . that was heartbreaking. Clara secured a few shillings from the coin purse on her chatelaine and discreetly slipped them to the forlorn girl.

Any light the child's tooth-sparse grin might have sparked was stamped out by the persistent clank of a metal boot. Clara huffed. No matter how fast she walked or how much she willed him away, Mr. Arthur remained on her heels like an irritating street hound begging for scraps. She would be tempted to report him to a constable, but the last thing her family needed was more attention from the very authorities who thought them mad.

Clank-tap, clank-tap.

Stars, did he intend to follow her all the way home? Clara hazarded a backward glance. Mr. Arthur offered her a crooked grin, which she promptly threw in the gutter as she stared ahead once more. Apparently, that's exactly what he intended. But why? He couldn't sincerely care for Grand after so short an acquaintance. A suspiciously formed acquaintance, at that. He must have an ulterior motive, and although he'd sworn to the contrary, she couldn't shake the suspicion that it involved her ex-fiancé. Mr. Arthur *must've* been sent to steal the letter signed by a respected member of Her Majesty's army, which would give Mr. Forrester written corroboration of his insanity claims. With that letter, Mr. Forrester would have tangible leverage to bend her to his will. After all, had it not been the word of a respected member of Her Majesty's army that had doomed Uncle Fritz to his fate in a madhouse cell?

It was the only thing that made sense.

Clank-tap, clank-tap.

Botheration. The time had come to change tactics. If she let the street hound follow her home, Mum would want to keep him, and she didn't need the distraction of worrying when the mutt would bite. Turning onto the next street, she spotted an alley betwixt an apartment building and a grocer's shop. Hmm . . . perhaps the best way to be rid of the mutt was to bite first.

Dashing into the alley, Clara pressed herself flat against the grocer's shop and lay in wait. Her heart slowed, pounding in unison with her quarry's ever-nearing clank-tap-clank. Just as Mr. Arthur peered into the alley, she smashed him in the face with the ledger, and he dropped his crutch to grasp his nose. Taking advantage of his disoriented state, she grabbed the collar of his ratty overcoat, dragged him into the alley, and shoved him against the nearest brick wall. She pressed the edge of the ledger against his throat as though it were a blade, standing her ground even when she caught a whiff of his regrettable cologne.

Mr. Arthur gawked with eyes of green, stunned by her actions and the impending threat of papercut. "I've been warned against the sort of women who lure unsuspecting lads into alleys and have their way with them, but I'd never have thought it of you, Miss Stanton. Your grandfather would be horrifi—"

"My grandfather is gone." The hollow words fell from Clara's lips like a vase shattering to the floor. "And you've brought him and the rest of this family quite enough trouble as it is, so tell me. How much will it take for you to leave my family be?"

Creases pinched the edges of Mr. Arthur's eyes as he made a study of her face. "Your parents are optimistic folks. As is Drosselmeyer. Who was it, then, who made you think the world is populated by naught but spies and villains? Was it that Forrester bloke?"

Clara flinched.

Keeping the ledger firmly against Mr. Arthur's throat, she reached into her purse and from a hidden slit in the lining withdrew the twenty-pound note Papa insisted she keep on her person in case of emergencies. She slipped the currency into one of the interior pockets of Mr. Arthur's overcoat. He could never hope to get as much from Mr. Forrester, especially now with the letter in Grand's pocket out of reach. "Your apprenticeship is nullified. Henceforth, you will not speak *with* my family. You will not speak *of* my family. You will simply use this note to leave Greater London, or I shall hire a private investigator with low fees and lower morals to uncover the past you're so keen to hide."

Leaving the deception and money behind, Clara fled the alley. Only when she found a hackney carriage for hire, climbed inside the glorified tinderbox, and pulled the ragged curtain over the window, did she allow the tremors rattling within to move without and shake free a restrained tear. She slumped against the torn seat. Here, amid the shadows of isolation, she could lower her guard and breathe. Just breathe. Just for a moment.

Until the carriage came to a halt outside the Stanton home. Time for Little Atlas to once again don her load.

Upon opening the Stanton home's cheery red door, Clara was greeted by the wagging tails and slobbery tongues of two spaniels, one bloodhound, and a solid black Great Dane named Dudley, whom Mum had saved from having his ears docked. She patted each canine in turn and headed for the parlor, where Papa sat in his usual chair, reading the business section of the paper whilst the baby goat on his lap ate through the obituaries. Across the way, Mum was occupied in the knitting of a four-legged sweater, her progress overseen by Fred as he lounged about her neck. Such a tranquil scene of hearth and home. One that ought to include the presence of clockwork butterflies.

"You're rather late, Clara Marie." Papa remained fixed on the paper as he absently scratched his beard, the graying facial hair held up by muttonchops on his otherwise bald head. "I've never known you to not be home in time for tea."

"She and Father must have been enjoying quite the adventure to lose track of the hour." Mum peered up from her knitting, though her needles still moved. "Where did the pair of you go this week, ducky? You get lost in the pyramids again?"

Clara dug her nails into the ledger. "No, I . . . I didn't get lost, but I'm afraid Grand did." She opened the flight log to the page with Grand's letter and placed it atop the yarn on Mum's lap.

Exchanging a look with Papa, Mum lowered her needles and proceeded to read the proffered page. Her eyebrows raised in gradual increments, and then she passed the ledger to Papa, who repeated the routine entire. Raised brows aside, neither exhibited much of a reaction. No frowns, exclamations of fright, or shedding of tears. They must be in shock.

Clara sat beside Mum, placing a reassuring hand on her knee. "I'm sorry I failed to reach the docks in time to stop him, but I promise, I'll set this right. Grand has a good head start, and the owl is swift, but if I leave within the hour, I think—"

The doorbell's *priiing* echoed through the house.

Clara's heartbeat tripped over itself as she shot to her feet. Merciful heaven, let that be Grand. Rushing to the entryway, she flung open the door and came face-to-face with Mr. Arthur.

His mouth tilted in a lopsided grin. "Hello, Miss Stanton. Pardon the intrusion, but I've come to return this scrap of paper that's fallen from your reticule." With a carefree air, he reached into his overcoat and produced her twenty-pound note.

Clara's jaw hung from its hinges. "Th-that's impossible, sir. I don't carry a reticule."

"Odd. I could've sworn you did, but then again, I have been seeing all sorts of inexplicable things today. Perhaps I should consider spectacles."

"Who's that at the door, ducky? Let them in, will you?"

"Aye, let us in, will you?" Mr. Arthur winked as he slipped the note between the doorknob and Clara's palm and clank-tapped toward the parlor.

Unbelievable. Had the man truly just given back her bribe? Clara studied the note as the door swung shut of its own accord. Indeed. He'd returned every shilling of a twenty-pound note that he might have pocketed without consequence.

Miserly Mr. Forrester wouldn't have offered Mr. Arthur as much, so why didn't the stray just take the money and run?

Restoring the note to her chatelaine purse, Clara returned to the parlor, where Mr. Arthur had made himself obnoxiously comfortable on Mum's right. In an act of betrayal, the canine quartet gathered around the man, accepting him into their pack with unfettered adoration. Dudley the Dane, sitting tall as a floor lamp beside the couch, rested his chin atop Mr. Arthur's head. "Excellent timing, Miss Stanton. I was just outlining my plans for retrieving Drosselmeyer. As his apprentice, I feel it is my duty to—"

"*Former* apprentice, Mr. Arthur. I terminated your employment, remember." Clara claimed the seat on Mum's left and looked to Papa, willing him to heed the plea in her gaze. "Do send him away. This is a family matter. Grand asked me to come after him, and I am more than capable of bringing him home. Once I fetch my maps and travel guides from the attic, I can outline Grand's most logical flight pattern and—"

"Beg pardon, Miss Stanton, but you seem to be forgetting Drosselmeyer's postscript." Mr. Arthur held aloft the ledger book. "The one in which he asked me to come after him."

Clara snatched the ledger back, gaping at her parents. "How could you let him read—"

"Perhaps because they know I have experience traveling abroad." Mr. Arthur shifted on the sofa, displacing Dudley's chin as he angled for a face-off. "It seems to me that the expertise you profess is limited to paper and ink, and while your maps and travel guides are well and good, knowledge does not trump experience. I know how to handle the sort of unforeseen obstacles that aren't charted on maps. Strategize alternate routes. Think on the move. Make up for any knowledge I lack by gleaning information from the terrain, locals, and newspaper reports."

Clara's mouth went dry. "N-newspaper reports?"

"Aye, Miss Stanton." Mr. Arthur slapped his knees and leaned forward. "You think a larger-than-life automaton owl soaring over cities, villages, and international borders isn't going to be noticed? By this time, a dozen or so longshoremen are selling their firsthand accounts to newspapers across London. Come morning, Drosselmeyer's machine is bound to be front-page news."

Front-page news. Each word plunked to the pit of Clara's stomach with the unsettling effects of an underdone potato. These past few hours she'd only thought to be worried for Grand's safety, but now . . . now there were the unmerciful, unpredictable, unrelenting members of the press to consider.

If the papers got wind of Grand's identity—that the owl's pilot was accused of lunacy—the repercussions could land dear Grand in an asylum and her parents in the gutter. Especially if the letter were to be discovered on his person. Oh, there was no room for debate now. She must go after Grand. For Mr. Arthur could not be trusted with secreting Grand's incriminating trail of clues and bringing him and the letter home undiscovered.

Leaning across Mum, Clara met Mr. Arthur nose-to-nose and refused to recoil from the stench of the Thames that unaccountably clung to his person. "He's *my* grandfather, and *I* will bring him home. End of discussion."

Mr. Arthur arched a blond brow. "Relation does not make up for a lack of qualifications."

"Qualifications without verification do not signify."

"Mulish stubbornness doesn't make one in the right."

"Smelling like the backside of a mule doesn't win people to your way of thinking."

"Enough pecking and squawking, chickies! You're crushing mother hen." Mum emerged from betwixt them, pushing them to their respective corners of the sofa. "Now. George and I have both read Father's letter and listened to your differing opinions. Since the pair of you can't seem to agree on a course of action, we shall decide how the situation should be handled. What do you think, George?"

Stroking the goat, Papa knit his brow. "I think . . . you should have the final say in this matter, Heidi dear. C. E. is your father, for one. For another, I cannot be away from the London office for an indeterminate length of time."

"Very well, George. If I am to decide, I say let the three of us set off at once."

But if Papa couldn't join them, who was the . . . ? Clara's head popped up. "Oh, Mum, you cannot mean—"

"Indeed, ducky. Our party of three will include Mr. Arthur. I believe his travel experience *and* your knowledge of geography are needed to make our journey a successful one. Besides, Father did mention you both by name in his note. While my name was omitted, I shall join the pair of you as your chaperone and revel in the entire escapade."

Mr. Arthur stood, taking up his crutch. "Right-oh, Mrs. S. If that's what you feel is best, that's how it shall be. I'll return to the shop to grab a few supplies and lock up." With that, he saw himself out.

The moment the front door thudded shut, Clara seized Mum's hand. "You can't possibly be serious about traveling abroad with a man we've known all of one month. What if he's working for Mr. Forrester? What if he's making up all these stories of his travel experience? What if—"

Mum placed a finger over Clara's lips. "What-ifs are not acquainted with what-is, and they spread horrid falsehoods about what-will-be, so why bother entertaining them? I'd sooner invite hope into my home—for even when her predictions miss the mark, she makes for pleasant company and eats far less food."

Hope might be pleasant company, but she didn't protect against vandals. Clara knelt before Papa. "Make her see reason. We hardly know this person. Traveling with him . . . it's not safe."

A smile quirked Papa's whiskers as he cupped a warm hand to her face. "Oh, Clara Marie. The Lord never promised that life would be safe. But He *did* promise to be with us always. Whatever the harrowing journey of life may bring, rest assured, you shall never be left to face it alone."

She sank to her haunches. Traveling with the Lord was one thing, but with her Mum and Mr. Arthur? This would be no merry adventure as Grand wished.

This would be a disaster.

CHAPTER

7

"Are ermine prone to seasickness, do you think?" Mum's question rattled about the dilapidated hackney carriage conveying them to the docks.

Clara massaged her temple and heaved her longest sigh of the day. Quite a feat, that, considering this had no doubt been the longest day in the whole of her three and twenty years.

A spring poking through the seat cushion jabbed her posterior with every jostle. If only Grand hadn't decided to fly off on a Thursday, they might be riding comfortably in their own carriage right now. Alas, it was the horses' day off, and Mum flatly refused to harness their beloved team of four. Clara had reasoned that the girls would understand, given the extenuating circumstances, but Mum held firm. If God saw fit to give man a day of rest, then Apple, Cherry, and the other blossoms should enjoy their customary back massages and hoof polishing undisturbed.

"Perhaps I should moderate Fred's diet our first few days

at sea until his stomach has grown accustomed to the ocean's undulation. What do you think, ducky?"

This ducky's opinion doesn't carry much weight anymore. Swallowing the thought, Clara responded with a very mature shrug of her shoulders, knowing well that Mum couldn't see her in the night's darkness. She was too peeved to care about Fred's diet at present. How could she not be after having been ignored and pish-poshed all evening?

During their rushed travel preparations, Mum had been fixated on giving Mudgett and Mrs. Collins detailed instructions for the care of her menagerie, whilst Papa arranged their passage on one of his mercantile ships scheduled to depart that evening. Both parents had refused to hear—let alone heed—her continued protestations against Mr. Arthur serving as their escort.

Clara bored a glare through the carriage wall that separated them from Mr. Arthur, now seated beside the hackney driver. While her wary nerves wished to convince Mum to maroon him once they set sail, such an attempt would be a futile expenditure of breath. Mum liked the scamp too much. At this point, her energy would be better spent by focusing on what mattered most—keeping Mum safe and bringing Grand home without discovery.

With a bounce, a screech, and a lurch, the hackney gasped to a halt. Clara gripped the wall and seat to keep herself upright. Sailing would feel like a languid stroll through Hyde Park after riding in this cursed contraption. She pressed her fingers to her stomach, trying to convince her body the carriage had in fact ceased moving, but the noxious odor of the Thames seeping through every board did little to aid her efforts.

The door opposite her flew open, revealing a masculine silhouette against a backdrop of moonlight. "Right-oh, Mrs. Stanton." Mr. Arthur extended a hand. "The SS *Heidi* awaits her lovely namesake."

Fred raised his head from his place on Mum's shoulder with an eager squeak.

Chuckling merrily, Mum took Mr. Arthur's proffered hand. "I do believe Freddy has taken a fancy to you, Arthur."

Of course he had, the adorable little traitor. Was Clara the only creature on God's green earth immune to his charms?

Mum alighted from the carriage with a hop. The displacement of weight set the rickety conveyance to rocking and Clara to falling against her seat's loose spring. "Ow!"

"Hurry along, ducky. We don't want to take up this gentleman's evening. I'm sure he has more fares to transport before the night is through."

May God have mercy on their souls if they hired this overstuffed pincushion. With a groan, Clara righted herself and staggered out of the carriage, shutting the door none too gently. She paid the driver, begrudgingly, then stood for a moment on the dock and arched her aching back. Just ahead, Mum and Mr. Arthur walked arm in arm toward the ship, following a dockhand carrying their luggage. She drew a steadying breath and grimaced at the less-than-fresh air. If she prayed for patience, would that make this evening better or worse?

Definitely worse.

Much safer to pray for strength to bear her load. She shut her eyes, reveling in the quiet solitude of night and the sensation of steady ground beneath her feet. *Whatever the journey ahead brings, keep a stiff upper lip, Clara Marie. For Mum's and Grand's sakes. You cannot afford to let them down this time. The stakes are too high. The danger too great.*

"Good evening, darling."

Clara's eyes flashed open. A yellow waistcoat, blindingly garish even in the darkness, turned her stomach to stone. How did Mr. Forrester know to find her here? Was he still "watching out for her," as he put it? She clenched her jaw. It didn't matter. She refused to be frightened or intimidated. Steeling herself from head to toe, she marched toward the SS *Heidi*.

Mr. Forrester darted into her path. "Clara, please. I know our last encounter was less than pleasant, but are you not even going to bid me farewell?" With a glance over his shoulder, he removed his bowler hat, clutching the brim in his hands as he faced her again. The moonlight revealed a black eye and split lip.

Clara winced. "Who did that to you?"

A change came over Mr. Forrester's countenance. An expression—half fear, half agony—that displaced his tailored mantle of suave self-assurance and revealed tattered remnants of the young boy she once *thought* she knew. Thought she loved. "I told you, my dear, creditors have no patience or scruples." As quick as it came, the look was gone.

He donned his hat, obscuring his eyes in shadow. "That doesn't matter now. All that matters is I've caught you in time."

Unease crept along Clara's skin, raising gooseflesh. "What are you going on about?"

Mr. Forrester took possession of her gloved hands. "Please, marry me, Clara. Tonight. It will solve everything."

Her tense shoulders sagged, laden with weariness. "My family's *money*, you mean. That will solve everything."

"Yes, yes, Clara. Money is the only thing that solves problems, that brings security in this world. Why can't you comprehend that simple fact?"

"Why can't you stop being so underhanded? Why not just ask Papa for the money or get a loan—"

"Paying off one man with another man's money still leaves you under a burden of debt. And I refuse to be indebted to anyone ever again. Marriage will make your fortune mine in the eyes of the law, and I'll finally have the means to make my own way. Don't you see? Once we're engaged, the creditors will be appeased with assurance of payment, and I can be free of their blighted faces and fists. Free to learn to love you the way you love me. Free to be my old self again." Pulling her close, Mr. Forrester kissed her hand with the awkwardness of a child who'd never been shown such affection. "Everything will be as it was before."

A sigh bled from her lips. He was either completely delusional or the greatest actor to perform off a London stage. "You have conspired to wed me under false pretenses. You have slandered those I hold most dear. You've sent spies into our home—strangers who might've done us harm—all so you could steal the evidence of my family's greatest heartache and use it to manipulate me for personal gain. Even now, you choose to deceive and make empty promises rather than tell me the truth of your circumstances. Things can never be as they were before."

Prying her fingers from his desperate grasp, Clara restored a healthy distance between them. "Now, Mr. Forrester, I bid you farewell and good night." She skirted around his stunned form and made for the ship.

"Drosselmeyer should've been more careful." Mr. Forrester's voice, a hollow, haunting specter, reached out through the gloom. "Taking flight midday when the docks were crowded with onlookers was a mistake he's sure to regret."

A quiver unsettled her lips, but Clara kept moving. She should've known reports of the owl's departure would reach Mr. Forrester quickly. He had men working the docks from end to end.

"The moment Drosselmeyer sets foot on British soil, I'll see him carted off to Bedlam."

The threat's icy hand yanked her worst fears to the surface, and she whirled, fists balled. "On what grounds, sir? Your bumbling spies have failed to find the letter."

Mr. Forrester's dark silhouette remained still and calm. Too calm. "Who needs a letter about the deranged son when the father is crazy enough to take to the sky in a machine of war?"

Her jaw slackened. "You're mad."

"No, my darling. Just desperate, thanks to you and my old man. Before the break of dawn, I can buy a dozen respectable witnesses who will testify your unhinged grandfather threatened to attack the Palace with his flying machine. Carry off the little queen and her brats like so many mice in its talons. Yes, those were his very words. With the rumors of Drosselmeyer's lunacy and his son's death in an asylum already swirling about London, who will doubt such testimony? Not a single soul who's loyal to the Crown. Just think how easy it will be for the papers to play on the public's fears, goading them into a hysterical mob. For the good of queen and country, the crazy pilot of the owl will have to be locked away in a government institution. Safe and sound."

Mr. Forrester stalked toward her slowly. "Ah, but you and I know what those places are really like. How unsafe they are for the pitiful wretches who find themselves there. Lieutenant Harbinger's letter about your poor uncle made that plain enough."

Her blood ran cold. "Don't—"

"*Shackles hang from the ceiling to restrain the deranged patients, all skin and bones.*"

At that line, Granny had begun to weep. Clara retreated, without care to where the dock ended and the Thames began. "Stop."

"*Brutish guards maintain order with the crack of whips.*"

At that line, Granny had collapsed, never to rise again.

"Enough!" Her back slammed against a stack of crates as tears pooled in her eyes. She looked about for help, but none was to be found. The solitude she'd once craved was now an enemy, and the quiet of night a menacing accomplice.

Moonlight cast Mr. Forrester's looming shadow over her with the ominous effect of a hand to the throat. "Lest you think the lieutenant was exaggerating, let me assure you, dearest. There is no darker hell than a government institution. I've been inside the four walls of a debtor's prison. Seen the dank stone cells, untouched by sunlight or fresh air. Heard the coughs of illness, felt the heat of fever left untreated."

Seen? Heard? Clara gawked at him. "When did you have cause to visit a debtor's prison?"

"Visit." He spat the word like a bit of spoiled meat.

"What are you not telling me? Have you—"

"If that's the sort of care the government gives to its poor, imagine what hospitality they show to their insane. Drosselmeyer won't last a month in one of those places. Marry me, and you'll save him from that fate. Marry me, and I'll call off my spies, cease my search, and keep quiet about what I know of your uncle's death and your grandfather's machine."

Clara shuddered, pressing against the immovable crates at her back. A wedding band would not protect her family from a man like this. A man callous enough to corner her alone . She needed to get on that ship. Now.

A splintering crash resounded behind Mr. Forrester. He startled and turned away from her in the direction of the noise, fists raised as though to fend off attackers.

Clara ran for the ship. Mr. Forrester called after her as unseen longshoremen cursed the loss of cargo, now shattered, but she didn't look back—didn't stop—until the steel door of the SS *Heidi* barred out the night.

Mum's stockinged feet dangled overhead, kicking in unison like she was perched on a tree swing rather than the upper berth of their confined cabin aboard the SS *Heidi*. "You've been awfully quiet since you boarded the ship, ducky. Are you seasick?"

No, just heartsick. And oh so very tired.

Wedged on the lower berth, Clara stared at the metal wall that separated their cabin from Mr. Arthur's. Since boarding the vessel, she hadn't uttered a word to her mother about what happened at the docks, partly because she couldn't bring herself to speak of it just yet and partly because there seemed no point in robbing them both of sleep. "I'm fine, Mum."

At least she would be, given more time and distance. When they'd reached the Thames Estuary, Clara's heart had stopped racing, and now, an hour into open sea, the tremors coursing through her body had finally stilled. Yes, she would be fine soon enough. As long as she didn't let her thoughts stray back to Mr.

Forrester's threats. As long as she was able to find Grand and convince him that the letter and the owl must be destroyed.

Slipping a hand into the pocket of her brown corded silk dress, Clara removed the journal she'd been gifted—not to engage in Grand's wild suggestion of composing her own travel guide, mind, but rather to serve as a convenient hiding place for the clues she must now collect. Opening the journal to where clue number one now dwelt amongst the blank pages, she ran her fingers over the cryptic words that Grand had inscribed and she had deciphered. The words that even now had them sailing across the North Sea, bound for the city of Amsterdam.

You shall find my next clue in the capital city where your mythical namesake holds the firmament upon his shoulders within a mapped marble hall.

Clara yawned. She really ought to change into her nightdress, but the thought of rising from her berth to do so was enough to incite another mouth-stretcher. She returned the journal to her pocket and shut her eyes. Her nightdress could have a holiday. For she was not taking to her feet again until they docked. And perhaps not even then. Perhaps she'd tell Mr. Arthur to make himself useful and carry her across Amsterdam to the—

Feet smacked against the cabin floor. "Care to join us for a moonlit stroll?"

Please be a dream. Clara pried her heavy eyelids open and found Mum standing by the door of their cabin, boots on and laced. Fred was draped about her neck, playing with the pink ribbons dangling from Mum's straw bonnet. Clara groaned and rubbed her eyes. Why must reality be stranger than her dreams? "Can't a stroll wait until morning?"

"I should think not. Moonlit strolls hardly ever happen in the morning. For that shy maiden moonlight has a habit of running away at the break of dawn."

"And ship decks have a habit of being slick and littered with a tangle of ropes. It would be safer to take a turn about in the morning when you'll have enough light to properly see where you're going." *And a rested daughter to keep you out of trouble.*

"Rubble and rot. I've been aboard these sorts of vessels with your father more times than I can recall and have navigated them with surefootedness no matter the weather or hour. Which is precisely how I know there's no substitute for taking in the sea air whilst the sky is aglow with maiden moonlight's silvery blush. It is simply magical."

It was simply reckless. "Be that as it may, I must beg we retire for the night. My current state of exhaustion surpasses that of a perpetually napping hedgehog."

"You would forgo a magical moonlit stroll and take to your bed at half past eleven?" In a trice, Mum's fingers were pressed upon Clara's brow, checking for a fever, then upon her wrist to search for a pulse, then upon her cheek as if to reclaim a lost treasure. "What happened to the little girl who'd steal away from the nursery every night at a quarter past three to play intrepid explorer? The little girl who'd awaken her parents with squeals and laughter as she slid down a 'waterfall' banister? What happened to Little Atlas, who once charted courses to exotic lands and daydreamed of romantic adventures?"

Clara pulled her bottom lip between her teeth. She'd grown up and realized her folly too little, too late, to the detriment of those she loved most. A tattered sigh tore itself from her chest. "Romance and adventure are the idealistic scribblings of Austen and Dumas. Like Elizabeth Bennet and Athos, they are not real. Nor do they exist off the page. To believe otherwise is to suffer disillusionment and heartbreak."

The saddest of frowns draped itself over Mum's face, bleak and delicate as a mourning veil. "Elizabeth Bennet's happily-ever-after might be a work of fiction, but love is real enough. Sometimes it takes idealistic scribblings to remind us of that truth when the whole of our very real, very dark world makes it feel like a lie."

Allowing no time for contradiction, she walked out the door.

Clara stared at the rivets lined in neat rows on the cabin wall. Now she'd done it. She'd let her foul mood get a hold of her mouth and cast a bitter shadow over the most cheerful woman to walk the earth. Should she chase after Mum or allow her a moment alone with maiden moonlight? Mum might prefer the latter, but guilt and fear made a sound argument for the former. What if Mum was so upset that she failed to watch her footing on the slick deck? Clara pursed her lips. Or perhaps Mum was right, and she was worrying for naught. Perhaps, this once, she should leave Mum to her own devices and relax.

A scream on deck pierced through the cabin walls.

Clara snapped upright. Good heavens, was the ship going down?

"Murderer!" The all-too-familiar, all-too-loud denunciation seemed to rattle the steamer's iron hull.

Stars above, what species of trouble had Mum found this time? Catapulting from her berth, Clara flew toward the port bow, where her mother's indignation combated with the refutations of a gruff male voice.

"I demand you release the prisoners at once!"

"I'm just doin' me job, marm. 'Tain't no concern of yours."

"When God charged humankind to tend the creatures of the garden, it became my concern."

Beneath the brilliant glow of moonlight, Mum stood boot-to-boot with a squat sailor who held a gas lantern at eye level. The man's broad chest was a solid mass of muscle, and his patience appeared to be wearing as thin as the strands of hair greased flat across his brow. Clara's nose scrunched. Of all the sailors to pick a fight with, Mum would pick the snarling bulldog of the sea.

Said bulldog gave the metal cage in his opposite hand a sound shake. "These varmints are goin' overboard, and so 'elp me, if you don't get out the way, you're goin' with them."

Mum planted her hands on her hips. "I'd be amused to watch you try it, lard gut."

"Mother!" Clara seized Mum's shoulder and whispered in her ear, "Papa may have christened this ship in your honor, but that doesn't make you the captain. Let the man do his job."

"But his task isn't honorable. He intends to drown those innocent creatures. Just look at how frightened they are!"

Clara made the mistake of glancing at the rickety cage, where a furry family of stowaway mice huddled together aquiver. Seven little heads with large dark eyes and even larger ears. Drat it all, why must they be so darling? *Snuff the flame of sentimentality, Clara. They're just rodents. Just nasty little beastie rodents.* She severed her gaze from the mice only to have Fred nudge her cheek with his twitchy nose, as though to implore on his fellow creatures' behalf.

She sighed, defeated by darlingness. "Sir, would you please consider—"

"I ain't got time to haggle with hysterical women." Squaring his shoulders, the bulldog invaded their personal space bodily. "Shove off afore I make ye shove off."

"Such a boorish turn of phrase, that." Awash in a combination of golden lantern and silver moonlight, Mr. Arthur approached with the aid of his crutch and an air of nonchalance. "'Shove off' is definitely not the sort of idiom that should be bandied about in front of ladies. Why, I imagine refined women like the Stantons aren't even familiar with the vulgar term." He set his gaze upon Clara, green eyes gleaming with a suppressed smirk. "Can I be of assistance, Miss Stanton?"

Heat that not even the crisp sea air could cool singed Clara's cheeks. "I shouldn't think so, Mr. Arthur, as we are merely engaging in a civil debate with this gentleman."

"Gettin' in my way, more like," the man growled under his breath.

Mum jabbed a finger at the bulldog's snub nose. "Your way being the corpse-strewn crossroads of injustice and tyranny."

Clara swatted her mother's finger out of the air. "I have this well in hand, Mr. Arthur."

"That so, Miss Stanton? From what I've observed, you might have the clock in hand, but you're struggling to make it tick. You see, you'll never convince a pair of gears to work together by trying to force them to agree and turn in the same direction. Gears must be allowed to go their separate ways and thus turn one another through the interlocking process of compromise. Only then will the clock tick."

The bulldog shifted his glower between her and Mum. "What the devil is he goin' on about?"

"Just this, my good fellow." Without regard for health or cleanliness, Mr. Arthur slapped a hand on the bulldog of the sea's grimy shoulder. "When push comes to shoving off, you're not opposed to these mice living to see another sunrise. You don't care a whit about them one way or the other. What you care about is avoiding the boot of your captain, who, I take it, has ordered you to keep this ship rodent-free. A task that is nigh on impossible with faulty equipment, am I right?"

The sailor relaxed into a noncombative stance, broad chest and shoulders slumped. "That's sure enough. Only thing the cap'in likes more than a clean ship is full pockets. The tight fist won't give me a farthin' for proper cages, and since these varmints won't keep in busted ones, I got no choice but to toss 'em over. I ain't gettin' sacked o'er a lot of mice."

"Nor should you, my man. Hard workers like yourself ought never to fear getting the sack over something beyond your control. That's why I want to help secure your employment. What if I were to repair all your cage traps—free of charge, mind—so stowaway mice can be secured on ship and released on land, thereby making your job easier and getting your captain's boot off your back? Could you find your way to agreeing to that sort of arrangement?"

Clara's eyes rolled so hard she felt they must have gone right off the ship. Did Mr. Arthur really think he could just saunter up to this obstinate bulldog, change his mind with flattery, and—

"You got yourself a deal." The sailor extended the cage toward Mr. Arthur.

The ship swayed beneath Clara's feet. Apparently, he could.

"Right-oh, sir." Mr. Arthur accepted the cage and gave the bulldog's free paw a hearty shake. "Always a pleasure to do business with a man of intelligence. Now, with your concerns allayed, let's attend to those of the lovely lady here. Mrs. S., if this family of mice are assured safe passage and given unto your care for the duration of our voyage, could you abide by the condition of keeping them caged?"

Now Mr. Arthur had found himself an impossible task. Clara crossed her arms. If her experience was any indication, Mum would never consent to leaving an animal behind bars.

"To save their lives, I suppose I can tolerate a temporary incarceration."

Clara's arms fell in tandem with her jaw. This never-ending day was naught but madness.

"Excellent, Mrs. S. Thank you for being so understanding. Let's get this temporary prison secured straightaway, shall we?" Kneeling upon his good leg, Mr. Arthur set the cage in front of him and then laid his overcoat alongside, revealing a lining of pockets nigh bursting with various bits and bobs. Unbuttoning each cuff of his white cotton shirt, he started rolling up his sleeves. "Shine that light here, sir."

Over the course of a few minutes, Mr. Arthur tinkered and toiled upon the mouse family's cage whilst Clara stood by, wondering what to do with her useless self. How had the man unraveled the knotted situation with such ease? Why had his efforts succeeded while hers failed? Oh, but he was infuriating. And irritating. And . . . remarkably inventive.

She studied his work on the cage more closely. Grand was right about the man's creativity, at least. Mr. Arthur enacted unconventional solutions with whatever resources could be found within reach, whether it be the expected implement of pliers or the unusual employment of a rubber band. He labored with ingenuity and a surprising amount of care. When Mum requested that he not jostle the mice about in his work, Mr. Arthur altered his methods to set her at ease.

When the cage was repaired, Mr. Arthur stood with the aid of his crutch, reassuring the bulldog that the other cages would be mended at dawn's first light. Satisfied with that promise, the sailor walked off with a lumbering swagger. Mum clutched the cage to her ample bosom, making introductions between Fred and the "little dears" as she hurried off to their cabin to prepare a banquet of cheese.

Her mother's departure left Clara quite alone with Mr. Arthur amid a moonlit atmosphere of awkward silence. She gnawed her lip. While she'd like nothing better than to withdraw, collapse on her berth, and awaken to find this whole topsy-turvy day had been but a dream, there was one Herculean task she must perform first.

Presenting Mr. Arthur with a word of thanks.

Clara pried her lip out from betwixt her teeth. "I appreciate what you did just now, Mr. Arthur. For Mum. Thank you."

Mr. Arthur slipped on his overcoat and offered a bow. "My pleasure, Miss Stanton."

There. She'd been civil. He'd been civil. She could retire now.

"Did Drosselmeyer create all those contraptions?"

Clara paused on her turning heel and faced Mr. Arthur, who gestured toward the objects hanging from her chatelaine. Dratted civility. One pleasantry voiced in obliged politeness and people thought you wished to engage in a conversation that outlasted a meeting of Parliament. "Indeed he did. Now if you'll excuse me—"

"I'm terribly sorry, Miss Stanton."

The complete lack of tomfoolery in Mr. Arthur's voice prompted Clara to draw close enough to inspect him in the moonlight. His entire countenance now bore a heavy mantle of seriousness that she'd never seen him wear before, nor thought him capable of donning.

Raking a hand through his untamed mane, Mr. Arthur heaved a sigh. "It was my fault Drosselmeyer took off the way he did this morning. I should've paid more attention to the nuance of his words. Insisted he stay put until your arrival so you might've been spared the shock of it all. But I didn't, and for that I'm sorry. Despite what you may think, the last thing I want is for your family to come to harm. Whether or not you take my word for it, I swear to do everything in my power to reunite you with your grandfather."

Either this man without a surname was the most skilled liar she'd ever met or she had grievously misjudged his character. "I blame you for many things, Mr. Arthur. But my Grand's departure isn't one of them." For she was the one who'd failed to notice the nuance of Grand's words back at the Globe.

"He's a rare man, your grandfather." Something akin to fondness grounded Mr. Arthur's words. "I've worked with many a clockmaker in my time, but Drosselmeyer has the sort of skill that can't be learned. The sort of talent that's built into the movement of a man by the Almighty Maker Himself. Drosselmeyer's impeccable clocks and incredible inventions are fit for the collections of royal palaces. His work is that fine. His attention to detail that meticulous. Which is why I'm surprised that compass he made you looks in such poor shape. Why hasn't Drosselmeyer attempted to repair it?"

Because she'd told him to leave it alone.

Clara brushed a finger across the broken compass. The one Papa had commissioned Grand to make as a gift for her sixteenth birthday. The one Mr. Forrester had yanked from her chatelaine the evening she'd broken off their engagement. She'd never forget his words from that night.

"I'm not stealing from your precious family, Clara. Stanton Shipping and Forrester Freight will merge eventually when your father dies and you inherit. I've every right to put up my future property as collateral in order to appease these creditors, and as my future wife, you've no right to involve yourself in my business affairs."

"I could repair the compass, if you like, Miss Stanton."

A chill breeze laced with salt caused Clara to shiver. Wrapping both arms about her in lieu of a shawl, she braced herself against the cold. "Thank you, Mr. Arthur, but I'd rather you didn't. Even in its current condition, it serves me quite well." As a tangible reminder that it was far better to misjudge than to be misused.

Once again, he'd have to watch them die.

Once again, the nightmare would win.

Bereft of saber and steed, Theodore raced across Balaklava's valley of death on legs intact and unscarred. Sweat poured down his brow and saturated his uniform. His muscles burned, and yet the strength he exerted failed to produce momentum, produce movement. Burdened by a heaviness that could not be shaken, his sprinting legs remained in the exact same location. Stuck. *Always* stuck. Shells careened toward him, exploding left and right. Each blast tossed fellow members of the Light Brigade into the air like bits of chaff. He tried to catch them, knowing all too well that it would do no good. In the nightmares, they always fell out of reach.

Broken.

Like him.

Because of him.

And there was nothing he could do to repair the damage that had been done.

Screaming without audible sound, Theodore collapsed on the bloodstained soil and clutched his right leg, now severed below the knee. Like every dream prior, he did not feel the injury. It was the slap yet to come that inflicted pain, and if this night terror progressed in the same manner as the others, it would happen soon.

Father strode onto the battlefield in a pristine suit, unfazed by the surrounding carnage, and looked down on him with that familiar expression of disappointment spiked with disdain. "How could you have misinterpreted a written order so grossly? How could you misdirect your men toward an artillery battery they'd no chance to withstand? How many more people must die because of you?"

In a blink, the scene changed, and Theodore was in the study at Kingsley Court, standing before Father on the day that had changed everything.

"Be a man and join the cavalry as is tradition. And if you can't live up to your name, then don't bother coming back." Father's palm struck fast and hard.

The pain scorched Theodore's cheek as his head snapped to the left.

He was on the battlefield once again, lying beside a comrade-in-arms, now cold in death. *No.* Tears wet his cheek, still stinging from Father's strike. *I have to make things right. I have to fix this.* Theodore turned the soldier over, and Drosselmeyer's face lolled to the side with vacant eyes that chilled the soul.

Theodore bolted upright. Awake.

At last, awake.

Shivers racked his body despite the perspiration dripping from his brow. Every breath was a splintered fragment, jagged and short. Theodore gasped and took in his surroundings—narrow berth below, narrow berth above, the riveted metal door of a steamer cabin ahead—each solid object grounding him to reality.

The nightmares had grown worse in recent weeks. More frequent. And tonight, the demons haunting him had chosen to rewrite the dream's end—a change more troubling than the nightmare itself. After years of enduring the same terror over and over again, he'd become numb to its effects. Resigned to the sights and sounds that would forever plague his sleep. There was a small measure of comfort in knowing what to expect. Knowing how to cope. Knowing how to hold it together.

Not knowing, on the other hand . . . that was a nightmare in and of itself.

His eyelids sagged and vision blurred, fatigued by countless nights of slumber without rest. How was he to protect the Stanton ladies in this state? Today the SS *Heidi* was to dock at Amsterdam, and he needed to be ready to move out. He *must* be in fine form. But that was impossible. Theodore Kingsley was too shattered a man to ever be *fine* again, which was why he'd constructed Arthur in the first place—to conceal what he could never mend.

To distance himself from the name he was unworthy to be called.

Lumbering out of the ill-fitting berth, Theodore dressed and reattached his metal prosthetic. After splashing cold water on his face and combing it through his hair, he mentally gathered up every raw emotion and bloody memory the nightmare had jarred loose, shoved them back in their encasement with the rest of his broken past, and locked the door. He took up his crutch. Right-oh, time to forget the night and greet the day.

An amber sun crested the horizon as Amsterdam's harbor greeted them with a welcoming party of vessels—wooden-hulled grandfathers with sinewy masts waved sails of wizened white, while strapping, iron-hulled chaps stood at attention in rows of tall funnels, saluting them with billows of boiler steam and smoke.

As the SS *Heidi* joined its fellow seafarers, a door creaked behind Theodore, and Miss Stanton emerged from the adjacent cabin. Failing to notice him, she took in a long breath, as though reveling in the fresh air. She wore a simple brown dress and a straw bonnet with a large, rounded brim that crushed black ringlets against her fair cheeks. Was he imagining things, or did she appear even paler this morning? Had sleep evaded her as well?

"Morning, Miss Stanton."

She startled upon hearing his voice and then swished toward the ship's railing, pretending as though she had not.

So the pretty grump still wasn't speaking to him, aye? Theodore scratched his head. The night they'd set sail, he thought he'd finally made a sound step toward securing Miss Stanton's good opinion. She'd seemed to accept his apology and had spoken to him in a manner *almost* congenial. She had even thanked him! But then, all at once, she'd reverted. For some blasted reason he couldn't deduce, she'd shunned him for the duration of their voyage. Either he'd inadvertently said something offensive, or she was determined to loathe him until the return of Christ.

"Liberation day at last!" Bursting onto the deck, Mrs. S. flung a hand toward the sky and performed a flamboyant twirl. When she stilled, her full skirts continued to swing back and forth like a ringing bell. Ermine round her neck and cage full of mice in hand, she shone the brightest of smiles his way. "Be a lamb and fetch our luggage, Arthur. The time has come to free the prisoners!"

"Right-oh, Mrs. S." Theodore strode into the Stantons' cabin and secured the hefty carpetbags on the lower berth, one embroidered with fuchsias and hummingbirds and the other with violets and bumblebees. He still couldn't believe the women had brought only two bags between them. While he'd always preferred to travel light—carrying all he required in the numerous pockets of his overcoat—most ladies tended to enlist a heavy brigade of trunks laden with all the comforts and fripperies of home. But then again, the Stantons weren't exactly like most ladies.

After returning with the bags, Theodore struggled to make haste as swiftly as the women he was meant to escort. Like a duo of dormice, the Stantons scurried down the gangplank and scampered across the shipyard, always several paces ahead of him, despite their petite stature. While his automaton prosthetic had restored a sense of ease to his stride, it simply couldn't match their light-footedness. Not that he minded. After five days and four long nights at sea, he was just glad to have solid ground beneath his boots again. The consistent feel of pavement provided an illusion of stability, which he craved after so many shaky nights.

Once the shipyard was in their peripheral, Mrs. S. set about finding a place to liberate the prisoners. And of course not just any location would suffice. The mice must be transported to a suitable habitat, which she expounded upon at length for the benefit of his and Miss Stanton's education. There were dietary needs to consider. The matter of shelter against inclement weather. And apparently potential habitats were also to be judged on their "conduciveness to pleasant procreation practice." An issue which, evidently, was of grave concern to Miss Stanton as well, judging by her sudden fit of coughing.

All the while their search progressed, the Stantons remained arm in arm, and all the while—coughing fit aside—Miss Stanton remained the ever composed and levelheaded voice of reason to her mother's seeming madness. No matter how many times her mother changed direction or fretted over the welfare of the wee mice, Miss Stanton's patience didn't waver. Rather, she assisted Mrs. S. in her eccentric endeavor with an air of protective and loving devotion, the likes of which Theodore had never seen. In the upbringing he'd known, family only watched your back in order to find fault with your posture.

As they crossed yet another bridge, over yet another canal, the hair along the nape of Theodore's neck raised. Stirred, as if by the breath of someone following much too closely. Lungs seizing, he spun around and—nothing.

No one.

Just a breeze rustling the cloaks of the few pedestrians ambling along the bridge. He exhaled a shuddering breath. *Get a grip, man. No one is watching us. Don't let the night's terrors distract from the day's task.*

Pivoting, he marched after the Stantons. Somehow, he needed to sleep. Shake this looming paranoia before it consumed his senses. After all, they weren't on the battlefield evading enemy soldiers. They were scouting out lodging for a family of mice. Why would anyone follow them?

CHAPTER

10

A msterdam simply isn't a suitable habitat for a growing
family of mice."
Medicating her weary nerves with a deep breath,
Clara managed to keep her smile intact and not throttle
her dear, sweet, doggedly determined mother. She'd been
happy to assist Mum in finding the stowaway mice a *suitable
habitat*—three hours ago. But now? Now her feet throbbed
from traversing up and down cobbled streets while Mum
hemmed and hawed beside every single one of Amsterdam's
winding canals to examine the natural surroundings for adequate rodent resources.

A dull headache prodded Clara's temple with a persistent
reminder that luncheon had come and gone without their
participation. When Mum was on one of her sacred missions,
eating plummeted down her list of priorities.

Taking another large dose of fresh air, she patted Mum's
arm, linked with her own. "Mice have thrived in cities for
hundreds of years. I see no reason why these mouselings

should be any less hearty and resourceful in a metropolitan environment."

"I suppose that's true." Mum glanced at the cage cradled in her left arm. "Ah . . . but I'd feel much better if the little dears had a home unmarred by the edifices of man. Can we not take them to the countryside?"

And delay us by how many hours more? The retort dissipated in a lengthy sigh. Mum's zealous compassion had never been limited by the possible or bound by the practical. It was a trait Clara had always admired . . . and failed miserably to emulate. "Mum, I love you with all my being, but we cannot afford to dally any longer. Not if we are to locate Grand's next clue before nightfall."

"There's no need for such haste, ducky. After all, the purpose of this trip was for you to have a merry time exploring new places. Are we not doing as much?"

Oh, Mum. Even if she wished to make merry, how could she possibly do so whilst consumed with worry for Grand?

"What say you to that jolly park we just passed, Mrs. S.?"

Clara returned Mr. Arthur's suggestion with a raised brow. She'd almost forgotten the man was trailing behind with their bags, for he hadn't spoken a word since disembarking the ship. Not even a complaint about missing luncheon. She had been most grateful for his silence. How unfortunate that, like all good things, it must come to an end.

"I suggested that park half an hour ago, Mr. Arthur. If you'll recall, Mum declared the grounds 'insufficient for a rodent's romping needs.'"

"I do recall the romping concern. A valid consideration on your part, Mrs. S. Most important, physical exercise. However, I think the park—a most excellent suggestion on your part, Miss Stanton—warrants a second examination. Consider this, ladies." Placing their bags upon the cobbles, Mr. Arthur waved a hand through the air, as though he were setting the scene of a play. "Sturdy trees and romantic shrubbery as far as the eye can see, there's your shelter and reproductive necessaries. A glistening lake surrounded by picnic goers with luncheon crumbs, there's your dietary musts. As for adequate romping space, we need only to factor in scale, and suddenly this small park becomes a massive rodent gymnasium. Why, if I were a mouse, I'd be delighted to live in such a park. What say you, Mrs. S? Shall we release the prisoners into this paradise and find ourselves a well-deserved celebratory meal?"

Mum scrutinized the park behind them. "Hmm . . . the challenge of scavenging in an urban environment might be a boon to the little dears' physical fitness and mental agility." A smile smoothed the lines from her forehead. "On second thought, I think this park will serve quite well. Thank you, my boy, for helping me to see it for its possibilities."

A huff deflated Clara's chest. Unbelievable. Any notion she presented in matter-of-factness was opposed with vehemence, but let the very same notion be put forth in Mr. Arthur's grandiloquence and suddenly all within hearing were gladly persuaded. Stars, his silver-tongued prowess was irksome. Dragged along by Mum through the gates of the now perfectly suitable yet completely unaltered park, Clara glowered at Mr. Arthur, who had the nerve to wink in reply.

After Mum bid the mice farewell with a dramatic wave of her tear-wetted handkerchief, the travelers quit the park in search of much-needed nourishment. Mr. Arthur assumed the lead of their procession with assurances that he knew the "perfect place to grab a bite" since he'd—allegedly—traveled through Amsterdam years ago. Keeping a firm hold of Mum's arm, Clara allowed him to lead on, since her headache had grown too severe for protest.

Crossing a stone bridge, they passed townhouses with colorful shutters, which seemed to spring up from the canal's placid water like so many tulips. On the other side, Mr. Arthur stopped at a quaint café where alfresco dining took advantage of the picturesque waterway. A waiter soon arrived, but before Clara could request a menu, Mr. Arthur ordered for their party in Dutch.

Her eyebrows vaulted. Perhaps not *all* the man's wild stories were falsehoods.

In due course, the waiter returned with two plates of *bitterballen*, a fried bite-size appetizer accompanied by a dish of mustard for dipping. While she and Mr. Arthur shared from the first dish of crispy, traditional bitterballen filled with savory beef and gravy, Mum enjoyed a dish all to herself that had been prepared with mushrooms, per Mr. Arthur's special request. A thoughtful consideration that warmed Clara's heart despite herself.

Appetizers thus dispensed with zest, they proceeded to dine on a main course of *stamppot*, which Mr. Arthur informed them was a Dutch staple made from a combination of potato mash, spinach, sauerkraut, and other assorted vegetables. The creamy stew, served with a wedge of gouda, was most satiating, and by the time Clara had scraped the bowl clean with her spoon, her strength was quite renewed. Along with her determination to be about their purpose.

She stood and began slipping on her brown gloves. "Let's settle the bill and be off, then."

Mr. Arthur gave a mock gasp. "But, Miss Stanton, we've not yet had dessert."

"We haven't the time to indulge, sir. The hour grows late, and Grand's next clue is yet a long walk away."

Like a cat sprawled in the sun, Mr. Arthur didn't stir from the comfort of his chair. "There is absolutely always time for dessert. Besides, one cannot travel through the city of Amsterdam without reveling in one—or two or three—fresh *stroopwafel*. Think of this: two flattened waffle biscuits, round and crisp and golden as the evening sun, joined together by the perfection that is caramel. It is resplendent. Especially when you place the stroopwafel atop the rim of a piping cup of tea and let steam warm the cara—"

"I don't care for a lecture on proper biscuit consumption, Mr. Arthur. I care about Grand. Remember him? The lovable, stubborn old man who is currently wandering about the globe in a bizarre invention that could get him committed? We're here for *him*—not a jolly holiday."

"Ducky, ducky . . . you are anxious and troubled by many things." Mum observed her with an expression equal parts pity and amusement as Fred rubbed his little face against her cheek. "Father will be fine. He's as hearty and resourceful as the mice we freed today. Perhaps more so, since he's significantly older. What's more, your Grand intended for this journey to be a pleasurable stroll, not a harried race. Therefore, you are going to be an agreeable granddaughter and indulge him, so sit your rump back in that chair. We are getting the biscuits, and as your mother, I am ordering you to eat one."

Of all the ridiculous commands. Clara crossed her arms. She was not a child to be ordered about. She was a woman, fully grown, who could make her own decisions. Clara remained standing while Mr. Arthur requested the infernal biscuits and tea. She remained standing while the waiter served said infernal biscuits and tea, and she had every intention to remain standing while Mum and Mr. Arthur ate their infernal biscuits and tea. That is . . . until Mum's blue eyes sharpened in that authoritative manner that, in her formative years, had never failed to melt her childish obstinance into a puddle of remorse.

Apparently, the trick also worked on women fully grown.

With a downcast frame, Clara sat. Removing the warm stroopwafel from atop her steaming cuppa, she took a bite and—dash it all, Mr. Arthur was right! The biscuit *was* resplendent. Setting the stroopwafel upon her Delftware saucer, painted with cobalt windmills on a glazed background of white, she sipped her tea.

The chair to her right scraped against the cobbles. Propping an elbow on the table, Mr. Arthur leaned quite close and whispered in her ear provocatively, "Best biscuit you ever had, aye, Miss Stanton?"

Clara sent the man a sideways glance over the rim of her cup. "It's palatable."

She felt more than saw Mr. Arthur's smirk. "I wonder, Miss Stanton. Do you judge anything on its own merit, or are all your views blinded by prejudice?"

The question plucked a vein along her temple.

"*Krant te koop!*" The shout came from a young lad walking by the café with a stack of newspapers tucked under his arm. "*Krant te koop. Het laatste nieuws.*"

"Right-oh, just what we need. A newspaper to enlighten our limited viewpoint." Jumping from his seat, Mr. Arthur ran after the newsboy for a paper.

Mum offered the last of her stroopwafel to Fred, and the ermine nibbled away, raining crumbs upon the embroidered buttons that fastened her fuchsia bodice. "Anything interesting happening in the world, Arthur?"

"I should say so." Mr. Arthur perused the pages with an unperturbed air. "Our clockwork quarry has landed himself on the front page."

Clara's heart stilled, and she lowered her cup and saucer to the table with a clink. She'd known it was inevitable, the owl hitting the papers. She'd known better than to hope otherwise, but just this once . . . she had wanted so much to hope.

"Apparently, Drosselmeyer's dramatic departure hit the London papers the morning after our ship set sail."

So soon? "Does . . . does it mention Grand by name?" *Or refer to his invention as a war machine?*

"Not thus far. Here, allow me to translate."

As Mr. Arthur proceeded to read the headlining article aloud, Clara envisioned each word printed in bold black ink.

"'Second of April, 1860. Mechanical Marvel Wings Across the Sky. Days ago, dozens of London's longshoremen sighted a giant mechanical owl as it emerged from a warehouse and flew over the Thames. Their story was taken for fiction until corroborating reports trickled in from across Greater London, and later, from England's southern coast, where fishermen witnessed a great owllike machine venturing across the North Sea. As each additional account confirmed its predecessor, frenzied fascination engulfed the city of London, from Cheapside's pubs to the elite parlors of the *ton*. Speculations have run the gamut from a publicity stunt to a deranged daredevil, but nothing has been confirmed, leaving many questions unanswered. What exactly is this mechanical marvel? Is it a weapon or simply a new form of transport? Where is it bound for, and most importantly, who is the madman at the helm?'"

An aching emptiness swept over Clara as though she had not eaten a bite. *Madman.* That label, manipulated in the hands of her cruel ex-fiancé, was all it would take to have Grand locked away, should he be found out.

"By jove!" Mr. Arthur gawked at the paper.

Mum tossed a stroopwafel crumb at Mr. Arthur and hit the target of his nose. "Don't keep it to yourself, boy. What else does it say?"

"Apologies, Mrs. S. But you're not going to believe this." Shifting to the edge of his seat, Mr. Arthur propped his elbows on the table. "'The identity of the owl's mysterious pilot is now a valuable commodity as the subject of countless wagers placed in gambling houses, society clubs, and corner pubs across London. Numerous prize purses are at stake for those wishing to hazard a guess at the pilot's identity, but the grandest prize of all is that offered by Buckingham Palace.'"

Clara's chair seemed to tilt beneath her.

"'Greatly fascinated by the owl and its scientific implications, HRH Prince Albert made an unprecedented announcement on the third of April—if the owl's pilot will present himself and his invention at the palace, he shall, at that time, receive a royal commendation and patronage purse of ten thousand pounds per annum.'"

"Ducky, just think of all the animals we could rescue with such a sum!"

All Clara could think of were Mr. Forrester's threats and the glaring limelight the prince's fascination would cast upon her family. Once the palace learned of the allegations of insanity, the prince's offer would most assuredly be withdrawn to protect the palace from scandal and Grand would be thrown in Bedlam to keep him quiet.

"'With the prince's announcement augmenting public interest here and abroad, betting on the Clockwork Owl, as it's now being called, commenced in Amsterdam when the machine was spotted flying over the city on . . .'" Mr. Arthur drew the paper closer, his smile now disturbingly absent.

Clara wrung her hands in her lap. "Go on, then. When was Grand spotted in Amsterdam?"

"Two days ago."

An unsettling but not surprising bridge of time and space. After all, Grand could travel swifter by owl than they could by ship. Why, then, was Mr. Arthur's expression so dour? "What else does the article say?"

Mr. Arthur tucked the paper into his overcoat. "Nothing to trouble yourself over, Miss Stanton."

And blatant avoidance of her question was supposed to be less troubling? "I will have an answer, Mr. Arthur. What else does the paper say about Grand? What are you so reluctant to tell me?"

Mr. Arthur's throat bobbed as he met her gaze. "Competition for the latest information on the owl has spurred countless papers to anticipate its movements. As of this morning, parties of reporters await the owl in nearly every major city in Europe."

CHAPTER

11

S tanding before a looking glass in the Dancing Clog Inn, Clara attempted to arrange her uncooperative locks in a halfway presentable manner and ignore the disheartenment aching in her chest. The one she'd gone to bed with last night and awoken to at dawn. The one that would remain until Grand was safe in her care once more. An event that would not occur any time soon.

She smoothed her black hair with a brush and then plaited the length, leaving a few natural curls loose to frame her face. Twisting the plait into a simple chignon that would tuck snugly into her bonnet, she began pinning it in place. Her gray eyes strained to focus on the task, so weighted were they by crescents, shadowy and stark. Sleep might have brightened her complexion, if it had come.

As she reached for hairpins strewn on the washstand, Fred scuttled up the furnishing and squeaked for attention. She smiled despite her exhaustion and scratched his wee ears. "Hush, sir. You're not here, remember?"

Finding an inn that would permit the ermine had proven an impossible task. In the end, Fred had played dead in order to sneak into *De Dansenklomp* under the guise of a stole. At least Mum had taught the rascal one useful trick. She stuck a final pin in her chignon and covered it with a fine silk hairnet for added security. Coiffure complete, she turned from the mirror and transported Fred to his usual perch about Mum's shoulders.

Sitting on their shared bed, Mum finished buttoning her boots and passed the buttonhook to Clara, who then packed it in the hummingbird bag. While most of her suggestions regarding this trip had been ignored, thankfully Mum had agreed that it would be advantageous to limit their luggage to the bare necessities. Toting a pair of carpetbags was much simpler than arranging for the transport of numerous trunks, especially when one considered that they hadn't the slightest notion where Grand's clues might lead from one day to the next, or how long they'd remain in any given city. On this unconventional scavenger hunt, agility was of greater importance than having a new frock to wear every day. A single, sturdy traveling dress could serve a lady quite respectably, if care was taken. And if there was one thing at which Clara excelled, it was taking care of things.

As she checked through a mental list to ensure not one bare necessity was left behind, Mum patted her shoulder comfortingly. "It'll be all right, love."

She pursed her lips. Would it? Deep inside, she believed the worst was not only possible, but quite probable.

Begoggled Grand ensnared by a hunting party of journalists who prized newspaper sales above people.

Grand's name emblazoned in printer's ink—on the front page of every paper in Europe—alongside the headline *Madman behind the Clockwork Owl Committed to Asylum. Family Left in Ruins.*

The thought that she might not be able to prevent the worst from occurring terrified Clara to the core. She'd been in such a state of shock after listening to the newspaper accounts that Mum had insisted they call it a day, retire to an inn, and recuperate from their time at sea before commencing with the scavenger hunt the following morning. Clara had protested, wanting nothing more than to carry on and find Grand as soon as possible, but she'd been outvoted when Mr. Arthur and Fred took Mum's side. An unfair vote to say the least.

However, today was a new day, and Clara was determined to keep a stiff upper lip moving forward. She couldn't allow fear to override her faculties. She must focus on tracing Grand's movements and shielding his identity by securing every clue that proved he was the owl's pilot. A task that today would take them to Amsterdam's Royal Palace.

With their bags packed and Fred playing stole, Clara and Mum joined Mr. Arthur for a quick breakfast, then set forth to retrieve Grand's second clue. Elbow linked with Mum's as they walked down the cobbled street, Clara felt the heat of an unwavering gaze threatening to tan the right side of her face. Why couldn't Mr. Arthur leave her be so she could pretend he wasn't there? She was worried enough about Grand. She didn't need the additional headache of having to guard herself around his clanking apprentice.

Mr. Arthur opened his mouth as if to speak, and Clara rankled. "Say anything within a fraction of 'it'll be all right,' and I shall dispatch an ermine assassin to end you in your sleep."

"Does this ermine assassin have a tiny sword, or would the fiend nibble me to death?"

Mum chuckled, and Clara shot Mr. Arthur a well-aimed glower.

As he hoisted their carpetbags and his crutch above his

shoulders to indicate surrender, Mr. Arthur's grin diminished. "As you like, Miss Stanton. I promise you'll not hear another comforting comment or reassuring remark from me."

The trio soon entered a large square bustling with people and surrounded by edifices that felt remarkably familiar to Clara. And no wonder, for she and Grand had been here often. This was Dam Square, "the central heart of the city of Amsterdam," or so said the travel guide they had read at the Globe. The still life she'd painted on the canvas of imagination had captured the square's basic components but could not begin to convey the vibrancy of the real thing. Musicians played for coins in the street, and children tossed breadcrumbs for flocks of pigeons that strutted awkwardly along the cobbles and then all at once shot to the cloudy sky in a cacophony of flapping wings.

Mum tilted her head toward the heavens. "Look how they soar into the firmament. Aren't pigeons majestic creatures?"

Clara smiled despite her weariness. Every creature was majestic in Mum's eyes, no matter its frame, and therefore every creature gave her cause for awe. A beautiful gift of perception that was too often labeled as an oddity. "Indeed, Mum. I do believe they're the most splendid pigeons I've ever beheld."

The Nieuwe Kerk's Gothic spire came into view as it stretched to touch the clouds, and just below it on the western wall, the church's signature sundial overlooked the square. Beside the fifteenth-century house of worship stood the reason for their coming to Dam Square—de Paleis Amsterdam. As she stood arm in arm with Mum before the sandstone façade of the grand Royal Palace, conflicting emotions swelled within her. Delight, wonderment. Loss, regret.

Grand should be here. She should have let him bring her here.

Clara clutched the journal in her pocket as if to hold Grand's hand. She could almost hear him reading aloud from one of her travel guides in that comforting timbre that never failed to take her imagination where she longed to be.

"'On top of the Royal Palace rests a large domed cupola, topped by a golden weathervane in the form of a cog ship—a symbol of the city of Amsterdam. Nestled within the cupola is a carillon cast in 1664, and affixed to the cupola's exterior, facing Dam Square, is a skeleton clockface whose golden numbers and hands appear suspended in midair.' Remarkable, remarkable. I should like to see that for myself."

A tug on Clara's arm pulled her down from the heights of imagination. "Hmm? Did you say something?"

"Not me, ducky. The boy. He made a suggestion."

Of course, he did. "And what was your suggestion, Mr. Arthur?"

"Just that we ought to head round to the back of the palace. You said Drosselmeyer's clue referenced Atlas, and if I recall from my previous visit, the statue of Atlas is somewhere on the palace's rear wall."

Apparently, he had failed to memorize Grand's clue word for word, as she had done. Although, in Mr. Arthur's defense, he had only read it once before she'd snatched it from his hands. "The clue does reference my 'mythical namesake,' and there is a bronze statue of Atlas on the far side of the palace, but it is not the one we seek. Grand's clue also mentioned 'a mapped marble hall,' and that is where we shall find our Atlas."

"Are you certain, Miss Stanton? I don't remember seeing a second Atlas when I toured the city."

Clara made a mental notation never to entertain the thought *in Mr. Arthur's defense* ever again. "When you toured the city, did you happen to venture *inside* the Royal Palace?"

"Well, no—"

"Then you shall just have to rely on my expertise. Limited though it may be to paper and ink."

Following the map in her mind's eye, Clara led the way to Citizens' Hall, the center of the palace that had served as Amsterdam's Town Hall before Napoleon converted it into a royal residence during his brief imperial reign. She'd read in *An Englishman's Comprehensive Guide to Amsterdam* that the hall was freely accessible to citizens and visitors alike, and this proved true, for no one stopped her as she navigated the interconnected galleries of white marble and passed through arches intricately carved with personifications of the planets and four elements. Mum was particularly taken by the depiction of Earth as a woman feeding her child whilst surrounded by animals, including a dromedary, a lion, and a monkey, which provoked comments about Bartimaeus and candied oranges.

The galleries led them at last to Citizens' Hall. Upon entering the imposing room, Clara was whisked away by the surreal sensation of floating between heaven and earth. Sunlight, summoned by dozens of windows, gave the white marble walls and pilasters an ethereal glow. And there, laid at her very feet, were the earth and sky. Inlaid in the marble floor, three maps depicted the world and a celestial hemisphere with such stunning beauty and realism that she dared not tread upon them. Rather she edged around them with care, unable to tear her gaze from the floor. Her heart constricted. What had Grand thought of this place? Did he miss her as much as she missed him?

"Surely Drosselmeyer didn't place a clue up there?" Mr. Arthur's voice put an end to her musings.

Clara and Mum joined him at the western end of the hall. High above their heads . . . high above an archway crowned with a pediment of statuary . . . higher still than a pair of glittering chandeliers hanging from the vaulted ceiling . . .

was her mythical namesake. The white marble figure of Atlas stood upon a ledge carved into the wall, straining not to drop an aquamarine globe dotted with golden stars. La, she'd expected the Titan to be elevated, but she hadn't anticipated it being so completely and ridiculously out of reach!

"If only we had a mountain goat." Mum shook her head, no doubt grieved more by the absence of a goat companion than by the predicament at hand.

Clara gnawed her lip. Had she taken Grand's clue too literally? "Perhaps the clue isn't hidden on the statue itself but somewhere in the surrounding vicinity?"

Splitting in three directions, they scoured the hall from end to end. They searched the great marble floor. They searched the two walls segmented by pilasters and windowed alcoves. They even searched beneath the upholstered benches tucked in said alcoves, but they did not find a slip of paper bearing precious words from Grand. As they searched, an elderly couple strolled in, took a turn about, and strolled out again. A class of young women carrying sketchbooks made a study of the sculptures while their bespectacled teacher lectured in English on Dutch classicism and the legacy of the palace's architect, Jacob van Campen. Then they, too, left.

Clara's stomach began to implore for luncheon. Still, they'd found nothing.

After tucking Mum safely away in an alcove to feed her "stole," Clara wandered back to the lofty statue of Atlas. She was missing something—some nuance in Grand's clue she'd failed to perceive—but for the life of her, she could not think what. She rubbed her right temple before that troublesome vein could start to twitch. "Where did you put it, Grand?"

"Perhaps it's not here." Mr. Arthur appeared on her left, carpetbags at his feet, crutch under his arm.

The troublesome vein tugged on Clara's eye. "Cheery thought."

"I was under the impression you detested cheery thoughts, Miss Stanton. You did instruct me not to be comforting, remember? Death by ermine assassin and all. I take such threats on my life quite seriously. I promised not to offer you one word of consolation, so not one reassuring word shall you have. For I always keep my promises."

Could any man make such a bold claim? Clara faced Mr. Arthur. "Do you, now?"

Mr. Arthur didn't deflect or hesitate. "Indeed I do." He resumed his study of the statue overhead. "I wonder why the palace architect chose to depict Atlas in two places of prominence. Why a Titan and not one of the more renowned Greek gods?"

"Could it be you were so unfortunate as to have missed this morning's stirring lecture?" Clearing her throat, Clara mimicked the bespectacled teacher's voice, which had conveyed the enthusiasm expected when discussing the price of corn. "'In the Dutch Golden Age, Amsterdam was one of the most important ports in the world. A hub of finance and trade. The presence of mighty Atlas in Citizens' Hall, bearing the sky on his shoulders, illustrates how Amsterdammers saw themselves as the center of the universe. Generations of Amsterdammers warned their children that if ever Atlas was to drop the heavens, Amsterdam too would fall.'"

Mr. Arthur leaned against a nearby column. "Fancy that, Miss Stanton. We've just managed to have half a conversation without you running away, terminating my position, or threatening my life. Perhaps there's hope of you being civil to me for the span of an entire day?"

Clara squelched the barest hint of a smile before it graced her lips. "The day's not over yet."

"True enough." Withdrawing a watch from his pocket, Mr. Arthur made a show of checking the time. "'Tis only noon just . . . now." At his pronouncement, the pocket watch began to herald the top of the hour with delicate, metallic chimes that sounded very much like a music box's melody. A melody that was somehow familiar.

Clara looked closer at the golden timepiece in Mr. Arthur's hand, and her pulse slowed. "That is *Grand's* pocket watch." The watch from the story about his wedding tour with Granny.

"I didn't pinch it, Miss Stanton, if that's what you're thinking. Drosselmeyer gave me the watch just before he left for the docks, but—"

"Grand wouldn't give away that watch! Not to you. Not to anybody. It's—" *Not an ordinary watch.* Clara's tongue stilled as the watch chimes echoed through the hall, as she recalled the story she'd heard so often in the voice she loved so dearly.

"One morning, I snuck out while Norma slept and hid an automaton on the bear fountain that was just outside our window. When we left later in search of food, my pocket watch struck the hour as we passed the fountain and activated the automaton. Norma nearly jumped out of her skin when one of the bear cubs came to life and began dancing around its bronze mother's claws. My, how she laughed."

That's how Grand had done it. That's how they were meant to find his clues.

Gesturing for Mr. Arthur to be silent, Clara lifted her gaze to the Titan statue. There. Something moved near the feet of Atlas. It was a pigeon, strutting to the edge of the marble ledge on which Atlas stood. As the golden timepiece continued its tinkling song, the pigeon alighted from the marble edifice and glided the long distance downward, perching on the shoulder of a rather startled Mr. Arthur. Clara cupped a hand over her mouth. The pigeon was, in fact, a life-size clockwork masterpiece covered in tiny shards of white porcelain to resemble overlapping feathers. An automaton. Just like in Grand's favorite story.

The mechanical pigeon tilted its head one way and then the other before parading down Mr. Arthur's arm to the watch in his hand, beckoned by the song of his maker. The pigeon roosted upon the pocket watch, and the melody ceased.

All was again silent and still but for the rapid beating of Clara's heart. This was why Grand's note had said she would require Mr. Arthur's assistance. The dear old man had engineered his scavenger hunt so she would need Mr. Arthur along in order to locate his clues. But why would Grand arrange things in such a way? Why not leave the watch with her?

Out of the corner of her eye, she saw Mum hastening toward them. "Did I hear—"

"One of Drosselmeyer's inventions. Indeed you did, Mrs. S." With a lopsided grin, Mr. Arthur raised the automaton for closer inspection. "By jove, the thing has almost no weight at all. As if the bird's bones are actually hollow. How did Drosselmeyer train this mechanical carrier pigeon to respond to the watch's chimes?"

That was one part of the story Grand had never explained, and one she had never wished to have elucidated. When it came to Grand's inventions, it was so much more delightful to stand in wonder than to understand.

"Look, ducky. The next clue is wrapped around the pigeon's leg. How exciting!" Mum burst into fleeting applause and then clasped her hands to her chest. "Go on. See what it says."

Clara unrolled the scrap of paper.

Dear Little Atlas,

I pray that having the world laid at your feet, here in Citizens' Hall, has opened your eyes to the endless possibilities creation has to offer. Possibilities for joy and beauty, adventure and wonderment. Can you not see now that there is more to life than the pain and sorrow we've experi-

enced? Yes, we have known the sting of betrayal. The ache of loss. But we are not without hope, Clara. For it never ceases to exist. Hope's light lives on in the One who ignited its flame through His resurrection. The One who even now dwells within us and we in Him.

With a new awareness of that unextinguishable hope, let's continue our scavenger hunt. My next clue can be found where an imperial crown rests atop Amsterdam's loftiest spire and leans in deference to the King of Kings. It is my sincere hope that a turtle dove's view will enable you and my apprentice, who I've come to view as a son, to tick in harmony.

> Your devoted,
> Grand

Clara gawked at the note, now keenly aware of Mr. Arthur's proximity. She'd misinterpreted the clue, surely. Grand must be hinting at something else that she'd failed to comprehend. She read the note again, then a third time, heat stoking in her cheeks as she pieced together the words of Grand's clues. *Be sure to invite Arthur along. Tick in harmony. Come to view as a son. Turtle dove.*

She gulped. That's why Grand had given the watch to Mr. Arthur. Her mischievous grandfather wasn't just acting as tour guide—he was bent on playing matchmaker.

Theodore had finally won the pretty grump over.

For all of three minutes.

Now Miss Stanton strode ahead of him on the cobbles, refusing to acknowledge his presence with renewed zeal. Theodore studied the back of Miss Stanton's bonnet, digging his fingernails into the handles of the carpetbags he toted. What the deuce had happened? One moment he fancied himself making progress—he could've sworn she had almost cracked a smile—and then, bang, he was right back where he'd started. Worse off, actually. For ever since she'd read Drosselmeyer's second clue, Miss Stanton had adopted an extreme form of her reclusive nature. Gone were the cold glowers and biting remarks, and in their place was a wall of impenetrable silence.

And for the life of him, he couldn't fathom why.

Mrs. S. offered a sympathetic smile that seemed to say, *"Don't worry, lad. You'll figure it out."*

An assurance he highly doubted. Theodore whacked a

stray pebble with his crutch and sent it skittering out of sight. What had that blasted note said? Miss Stanton had refused to let him see it, of course. Having surveyed its contents, she'd announced they must head for Westerkerk church, and off she'd gone without so much as a glare in his direction. He'd been left with the automaton pigeon, which he'd shoved into one of the carpetbags. When Mrs. S. had insisted on stopping for luncheon, Miss Stanton had acquired a table for two at which he was not welcome. When he'd cracked a joke about rampant chair shortages sweeping across Europe, Miss Stanton had turned her back to him as an almost imperceptible shudder disturbed her frame.

Theodore had learned to accept Miss Stanton's perpetual anger at his existence, but for her to shudder as if afraid of him . . . that he could not accept. He'd allowed Miss Stanton her separate table during luncheon and now kept his distance as they traveled to Westerkerk, but at some point, the matter must be confronted. The old order restored. For though he'd be loath to admit it aloud, he was already beginning to miss being the object of Miss Stanton's ire.

As they made their way over a second canal bridge, the Westerkerk and adjoining Westertoren clock tower came into view. When he'd wandered through the city years ago, a few locals had mentioned their beloved *Ouwe Wester*, but ever since the Charge, he'd made it a practice to stay well away from places of worship. No matter how renowned. No matter how much he might long to venture in . . . he couldn't. Wouldn't. He respected the Almighty too much to soil His house.

In contrast, the Westertoren rose unabashed into the heavens, assured that it belonged. The hull of the tower was constructed of modest brick, but as the structure neared the clouds, its impressive sandstone spire assumed a regal air crowned by the blue *keizerskroon*—the Imperial Crown of Austria featured in Amsterdam's coat of arms. Just below the crown, a carillon of bells was situated atop a red clockface whose numerals and hands shone of gold.

After crossing a third and final bridge, they traversed a stone street with the church to their left and a canal to their right. Iron lampposts and trees stood at attention along the canal, but the gentle hush of flowing water couldn't be heard over a din of flapping and twittering. Theodore gaped at the uninhabited trees and then craned his neck to see farther down the road. Just ahead, beneath one of the lampposts, an elderly woman in homespun clothes sat on a crate, surrounded by sparrows. Not just surrounded—positively festooned. Little brown birds perched on almost every inch of her person, from tattered bonnet to patched apron to scuffed boots.

Greeting them with a weathered smile, all wrinkles and kindness, the woman gestured toward a row of small canvas bags. "Feed the little birds. Feed your anxious souls." She echoed the plea again and again, alternating between Dutch and accented English. "Feed the little birds. Feed your anxious souls. One heavy burden for one bag of seed."

Mrs. S. rushed to shake the bird woman's hand. "Blessings upon you, fellow soldier. I must commend your efforts to carry out the great commission outlined for Noah in the book of Genesis to preserve God's creatures from extinction. You're here every morning, I gather?" The bird woman's answer had no time to reach her lips. "Of course you are, dearie. Our fight is far from over, but our resolve is far from shaken. As long as tyrannical taxidermists seek to stuff and mount mammals to walls, we shall fight. As long as malevolent milliners seek to pluck and pin feathers to hats, we shall fight. As long as the tides of fashion seek to reduce God's creation to a mountain of pelts, our fight shall continue. And we shall never surrender."

Mrs. Stanton raised her fist as if to seize victory.

Miss Stanton slapped a palm over her face as if mortified.

And the bird woman tilted her head as if befuddled by bizarre foreigners.

Theodore choked back a chuckle as Mrs. S. jabbered on. "I should consider it an honor to contribute to your efforts. Come, ducky, let's purchase a few bags of seed and feed the birds."

Prying her gloved hand from her face, Miss Stanton looked toward the sky as though imploring for aid and then pulled her mother aside. "We haven't the time. If we don't make haste, we're sure to miss it."

So the pretty grump had looked up to check the hour, not to inquire of the Lord. What exactly did she not want to miss?

"I'll not be joining you, ducky. The tower is much too high for my liking. I shall stay on solid ground while you and Arthur make the upward trek. No doubt you'll need his pocket watch to locate Father's next clue."

Miss Stanton's lips pinched so hard they blanched. "It's not *his* pocket watch."

Heat emanated from the watch in Theodore's pocket. Was that why Miss Stanton's behavior had altered at Citizens' Hall—because she'd learned Drosselmeyer had given him the watch? No wonder the woman was incensed. Heirlooms ought to be kept in the family, and he'd tell her as much. He set down the bags and reached into his pocket.

Holding her daughter's gaze, Mrs. S. laid a hand on his coat sleeve. "Clara, your grandfather gifted the watch to Arthur for reasons of his own, and we must respect his decision."

A slight quiver disturbed Miss Stanton's delicate jawline, but she nodded in acquiescence. She kissed her mother on the cheek and her stole on the whiskers. "See to it she behaves, Freddy. I'd better find Mum on this exact cobble when I return." With that, she entered the Westertoren.

Mrs. Stanton tossed him a wink. "Go on, then. Don't let her get away."

Not sure he wanted to dissect the double entendre contained in that wink, Theodore handed the luggage to Mrs. S. and dashed into the Westertoren. He soon caught up to Miss Stanton, and in single file, they ascended the clock tower's series of wooden staircases, some spiraling, others vertical, all so steep and narrow as to feel more like ladders. Only half of his automaton boot fit upon the shallow steps, forcing him to climb at an awkward angle. How Miss Stanton's full skirts managed to squish between the railings, he couldn't guess, but they certainly weren't slowing her down.

By the time they reached the sixth floor, Theodore's burning calf and thighs felt all one hundred and eighty-six steps. Hardly seemed worth it . . . until they ventured onto the viewing platform and were rewarded with a panoramic view of central Amsterdam. Sunlight glinted off the Prinsengracht canal as a pair of boats saluted each other in passing. Homes in the neighboring Jordaan district clustered together in comradery, some with tiled roofs the color of slate, others the color of cinnamon. In the opposite direction, he could just make out the bronze statue of Atlas on the Royal Palace's rear gable, holding a huge globe against the vast firmament.

Theodore was about to remark to Miss Stanton on the breathtaking blueness of the sky when a triumphant clang of bells resounded from the carillon overhead. Knocked off-kilter by the ensuing vibration, he dropped his crutch and caught himself on the balcony's chest-high railing of sandstone. The bells continued to toll with increasing jubilance as a carillonneur, unseen within the tower's frame, played Bach's classic chorale "Jesu, Joy of Man's Desiring." The stirring music joined forces with the wind and swayed the Westertoren gently, recreating the sensation of sailing on the North Sea, this time aboard the mighty cog ship of Amsterdam.

How long the chorale filled the air with joy and life, Theodore didn't know. Nor did he care. All he knew was that he never wanted the song of worship to end. Though his bowed head knew he was unworthy to hear it, though his quaking legs knew he was unworthy to stand in this place, his chest yet swelled, desiring the Maker he dared not seek. Perhaps staying away from the Lord's house had been a mistake. Perhaps . . .

The bells tolled the chorale's finale, and the last soaring note was carried away by a spring breeze. All that remained in its wake was a jarring hush. Theodore righted himself, running a palm over his face and through his hair. The unrelenting nightmares were corroding his faculties, his senses. That's all that swell in his chest had been. Exhaustion and emotion. That's all it could be. Nothing had changed, and he shouldn't expect otherwise.

Turning on the heel of his leather boot, Theodore retrieved his fallen crutch. "You might've warned me about the carillonneur, Miss Stanton. Unless, of course, the plan was to startle me right off the tower."

Sequestered on the opposite end of the viewing platform, Miss Stanton kept to the shadows, clinging to the tower wall, and disregarded his quip.

Come on, woman. Don't make of me a fearsome hobgoblin. Just tell me what I did to offend. "How did you know when the carillonneur's performance would take place? Did Drosselmeyer mention it in the clue that led us here?"

Miss Stanton remained mute.

All right, he'd had about enough of this rot. The time had come to surmount the blasted wall between them. But how to go about it? He rubbed a hand along his beard. Casual air with a dash of humor, perhaps? His tried-and-true tools had yet to succeed with Miss Stanton, but perhaps they could gauge the height and breadth of said wall. Ascertain if it had been constructed with a drawbridge or if he'd have to scale the thing with his bare hands.

He approached Miss Stanton, reclined against the tower, and put both hands in his overcoat's outer pockets. "Where do you think Drosselmeyer will have us go next? Any particular destination you're hoping to see? I'd fancy Paris myself, but then again, I've always been a romantic sort of fellow. You know, I once composed a poem about my unrivaled affection for raspberry trifle."

Miss Stanton's posture went rigid, hardening more than the bricks at her back.

Right-oh. Humor was a bad move, a very bad move indeed. Theodore tugged at his shirt collar. No sign of a drawbridge. Perhaps he needed a more direct approach. Like the battering ram of complete honesty.

"I know you're angry with me, Miss Stanton. And I can't say that I fault you for it. By all rights, you ought to be the inheritor of your grandfather's pocket watch. I tried to tell Drosselmeyer as much when he presented it to me, but he was rather . . . focused. I only intended to keep the watch safe until he came back, and that is still my intent. The moment we catch the dear old codger, the watch will be returned. You have my word on that."

The slope of Miss Stanton's shoulders relaxed ever so slightly.

Better, much better. Now that the wall was teetering, he might be able to knock it down by employing one final tactic of biblical proportions. The trumpet blast of absurdity.

"So . . . what's your favorite color?"

She finally looked at him, then, in perplexed perusal, as if to discern how his brain had fallen out of his head.

"There you are, Miss Stanton. I was beginning to think you'd gone deaf."

Her intense gray eyes sharpened into blades of steel.

By jove, but they were stunning. Captivating, really. Was it a wonder he'd missed the company of such eyes, however menacing? "Now that I have your attention, would you care to explain how exactly I came to be transformed into a hobgoblin at Citizens' Hall? Was it the matter of the watch only, or did I commit some other trespass? If so, I should very much like to be made aware of my offending actions."

Miss Stanton's right eyebrow arched. "If you're so unaware of your own actions, perhaps you're equally oblivious to the fact that you've been a hobgoblin all along."

"Or . . . perhaps it was not I who transformed, but yourself. For prior to entering Citizens' Hall, you always parried the hobgoblin with quick-footed swordplay instead of cowering from him in the shadows of lofty towers."

"I never cower, sir. No matter the circumstances, I always stand strong, on my own." Her voice wavered as though she were reassuring herself rather than stating a fact.

All on her own, aye? "I'm glad to hear it, Miss Stanton, for I would not see you cower before anyone. Least of all a mischievous hobgoblin. Although . . . I must say, I find it odd that you should always stand on your own when you've four people and one God standing at the ready to lend you support."

Miss Stanton's arched brow slipped, and for just a moment revealed a softness in the planes of her face that he never knew they possessed. But all too soon, tension pulled taut the sharp angles of her jaw and cheekbones. She moved to the railing. "'As the birds are to the sky, so are bells to the city of Amsterdam.' That is a quote from *An Englishman's Comprehensive Guide to Amsterdam*, the same book that also recounts how the Westertoren carillonneur performs every Tuesday. That, to answer your question, is how I knew when the performance would take place."

Now that she was speaking to him again, he wasn't about

to let her stop. "And you knew to come to the Westertoren because . . ."

"Grand's clue said to find the place where 'an imperial crown rests atop Amsterdam's loftiest spire and leans in deference to the King of Kings.'"

"'Leans in deference' . . . is that some sort of metaphor?"

"No, in this case, the phrase is factually applicable. According to the guidebook, Westertoren is eighty-five centimeters out of plumb. The tower literally leans before the church."

House of the King of Kings. "Your grandfather is a clever—"

Chimes sprang from the watch in Theodore's pocket. As he produced the timepiece, the Westertoren clock marked the top of the hour with the tolling of bells, drowning out the watch's delicate dings. Miss Stanton furrowed her brow, no doubt fearing the clock would prevent Drosselmeyer's invention from responding to the watch's call.

Just when Theodore was starting to think that fear justified, the bells fulfilled their purpose and their tolls faded into stillness. But the pocket watch chimed on. For it was not designed to merely proclaim the hour, but moreover, to summon ingenuity out of hiding.

Miss Stanton pointed upward. An automaton sparrow fluttered down from the carillon and landed atop the timepiece, immediately silencing its chimes. Although he was beginning to expect such marvels, Theodore couldn't help but be amazed. The life-size sparrow in his hand was plated with layers of finely hammered brass feathers. Strapped to its back was a tiny leather tube, the sort that would protect works of art or important documents in transit.

Miss Stanton removed the tube, which most likely contained her grandfather's next missive, and tucked it away in her skirts.

"You know . . . if you let me read Drosselmeyer's clues, I could lend that support I spoke of earlier."

"Oh, I wouldn't want to trouble you with matters of paper

and ink. Your vast experience is much better suited to handling unforeseen obstacles—like transporting a mechanical
menagerie." Unfurling a sardonic smirk, Miss Stanton patted
the automaton sparrow on the head and disappeared into the
tower. "See you outside, hobgoblin."

Theodore attempted to catch up to her, but the climb down
with his cumbersome boot proved to be even more challeng-
ing than the climb up, allowing her to gain a significant lead.
Back outside Westertoren, he found Mrs. S. seated on the
ground, so covered in twittering sparrows that he almost mis-
took her for the old bird woman to her right. Miss Stanton
was speaking with the pair, trying to convince her mother it
was time to leave the birds behind.

A smirk tilted Theodore's lips as he tucked the mechanical
sparrow into the carpetbag with its pigeon friend. He'd let
Miss Stanton have that battle. As the women parried, something down the street moved, and he snapped to attention. A
man stood near the canal, half-concealed behind the trunk
of an elm tree, intently watching them.

Chills pricked Theodore's neck. This wasn't the lingering
effects of nightmare. He'd been spared his usual terror last
night, and with it, the residual haze of fear, exhaustion, and
paranoia that caused him to startle at the touch of a breeze.
This man was *real*. And he was eyeing the Stantons like a hungry fox on the scent of an unsuspecting sparrow, or perhaps
. . . an *owl*. Had they been sniffed out by one of the reporters
hunting for Drosselmeyer?

Theodore's grip tightened on his crutch. He needed to investigate, and if need be, throw this fox off their scent. He
moved in the direction of the man, but the clank of his prosthetic startled the sparrows, who took to the air en masse,
creating a whirlwind of feathers that obscured his view.

When the birds cleared, he rushed down the street. But
the man was gone.

Dear Little Atlas,

    I hope you lingered at Westertoren long enough to enjoy a performance from the carillonneur and allow the bells to resonate in your soul. The beautiful and formidable sound, I thought, was almost like hearing the voice of God. I couldn't help but smile. I couldn't help but weep. I'd have taken to my knees if I could have got up again! Oh, how I pray you were awed in equal measure. For though these old knees grumbled all the way up the staircase, the experience of Westertoren was well worth the temporary discomfort.

    In my two and seventy years, I've discovered that oftentimes life's greatest joys are found on the other side of discomfort. We must fall before we can walk. We must look the fool before we can learn. We must labor before we can feast. We must travel the distance before we can see the destination. With that said, I urge you to gird yourself for *the discomfort that lies ahead with the assurance of worthwhile joy.*

The first leg of our merry scavenger hunt has come to an end, and the second leg will take us further abroad. Make your way to Station Amsterdam Willemspoort and acquire a ticket to Prague, Bohemia. Yes, dear one, you shall travel by train. Now that we've a renewed outlook of hope and possibility, it's time your fear of locomotives was overcome by the thrilling rush of traveling clickety-clack over the rails.

Clammy palms trembling, Clara read Grand's note for the hundredth time. Rush indeed. One would feel a rush while traveling at the ungodly speed of forty miles per hour—a blood-chilling rush of panic as the railway carriage packed with all manner of strangers swayed, bounced, and clickety-clacked right off the track.

A shudder rattled her spine. Storing the note with the others in her journal, Clara pocketed the leather book and reclaimed her tight grip on Mum's gloved hand. Fumes belched from the waiting steam engines of Station Amsterdam Willemspoort, polluting the air with coal dust and dread.

Why must Grand put her through this exercise? He knew how terrified she was of locomotives. When the Tottenham Station railway disaster rocked the London papers back in February with horrific eyewitness accounts and a list of fatalities printed in mourner's black, her wariness of railway travel had been validated, and she'd vowed never to set foot on a train.

Yet here she stood, waiting in a long ticket queue at Grand's request. White columns gave the train station's classical façade the appearance of an ancient Greek temple, while the sails of a windmill, waving over its right shoulder, reassured impressionable imaginations that they yet stood on Dutch soil. A quaint sight she might have enjoyed, were it not for the imminence of being locked in a smoke-spewing death trap.

Dazzling morning rays elbowed through the clouds, prompting parasols to raise as the queue slugged forward. A boisterous party of spiffed-up dandies, five tickets to Paris. A couple of middling years, two tickets to Rome. A subdued gentleman with naught for company but a briefcase, one ticket to Brussels. On and on travelers became passengers, and on and on the line stretched before them, seemingly unaltered. The shrill whistle of a departing train pierced her senses like the incisive claws of a startled cat. Tremors coursed through her veins. How could Grand call this terrifying prospect a temporary discomfort? How could she go through with this?

Mum gave Clara's hand three quick squeezes. *I love you.*

Warmth traveled up Clara's arm, spreading over her lanced nerves as a soothing balm. She squeezed Mum's hand four times in return. *I love you more.*

Mum responded with a prolonged squeeze of rebuttal. *Most.*

At last, Clara breathed with a measure of ease. Thank heavens, she was forgiven for the sparrow debacle. Yesterday at Westertoren, Mum and Mr. Arthur had purchased bags of seed to feed the birds, but when she'd been pressed to follow suit, Clara had refused. She simply couldn't consent to the bird woman's requested payment—*one heavy burden for one bag of seed.* Others might find pseudo-confession to an octogenarian birdwatcher an amusing exercise, but she knew the weighty cost of such openness. Divulging cares of the heart rendered one vulnerable, and she couldn't hazard vulnerability in the presence of a stranger . . . or Mr. Arthur.

Aloft in Westertoren, Clara had allowed Mr. Arthur's promise to return Grand's watch to lure her into conversation, but she couldn't afford to repeat such an exchange. Not with Grand penning allusions to romance. Not with Mr. Arthur making a study of her face. Henceforth, any words exchanged between them must be starched with formality. While she might not be able to prevent Grand from viewing Mr. Arthur as a son, she could most certainly prevent him from viewing the man as a grandson-in-law.

Besides, the burden she carried was hers alone. How could the responsibility of protecting her family belong to anyone else? Were they not her own blood? Indeed, they were the very heart beating in her chest, which was precisely why her tender heart must be bricked over.

After dragging Mum away from Westertoren, they'd settled at a nearby inn, which had saved them the trek back to the Dancing Clog on the other side of Amsterdam. Mum had wanted to explore the city, but Clara reasoned it was best to save their strength for the morrow's travels, and oddly, Mr. Arthur had agreed that they ought to seek shelter straightaway. That's when Mum had gone silent. Uttering not a word through dinner, nor bidding her good night. Poor Fred, perceiving they'd quarreled, had wedged himself betwixt them in bed like a furry bolster.

As the ticket line progressed another step, Clara rubbed her thumb along the back of Mum's hand. It was such a relief to have the spat ended and the lines of communication restored.

Finally, they reached the front of the queue. Once their tickets to Prague were in hand, Clara made to leave and bumped straight into Mr. Arthur, whose gaze was fixed on the people behind them. "Do move along, Mr. Arthur. You're holding up the queue."

Mr. Arthur seemed to come to himself as one woken from a dream he was keen to have ended. "Right-oh. My apologies. Just sad to bid Amsterdam farewell, I suppose." Adjusting the crutch under his arm and the trio of carpetbags juggled in his hands—the newest of which had been acquired to transport their automaton souvenirs—he gestured for them to lead the way. "Let's be off, then, ladies. New sights to see and all that."

With Mr. Arthur bringing up the rear, the three approached the great iron beast huffing and puffing on the tracks. Burning coal wafted through the air in swirling clouds of black, while a fog of steam, dense and moist, rolled along the ground. Behind the mammoth locomotive, a procession of railway carriages formed their own neat queue in order of social class. A portly conductor stood at the entrance of their first-class carriage and requested their tickets. Each was produced, marked, and returned. Having verified their passage, the conductor offered a hand of assistance to Mum. "Watch your step, *mevrouw*."

Mum returned his offer with a smile that grew more strained and awkward with each passing second that she failed to move. She turned to Clara, softening the lines of her mouth as she whispered. "I can't accept the man's hand if you don't let go of mine, ducky."

"Hmm?" Clara's gaze fell to her strangled grip on Mum's glove. Oh, right. Heat from the locomotive's billowing steam rose from her boots to her pearl-studded ears. She forced a wobbly smile at the conductor, and one by one, pried her rigid fingers from Mum's hand. Thus liberated, Mum boarded the train with the agility and swiftness of the mountain goats she so admired.

Then the conductor extended his hand to Clara, his thick brows curving in a pair of question marks. "Ready, miss?"

Not in the slightest. Trepidation threatened to suffocate her from within, but she refused to let it win out. By might and main, she would do this thing. For Mum and for Grand.

Grasping the conductor's hand, Clara hefted herself up the carriage's ominous black steps. Mr. Arthur followed, and together, they proceeded down a narrow passage in single file. The interior of their designated carriage was not dissimilar to a traditional horse-drawn one. Two seats faced each other with a window situated betwixt. Each seat was upholstered with tufted velvet that matched fringe-trimmed pillows and short curtains drawn back with tasseled cords. Yet unlike its horse-drawn counterparts, this carriage contained an inherent danger that raised more gooseflesh on her skin than even the thought of a fiery crash.

Railway madness.

Just the sort of malady a family accused of lunacy ought not to hazard.

The last few travel guides Clara had added to her library had included excerpts from medical journals, cautioning travelers against the dreaded condition. The jarring motion of a speeding train was alleged to unhinge the mind and shatter the nerves, causing violent outbursts. She recalled the accounts of sane individuals turned mad and the recommendations for avoiding such a fate. Minimizing sensory exposure was the number one advisement. As Mum made herself comfortable and Mr. Arthur situated their bags, Clara drew the curtains. There. No fast-moving landscapes to overwhelm the eye.

The clanking of iron drew her attention to a lanky, uniformed guard with a set of skeleton keys. He addressed them in Dutch, then again in English. "Good day. If you require assistance during our journey, please knock on the door. I'll be locking it now for your privacy and safety."

Clara gulped as the lock bolted. For their safety. Isn't that what the Tottenham victims had been told—the ones who'd perished because they couldn't escape their confined carriages? The train whistle blew, strident and startling, and with the ear-grating screech of iron grinding iron, the carriage lurched forward. As did her thrashing heart.

Why couldn't they have hired a team of grays?

A pair of draught horses?

One incredibly robust mule?

Why, oh why, did Grand have to insist on the train?

Grasping a handful of velvet in either fist, Clara braced herself as the carriage rolled along the tracks. On her left,

Mum reclined with gloved hands folded in her lap, and soon her head lolled against Fred on her shoulder, her snores competing with the locomotive's percussive clickety-clacks. Sweat beaded along Clara's temple as her right eye twitched incessantly. She ought to have brought cotton to protect Mum's ears from the thunderous sounds. Ought to have brought something—anything—to safeguard her against harmful jolts. Was Mum's mind even now becoming unhinged?

Prying her hands from the bench, Clara wedged a pillow on either side of Mum's hips in a vain attempt to keep her secure. Then she reaffixed herself to the bench with whitened knuckles.

Mr. Arthur eyed her from the adjacent seat, posture annoyingly relaxed. "If I try to comfort you, will you bite my head off?"

Clara's response came out short. "I'd never do anything so unsanitary."

"So I'll come to no harm if I offer you another pillow?" Mr. Arthur held up the solitary pillow on his side of the carriage.

Was he insinuating that she hadn't done enough? That her efforts to shield her own mother were insufficient? The trembling within swelled against her chest, and her words spewed forth in a scorching flood. "I don't want your stupid pillow. I don't need your stupid pillow. Neither do I need your comfort or your charity. I may be forced to endure your company, Mr. Arthur, but I have no need of you. I can carry on quite well without your assistance, so please. Leave me be." Her chest heaved, out of breath. Out of words.

Mr. Arthur's expression remained unmoved by the torrent. "You know, Miss Stanton. There's a drawback to spurning the assistance of others." He propped Mum's head with the cushion so it no longer lolled precariously, and then sat once more. "If you constantly profess to have no need, eventually people are going to believe you."

CHAPTER

14

Fortunately, Mum survived the perilous locomotive journey to Prague without succumbing to railway madness. Unfortunately, that meant her mental faculties were well equipped to conduct a stern interrogation the morning following their arrival.

"Out with it, ducky. What did you say to Arthur?"

Holding on to a bedpost in their room at the *Sto Věž* Inn, Clara stared at the butter yellow quilt where Fred slept while Mum laced her corset. She normally performed the function herself, but her mother had insisted on "lending a hand" this morning. No doubt because the task kept Clara tethered on a leash of sorts, which prevented her from escaping Mum's questions.

"I said nothing of consequence."

"Deception does not become you, ducky. You must have said something severe while I dozed on the train. From Amsterdam to Prague, the lad was a confirmed mute. He didn't utter a word for days. Just nodded and smiled, smiled and nodded. I don't like it when you meet that genuine smile of his with acrimony. You've no reason to treat the boy as you do. I raised you better than that, ducky. Your Granny raised us both better."

After the corset was properly fitted and laced over her chemise to provide comfortable support, Mum wrapped her arms about Clara in an embrace warmed by affection and the powdery scent of violet perfume. "Can you not try to be kind to the boy? For me."

A sigh fled from Clara's lips. "I'm civil to him . . . most of the time. Isn't that enough?"

"Civility is a lonely lass who smiles at the world as it passes by her window."

What was so wrong with that prospect? "Civility smiles because she's content, and more importantly, because she and her household are safe. No one can take advantage of you if you keep the door bolted."

"True, but no one can take care of you either. Bolted doors are poor judges of character, keeping out friend and foe alike. I don't want you to forfeit the former for fear of the latter." Mum cupped soft hands to Clara's face, preventing avoidance of the insightful blue eyes that too often discerned more than she wished to divulge. "Arthur is not Rupert, you know."

Clara pulled away from Mum's touch. She'd asked the family never to mention that cad's name. "It doesn't matter who Mr. Arthur is or isn't. I don't need companionship from him or any other outsider. I have you and Papa and Grand." *And Granny's memory.*

"Yes, you have us, ducky. But you no longer let yourself lean on us."

Mr. Arthur's words rose from the mental grave, the one she'd buried them in atop Westertoren. *"I find it odd that you should always stand on your own when you've four people and one God standing at the ready to lend you support."*

Her throat clogged. Why couldn't anyone understand? Why couldn't they see? Leaning on others for support was where all their troubles had begun. Standing on her own was the only way she knew how to bring those troubles to an end. To protect those whom she'd previously endangered through her naïveté. She just wanted to be a good daughter, a good granddaughter. If she wasn't capable of that much ... if her might and main weren't sufficient ...

Dressed.

She needed to get dressed.

Once she was properly attired, they could leave this suffocating room and conversation behind. Fleeing in a swirl of petticoats, Clara rummaged through the bumblebee-embroidered carpetbag she'd left on the wooden rocker. Spare stockings and chemise. Hairbrush and pins. Where was her traveling dress?

With a gentle clearing of her throat, Mum appeared on her right with the missing bodice and skirt. The ones she'd forgotten she'd hung to air out overnight. She grasped the skirt, but Mum held it fast, refusing to let go. "At some point, you must open the door, ducky. You must allow someone to help shoulder the load you strain to carry when you think no one's looking."

And here she thought she'd done a fine job concealing her perpetual state of *overwhelmed*. She must do better. Be stronger. Reassure Mum of her capabilities and prove she could take care of herself and the family that mattered so much more.

Clara snatched the skirt from Mum's hand and attempted to slip it over her head, but the billowing fabric snagged on a hairpin. Vision obscured by a veil of brown, she struggled to free the skirt without damaging the costly silk. After a great deal of exertion, the skirt fell free to her hips, undamaged. A dash to the looking glass confirmed her coif was also intact.

She aimed a smile of victory at Mum's reflection. "I do well enough on my own, and if I require help, I always have my faith to lean on."

"Do you, ducky?" Mum crossed her arms, an uncharacteristic heaviness in her tone. "Because it seems to me that God's on the outside of your bolted door, along with the rest of us."

Nonsense. Mum might be right about most things, but in this matter, she was way off the mark. Clara put on her bodice, unaided, and once fully dressed, withdrew to a window seat on the other side of the room. Cheek pressed against the windowpane, she waited for Mum to finish her toilette and tried to put their conversation out of her mind by focusing on the lovely sunrise.

Pastel shades of pink, lavender, and yellow swirled across the horizon and tinted clusters of fluffy clouds, which glided on the gentle current of a westerly breeze. Like dandelion seeds scattered by a heartfelt wish, one cluster of clouds suddenly burst, and from the fragments of fluff emerged a glimmer of light.

A massive creature with outstretched wings that reflected the sun.

Awestruck, Clara rose to her knees on the bench and pressed a palm against the glass pane separating her from the sky. Grand?

She blinked, but the owl machine didn't vanish. It soared high and majestic amid a watercolor sunrise that transformed its brass body into a glittering, opalescent gem. Her chest swelled. Surely, the flights she and Grand had taken under cover of night couldn't compare to the wonder of this. What must it feel like up there, flying with fearless unabandon in the light of day?

Was he close enough to heaven to hear Granny laugh?

Clara's heart ached with longing. Watching the world pass by her window had never felt so lonely. *Wait for me, Grand.*

I'm coming. Dashing across the room, she leapt over a stray carpetbag and nearly slammed into the door.

"Great grasshoppers! Where are you going, ducky?"

"To flag down Grand. The owl's flying this way!"

Unlocking the door, Clara turned the knob and pulled, but the door pulled back. The bolt hadn't fully retracted. She tried the lock again, but the door held fast. No, no, no. It couldn't be stuck. Not now. She glanced over her shoulder at the window. *Please don't leave me, Grand.*

"Ducky, let me—"

Clara turned the lock back and forth, back and forth, willing the rusty bolt to move. The blasted door to open. With every precious second wasted, her heart rate increased until her frantic pulse whooshed in her ears. Finally, she felt the bolt give with a clank. She swung the door open and ran down the hallway. *Please don't be gone.*

She bounded down two flights of stairs and sprinted past the desk on the inn's main floor. Bursting through the front door, Clara joined the group of people gathered on the cobbled street. Excited voices chattered in Czech, and outstretched hands pointed toward the heavens. Her gaze followed the direction of interest just in time to catch a glint of metallic tail feathers swiftly shrinking in the distance. Her heart faltered. She was too late.

The owl had winged away, once again, without her by Grand's side.

Once you arrive in Prague, follow a saintly pathway of stone to a wizened town, and you shall find my next clue where the Jesuits watch over great treasures of mind and eye.

Clutching Mum's hand, Clara pushed through the crowd making their way across Prague's famous Stone Bridge.

Dozens and dozens of strangers heading toward or away from Old Town. Dozens and dozens of bodies clogging the bridge like too many autumn leaves attempting to float down the same narrow stream. She tucked her free hand in a pocket, grasping the journal that contained Grand's note and promise of great treasures, the thought of which held no allure. All she desired was to reach Old Town and locate Grand's next clue before day's end. Perhaps that tangible victory would relieve the ache of watching the owl leave her behind, or at least offer a distraction from the reproof she couldn't get out of her head.

"Arthur is not Rupert, you know."

Of course she knew. Logically, no one else was Rupert . . . and yet, in the murky depths of emotion, somehow . . . everyone was Rupert. Names might vary, faces might possess different features, but the sense of trepidation they evoked felt the same. Once stung by a hornet, it was natural to shy away from anything that buzzed, was it not?

A yank on Clara's arm brought her to an abrupt standstill, and Mum's hand slipped from her grasp—for the tenth time since they'd stepped on the bridge. Stars above, was Mum going to straggle the entire sixteen hundred and ninety-two feet across?

She turned to find Mum becoming acquainted with yet another avian. This time a great cormorant with dark feathers and beady eyes, roosting on a statue of Saint Augustine. Carpetbags in hand, Mr. Arthur leaned against the crutch pinned beneath one arm and watched the interspecies exchange with an exuberance that sparked that "genuine smile" Mum so loved. And Clara distrusted.

As Mum made introductions between Fred and the cormorant, Clara tapped her boot. If they continued at this snail's pace, the whole day would be wasted on the bridge. "We ought to keep moving. The bridge will only draw more of a crowd as the day progresses."

With a guttural grunt, the cormorant bid Mum farewell and alighted from the bridge. Excellent. Now they could be on their way. "Let's—"

"Just a few more minutes, ducky. Come here." Mum drew Clara to her side. "What did your granny always used to say when you were fixated on a task?"

A smile tugged Clara's lips even as her heart ached anew. "'Don't get so busy tending the garden that you never sit back and enjoy the view.'" She could still hear the words in Granny's voice. Still feel the touch of her hand, soft and warm, as it gently tapped her chin, encouraging her to look up from her work and admire something of beauty she'd been too occupied to notice. The ache intensified into a cavernous vacancy. *Oh, Granny. How I miss you.*

Mum wrapped an arm about Clara's shoulders and turned her to face their destination waiting on the other side of the river. "Mama wouldn't want you to miss this view, ducky. Not after Father went through so much to get you here. Not after you've dreamt of it so long."

A quiver unsettled Clara's jaw. Perhaps . . . perhaps Mum was right. It wouldn't hurt to pause just a moment longer, to honor her grandparents. She closed her eyes and took a deep breath, embracing the memory of Granny's words. *"Sit back and enjoy the view, child."* Exhaling slowly, she opened her eyes.

If London was an icy lake shrouded in gray mist on a winter's day, then Prague's Old Town was a field of orange poppies at summer's peak. The city's vibrant terra-cotta roofs contrasted against the serene Vltava River and a cloudless azure sky. In the midst of the poppies stood Prague Castle, enthroned in history and fairy-tale enchantment. The gothic spire of St. Vitus Cathedral emerged from the majestic castle complex, towering over the city like the cross in its jeweled crown.

An awestruck sigh relieved tension in Clara's shoulders.

To think, that cathedral had seen centuries of worship. The coronations of kings and queens, and just recently, the flight of a clockwork owl. As wonderous as the prospect was below, Grand's view must've been—

Someone bumped into Clara, knocking her and Mum against the bridge wall.

Clara's gasp soured to a groan. It wasn't even noon and already she was quite done with humanity. No matter how lovely the view, she needed to get them off this bridge. Posthaste. Perhaps one of Mum's favorite chants would provide incentive.

"'The well-being of webbed feet and paws takes precedence over convenience, custom, and laws.' Consider, Mum. If we're jostled by this crowd, so too is Fred."

Brow furrowing beneath the shade of her bonnet, Mum stroked the ermine's lame legs draped about her shoulder. "Perhaps it is time to move along. I'll not see Fred suffer another grievous injury."

The trio reinserted themselves in the flow of pedestrians. Countless strangers brushed and bumped against Clara on all sides, each unwanted touch seeming to wrap a clammy finger around her throat. Attempting to blot the pressing throng from her conscious, she focused on the sandstone blocks that suspended them over the river, the rich statuary and decorative lamps adorning either side of the bow bridge's gothic structure. Like the statue of St. John of Nepomuk, one of the city's most significant saints. She recalled reading a legend about him in *A Practical Guide to Prague for Pennywise Persons*. In 1393, St. John of Nepomuk refused to divulge the queen's confessions to Wenceslas IV and was then . . . tortured to death, trussed up in armor, and thrown bodily off the Stone Bridge.

The imagined fingers constricted, and Clara gulped. Noted for posterity: Examining medieval sculptures and lore did not soothe agitated nerves. She rubbed a gloved thumb back and forth along Mum's hand, redirecting her concentration to the task of breathing. Of moving.

Ahead, the triumphal gothic arch of the Old Town Bridge Tower drew nearer, signaling the end of the Stone Bridge. Almost there now. Just keep breathing. Just keep moving.

A Goliath of a man striding away from Old Town bumped Mum in passing. Mum teetered and would've fallen if not for Clara's swift reflexes. The brute, who seemed as tall as he was wide, tramped off without so much as a "beg your pardon." Seconds later, he was absorbed into the crowd. Clara clenched her jaw. The sooner they were off this bridge the better.

"Wait a moment, ladies."

Wait? Was Mr. Arthur daft? She trudged onward. "We need to keep moving."

"Not just yet, Miss Stanton."

Like a persistent sheepdog, Mr. Arthur herded them toward the bridge's edge, where a brave—or out of his mind—artist had stationed an easel that bore an unfinished painting of the nearby statue of St. Joseph. Mr. Arthur thrust all three carpetbags into Clara's arms and propped his crutch against the bridge. "Wait here."

As Clara flailed to grasp that command, along with the luggage, Mr. Arthur dove into the current of pedestrians and ran back the way they'd come.

Mum rose onto the tips of her toes, watching the departure of Mr. Arthur with rapt curiosity. Unsatisfied with her limited perspective, she proceeded to mimic a rabbit, hopping in place and startling poor Fred, who changed his stance from stole to fur collar. When that exercise failed to provide an adequate view, she stilled and scrunched her pert little nose. "Drat my height deficiency. I can't see where the boy's gone. What's Arthur doing, ducky?"

Oh, I don't know. Wasting precious time, subjecting us to danger, driving me mad as a hatter. She situated the bags in her grasp and located Mr. Arthur amongst the throng.

Confronting Goliath without a slingshot.

What was Mr. Arthur thinking? "He's conversing with that last man who bumped into us. Though only heaven knows why." He couldn't possibly mean to confront everyone who'd accosted them today. That could take all year.

"Conversing? That's a riveting description, I must say. Details, love. I need details."

"But they are just conversing . . . albeit rather intensely. The man appears to be glowering, but Mr. Arthur is still smiling." Because of course he was. "Oh dear . . . The man is expanding his chest and broadening his shoulders. He's advancing on Mr. Arthur. There's no polite space left between them now. My stars, that giant truly does make Mr. Arthur resemble a shepherd boy."

"Thrilling! Are they going to engage in fisticuffs?"

"Surely not. Mr. Arthur must realize they're unequally matched and such a row wouldn't result in his favor. Although . . . he doesn't appear to be retreating." Not one step. Despite the giant's aggressive stance, Mr. Arthur was standing his ground.

And he no longer smiled.

Clara's stomach sank into the river. *God, please don't let there be a—*

The giant's knuckles connected with Mr. Arthur's jaw, snapping his head backward.

A gasp flew from Clara as if she'd been the one struck.

Mum beamed a hopeful smile. "Fisticuffs?"

Clara pursed her lips and nodded, fixing her gaze on what was now a full-blown brawl between Mr. Arthur and Goliath. Pedestrians dodged the flying fists, scattering in all directions. Young men tossed goading hurrahs into the fray, while their elders trudged by with unimpressed grunts. Mr. Arthur proved to be swifter than his rival, getting in a few punches, then darting just out of reach. But the giant soon perceived this tactic. When Mr. Arthur bobbed, the giant weaved and locked a brawny arm around Mr. Arthur's head, dragging him under and out of sight amid the sea of bodies.

Seconds ticked by, then a minute. Still the men did not resurface. Clara elevated to the tips of her boots but could see no better, thanks to the crowd of onlookers who'd encircled the brawl with morbid curiosity. Two minutes. Still no sight of Mr. Arthur. The vein along her brow began to pulse faster and faster, plucking at the corner of her eye. She didn't know whether to pray for Mr. Arthur's safe return or for the brute to knock some sense into him.

"Well, this is a moldy apple tart. My first bout of fisticuffs, and I can't see the action."

Clara rolled her eyes in her mother's direction. "What happened to your moral stance against senseless violence?"

"My stance still stands. Nonetheless, I must admit, watching a prime male specimen duel in defense of a lady's honor is rather . . . rousing."

"Mother!" Clara gasped, cheeks awash with the flames of mortification, and placed a hand over Fred's innocent ears. "For the love of all, never use the word *rousing* in reference to yourself. Not within my hearing, I beg you. For the sake of my digestion and sanctity of mind, just . . . don't." A shudder racked her stomach. "As to defending a lady's honor, we both know this is not that. Our honor didn't require defense from a mere bump on a congested bridge. It would've been far wiser for Mr. Arthur to see us to our destination. This skirmish was provoked by his pride and for his pride, nothing more."

"Ruled the judge without hearing the accused's testimony." Mum shook her head at Clara, and turning back toward the fisticuffs, broke into a smile. "Ah, here the boy comes! Just you wait, ducky. Arthur will have a logical explanation for his actions, I'm sure."

A flimsy excuse, more like.

Head downcast, Mr. Arthur made his way to them with a noticeable hitch in his stride. The collar of his shirt was torn, his overcoat was smeared with dust, and blood trailed from his nose in a scarlet mark of defeat. He met them with a ragged sigh. "Apologies for the delay. I had a matter of business to tend to."

Matter of business, her foot. She strangled the carpetbag handles in her grasp. "What were you thinking, inciting a row on a public street?"

"That Mrs. S. might like to have this back." From a bruising hand, with cracked and bloodied knuckles, Mr. Arthur produced a coin purse with a distinctive gold clasp in the shape of two squirrels with interlocking fluffy tails.

The carpetbags slipped from Clara's grasp and fell to the sandstone with a thwump, right along with her jaw and preconceived notions. She took Mum's coin purse from Mr. Arthur, but even with its weight balanced in her gloved palm, right before her eyes, she still couldn't believe her senses. "How?"

Mr. Arthur indicated over his shoulder with a nod, immediately regretting the movement with a wince. "That chap acquired the purse through the old push-and-pocket maneuver. I recognized it straightaway. Travel the world in a coat that's all pockets, and you're sure to learn many a trick of the pickpocket trade firsthand. Anyhow, I confronted the thief in question. Politely requested he return what wasn't his. When I realized the fellow wasn't inclined to oblige my request, I created a situation that would, erm . . . bring us closer together."

A gleam sparked in Mum's eyes. "You pinched it back? You darling scamp!"

Mr. Arthur's grin turned to a grimace when his split lip stretched too far. "I just employed the old snitch-back-what's-yours shuffle."

Producing a handkerchief, Mum fussed over Mr. Arthur,

cleaning the blood from his face. "As much as I admire your pluck, you must take more care with yourself. You shouldn't have let the brute pummel you for so long. You might've suffered more serious injuries."

"Better me than you, Mrs. S."

Clara blinked, unable to heft her jaw off the ground. She couldn't believe what she was seeing, absorb what she was hearing. Mr. Arthur had taken a beating for the sole purpose of retrieving *and* returning Mum's money? *All* of her money?

While Mum nursed Mr. Arthur's wounds, Clara discreetly examined the purse's cache. Nothing was missing. She didn't understand it. First, Mr. Arthur had returned her bribe, and now he'd passed up the perfect opportunity to dip into their coffers and blame the theft on someone else. A temptation her own fiancé had been unable to resist.

"Arthur is not Rupert, you know."

The hot coal of prejudice Clara had kept burning turned cold and crumbled to ash. *Good heavens . . . I might just be wrong.*

Secreting the coin purse into her skirt's deep pocket, Clara faced Mr. Arthur. The man was still being tended by Mum, a scrupulous nurse equipped with aforementioned handkerchief and the tried-and-true medicinal salve commonly known as saliva, which she applied with the pad of her thumb and a dose of maternal cooing.

To his credit, Mr. Arthur endured these questionable ministrations with remarkable patience, all the while minimizing the import of his actions. He caught Clara's observing gaze and offered a lopsided grin.

This time, Clara didn't throw it away. Perhaps she'd judged the hobgoblin too harshly. Perhaps he was neither a thief nor a spy. Perhaps it was time to give him half a chance.

CHAPTER

15

The Klementinum library stole Clara's breath with a rush of unrestrained wonderment. Less than a minute prior, she'd wanted nothing more than to find Grand's clue and escape to the solitude of the next inn posthaste. Yet now, enveloped in the musty incense of nigh on twenty thousand books, she didn't want to hasten. She wanted to linger.

For just a little while, she wanted to be Cinderella at the ball with the Klementinum as her castle. Instead of waltzing in glass slippers, she wanted to revel in the collection of geographical and astronomical globes, ceiling frescos, and illuminated volumes. Instead of having until the stroke of midnight, she'd allow herself until the chimes of Grand's pocket watch beckoned an automaton from hiding.

Clara sought the time from her chatelaine's watch. It was now a quarter past the hour, which meant Cinderella had exactly five and forty minutes to put aside all thought of cinders and striving.

Someone gave her a good shake as though to waken her from sleep. "Are you listening, ducky?"

"Yes . . . no." Reverie faded to reality as Mum eyed her with a quizzical expression. "I apologize. For what am I listening?" And at what point had she released Mum's hand?

"Not for what, ducky. To *whooom*. In this instance, I am the whom and you are the impolite ignorer of the whom."

Mr. Arthur snorted behind Clara's back, his amusement rankling her nerves. Reflexively, she turned to pin the man with a scowl, but at the sight of his split lip and bruising skin, she couldn't bring herself to do so. Instead, she redirected her gaze to Mum. "I beg your pardon, Mrs. Whom. You now have my full attention." Minus her peripheral vision, which kept flitting to the books shelved just out of reach, yet enticingly close.

"I said, this room is so vast we might have better luck finding Father's clue if we divide and conquer. I thought the boys and I might take the west wing and you the east."

"I don't know. . . ." After their encounter with Goliath the pickpocket, she wasn't keen on separating. She surveyed either end of the library. The lengthy hall was quiet and, aside from them, completely unoccupied. There was no need to squander her five and forty minutes to worry. Mum ought to be safe from giants here. "Very well. I suppose that plan will suffice."

Especially as it would permit her a chance to examine those tantalizing books.

Parting from Mum and the boys, Clara wandered down the baroque hall, lined on either side with expansive wooden bookcases. Each case was bookended with elaborate columns, some of which had been carved into dramatic whirls, all of which were topped with Corinthian caps of gold. Leather-bound books in varying shades of white and brown were arranged in neat rows along every shelf like so many jewels on a slide bracelet. Great treasures of mind and eye, indeed. What a blessing for the people of Prague that the Klementinum's library—once part of a private university for the Jesuits—had been converted to a public library.

What a shame that for all the volumes housed in its walls, she couldn't find one to read.

Alas, every book Clara strolled past, every volume she admired, was written in a language she couldn't understand. A scattered selection in Latin and Greek, the vast majority in Czech. While the library's enormous collection might contain works in her native English or learned French, the odds of locating one amid the myriad tomes in her limited time here were painfully slim. She traced a gloved finger down a book's embossed spine. To be encompassed by so many books was the best kind of bliss, but to not be able to read one was the worst sort of torture. It was as if Cinderella had arrived at the ball only to find she couldn't hear the music.

Clara sighed. Ah well, nothing could be done about it now. If she couldn't enjoy the treasures of the mind, she'd content herself with the treasures of the eye. *A Practical Guide to Prague for Pennywise Persons* had devoted several pages to the library's ceiling frescoes by Jan Hiebl. Perhaps she might study their allegorical representations of education and wisdom, attempt to identify the portraits of Jesuit saints and university patrons.

With a steadying hand to the crown of her bonnet, Clara tilted her head backward, but her gaze snagged on something odd before it could reach the fresco. Something out of place amid the hall's pristine order. A single book on a lofty shelf tilted forward, threatening to topple from its perch and dash against the floor. Such desecration she simply could not allow.

Locating a nearby ladder fitted with wheels, Clara rolled it toward the shelf in question and proceeded to climb to the rescue. She righted the book so it stood flush with the row of tomes, and the glint of gold leaf lettering along its spine held her gaze. Stilled her breath. For the words were gloriously legible!

She snatched the book from the shelf. *Tour of Athens: A Complete Handbook for the Use of Lady Travelers with Experiential Advice from One Such Lady, Miss E. Cochrane.*

A travel guide written in English and by a woman, no less—what were the odds?

Clara smiled. Only one "odd" could explain such a remarkable coincidence, and his name was Grand. That dear, sweet man. How many inquiries had he made, how long had he searched before finding this gem? A gem specifically chosen, cut, and set to her liking. When next she saw him, she must remember to thank Grand for his thoughtful selection.

Book in tow, Clara descended the ladder with care and returned it to its proper place. Then she walked farther down the hall, searching for the perfect spot to read. Windowed niches with built-in wooden seats were interspersed amongst the great bookcases, each one swathed in golden curtains that softened daylight's dazzling presence.

She selected one of these reading nooks, sat upon the hard bench therein, and leaned against the cold marble relief that formed the alcove. Yet the grandiose space did not suit. It chafed. It confined. It imposed reality upon imagination. How could one read thus, sitting staunch and upright? It didn't feel natural.

Why, when she was a girl, she'd taken books under Papa's desk and made of it a cave wherein she lounged as if a bear in hibernation. She'd transformed the library sofa into a tree from which she'd hung upside down and read as a monkey, and her bedroom floor had many times become the sea and she, with legs outstretched beneath an iridescent skirt of *changeante* silk, a mermaid.

My, but she had been a ridiculous child. Silly and naïve and . . . whimsical.

Her throat clogged. Eyes misted. Before grief had made life hard and betrayal had complicated its days, there was once a young girl named Clara Marie who was exuberant and carefree and longed for the delight of adventure. She'd almost forgotten that smiling child existed, but now that she recalled, she desperately wished to pay her a visit. Just once more.

Directly across the hall, a second alcove beckoned. It had no bench, only a great window with curtains that cascaded to the floor like a golden waterfall. A ridiculous notion revived her smile. The library was still theirs alone. Mum was safe, chatting away with Mr. Arthur or Fred or both, as they searched the western wing. Perhaps her ridiculous notion might be indulged?

Book in hand, Clara scurried across the width of the hall, slipped behind the billowing drapes, and settled upon the floor with her knees tucked against her chest. She suppressed a laugh. Nestled between the window and the golden curtains was a world of warmth and light, soothing and cozy. This was no waterfall, as she first supposed. Nay, this was the castle ballroom illuminated by the glow of a hundred thousand chandeliers, and here Cinderella would dance—or read, as it were. She opened the travel guide and proceeded to twirl through it, word by word.

Page by page.

Chapter by chap—

The curtains flew open, and a man loomed over her.

Clara's heart leapt to her throat, shoving out a shriek. The high-pitched noise echoed through the hall, and she clamped a hand over her mouth. Pulse pounding, she blinked, and her vision clarified on Mr. Arthur, who looked down on her with a countenance both dumbfounded and amused. Heat engulfed her cheeks. "Good heavens, sir! Why must you sneak about thus?"

Mr. Arthur gaped. "I never sneak. Makes a chap look suspect. Why did you screech at me like a banshee?"

"I didn't screech. I cried out in warranted fright."

He quirked a fair eyebrow. "You screeched. Vociferously. Prague's dead have thus been awakened to roam the streets in confusion."

The flame of embarrassment grew scalding, and Clara fumbled for the book she'd dropped. "I merely startled. As would anyone who thought themselves alone, only to be set upon by a looming shadow."

"Set upon? You make it sound as though I ambushed your village with torches and pitchforks in the dead of night. If one of us has the right to be startled, it is I, my lady. One moment I'm sent forth by Mrs. S. to ascertain your whereabouts, and the next, my unsuspecting ears are impaled by a piercing scream. All because I made the unfortunate decision to investigate the incongruous protrusion of these curtains. Now that we've established who frightened whom, would you care to explain what exactly you're doing down there?"

Making a fool of herself, that's what. "Nothing . . . nothing at all." Her bungling fingers at last grasped the book, and she clutched it to her chest.

"And so engrossed were you by 'nothing' that you failed to hear a man with a metal leg clank in your direction? Come now, Miss Stanton. If you're going to spout falsehoods, at least fabricate a tale that's somewhat plausible. Unless . . . you'd rather save yourself the trouble by telling me the truth, which is usually more interesting in any case." One hand resting atop his crutch, Mr. Arthur knelt upon his good leg and met her gaze, green eyes brightened with curiosity. "What were you doing down here? Really?"

Trying to relive a simpler time long past . . . to recover a part of herself long gone. Neither of which was possible. Neither of which she wished to share with him.

Clara pulled back her shoulders, willing her rectified posture to restore a measure of decorum, and thus, a fraction of her dignity. Something Mr. Arthur's unwavering gaze seemed intent to deny. If only he would take his inquisitiveness and leave so she might flee to a darkened corner and snuff her flaming cheeks in the pages of a book. "Where have you left my mother?"

The question sliced with a hidden blade of accusation she'd not intended to brandish, but Mr. Arthur didn't withdraw from its sharpness. On the contrary, he inclined toward her and stripped his voice of jest. "Miss Stanton, do you still truly believe I'd intentionally place that precious woman in harm's way?"

Her gaze fell to Mr. Arthur's arm draped across his knee, to the cracked knuckles that had not yet begun to scab. Rose to his bruised face, now a deeper shade of purple. *"Better me than you, Mrs. S."* Gracious, she was being unfair. What had happened to giving the man a chance?

She exhaled a long breath that took the starch right out of her posture. "No, Mr. Arthur. I can't say I believe you capable of such actions any longer. Please forgive my curtness. I . . . I'm afraid I have an unpleasant tendency to lash out in fright or fury when jarred from an engrossing book." She held up the copy of *Tour of Athens*.

A grin tugged at Mr. Arthur's split lip. "Done. And noted. You know . . . I toured Athens myself, once. Years ago. Sailed into the port of Piraeus." He nodded toward the book. "Have you visited the Parthenon yet?"

Clara couldn't curtail a sheepish smile as she presented her place in the handbook, a chapter entitled "Lessons Learned at the Parthenon: The Necessity of a Parasol."

"Right-oh, then. Far be it from me to keep a lady from ex-

ploring the wonders of the ancient world." Mr. Arthur tossed
her a wink and closed the curtains upon her in a dramatic
swoosh of silk. The familiar pairing of his prosthetic boot and
crutch echoed through the library, signaling his departure.
Clank-tap. Clank-tap. Clank-tap.

Alone once more, Clara stared at the golden drapery. She
ought to put this mortifying incident behind her and pray it
be soon forgotten. She ought to dust her skirts, return *Tour
of Athens* to its assigned shelf, and position herself for the appearance of Grand's next invention. After all, she'd frittered
away enough time as it was, and the pocket watch was sure
to sound at any moment.

Her gaze dipped to the open book propped on her knees.
But it had not chimed yet . . . had it? She pursed her lips.
Perhaps Cinderella might twirl through a few pages more.
The first chime of Grand's watch would return her to reality
soon enough.

Clara leapt back into chapter six and flitted about the
Acropolis. She pirouetted through the Athens Observa-
tory, admiring constellations that shone with beauty and
mythos, though not brightly enough, for her eyes squinted
and strained amid the darkness. Her stomach gurgled. How
could she be hungry? Had she not just dined on fish with
olives and—

Her stomach growled, demanding to be noticed.

Clara clutched her bodice and something thudded at her
side. Bother, she must have dropped her book, but where
was it? She couldn't make it out amid the shadows. Shadows?
Good heavens, where had the daylight gone?

Flinging curtains left and right, Clara reoriented herself
by the glow of dozens of candles now flickering throughout
the Klementinum library. She blinked. Oh no . . . she couldn't
have wasted an entire day without noticing. Could she? She
snatched up the watch on her chatelaine and checked the

time. She gulped. Apparently, she could. Why hadn't Grand's watch chimed? Unless . . . had she failed to hear it?

Clara stood on shaky legs that pricked and pinched with every movement and wobbled across the library in search of Mum and Mr. Arthur. She found them seated in an alcove, playing a game of cards by candlelight. As she approached, she stumbled over the trio of carpetbags situated nearby and barely managed to catch herself before her face crashed into the wall. "Why didn't you fetch me?"

Without lifting her gaze from the game, Mum placed a five on a six. "Because you don't need a third in double solitaire, and we lacked a fourth for whist." Fred squeaked, nudging her chin with his nose. "We've been through this, Freddy. The last time you played fourth at the whist consortium, you beheaded the queen of hearts, and that ended badly for all concerned. Alice still isn't speaking to me, so proud was she of that hand-painted deck from Italy."

The vein along Clara's temple began to twitch. "Mother. It's nearly eight o'clock."

Mr. Arthur topped a two with an ace and casually consulted Grand's pocket watch. "Right you are, Miss Stanton."

Why were they being so maddeningly calm? They ought to be berating her for her foolishness. "I'm sorry. I never meant to read so long . . . just a few pages more, and now I've left you to sit here for hours and hours and—" She gasped. "Stars, we haven't had dinner! Or lunch. Or teatime. We completely missed teatime. Oh, poor Mum, you must be famished."

"Not in the least, ducky. While you were engaged with your book, Mr. Arthur escorted me to this lovely little restaurant and saw that I was well taken care of."

Clara's mind reeled. "He did?" Her voice waned as she addressed Mr. Arthur. "Y-you did?"

After setting a ten of clubs atop a matching jack, Mr. Arthur met her with a direct gaze and matter-of-fact tone. "I couldn't let our beloved Mrs. S. go hungry, now could I?"

Our beloved? "But Grand's clue . . ."

Mr. Arthur nudged one of the carpetbags with his leather boot. "Apprehended and stored with the others shortly after our arrival."

They'd been in possession of Grand's clue all this time? "Why didn't you tell me?"

"Because, Miss Stanton, you looked so . . . happy. Smiling like a schoolgirl who'd slipped away from her austere governess to pick wildflowers. Drosselmeyer would've boxed my ears if I'd put a stop to the first bit of fun you'd had since we left London, so I had a chat with the library's rather amiable custodian, and here we are."

"We thought it best to let you be, ducky. For as long as you'd let yourself be." Mum rubbed noses with Freddy. "All three of us."

Clara shook her head, utterly flabbergasted.

Mr. Arthur smiled at her then, mustache and chin whiskers tilting upward in their accustomed way, and for the first time in their acquaintance, his lopsided grin failed to irritate her.

Clara simply couldn't puzzle out the man with the mechanical leg and steadfast smile. No amount of rumination made sense of him. He was an anomalous grouping of stars that refused to form a cohesive constellation. A foreign city she couldn't map. Oh, how she tried, though.

As she dined at a quaint restaurant in Old Town, Clara stared at the man conversing with Mum and Fred. She studied and thought, she analyzed and examined. She dissected his every action for logical motivation. Why had Mr. Arthur put himself in harm's way to recover Mum's purse? Why hadn't he stolen from them when given the chance? Why had he let her read for hours on end without complaint? Why had he tended to Mum's needs in her stead?

Could any man—other than Papa and Grand—truly be so selfless and kind?

Dusk tucked the sun in for the night, and the candles placed throughout the restaurant glowed all the brighter, each little flame undulating in a dance all its own as wax pooled and dripped. Clara enjoyed another bite of *vepřo knedlo zelo*, the regional dish Mr. Arthur had recommended. The tender pork loin roasted in onion and caraway gravy, then served over sauerkraut, was every bit as delicious as he'd promised. She dipped the last piece of *knedlíky*, a boiled bread dumpling, into the gravy and savored the final morsel's warmth.

Mr. Arthur, now cradling Fred as though he were a newborn babe, broke into a lilting song with a baritone voice that was endearingly out of tune. "La-la-lu, la-la-lu . . ."

And now the man sings lullabies to ermine. Yet another random star that failed to create a clear pattern in the befuddled firmament. Mum began to harmonize with Mr. Arthur, each taking a turn with improvised lyrics that somehow flowed together without rehearsal.

Clara couldn't help but smile at the pair. At him. How could she not, when Mr. Arthur showed Mum such unwavering respect, such earnest affection? *"I couldn't let our beloved Mrs. S. go hungry, now could I?"*

Another voice, from long ago, invaded her musings. *"I couldn't possibly allow your mother to visit my offices. Not so long as she insists on wearing that animal. One whiff of vermin could do irrevocable damage to my business. You understand, don't you, darling?"*

Her smile fell. Yes . . . at last she was beginning to. Mr. Arthur really was *nothing* like Mr. Forrester. Instead of conspiring to use her family to save his own skin, Mr. Arthur put himself at risk and fought on their behalf. He didn't steal, spy, or wreak havoc when her back was turned. He restored, protected, and took care. Heavens above, what was she to do with this?

A waiter interrupted the lullaby, carrying a plate of the dessert Mr. Arthur had requested. *Větrník*—puffed choux pastries baked a golden brown, enhanced by a sheen of caramel icing, and filled with swirls of cream.

As the waiter took his leave, Mr. Arthur sought her gaze. "Care to have the first selection, Miss Stanton?"

Clara pursed her lips. Perhaps . . . perhaps the most sensible thing to do was simply to declare a truce. Give Mr. Arthur the chance he was due. "That's very kind, sir. Thank you." She infused as much feeling as she dared into those small words of gratitude and hoped it would amend their belated utterance. Hoped he would perceive the interwoven apology.

With a smile that spoke of understanding, Mr. Arthur nudged the plate in her direction, extending her a fresh start sweetened with caramel. Solidifying their truce, Clara selected the *větrník* with the most filling.

Now that she'd replenished her strength, it was time to undertake a puzzle she might actually be able to piece together. "Might I have a look at the clue from the Klementinum, Mr. Arthur?"

"Right-oh. Perhaps you can figure out where it leads, 'cause I'm stumped as an oak felled for kindling." After rummaging through the carpetbag at his feet, Mr. Arthur placed the object on the table—an automaton moth.

Clara held the contraption to nearby candlelight. Almost weightless, the mechanical moth was life-size and fit neatly in her palm. The body appeared to be crafted from brass, including its dainty legs and antennae. Delicate wings were inlaid with enamel to create a distinct pattern of bright pink along the edges and yellow toward the center, each accented with a pair of symmetrical white spots. Interesting that Grand had taken such care with the details of color and pattern. She couldn't help but wonder if there was a reason. "Mum, do you recognize this moth?"

"We're not personally acquainted, but I'm familiar with the species. Read about it in an entomology journal when it was discovered just two years ago. It's called a pink star moth and is native to the eastern portion of the United States."

Pink star moth. Very interesting, indeed. Clara turned the automaton over. On the underside of each brass forewing, a word had been engraved. *Spectare*, on the left. *Polaris*, on the right. Both Latin in origin, only one familiar. She knew well that Polaris was the guiding North Star, but she couldn't begin to guess the meaning of *spectare*. She squinted at the word that neither her knowledge, nor the gleaming candlelight, could illuminate. Perhaps Grand's enclosed note would have a corresponding hint required to make sense of his riddle.

Clara extended her hand toward Mr. Arthur. "I should like to read Grand's note now, if you please."

Mr. Arthur held his hands up. "There wasn't one this time. That's what has me stumped. The watch chimed, the automaton appeared, but no note. Not on the moth. Not on the shelf from which it descended. All we have to go on is the device itself and the two words inscribed on its wings."

Botheration. Leave it to Grand to do the unexpected. She deflated with a sigh against the slatted back of her chair. "Such paltry information is hardly enough to go on, especially seeing as Mum and I have a meager understanding of Latin at best."

"Translation won't be an issue, Miss Stanton. I'm well versed in Latin."

She arched an eyebrow wryly. "You are not, sir."

Mr. Arthur parried her with a raised brow of his own. "*Polaris*. Shortened from the Neo-Latin, *stella polaris*, meaning 'polar star.' *Spectare* from the Latin, meaning 'to look at or see.' As in, 'Look at Miss Stanton and see her proven wrong.'"

Clara gaped at this newest puzzlement. How had Mr. Arthur come to acquire a working knowledge of Latin? A classical education wasn't something afforded to nameless vagabonds in patched overcoats. What sort of life had Mr. Arthur led before he'd arrived at Grand's door?

"Bravo, Arthur. It's not just any man who can render my ducky speechless."

Her slackened jaw slammed shut. If she didn't know any better, she'd think Mum had caught the matchmaking bug—assuming she hadn't been infected along with Grand before this whole journey began. Had the two of them been in league together this whole time?

A mischievous glint danced in Mum's eyes, one that couldn't be explained away by the candlelight. One that sparkled with significance as Mum's gaze waltzed merrily between her and Mr. Arthur.

Clara tensed, face burning despite her distance from the candle's flame. Heavens above, she'd been bamboozled! For as surely as they were blood kin, Mum and Grand were aligned in a matchmaking conspiracy.

A bead of perspiration formed along her twitching temple. She needed to steer this conversation back to the topic at hand before Mum's oblique quips took it to a place she didn't wish to venture. "Pink star moth. Spectare. Polaris. Two references to stars cannot be a coincidence. Our next destination must have something to do with constellations or . . . astronomy."

Her gaze drifted to the restaurant's four-paned window, framing the dark silhouette of the Klementinum backlit by the moon's silvery luminance. A tower rose from the vast building complex into a sky of sapphire blue, standing tall amid inky clouds and glittering stars. The familiar figure of an overburdened Titan adorned the tower's cupola, and in the shadowy haze of night, she could almost imagine a clockwork owl perched upon the globe.

Almost hear Grand's voice beckoning Little Atlas to spectare polaris.

"The Klementinum's astronomical tower." She faced Mum and Mr. Arthur, setting the automaton moth on the table with confidence. "That is where Grand wishes us to go next."

Comprehension dawned on Mr. Arthur's face. He consulted Grand's pocket watch, and then stood, a broad grin stretching from ear to ear. "Right-oh, ladies. Let's go look at some stars."

Together, they strolled back to the Klementinum, sights set on the astronomical tower's looming shadow. Once inside, Mum made herself comfortable at the bottom of a staircase, propping her boots atop two of their carpetbags and placing the third on the step just above to support her back. Leaving her in Fred's company, Clara and Mr. Arthur began their ascent. On their way up the tower's winding staircase, they passed various workrooms cluttered with instruments for astronomical and meteorological study.

When they finally reached the top, Clara pressed a hand to her bodice. She hoped Grand wasn't overtaxing himself with all this travel and scaling of lofty towers. Catching her breath, she took in the tower's uppermost room. Moonlight shone through a single round window like crystalline water pouring into a washbasin, simple and small. No furnishings lined the wooden walls. The only thing of note was said window and the door in which it was fixed.

Mr. Arthur opened the door. "After you."

She stepped onto the tower's viewing balcony and was greeted by a twinkling canopy of stars that awakened the soul.

"I'd wager Drosselmeyer had something to do with this." Mr. Arthur assessed a standing telescope tilted toward the heavens.

A smile touched her lips. "I wouldn't doubt it."

Before Clara could set her eye to the scope, metallic chimes broke the night's stillness.

Mr. Arthur held aloft Grand's watch, searching here and there for the emergence of wonderment.

A shadow stirred. Came alive. Breaking away from the tower wall, it dove through the darkness, weaving through silver moonbeams until it came to rest upon Mr. Arthur's hand. The moment it touched Grand's timepiece, the chimes quieted. The living shadow stilled.

Clara drew closer to inspect this latest marvel. It was not a shadow come to life, as first appeared, but rather an automaton bat with large ears, a flattened upturned nose, and flexible wings of black leather spanned betwixt tiny pewter limbs. A cylindrical satchel strapped to the bat's back most likely contained the next note from Grand.

Mr. Arthur tucked the mechanical bat into one of many patchwork pockets. "Right-oh. We've got what we came for. No doubt you wish to return to Mrs. S. and secure lodging in Old Town before the hour grows later still. Shall we be on our way?"

"Actually . . ." Clara bit her lip, surprised at the words edging to the tip of her tongue as she sidled up to the telescope and placed a gloved hand on its shining surface. "Seems a shame not to make use of this after climbing all those stairs. Besides, Grand did instruct us to look at the stars, did he not? I should hate to disappoint him by not sparing a moment to gaze upon Polaris."

The moon caught a pleasantly surprised expression on Mr. Arthur's face. He waved a hand toward the telescope. "Gaze away, Miss Stanton. I'm in no hurry."

Clara tempered a surge of glee and peered demurely into the telescope's eyepiece. In a blink, every celestial map she'd ever studied became three dimensional in a juxtaposition of darkness and dazzling light. Constellations she'd only ever observed on parchment and globes, due to London's impenetrable smog, now glittered before her eyes, stitching images across the heavens with silver thread and stardust. There was Draco to the west, the slain dragon tossed into the sky upon his defeat, and there, near the dragon's looping tail, sat Ursa Minor. The little bear constellation composed of seven stars. Polaris, the brightest of all seven, winked at her from the very tip of the bear's tail.

Clara's chest swelled at the polar star's brilliance—at its shining promise to bring those who wandered home again. Even absentminded grandfathers with a penchant for flights of fancy. A fine mist of tears blurred her vision. She stepped away from the telescope, blinking furiously. "Grand would wish you to see this, I think."

Mr. Arthur stepped forward and took her place at the telescope. "That bright one is Polaris, I take it?"

"Yes. 'The most comforting star in the heavens,' as Mum calls it." With Mr. Arthur suitably distracted, Clara quickly dried her eyes with the fingers of her cotton gloves. "When Papa used to travel on long sea voyages, before he'd built up Stanton Shipping to what it is today, I used to thank God for Polaris every night because I knew that even if Papa were to find himself lost, he could always follow the guiding North Star back to us."

Mr. Arthur's lighthearted tone dimmed. "I suppose that would be a comfort. For those with a home and family waiting for them."

She tilted her head, curiosity pitted against her better judgment. "Have you no family, Mr. Arthur?"

He stepped back from the telescope and into the shadows hanging about the tower. The darkness masked Mr. Arthur's expression, but she could feel him closing off. Withdrawing, as though he were a bat hiding from the light of day, wrapping himself in wings of silence.

"Come now, Mr. Arthur. Surely you have someone, somewhere, who misses you. Even if it's only a distant cousin who pops by to grate on your nerves and empty your larder every twenty-fifth of December."

Mr. Arthur's darkened silhouette removed an object from one of his pockets, made a quick study of it, and then, fisting his hand, shoved it back into the depths of his overcoat. "I'm just a spare part in this world, Miss Stanton." His prosthetic boot clanked on the stone balcony. "And a faulty one at that."

Brushing past her, he headed into the tower without a single smile or flippant pun.

Clara watched his retreating overcoat until it disappeared down the stairwell. Why was Mr. Arthur so reluctant to speak of his family? What had occurred to make the mere mention of his past alter his countenance so completely?

She shook her head, scattering her questions and desire to pry. To know. That was one desire she could not allow to flourish. For knowing had the potential of leading one to care, and while she no longer had any qualms about showing Mr. Arthur kindness, she couldn't allow herself to begin to care about him, especially with Mum and Grand scheming to entangle her emotions. Though she knew they meant well, the pair simply didn't understand that caring for another person would only give her overburdened shoulders yet another load to carry.

The nightmare was back, and it was changing.

Theodore stood once again on the battlefield of Balaklava, but this time, the carnage was already at its end. This time, he remained standing on one leg of flesh and one of bronze. Eerie silence and billows of black smoke choked the air. Bodies littered the ground around him, friend and foe alike, slumped atop sabers and crumpled over cannons. Death was the only victor here, and he didn't want to find out what its lingering shadow had in store.

Wake up, man. You have to wake up. The thoughts pounded his mind like frantic fists upon a prison door. He strained and twisted, yanked and pulled, trying with all his might to wrench his boots from the thick mire of sweat, tears, and blood. Yet his striving was to no avail.

The nightmare would have its way.

A slap came out of nowhere and knocked him to his knees. Plush carpet cushioned his fall, but the familiar Turkish pattern of crimson vines and golden birds raised gooseflesh on his skin. He was back at Kingsley Court.

A perfectly polished black shoe stepped upon the nearest woven bird, crushing its head. "Try to live up to your name, if you can. And if you can't . . . don't bother coming back."

Father's words landed on Theodore like an anvil, cold and crushing. *I have to wake up. I have to get out of here.* Theodore struggled to his feet and discovered that his seven older brothers now stood behind Father, their gazes as cold as his.

"You can't mean that." Theodore's voice cracked, shattered. "I'm your son as much as they."

Disdain dripped from Father's expression. "You're just a spare, and a faulty one at that. I've no use for broken pieces." Plucking a gear off a nearby desk, Father examined its missing teeth with revulsion and then tossed it at Theodore.

The gear struck true and lodged in Theodore's chest like a bullet. Pain exploded through his ribs. Kingsley Court vanished, and the nightmare dropped him back on the battlefield. Utterly alone beneath the noonday sun that glared without mercy. With trembling hands, Theodore attempted to cover the fresh wound above his heart, to apply enough pressure to stop the blood from seeping between his fingers.

Yet his striving was to no avail.

His feeble efforts healed nothing, mended nothing.

He collapsed to his knees as a shout tore itself from his chest. "I can't fix it!"

Something struck him hard, and he jerked awake.

Gentle sunlight peeked through gauzy curtains and warmed Theodore's skin where he lay amid a tangle of sheets upon a scuffed wooden floor. Though the inn they'd found last night had obviously seen better days, this morning it was a bit of heaven. He leaned against the room's shaky cot—now at shoulder level—and a shudder racked his sweat-drenched body. Rolling out of bed was sweet mercy. There was no telling how long the terror would've gone on otherwise.

"It's over." He repeated the phrase between deep breaths,

trying to ground himself to reality, but today, the exercise did nothing to shake the nightmare's residual effects. Because it wasn't really over. It wasn't really a dream. Not the parts that hurt most.

Nearby, his shirt and overcoat hung from a bedpost. Theodore reached into one of the coat pockets and withdrew a familiar gear with three missing teeth. The gear he'd been trying to repair when Father had confronted him in the study all those years ago. The gear he'd carried ever since as a tangible reminder of the one thing he could never mend.

"I've no use for broken pieces."

Though his father yet lived, the moment those words had been spoken with the cold finality of death, Theodore had become an orphan. Bereft of home. Bereft of family. Bereft of the hope of ever belonging to someone who cared to claim him.

"Come now, Mr. Arthur. Surely you have someone, somewhere, who misses you."

That conversation with Miss Stanton had been a wretched mistake. He ought to know by now that she never settled for casual banter. She always pushed. Always asked one question too many. He should've held his tongue. But no, he had to go and make some offhand comment about family and spark the woman's curiosity.

He fisted the gear. Dash it all, he'd been flabbergasted! Flabbergasted by the discovery of Miss Stanton reading on the floor at the Klementinum, by the rosy flush of her cheeks and the sudden appearance of a smile on her lips. He'd not thought her capable of such an endearing smile. At the sight of it, his mind had become muddled, and he'd forgotten to keep his past locked away when they'd lingered at the astronomical tower. Forgotten to keep her from seeing inside the clock casing called Arthur that held him together.

Theodore shoved the battered gear into his pocket. He

couldn't make that mistake again. No matter how pleasant her company had become—no matter how prettily those silver eyes of hers gleamed in the starlight—Miss Stanton must never know the truth of him.

Dear Little Atlas,

    You've clickety-clacked your way to Prague. Well done! I'm so proud of you. Thank you for trusting my love enough to take that step of faith and follow me into the frightening unknown. I hope the book I mined from the Klementinum library's myriad gems proved a worthwhile reward, and I pray, as we continue this second leg of our scavenger hunt, that you won't grow weary of the journey. No matter how many miles separate us, rest assured, we're on this adventure together. Every step you take I have taken first, choosing each location with care and priming the way before you with joyous surprises.

    In so doing, I hope to remind we two that there's One who precedes us both on the journey of life. There is a God who loves us more than we could ever love each other, and because there's no darkness in Him at all, we can trust His love absolutely. We can lean wholly upon it and follow Him into the unknown, trusting that He will carry us through sunshine and storm. Trusting that the Way, the Truth, and the Life is better than our way, our understanding, and our might. With this in mind, let us carry on, together. My next clue can be found where timely apostles parade above the heaven's expanse and the earth's days.

                                Your devoted,
                                Grand

The nightmares might rob him of sleep, but Theodore would be hanged if they ruined one minute of this day. Standing on a configuration of black-and-white cobbles, he gazed upward at Prague's Orloj, the medieval astronomical clock mounted on the southern wall of the Old Town Hall in the city's Old Town Square. It was an astounding bit of craftmanship! He'd studied the clock for over two hours now, and still, he'd not taken in half of its marvels.

Fatigue slumped his eyelids with the weight of a passed-out drunkard. He leaned into the support of his crutch and tried to blink off the unwelcome bleariness. Force his eyes to stay vigilant and survey the magnificent mechanism's every facet.

The clock tower was composed of three main components. At the base was a circular calendar dial with a background of shining gold, juxtaposed with painted medallions representing the months of the year. As a standard clock marked the time, so the calendar dial marked the day's date—April 11, 1860. A golden statue of the archangel Michael flanked the calendar, and just above it, an astronomical dial of equal size and shape possessed an astrolabe and a twenty-four-hour clock. This dial of overlapping blue spheres was haunted by a skeleton figure holding an ominous hourglass. Directly above the visage of death, at the tower's peak, the stone bust of an angel watched over all between a pair of shuttered windows.

Soon those windows would open and reveal their hidden wonders.

"Take care, Mr. Arthur. If you tilt your head back any farther, it's likely to roll right off. I should hate to have to explain your decapitation to Grand."

Theodore smirked but didn't lower his head, despite the burgeoning ache in his neck. "I'm certain Drosselmeyer would understand the reason for my untimely demise. I don't want to miss one blessed thing." He must remember to thank the old codger with the heartiest of handshakes. The simple gesture couldn't begin to convey the depth of his gratitude for this moment, but it was a start. One he'd endeavor to build upon for the rest of his life.

"What might you miss, pray tell? We've taken in the parade twice, and it won't begin again for another fifteen minutes. Surely you could rest your neck for that length of time without incurring some regrettable deprivation."

Something knocked against his leather boot. "You're welcome to join me down here, lad. The view is splendid!"

Prying his gaze from the Orloj, Theodore sought the origin of Mrs. Stanton's voice and found her looking comfortable as you please—on the ruddy ground! With carpetbags situated beneath her head and shoulders in lieu of pillows, Mrs. S. stretched upon the cobbles, skirt arranged modestly and bonnet tied neatly, while Fred curled about her gloved hands like an ermine muff. Just like, *except* for the matter of breathing.

Theodore gaped as he faced Miss Stanton, who seemed atypically unfazed.

Miss Stanton smiled at her mother with an expression that fastened a gear of annoyance to the stronger axis of love. "Mum's neck has always been in a fidgety way, and when it began to act up after the first parade, she decided to make herself more comfortable."

Right-oh, classic Mrs. S. logic. But why wasn't her overly protective daughter in a panic? "And you're fine with this because . . . ?"

"The number of people are few. I'm here to ensure no one treads upon her." Pausing, Miss Stanton adopted a hushed tone. "And because I've found it's beneficial to indulge Mum's whims whenever I can do so safely. Makes her more inclined to heed my 'vain imaginings of impending doom' when a truly dangerous situation arises."

Theodore arched a brow. He couldn't imagine Mrs. S. ever getting herself into any real peril. "Such as?"

"Such as the incident last summer when Mum shackled herself in irons to the door of a taxidermy shop."

A snort lodged in his nose. "She didn't."

"Mum's rallying cry for justice was 'You would not stuff your sons and daughters. You ought not stuff God's deer and otters.'"

Theodore choked back a laugh but couldn't keep from grinning. If he hadn't already been smitten by the amiable and unique Mrs. S., he was now, for sure and certain!

"Snicker all you like, Mr. Arthur. You weren't the one who was forced to pick the lock whilst attempting to convince a blazing mad taxidermist not to summon the constable. Oh, how that horrid man shouted in my ear, spewing profanities and spittle alike. We were lucky to make it out of that scrape unscathed."

Pick the lock, she'd said? "Didn't Mrs. S. keep the key?"

"Aye, she kept it . . . in her stomach." Miss Stanton grimaced with a shudder.

Theodore gawked at the mild-looking woman reclined on a chaise lounge of cobblestones. "You didn't swallow that key, ma'am!"

Mrs. S. grinned. "Knocked it straight back with a toast to the Creator and a swig of my husband's port."

Laughter seized Theodore with both hands and shook him with such exuberant force that tears sprung from his eyes.

"Keep hold of your head, Mr. Arthur. The timely apostles are about to begin their parade." A handkerchief fluttered white before his blurred vision. "Here. We wouldn't want you to miss anything."

Theodore accepted the cloth proffered by Miss Stanton and grinned at the chipmunks embroidered on its four corners. He swiped the handkerchief over both eyes, clearing his sights for the show. Clearing his mind of darker memories to make space for this bright one he could never deserve.

The merry clanging of bells announced the Orloj's show was about to begin. Theodore and the Stantons, along with a smattering of pedestrians, hushed. Activity on the street ceased as all looked up, eyes transfixed on the closed windows situated on either side of the angelic stone bust. The shutters, painted with a design of blue squares, slowly slid inward and disappeared into a partition hidden in the wall of stone behind the angel's wings.

Then the apostles commenced their parade. Peter with a key to the kingdom of heaven, Matthias with the ax of martyrdom. Two by two, the twelve elaborate statues passed the open windows and faced the city before continuing their procession and vanishing back into the tower. Below them, the skeleton was awakened by the tower's tolling and rang his own bell of mortality in a bony hand, nodding with grim pleasure as the hourglass in his opposite hand swung back and forth, shortening the days of man—a sight that might've struck fear into the hearts of onlookers, were it not for the stalwart presence of the archangel Michael, who remained unmoved by death's ostentation. Armed with spear and sword, Michael guarded the calendar dial, reminding those within sight that death had already been defeated by One it could not hold, by One who held the days of humankind in scarred and sacred hands.

The final two apostles, having blessed the people of Prague, now withdrew from sight, and the shutters once again slid across the windows, concealing the disciples in their fortress of stone. The clock struck noon, and death was rendered still by the triumphant heralding of a new hour. A bell tolled twelve times, the last peal hanging on the air before fading into awed silence.

The Orloj's feat of mechanical engineering and artistry had lasted approximately seven and twenty seconds. But the joy it evoked—the soul-stirring desire it inspired to create and transform and innovate — Theodore was quite certain would last a lifetime.

"Upon my word, Mr. Arthur, you are the very image of a boy at the fair. I do believe you could watch this show every hour of every day and never tire of the spectacle."

Theodore tore his gaze from the clock and found Miss Stanton making a blatant study of him. Instead of her well-worn glower of critical suspicion, she bore a refreshing raiment of amusement that softened the lines of her face.

"What is it, sir, that captivates you so?"

At the moment? A pair of silver eyes intent on sparring with his better judgment. Rubbing his sore neck, Theodore stared at the cobbles to purchase some time and sense. He ought to sidestep the question. Hold fast to the resolution he'd made at dawn and ignore the pull of the alluring gaze that tempted him to be honest and risk additional questions that might pry open the door to his past.

Miss Stanton's expectant silence rang in his ears.

Say something, man! Lengthy pauses could reveal as much as words. "Erm . . . I suppose I'm fascinated by the Orloj's precision and purpose. Every part has a specific function to perform. A specific place to belong."

A dangerous glint of insight flashed in Miss Stanton's eyes. "So that's why the roving vagabond tinkers with timepieces . . . to find a semblance of belonging?"

Theodore's jaw tensed. He should've risked the lengthy pause and thought twice before he spoke. The woman was too perceptive.

"Who taught you the trade? Were you a clockmaker's son?"

"I wish." He bit his tongue too late. The words were out and gone, leaving a bitter taste in their wake. Right-oh, definitely should've thought twice. After that stupid slip of the tongue, Miss Stanton's curiosity would require the mollification of a lighthearted anecdote.

He forged ahead as if his previous remark had gone unsaid. "My first apprenticeship was with a chap by the name of Whirling. A wiry and wise fellow, he was. Good old Whirling taught me how clocks work. How to care for them."

Until Father had discovered his youngest son was learning a trade and dismissed the faithful servant without warning. Theodore swallowed hard. According to the whispers of servants, poor Whirling had died destitute shortly after being sacked. Not many positions were available to an estate clock-winder without a reference. He rubbed a hand over his bleary eyes and sagged onto his crutch, weighed down by all the memories and emotions he'd suppressed over the years. Bah . . . so much for lighthearted.

"You know . . . since Grand's invention has yet to appear, we ought to explore the Orloj from a different perspective. One of my travel guides mentioned that the apostle figures can be viewed from a platform in the Town Hall's Chapel of the Virgin Mary. Grand might have hidden his next clue there."

The tension in Theodore's jaw lessened as he once again met Miss Stanton's silver eyes. So the woman could be as gracious as she was perceptive?

Popping up from the ground like a daffodil, Mrs. S. took hold of his free arm. "Let's be off then, chickees! There are more wonders yet to behold."

Theodore absorbed the warmth of the Stantons' smiles, the one demure and the other daring, and found himself no longer leaning upon his crutch. Nothing he beheld this day could compare to the wonder of his standing alongside this endearing family. Never in his life had he met such rare people, and never in his life did he wish to be parted from them.

Collecting the carpetbags, Theodore accompanied the Stantons into the Old Town Hall. Miss Stanton led the way through the Gothic structure, navigating its various corridors and assembly halls with the assurance of one who frequented them daily. His past disparagements of Miss Stanton's paper-and-ink expertise couldn't have been more erroneous. Not only was the woman well-read, but she was a veritable walking map! It was no wonder Drosselmeyer called her his Little Atlas.

As the ladies entered the vacant Chapel of the Virgin Mary, sunlight extended a warm welcome through an oriel window of stained glass. One that made Theodore drop the bags he toted in the arched doorway, suddenly chilled in its shadow. Unfettered, the Stantons climbed a short, curved stairway to the right of the chapel door, and standing upon a small platform, peered inside an alcove in the wall where the apostles must dwell.

Mrs. S. leaned into the niche, bonnet tilting downward, as Miss Stanton held fast to her arm. "Gracious me, it's the very heart of the Orloj! Whoever maintains the clock must use this little hatch and iron ladder to access the movement. Get yourself over here, Arthur! Dawdling is for snails and slugs."

Though everything in Theodore longed to see the Orloj's movement with his own eyes, he couldn't compel his feet beyond the threshold. For he knew he had no right. With its vaulted ceiling and prayer kneelers, the small chapel possessed a grandeur unassuming and pure.

One he daren't sully.

Theodore set Drosselmeyer's pocket watch upon the chapel floor, careful not to let his fingers brush the tiles. He retreated from the slowly closing door, withdrawing into the adjacent Council Hall with its elaborate wooden paneling, brass chandeliers, and row of alcove windows. Here, he could accept the sun's warmth. Bask in it without demeaning his Maker.

Tucking away in one of the alcoves, Theodore set down the luggage and unlatched a stained-glass window. He leaned upon the sill and drank in the fresh air. Latched on to the welcome distraction of observing life on the streets below. The top of the hour must be drawing near, for groups of people meandered in streams toward the Town Hall, pooling at the base of the astronomical clock in a swirl of browns and grays and . . . one blot of yellow that looked alarmingly familiar. Was that the man from Amsterdam?

Theodore rubbed his bleary eyes with his free hand, but the man remained on the street. This was no delirium born of nightmares and fatigue. This *was* the very same man who'd been watching them outside Westertoren—as real and certain as that waistcoat was hideous and startling. Dapper. Shifty. Vigilant. The man stood out among those gathered before the Orloj. For he was the one person *not* admiring the medieval clock with upturned gaze and rapt attention.

His gaze was fixed on the crowd.

Searching, as though hunting a specific quarry.

Examining, as though jotting down mental notes.

Theodore's hand fisted around his crutch, strangling the wood. The man *had* to be a reporter. Somehow he'd connected the clockwork owl to the Stantons and their swift departure from London. Now he was tracking them in the hopes of finding the machine and beating his fellow journalists to the story every newspaper in Europe was clamoring to print first. It made sense. It was the *only* thing that made sense. Why else would this man follow them to Prague?

The clock's chimes touted a new hour, and a hush fell over the crowd. All too soon, the parade ended. The chimes faded. And the reporter looked up.

Dangerously determined eyes seemed to find Theodore in the window, casting a grim shadow of dread that darkened the bell's lone toll into an ominous death knell.

Dear Little Atlas,

The time has come to ride the rails once again! I hope the memories you've made in Prague are the fond sort. The kind that, like a shiny curio, are tucked away in the mind's attic and taken out years later on rainy days and dreary nights to be enjoyed and shared with others. And shared they must be, child. For humanity was designed to share everything— dreams and memories, joys and sorrows, gifts and burdens. The Creator never intended for us to shoulder all alone.

Miss Clara Marie Stanton did not require smelling salts in the face of crisis. She did not swoon. She did not blubber. She was a resilient and self-sufficient woman because life had molded her into one after "sharing her dreams and burdens" proved disastrous. Grand *ought* to understand that. He ought to be proud of her for possessing the fortitude to carry on alone. He ought to know her shoulders were strong enough to bear life's yoke unaided.

After all, here she was, departing Old Town by way of the Stone Bridge with her head held high, having learnt from their previous experience. This time she'd secreted the coin purse containing their monies in the pocket of her traveling skirt, secured the firmest of grips on Mum's hand, and returned nudge for nudge as she cut through the bustling crowd with a self-assured pace. Soon she would have Mum conveyed to the other side, safe and sound.

Perhaps Grand might recognize her strength then.

Mr. Arthur glanced over his shoulder and met her gaze, then Mum's, before pressing onward. This wary practice, along with the shadows beneath his eyes, did not suit. Where was his jaunty saunter? His lopsided grin and carefree air? Mr. Arthur looked back again, this time without meeting her eyes. She had an eerie sense that he was looking behind them. More troubling still, as not once today had Mr. Arthur voiced a blandishment or jest.

Come to think of it, he'd hardly uttered a word of any kind since their visit to the Chapel of the Virgin Mary yesterday. When she had returned Grand's watch to Mr. Arthur's care, he'd given no explanation for leaving it upon the floor and declining to enter the chapel. When she had shown him the gold-plated rooster that had strutted out from behind the Apostle Peter, he'd shoved the automaton in the gadget bag without a hint of interest. When she had tried to make conversation during dinner last night, he'd replied in monosyllables and kept his gaze trained upon the inn's front door.

Something had disturbed him . . . but what? Her questions regarding his upbringing had clearly pricked a nerve, but he'd seemed to rally once she redirected the course of conversation.

No, something must have happened at the chapel itself, and while it was none of her concern, Clara found herself wanting to put Mr. Arthur at ease. Not because she cared for him, of course. She simply didn't wish to resume their former manner of taut silence. Despite herself, she'd grown accustomed to his voice. And at present, she'd appreciate a distraction.

Mr. Arthur's gaze darted to her again, his countenance becoming more intense. Frenetic. Might he also benefit from a diverting conversation? "Mr. Arthur—"

Like a horsewhip, he cracked to a halt.

Clara and Mum stuttered still, barely avoiding impact with the carpetbags Mr. Arthur toted. Gasping, Clara clutched at her bodice. "My apologies. I never meant to startle you."

"You didn't." The sheer whitewash over Mr. Arthur's tanned complexion contradicted his rebuttal, but in a blink, color returned to his cheeks as though they'd never paled. "What's wrong?"

"Nothing, lad." Mum smiled as Fred batted at the faux fuchsia blooms hanging from her silken bonnet of the same hue. "We're contented as a pair of sunbathing salamanders."

"I didn't mean to alarm you, Mr. Arthur," Clara added. "Only to remark that there's no need for you to glance back at Old Town as though you're bidding it farewell forever. You can always return. Visit the Orloj again." The air seemed to thicken as the flow of pedestrians split and veered around them begrudgingly. "Do let us keep moving."

Without so much as a "right-oh," Mr. Arthur walked on for perhaps a dozen paces. At which point, he froze mid-stride, and Clara collided with his rather solid back. The force of impact knocked her bonnet askew and flattened her nose, which fortunately sprung back to its customary pertness. Though the same could not be said of her good humor.

Clara set her delicate straw bonnet to rights. "Mr. Arthur. I feel it only fair to warn you that should any harm come to my favorite bonnet on your account, I shall be inclined to resume my loathing of you."

Rigid as the Baroque statues adorning the bridge, Mr.

Arthur gazed at the glistening Vltava River. "That man was here when last we crossed. I'd wager he paints in that exact spot every day."

Clara peered around Mr. Arthur's broad shoulders. A giraffe of a man with easel and paint-splotted palette was stationed beside the statue of St. Joseph. She vaguely recalled the same painter being here during their encounter with the pickpocket. "Why, exactly, are his artistic pursuits of interest?"

"Because sitting here every day makes him privy to all the comings and goings on the bridge. Passing conversations of locals and tourists. News from here and afar. Before we move on, I should speak with him. Acquire any information he might have about Drosselmeyer."

"Whatever for? We have Grand's clues to follow, and if need be, we could always purchase a newspaper." Once they were well away from the bridge's crowded confines.

Mum rubbed her thumb along Clara's hand. "Sometimes you can learn more from people than paper, ducky. There's something to be said for meeting an individual's gaze and listening to their unique perspective."

"Right-oh, Mrs. S." A flicker of a grin brightened Mr. Arthur's face. "There's also something to be said for pausing to evaluate the information at hand. Verify its accuracy. Corroborate its totality. Charging ahead on misinformation never ends well."

Before Clara could query his experiential tone, Mr. Arthur sidled up to the artist, who exceeded him in height despite being seated. Placing their carpetbags on a dry section of the sandstone pavers, Mr. Arthur flexed his fingers. Rolled his wrists. Then, with crutch propped atop his forearm like an ornamental cane, he made a show of examining the near-finished painting on the easel. "Jolly good work, my man. You've really captured the essence of Old Town."

Clara suppressed a snort. Essence? My, my. Mr. Arthur had certainly recovered quickly enough. And truth be told, she was glad of it.

The street artist expressed his thanks in heavily accented English and proceeded to converse with Mr. Arthur for several minutes about his work. Lighting and shading. Color and composition. Until, finally, Mr. Arthur indicated the right-hand corner of the artist's scenic landscape. "What is this object just above the Powder Tower?"

The artist's brush stilled over the canvas. "That is the great owl."

An ache gripped Clara's heart even as it quickened, and her free hand sought the journal in her pocket. "Did you actually see the owl, sir?"

The artist nodded. "It flew right over my head. Drew such a crowd onto the bridge as I have never seen—and I've seen many. My easel and I were almost crushed, but it was worth the pressing to behold such a sight. I only wish my brush could convey the wonder of it."

Clara gnawed on her lip. She only wished Grand had the sense to fly under the cover of night as he'd done in London. "Could you see the pilot?"

The artist shook his head. "The owl keeps its face to the clouds. How it flies, where it goes, no one seems to know. It is like a piece of art that people gather about but cannot understand. It evokes questions as well as awe."

Mr. Arthur rubbed a hand over his flaxen beard. "We're not the first to ask you about the owl, I take it?"

"Not the first. Nor the only foreigners. Another Englishman questioned me about the owl. Just three days ago, I think it was."

Odd coincidence. That was the very same day they'd arrived in Prague.

"I must admit, I'm relieved to see that not all Englishmen have his poor taste. Polished as a new penny he might've been, but as an artist, I found the young man's choice of color lacked sophistication."

Mr. Arthur shook his head in mock gravity. "Always a shame when a bloke fails to represent the fine tastes of his queen and countrymen. Tell me, what did the distasteful chap look like? Should I happen upon the fellow, I'd like to censure him severely."

The artist chuckled and blue paint dripped from his brush, splattering shoes already speckled with color. "He was about your age and height. Brown hair and eyes. Groomed to a fault. He wore a traveling suit of chocolate brown with a subtle pattern of cream plaid and the gaudiest waistcoat ever manufactured. Whoever produced that yellow aniline dye ought to be arrested for assaulting the senses."

The fine hairs along Clara's neck raised. It was a coincidence. It had to be. Surely more than one Englishman owned a yellow waistcoat. Surely—

"Rusted cogs." Mr. Arthur exclaimed under his breath, eyes flashing with heightened alertness. "He's right on our tail."

A vein along Clara's temple flinched. "What are you going on about?"

Mr. Arthur gave no answer. Instead, he propped his crutch under one shoulder, snatched up their bags, and thanking the artist for his time, shepherded them down the bridge and out of the artist's hearing. He tucked them against the low sandstone wall, shielding them bodily from the flow of pedestrians, which his darting gaze now searched. His hands fisted, primed to defend.

Unease churned in Clara's stomach. All those backward glances . . . he'd been watching for someone. Someone pursuing them. Someone he believed was dangerous. "Did you spot another pickpocket, Mr. Arthur?"

Focus intent on the sea of passing faces, Mr. Arthur spoke in tones hushed and foreboding. "Back in Amsterdam, I saw a man watching us . . . or rather, watching the pair of you. Unfortunately, he ran off before I could determine his intentions. When I spotted him again at the Orloj yesterday, I realized he was, in fact, following us. A fact confirmed by our artistic friend's narrative of the distasteful Englishman. His description matches the man I saw, right down to the painfully yellow waistcoat. It's no coincidence this chap was seen in Prague the same day we arrived. He's tracking our movements. And he's gaining ground."

The vein pulsed faster, plucking at Clara's eye. She pinned a finger to her temple. No. She refused to panic. She refused to think—let alone voice—that man's name. That would make it real. And she refused to let this be real. "Are you truly suggesting that someone is pursuing us?"

Mum cupped a hand over Fred's wee ears. "Like a hunter?"

"Near enough. I suspect the man is a reporter from London who's using us as bloodhounds to lead him to his real prey." Mr. Arthur met her gaze, brow furrowed. "He knows, Miss Stanton. Somehow he knows you have a connection to the owl."

A shudder coursed through Clara. There was no avoiding the man's name now. For, aside from Papa, the only other person who knew of their connection to the owl was Mr. Forrester. But why would he go to the great length and expense of following them across the continent? After her last adamant refusal to become his wife, what could Mr. Forrester possibly hope to gain?

Pluck, pluck, pluck. She shut her twitching eyes only to be confronted with a vison of bold, black newsprint. *HRH Prince Albert has announced that if the owl's pilot will present himself and his invention at the palace, he shall, at that time, receive a royal commendation and patronage purse of 10,000 pounds per annum.*

Of course. With Mr. Forrester, everything always came down to wretched money.

Clara pulled her lip between her teeth. Mr. Forrester was

following her once again. Lurking and scheming to get what he most desired. How could he be expected to resist the temptation of ten thousand a year? And so easily obtained? All Mr. Forrester need do was reach Grand first, steal the machine she had taught him to fly, and present himself to Prince Albert as its inventor. Who would have cause to doubt the word of he who landed the great owl atop Buckingham Palace? Who would believe the contrary claims of an old man accused of lunacy?

Not a blessed soul.

Mr. Forrester would bring ruin upon her family at last—all because she'd been fool enough to accept his proposal, weakened by the selfish longing to have someone take care of her for once.

"What I can't puzzle out is *how* he knows you and Mrs. S. are linked to the owl."

Squaring her shoulders, Clara forced herself to open her eyes. Face reality. Mr. Forrester hadn't won yet, and she did not intend to let him. "He knows because he's seen the machine before."

Mr. Arthur's brows vaulted. "I thought the machine was a secret. Known only by the family."

"The family . . . and my former fiancé, Rupert Forrester. I have no doubt that he's the man you saw following us."

"The Forrester bloke? How can you be so certain? Suppose he mentioned the machine to someone else?"

"I don't have to suppose. I know Mr. Forrester, and he's skilled at keeping secrets. He gives away nothing unless it will give him more still. He had no incentive to mention Grand's warehouse or the owl to someone else. The information held no monetary value—until Prince Albert named a price. When news of the owl hit the papers, and when he learned of the prince's patronage purse, Mr. Forrester would've seen a way out from under an anvil of debt. He knows I'd chase Grand anywhere to keep him safe. He knows how to follow my trail, and he knows how to fly the owl back to London and claim it as his own." Clara fisted her hands at her sides. "And I know he'd have no qualms doing so if it meant lining the pockets of his garish yellow waistcoat with ten thousand a year."

Mr. Arthur's brows furrowed over eyes of green. "Am I to understand, Miss Stanton, that this . . . former fiancé . . . has followed you before?"

The pity in his voice set Clara's cheeks aflame, but she didn't lower her gaze. "Twice, that I'm aware of. The last time, he accosted me at the docks in London the night we set sail. He knew about the owl. Threatened to leverage his knowledge and have Grand institutionalized unless I married him. He was so desperate . . . so cruel." Another shudder unsettled her frame. "If he hadn't been distracted by some clumsy dock-hands . . . if I hadn't been able to get away . . . I fear what he might've done."

A grave mixture of emotion deepened the furrows along Mr. Arthur's brow, and he nodded with resolution. "Now that we know what we're up against, we can give the scoundrel the old slip and dodge. Plant false trails. Shake him off our scent. As long as the three of us stick together, we'll be just fine. Never you fear, Miss Stanton. A little cat-and-mouse chase will just add a bit of excitement to this scavenger hunt. Wouldn't you agree, Mrs.—" He gawked at something over Clara's shoulder. "What the deuce! Where's she gone in such a hurry?"

Clara whirled around just as fuchsia blooms bouncing atop a silken bonnet disappeared amidst the crush of pedestrians. A tremor unsettled her fisted hands, now empty. Heart thudding in her ears, she numbed to all sensation except the pulse of a single, chilling word.

Gone.

Gone.

Gone.

CHAPTER 19

Helpless, that's how Clara felt as she dashed across the Stone Bridge. Helpless, although she'd no time for the paralyzing emotion. For she must run. Not hasten as proper ladies were taught, but hoist skirts clear of boots and *run*, pushing aside young men who reeked of fish and dodging old women slower than slugs. Run, unsure whether Mr. Arthur followed. Run, lest the wolf pack of fears nipping at her mind pounced on her sanity.

Oh, how the beasts were gaining ground.

Clara reached the other side of the bridge and, finding no sight of Mum, raced down the thoroughfare. People gawked at her unusual haste, but none were the face she sought. Where could Mum be? What if she got lost following a stray kitten? Her ankle wobbled. What if Mr. Forrester happened upon Mum first? Her chest ached. What if Mr. Forrester held Mum captive in exchange for Grand's machine? What if he hurt her in his desperation?

Her foot landed wrong on a loose cobble, and she fell, skidding across hot stone. Pain flared in her hands, her knees. Collapsed in a dusty heap, her world went still but for the heaving of lungs that didn't know she'd stopped running.

Have to get up. Have to find Mum.

Slowly, she rose onto shaky legs and eyed her torn gloves now stained with the blood of her scratched palms. Empty, stinging palms that weren't supposed to let go. Her eyes misted. She'd grown careless in Prague . . . selfish. The allure of books and stardust had distracted from her duty. If something happened to Mum today, it would be her fault.

Her lip quivered, but she bit the weakness into submission. *Clara Marie Stanton does not blubber. By might and main, Clara Marie Stanton takes care of her own.* Shoving the ruined gloves into a skirt pocket, she wove through clusters of strangers, gaze combing the narrow street lined with various storefronts until something ahead caught her eye. Snagged her breath.

A bobbing bouquet of fuchsia.

The epitome of serene, Mum sat on the steps of a boarded-up shop. A bulging canvas sack lay at her feet, and Fred peered from her shoulder to sniff a bundle of fur in her lap.

Clara heaved a shaky sigh. She was safe. Mum was safe. Now she could breathe . . . so why was it so hard to move? Forcing one foot in front of the other, she trudged until the distance between them vanished and then sank onto the stone step just below Mum. Clara seized her gloved hand, clinging to the fuchsia-hued silk with the last of her strength.

"Good gracious, ducky. Did you take a dust bath?" Mum chuckled as three fox kits nestled in the folds of her skirt. "While the practice does wonders for pachyderms, I wouldn't suggest it for a human's toilette."

Though she couldn't chuckle at Mum's oblivious remark, neither could she be irritated by it. Clara squeezed Mum's hand three times. *God, please forgive me for letting go of her. I'll never be so thoughtless again.*

Mum squeezed back four times and then gasped. "Mercy, where are my manners? I've neglected introductions." She gestured to each fox cub in turn. "Clara Marie, I would like you to meet Phileas, Honorine, and Todd."

The foxes, whose eyes were just beginning to open, squirmed in Mum's lap, nudging one another with tiny black noses. She scooped up Honorine and placed a kiss on her fluffy brown brow. "Our meeting was not by chance but rather a case of divine intervention. You see, back on the bridge, I saw a man with a canvas sack flung over his shoulder and noticed that the bag moved with life. I knew straightaway what the man was about, so I flew to intervene. I confronted the fellow—"

"By yourself?" Clara's stomach clenched.

"Of course not, ducky. I was led forth by the God of justice. As I was saying, I confronted the fellow just as he was about to toss the whimpering sack over the bridge. He tried to excuse his dastardly intentions, explaining that a vixen had made a den of his larder and was pilfering food. Can you believe he confessed to murdering the innocent creature, imagining I'd sympathize? Well, my sympathies gave his shin a sound kick and reveled in his yowl as the sack fell into my hands. Took us a while to lose him, but we did it. Didn't we, dears?"

Reuniting Honorine with her brothers, Mum shook her head. "The poor things have no idea they're orphans now." She whispered, "Mother fox is shrouded in the sack just there, and she will, of course, require a proper burial. Fred and I have already begun work on her eulogy."

Leave it to Mum to incite irritation with funeral preparations for a fox. Clara wet her grit-coated lips, her voice reduced to a croak. "Mum . . . you can't just go running off like that—in a foreign country, no less—without a word. I might never have found you. As we continue our journey, you must hold my hand. How am I to keep you safe otherwise?"

Mum chuckled. "Oh, ducky, your hands aren't the ones that keep me. That task is far beyond your control."

The terrifying notion wreaked havoc on Clara's nerves, and she grasped Mum's fingers tighter to keep her own steady. "Please, for my sake, just promise to hold my hand? I need . . . I need to know you're close. Your care and well-being are my responsibility."

Beneath the shade of her bonnet, Mum's gaze pierced. "Listen here. Little Atlas may be your nickname, but it is not your identity. You were never meant to carry the world on your shoulders. You are not God."

Clara's jaw slackened. "Of course not. When have I ever made such a claim?"

"In word, never. But in deed, you've proclaimed yourself to be without need of a savior—human or divine—every hour of every day since you broke things off with Mr. Forrester. In assuming the role of a self-reliant Titan, you've isolated yourself from the world and worn yourself ragged. Body, mind, and soul."

"I'm n-not worn ragged. I'm doing just fine." How could Mum say such things?

"Are you, now? Then explain what has done this to my ducky?" Mum directed Clara's gaze to the nearby shop window.

All of Clara's breath escaped her lungs in a single exhale, heavy and long. The woman reflected at her in the fractured windowpane was a stranger. A corpse she could not identify. Yet, somehow, she could feel the weary slump in her shoulders. The ache in her bones. She could feel the frailty of her ashen skin that exposed a graveyard of blue veins. A tear trailed down the woman's cheek, slicking across the broken pane, before it fell upon Clara's blanched knuckles. Heaven above, when had this happened? How could she have wasted away and not known?

A warm and steady hand cupped Clara's chin, lifting her gaze to glistening blue eyes. Mum rubbed a thumb back and forth along her jaw. "You need to embrace the starry-eyed wanderlust God has placed in you. Explore the wonders of the world and let *Him* be the one to carry it. Let Him be the one to carry *us*."

But if she wasn't capable of taking care of her own family, what good was she? Clara angled on the step to face the busy street, her clenched hand unwilling to relax its hold of Mum's. "We need to find Mr. Arthur and make our way to the station before we miss the day's last train."

"All in good time, ducky. Our first priority is the dearly departed vixen. I should like to consult with Arthur regarding the order of service. I have some hymns in mind, but if the lad doesn't know all the verses, he might prefer to read from the Psalms. Twenty-three is fitting but rather overused, so I'd be inclined to suggest forty-two. Oh, and after the funeral, we'll need to secure food and a manner of conveyance for the little ones."

As was its wont, the vein along Clara's temple twitched. "You cannot mean to take the kits along."

"You cannot mean to leave them behind? They're much too young to be released now. Of course, we'll have to release the dears before they come of age to hunt and consume meat." Mum covered Fred's ears with a protective hand and whispered, "Foxes being the natural predator of the ermine and all." Her hand lowered to her lap as her voice rose, resolute. "But for the time being, the kits must remain in our care."

A sigh took the starch out of Clara's shoulders. "They will never allow them on the train. We barely manage to smuggle Fred as it is. How do you mean to explain the presence of three wiggly, whimpering fox kits?"

Mum shrugged. "We'll figure something out."

Inevitably, that phrase always resulted in Mum throwing aside social convention and leaving Clara to extricate them from the consequences. On a normal day, she could manage, but today . . . today she was just so tired. "They can't come. Plain and simple."

Mum snatched her hand away. "If we don't bring the kits along and nurse them, they'll die. I shan't abandon them. If needs must, I'll stay behind to nurture them until they can be freed in the country."

"That would take weeks." And they couldn't afford to linger in Prague that long. Not with Mr. Forrester bent on tracking them down.

Mum held her head high as if she were Joan of Arc about to be burned at the stake. "Life is worth protecting at all costs. I'm willing to sacrifice my time to preserve it."

Perfect. Clara knew that look. Now Mum would never budge.

Unless she could think of a way to sneak three fox kits aboard a passenger train.

As a headache set in, Clara massaged her twitching temple. How could it be done? She scoured her mind for a solution, a means, a way, but none came. Try as she might, she couldn't figure something out this time. She looked at the derelict shop window, where fractured glass cut across her haggard reflection. Taut lines entrenching along her brow, shadows looming beneath her eyes. With a wobbly hand, she brushed aside a fallen tendril of black, now powdered gray with dirt and dust. Perhaps shouldering everything alone was taking a toll.

Perhaps her family's keeping really was beyond her control.

"There you are, ladies!"

Mr. Arthur clank-tapped toward them, panting as he carried their luggage along with his crutch. Setting his load down, he wiped a sleeve over his perspiring brow. "You two took a decade off my life! Do you know how dashed hard it is to run while hefting this lot? I never thought to catch up. From now on, warn a chap before you go gallivanting—" His gaze settled on her, and the corners of his eyes pinched. "I say, Miss Stanton, do you need help?"

Yes, she did. And for the first time in her life, Clara couldn't pretend otherwise.

CHAPTER 20

"That lad snores like a snub-nosed pug with hay fever, but he's a fine man."

For the first time, Clara could offer no refute to Mum's declaration of Mr. Arthur's good character, too wonder-struck was she that he had taken care of everything.

Without deferment. Without angling for something in return. Without so much as one patronizing remark, Mr. Arthur had assessed the situation and set to work. He'd acquired a picnic basket with a handle, dual lid, and soft gingham lining to use for the kits' transport. He'd negotiated with a widowed innkeeper to let them bury the vixen in her garden and persuaded Mum to condense the funeral to twenty minutes. He'd also taken measures to throw Mr. Forrester off their trail, including paying for a room at the widow's inn, departing through a back door, and taking a circuitous route to the station. Finally, he'd secured tickets for the day's last train and convinced a wary conductor that Mum's basket contained a litter of puppies being transported to cherub-faced nieces it would be a shame to disappoint.

Now here they sat in a first-class carriage, clickety-clacking alongside five other passengers who'd no idea the wicker basket nestled in Mum's arms contained wild foxes.

Clara endeavored to relax against the cushioned seat and not think about the locked carriage door, the speed of the train, or railway madness. Instead, she tried to divert her thoughts from her lingering fear of locomotives by envisioning the words of Grand's latest clue and imagining how they'd sound if read by his dear voice. *More curios of yet-to-be-memory await you on the Grande Île in Strasbourg, France. On this leg of our journey, we won't—*

A snore bellowed in the confined space, inciting peeved stares at their snub-nosed pug.

Clara snipped a budding smile before it could bloom, lest she provoke greater annoyance, and proceeded to study said pug. Mr. Arthur slept on her immediate right, beard drooped upon his chest and arms limp across his weathered overcoat. Bruises from the pickpocket still marred his face, and a new series of scratches glared red on the top of his hand, compliments of a startled Todd. Rather than being angered by the injury, Mr. Arthur had apologized to the kit for the rude awakening.

Her smile blossomed then, unpruned. He really was a fine man.

Another cacophony of congestion resounded from Mr. Arthur's sinuses. Clara bit back a chuckle. Did he always snore so spectacularly, or was the poor man *that* exhausted? Feeling the heat of glares directed Mr. Arthur's way, she shot their traveling companions an austere glower punctuated with a raised brow. After what he'd done for her today, Mr. Arthur could snore as loud as his snub nose pleased.

A nip to her finger drew Clara's attention to Fred, his long furry body curled about her bandaged hands like a muff. While his mouth remained ajar to appear pelt-like, Fred's black eyes had abandoned the pretense of lifelessness to gaze up at her with an imploring look that made his wee eyes shine. *Message received, little rascal.*

After confirming the other passengers were occupied with newspapers and needlework, Clara scratched Fred's tiny chin, her finger concealed beneath his body. The movement pulled at her fresh scrapes, now bound in white linen strips that Mr. Arthur had procured. He had insisted on cleaning and dressing her bloodied palms before the funeral, and she'd been too overwrought for argument. Hours later, she could yet feel the warmth of his calloused hands as they carefully tended her and could yet feel the strange, tranquil sensation of not needing to do . . . anything.

Of being held, rather than holding on.

Of being still, rather than striving.

Of being taken care of, rather than taking care of everything and everyone.

A lump formed in Clara's throat. She'd forgotten what that felt like. Since Granny's death and Mr. Forrester's betrayal, it seemed she had forgotten many things.

Mr. Arthur snored again, and his eyelids fluttered as though he were dreaming. His lips moved with unintelligible mumbles, and without thinking, Clara inclined toward him.

A grimace darkened Mr. Arthur's features as mournful words dropped from his mouth like unbidden tears. "I'm sorry . . . so sorry."

Clara's brows pinched. Never had she heard an apology laden with such sorrow. Such pain. Mr. Arthur flinched and shifted in his seat, reciting his regret with increased volume and despondency, as though in an act of penance. She turned to Mum, who eyed Mr. Arthur with concern. "Should I wake him?"

The other passengers had taken to gawking, some with brazen curiosity and others with pallid fear.

"Stop!" Mr. Arthur's scream jolted Clara's every nerve. She whipped around to find him writhing. Head thrashing against the carriage window, he sobbed. "Stop . . . please."

The broken plea chilled the blood in Clara's veins. This was no dream.

It was a nightmare.

"Ducky, wake the lad. Wake him now!"

The nightmare refused to set him free. Mired on the battlefield of Balaklava, Theodore could feel its charred darkness invading his every pore. His every thought. Eternal seconds made awakening seem less certain. Impossible. Smoke crept along the valley, reaching for him with gnarled fingers of ash. Tormenting his subconscious was no longer enough.

This time, the terror had come to claim the whole of his mind.

Father's polished shoe emerged from the smoke and crushed a bloodied saber. "If you weren't a faulty soldier, your comrades wouldn't have perished."

Theodore's gaze fell to an oriental rug in the study of Kingsley Court.

Breath scalded the back of his neck, reeking of sulfuric scorn. "If you weren't a faulty son, your mother wouldn't have died in my arms."

Theodore remained unmoving, face buried in the rug, for he knew what came next.

Some memories one could never forget.

Cold fingers gripped Theodore's chin in a vice and forced him to his feet, leaving him no choice but to stare into green eyes that flashed with rage. The eyes of his father.

Apprehension curdled in Theodore's stomach. *Just say it and be done.*

"I'd trade your life in a second if it would restore the life of my Theodora." Father shoved his face away like a dirty rag.

Theodore couldn't prevent the onslaught of tears, but he tried to hide them. Bury them in hands now quite small. Those of a child. When he looked up, Father was so much taller, looming over him with a shadowed scowl. From behind his back, Father produced a switch.

Theodore whimpered, his voice now that of his ten-year-old self. "I'm sorry."

"Stop your blubbering, boy." Father raised his arm above his head and brought the switch down. Once. Twice. The switch sliced into Theodore's chest.

Once, twice, he begged to be pardoned for being born.

For killing the mother he'd never known. "I'm sorry . . . so sorry."

But in the terror, as in reality, he was never quite sorry enough.

Never quite good enough to bear his mother's name.

The switch struck without sign of relenting. Shredding Theodore's shirt. Slashing his chest. As the first drop of blood trickled down, the study's plush carpet vanished. The valley of death reemerged. Still the switch tore into him. Thwack. Thwack. Thwack.

With a guttural scream, Theodore fell to the ground. "Stop! Father . . . please."

Thwack. Thwack. Thwack.

The switch found his heart.

Theodore wrenched awake and grasped for something solid. Something real. Something to prove the nightmare was over. *Please, let it be over!*

A hand patted his forearm. "All is well, Mr. Arthur. It was only a bad dream." Miss Stanton offered a reassuring smile.

When had he grabbed hold of her shoulders? Theodore released her, trembling from the inside out as he recoiled into his seat and leaned into the chill of a nearby window. A salty taste on his lips explained the dampness of his face. He'd wept. Rusted cogs, he'd wept! And Miss Stanton had seen everything. She'd seen the pitiful state of his broken soul.

Voices floated into his awareness, speaking English and French. The other travelers huddled in the far corner of the railway carriage, watching him wide-eyed and talking amongst themselves in hushed tones.

"He's succumbed to railway madness, I'm certain."

"We need to get out before the screaming lunatic murders us all!"

He'd screamed? Theodore's fingers dug into his cushioned seat. *Hold it together, man. Shove the faulty pieces back in the clock casing. Lock them away so all they see is the handcrafted face of Arthur. A man without nightmares. The man you used to be.* His lips parted to allay the fears of his fellow passengers, but no words emerged. No smile formed. The pieces were too heavy, too many. Too much.

He couldn't hold it together this time.

The door rattled. "Oh, why must they lock these carriages?"

"Hail the guard to let us out."

"Fetch a constable at the next station!"

Cold sweat slicked down Theodore's brow. If a constable hauled him off for lunacy, he couldn't look out for the ladies. He couldn't protect them from Forrester. That cad had already gotten to Miss Stanton once on his watch. He'd fail them just as he'd failed his men. His mother.

Pressure swelled in his lungs, making each breath shallower than the last. Air. He needed air. He stood and tried to pry open the carriage window.

"The madman's going to toss us from the moving train!"

A woman's shriek threatened to shatter glass.

"Oh, snort some smelling salts, will you!" Miss Stanton's voice cut through the pandemonium and enforced immediate silence. "Mr. Arthur isn't going to harm anyone, but if the lot of you don't pipe down, I just might box your ears. Stars, you act as though you're in a penny dreadful. Mr. Arthur has obviously experienced a nightmare, and your histrionics are only serving to prolong his agitation. He'll recover in due course, providing the rest of us remain calm. Ergo, do us all a grand favor and bite your tongues. *Gardez votre paix.*"

Bandaged hands appeared in Theodore's peripheral, coaxing his rigid fingers to release the locked window latch. "Come back to your seat, Mr. Arthur." As he sank onto the cushioned bench, Miss Stanton rubbed a thumb along his quaking fingers. "Just breathe. Nice long breaths. That's the ticket."

Theodore inhaled tremors, exhaled shudders. *Inhale, exhale, inhale.* Gradually, his breathing aligned with Miss Stanton's soothing cadence, and the trembling ceased. Miss Stanton fell into silence, but she retained her hold of his hand. Glancing to his left, he found that Miss Stanton's eyes were closed even as her mouth moved with inaudible utterance. Was she . . . praying . . . for the likes of him?

Withdrawing from Miss Stanton's touch, Theodore edged along the bench, as far away from her underserved prayers as possible.

He felt Miss Stanton bridge the distance he'd created, whisper in his ear. "Who were you talking to . . . in your sleep? You kept apologizing to someone. Telling them how you'd tried to be worthy of your name."

Theodore clamped his eyes shut. After all these years of trying to conceal his past, he'd been betrayed by a nightmare.

"Is that why you never acknowledge your surname? Because someone thinks you unworthy of it?"

No, that was why he never acknowledged the Christian

name bestowed by his dying mother. Leaving his surname on a headstone at Kingsley Court had been at Father's behest.

Miss Stanton's gaze lingered, awaiting an answer.

Theodore's nerves tangled in knots and scraped against one another. Fraying. Threatening to snap. He couldn't fall apart in front of her again. He needed to avert and redirect. He needed to be Arthur—the carefree part of himself the queen's war and Father's scorn had all but destroyed.

He forced a grin to turn on rusted hinges. "Was my madman act convincing, Miss Stanton? The lark sure fooled the lot of them, didn't it? I spent a whole summer with a circus learning that bit, but if I'm honest, I think your 'snort salts' speech was more impressive."

As the jostling train carriage clicked and clacked over rails below, Miss Stanton withheld expression. Not a single eyebrow did she raise in reproof. Instead, she leveled him with the constancy of her piercing eyes of gray. "All the quips in the world can't distract from the broken clock on the mantel. Not forever. Eventually, the jovial residents will notice the silence, look up from their merriment, and find the clock's hands unmoving."

Theodore's grin fell. The encasement he'd fashioned might yet hide his name and the details of his former life, but it could no longer conceal who he was. Could no longer contain all the shattered pieces of his true self. Theodore the disappointment. Theodore the weakling. Theodore the failure. "Some clocks can't be repaired, Miss Stanton."

The fair skin around her eyes pinched, and her mouth twisted to one side. "When I was a young girl, I once borrowed a costly leather-bound atlas from Papa's office and took it down to the kitchen for an imagined safari. A blazing oven does wonders to simulate an African summer. Erm, in any case, the atlas was the unfortunate victim of a lion attack." A becoming smile touched her lips. "Cook Collins stepped on my calico's tail, and the atlas was one of many things to suffer the consequences of her violent reaction. The beautiful illuminated pages were torn. Rent from the book's spine. I promptly rushed the atlas to Grand's shop because, well, he could fix anything. I didn't even cry, so confident was I that he could mend what I'd ruined. When Grand admitted he'd no idea how to mend books, I burst into tears. If Grand couldn't repair the atlas, surely all hope was lost."

One of Miss Stanton's bandaged hands slipped into her skirt pocket. "Grand put me in his lap, wiped my tears, and reassured me that everything could be set to rights again. All I had to do was take the atlas to the one who'd made it. For as he said, 'Any broken thing can be made whole again. It all depends on who you give the pieces to.'"

But shouldn't a man be able to manage his own emotions privately? Mend his own brokenness discreetly? Was that not what had always been expected of him?

Theodore tried to swallow, but his mouth was too dry. His voice too raw. "I'm a clockmaker. I ought to be able to fix any timepiece put in front of me."

"You are a maker. Not the Maker." Miss Stanton gave his hand a firm squeeze. "Just as Grand would never expect a clock to fix its own windings, God would never expect us to mend our own hearts."

The broken cog in Theodore's pocket pressed against his skin, cold and unnaturally heavy. *"God would never expect us to mend our own hearts."* But would He deign to mend one so tarnished?

His gaze fell to Miss Stanton's fingers wrapped about his, soft and warm and unsullied. Pulling away from her, he buried both hands in his overcoat. Perhaps one day he might gather the courage to find out. But not today.

He cleared his throat. "Very well said, Miss Stanton. Have you given this speech often?"

"This was its debut. I was inspired by a thought-provoking lecture on the sovereignty of God and the damage caused by our feeble attempts to do what only He can."

"Indeed? Who gave the lecture?"

Mrs. S. peered around her daughter's shoulder. "A wise woman so ahead of her time that the whole of London thinks her mad."

More curios of yet-to-be-memory await you on the Grande Île in Strasbourg, France. On this leg of our journey, we won't visit a single edifice depicting the Titan Atlas. Henceforth, that name is to be put behind you. When I first called you Little Atlas, I did so because you held the globe near to your heart—not because I wished you to shoulder it. The endearment was never intended to fetter you with false responsibility, and I'm determined to free you of that burden now with a new name. From this day on, I shall call you my Little Stargazer.

Lift your face to the heavens, granddaughter mine! Recall the joyous wonder of dwelling and dreaming beneath a canopy of stars, embracing the peace found in total dependence on Him who spoke their radiance into being. That is my wish for you. That is my prayer.

Your devoted,
Grand

Dreaming beneath the roof of the Canopy of Stars Hotel was a notion Clara could fathom, but total dependence on another—even the Maker of the heavens—was a thought her mind struggled to comprehend.

Nestled in a window seat, Clara admired the view of Strasbourg from their recently acquired quarters on the second floor. Just outside, a sign swayed in the breeze from a scrolled-iron hook. The circular advertisement for the hotel was painted the dark blue of an evening sky and embedded with shards of yellow glass. Brilliant rays from the afternoon sun streamed through the glass, which harnessed the light and arranged it on the cobbles below in a shining new constellation. A diminutive canopy of stars that twinkled during the day.

Leave it to Grand to remember the obscure hotel mentioned in one of her travel guides.

Clara withdrew the leather journal and silver pen from her pocket. Paging through the journal to where Grand's notes were sheltered, she traced a finger over the words he'd penned with loving prayer. She wanted to embrace the peace Grand said she might find, but releasing her long-held illusion of being in control was not so easily done.

Nor was changing one's name. For names came with an identity. A certain way of being and living, thinking and acting. A new name, then, required that one cease responding when the old name was beckoned and turn instead toward the sound of a different call.

With one bandaged hand, she grasped the compass on her chatelaine, tracing a thumb over the fissures that skewed the glass. With the other, she held the silver fountain pen, feeling the weight of its ornate reservoir filled with ink. What would the transition from Little Atlas to Little Stargazer entail, and how would it rewrite her story?

Lift your face to the heavens, granddaughter mine!

Clara opened the window, granting entry to the gentle

breezes of spring, and took a deep breath infused with the herbaceous scent of geraniums. *I shall try, Grand. By might and main, I shall try.* Setting aside the compass, she attached the pen's lid to her chatelaine. Then she turned to the front of the journal and pressed the nib to the first blank page.

Something arced over her shoulder, clacked against the open window, and ricocheted onto her skirt. Clara startled. She capped her pen and picked up the intrusive object, a small gray stone. *Where did you come—* Something struck the back of her skull. *Ouch!* Flinching, she dropped the pebble beside a second. Mouth agape, she turned to Mum, who sat on their bed, brushing Fred's fur while the ermine groomed the wriggling fox kits.

Clara placed a hand to her assaulted crown. "I think we're under attack. Should I inform the proprietor or—say, isn't that my hairbrush?"

Mum continued brushing without lifting her gaze. "Seventy-four. No. Yes."

"He ought to know, and Fred has his own hairbrush."

"Seventy-nine. It's no concern of his. Fred misplaced his hairbrush on the train."

"Why isn't it his concern? And for the love of all, can't Fred simply make do?"

"Eighty-five. Because the romantic pebbles are addressed to you. Freddy's fur mats if he goes without his daily one hundred strokes."

A third pebble crashed into Clara's nape and incited an unseemly yelp. She dove off the window seat, scattering pebbles and writing implements across the planks, and took cover against the wall. "Pray tell, Mother, how is being pelted with rocks in any way romantic?"

"Ninety-nine, one hundred." Mum placed the brush on the pale blue coverlet and met Clara's gaze with a smirk. "Look out the window, ducky."

Snatching a pillow to shield her face, Clara rose with caution to peek outside—just as a hobgoblin on the street below readied to hurtle another projectile.

"There you are, Miss Stanton." Mr. Arthur dropped a pebble and dusted off his hands, looking up at her second-floor perch. "Heaven be thanked! My arm was getting dashed tired. Mailing through the Pebble Post might spare a penny, but it extracts payment from a man's patience and taxes his brawn. Might I inquire, fair maiden in yonder tower, what the dickens took you so long?"

A flicker of a smile sparked on his lips, dim and wavering, as if the breeze might extinguish it at any second. But it burned. For the first time since the incident on the train snuffed it cold last night, it reflected a glint of jest in his eyes.

For the first time, Clara couldn't deny that she'd missed it. She'd missed crossing swords with Mr. Arthur as that lopsided grin of his goaded her to smile back. Lowering her down-feather shield, Clara challenged his smile to a duel with the arching of an impervious brow. "I was detained by a mischievous hobgoblin throwing pebbles."

Mr. Arthur gasped with mock horror. "Were you, now?"

"Indeed. Apparently, the creature is ignorant of the invention of doors and the human practice of knocking upon them."

"Tragic, that. Hobgoblins can be quite ill-informed creatures." Hiding both hands in his overcoat, Mr. Arthur tilted his head. "I'd thought to escort you and Mrs. S. to luncheon. Shall I have to scale the tower's thorny vine to retrieve the pair of you?"

"I think such exertion can be avoided if we make use of the stairs." Suppressing a smile, Clara latched the window.

Mum's smirk broadened, revealing a dimple. "You two make quite the pair."

Heat washed over Clara's cheeks. Oh dear. There could be

no more ignoring Mum's oblique attempts at matchmaking. Not now that a puckish dimple conspired with the impish gleam in her eyes. Retrieving her journal and pen from the floor, Clara tucked the former in her pocket and reattached the latter to her chatelaine. Her mother's notions of romance must be quashed before they led to matrimonial machinations.

Clara put on her bonnet, fingers fumbling to arrange the ribbons in a satisfactory bow. "Whatever scheme you and Grand have devised to usher me down the aisle can be put out of your mind right now. Mr. Arthur and I are not a pair. We are two separate and singular persons. I've accepted him as Grand's apprentice and as our escort, that is well enough. I have no interest in romantic entanglements. Not even the suggestion of one. Consequently, I won't abide any more talk of turtle doves or pairs or romantic pebbles. Am I quite clear?"

Mum's dimple deepened. "As blush-tinted glass."

Clara gave up on her mother and the bow in succession. "After luncheon, you're buying me a new hairbrush."

Leaving Mum to settle the fox kits, Clara strode out the door and took the stairs two at a time, eager for fresh air. Nature did not disappoint. As she exited the inn, red geraniums planted in window boxes on either side of the door greeted her with their warm green aroma. She took a deep breath.

Touring the Idiosyncratic Alsace had described Strasbourg's Grande Île as a charming conglomeration of French and Germanic cultures, but now, drinking of the geranium's fragrance, charming seemed an insufficient descriptor. For here, in the island's Petite France district, she felt as though she'd been swept into a fairy tale.

The River Île flowed through the district, irrigating the land with enchantment. One of the river's five arms wrapped in front of the Canopy of Stars Hotel, holding the narrow street's medieval paving stones in a tender embrace.

Colorful half-timbered houses with façades of pastel yellow, blue, pink, and orange flanked the hotel on either side and reflected upon the water as a sparkling rainbow.

Yet despite this enchanting prospect, Clara found herself tensing. Examining every male figure that strolled along the channel. Ever on the lookout for a garish yellow waistcoat.

The clank-tap of a mechanical boot and crutch approached. "We weren't followed."

One of the knots in her shoulders loosened. "Are you certain?"

"Fairly." His mouth quirked to the side. "Before we boarded the train from Prague, I talked the conductor into allowing me a glimpse of the passenger list. Assuming Mr. Rupert Forrester used his real name, he wasn't on board. It appears we've given him the slip for now."

If only *for now* meant *for good*. "How should we proceed, then?"

"We carry on, Miss Stanton. Enjoy the merry scavenger hunt your grandfather has planned. Since Drosselmeyer's clue led us to this hotel, his next invention must be nearby."

"What of Mr. Forrester? The papers have reported sightings of the owl on the Île. It's only a matter of time before he discovers our location." A group of men strode by the hotel, and Clara stiffened. "Mr. Forrester won't stop pursuing us. Not after he's come this far."

Mr. Arthur placed a hand on her shoulder. "You leave Mr. Forrester to me."

Clara exhaled, the knot unwinding as her unease melted away. Perhaps depending on others wasn't so difficult after all.

"My apologies for the delay, chickees." Mum appeared on her left, slipping on her gloves. "The kits began to cry whenever I tried to take Fred, so he agreed to stay behind and tend the children in our absence. Now, where are we bound for luncheon?"

Mr. Arthur pointed down the street with his crutch. "I thought you might fancy that quaint establishment on the corner, Mrs. S."

Located two doors down, the tavern he indicated boasted turquoise walls cut with dark beams and speckles of what appeared to be white paint—until one noticed the stork. A wooden platform constructed on the slanted roof welcomed the large bird's nest of broken tree limbs. Beneath the structure, a sign depicting a stork with a spoon for a body confirmed the tavern owner's zealous belief that a stork roosting on one's dwelling was an omen of good luck.

Clara arched an eyebrow. "Really, Mr. Arthur. I'd rather not entrust the preparation of our food to the proprietor of the Stork and Spoon. The sort of person who clothes their business with such a threadbare pun is liable to switch the salt and sugar for the sake of a laugh."

"And what's so wrong with having a laugh, Miss Stanton?"

"Nothing—assuming it's not at my expense. I recall passing a restaurant yesterday called Tavern on the River. The place was highly recommended by the author of *Touring the Idiosyncratic Alsace*. Why do we not go there?"

Mr. Arthur feigned a yawn. "Because it's dull, that's why. The sort of person who garnishes their business with such a bland name is liable to make food just as flavorless. The Stork and Spoon has character."

"Oh, it's a character all right. A veritable jester with jangling foolscap for brains."

"Hush, kids. I've had enough of your bleating and headbutting. We shall eat at the Stork and Spoon, and that's that. Any establishment that welcomes God's creatures is worthy of our patronage." Mum took off down the street, leaving

Clara and Mr. Arthur to trail behind, silent in the wake of her reprimand.

At the Stork and Spoon, Mum selected an outdoor table with a prime view of the tavern's namesake. Plane trees of great age and height provided shade and the hushed lullaby of rustling leaves. After discussing the menu with an amiable waiter, they opted to try a regional dish known as *flammekueche* or *tarte flambée*, depending on which half of the island's heritage one favored. When the flammekueches arrived, Clara's aspersions were pleasantly proven wrong. The thin and crispy pastry topped with tangy crème fraîche, sliced onions, and salty lardons reminded her of a rustic savory tart, although Mr. Arthur argued it was more akin to something he'd enjoyed in Naples called pizza. Whatever the name, it was quite delicious!

Never one to forgo dessert, Mr. Arthur ordered *kugelhopf* to complete their meal. The molded cake placed before them resembled a crown dusted with confectioner's sugar. Clara accepted her portion without protest. Filled with raisins and slivered almonds, the popular Alsatian treat was more brioche than cake. Rich and satisfying without being too sweet.

The chimes of Grand's pocket watch announced the top of the hour, and somewhere nearby, a metallic melody responded to its call.

Would they truly find Grand's clue so soon? The pocket watch struck one o'clock but continued to chime, stirred by the tinkling song of an invention that remained unseen. They waited. They watched. No automaton bird swooped from the trees. No mechanical fish leapt from the placid River Île. Aside from the duet of devices, all was normal.

Which was most unusual.

Clara pushed back her wooden chair. "Where is it coming from?"

Together, they abandoned their table. Wandered about the

premises, looking high and low. Thankfully, the other Stork and Spoon patrons dined inside, and the few people ambling down the street paid no mind to their odd behavior. For the moment, there was a chance of locating Grand's invention without drawing unwanted attention.

"I think the sound is coming from the stork nest, ducky. Give me a moment to investigate."

Investigate *how*, exactly? Clara turned to witness Mum's rapid ascent from chair to table to tree. Forget unwanted attention. They'd do well now not to make the papers. She hastened to the base of the trunk and planted a hand on either hip. "Mother, come down before you break your neck!" *Or make yourself a front-page headline.*

Hiking her skirts well above her ankles, Mum scaled the plane tree and perched on a thick branch adjacent to the Stork and Spoon's roosting platform. She grasped another limb and peered into the occupied nest. "Be not alarmed, Mother Stork. I shan't plunder your majestic plumage. Oh, oh! How wonderful!"

Mum beamed Clara a flushed smile. "Mother Stork is with child."

Somehow Clara managed not to roll her eyes. "Congratulations, you've discovered an egg in a nest. Now, for heaven's sakes, come down."

"There are four eggs, actually." Mum swung her boots in midair like a child on a swing. "You may be interested to know that one of the eggs is covered in fragments of white porcelain."

Clara's fists slid right off her hips. "Grand wouldn't."

Mr. Arthur laughed. "Wouldn't he, though? Drosselmeyer's a logical sort of fellow. Where else would he lay an egg but in a nest?"

"It's hatching!" Mum squealed as she peered over the nest. "The porcelain is cracking, and a brass bill is poking through. Ah me, the miracle of life is a wonder."

The stork inspected Mum with beady black eyes and clapped its pointed bill together, questioning her presence with a loud clack, clack, clack.

Clara gulped. If the stork took offense, this precarious situation could take a tumble. She turned to Mr. Arthur. "How are we to retrieve the egg without the stork attacking us?"

Mr. Arthur shifted the crutch under his arm. "We won't be doing the retrieving. Your mother will. Mrs. S. knows the most about animals, and I think she's more than up to the task. In any case, she's already up the tree."

"But what if the stork perceives Mum as a threat? That bill looks dreadfully sharp."

"Don't fret, ducky. I'm well versed on bird calls and avian customs. Perhaps if I can imitate Mother Stork's manner of communication, she'll perceive that I am friend rather than a predator." Snapping two branches off the tree, Mum proceeded to whack them together in mimicry of the stork's bill-clattering.

The stork rose on legs orange and gangly.

"See, Mother Stork has granted me permission to enter her home." Mum laid the branches upon the platform and clambered to stand on the tree limb.

Clara gritted her teeth, resisting the urge to dash to Mum's aid and holding fast to the promise she'd made Grand. *Lord, she's in your hands. Please don't let her fall.*

With a few tottering steps, Mum traveled from the tree limb to the nest platform. Once there, she retrieved the egg, holding it aloft as proof of success. "Warmest gratitude for your hospitality, Mother Stork."

The stork mounted to the air with a mighty flap and kicked Mum off the platform.

Clara gasped, knocked flat on the cobbles by the human anvil that was her mother. Aches permeated her every joint and muscle. My, but she was going to feel this rescue come the morrow. And the morrow after that.

"A more foolish stunt I never did see!" White petticoats parted to make way for Mum's outrage. Bonnet missing and coif in shambles, Mum glowered from where she sat on Clara's person. "What do you mean, diving in the way like that?"

In the way? Is that what Mum called swooping in to break her fall? Foolish though it might've been, she had expected a measure of gratitude for saving her mother's neck. "Who else was to catch you, I wonder?"

"Oh, I don't know, ducky. How about the big, strong man you shoved out of the way?" Mum flung her arm to the right.

What? Clara rolled her head to the side and locked eyes with Mr. Arthur. Oh . . . that man. Heat saturated her cheeks. Had she truly shoved him? There seemed no other explanation for his being sprawled on the stone pavers like a tin soldier cast aside by an ungrateful child.

Mr. Arthur retrieved his crutch, and a grimace flitted across his features before hiding behind a bearded frown directed at her. "I would've caught her, you know." With a shake of his head, he trudged toward the hotel.

Clara winced. She'd hurt him. After all he had done for them, how could she treat him so poorly?

Mum alighted from Clara and extended her hand.

Too embarrassed to accept it, Clara stood unaided and dusted off her dress. She situated her bonnet as people inside the Stork and Spoon stared at them through the window, laughing at her expense. Foolish stunt, indeed. What had she been thinking?

A pair of gloves secured Clara's face, forcing her to meet Mum's eyes. "Are you injured?"

"No. Merely winded and sore."

"Good." Mum placed a kiss on Clara's brow and promptly pointed a stern finger at her nose. "Never push aside a helping hand. Though pride says you're stronger alone and fear says you're safer alone, take it. Grasp it. The wise woman knows that strength and security are found in numbers."

Clara heaved a sigh. "It was a stupid reflex. I didn't even realize I'd shoved Mr. Arthur until after we hit the ground. All I could think . . . all I could see was that you were falling, and I couldn't let that happen. I had to *do* something." Her gaze fell to her hands, swathed in bandages and woefully weak. "I wanted so much to make Grand proud . . . strove so hard to depend on God as he bade."

"Oh, love. Dependence isn't about striving, it's about relying. It's assuming a posture of hopeful humility at the feet of a sovereign Lord. Conferring with Him before you move. Believing that He is moving on your behalf when you're instructed to be still."

"You make it sound so easy."

A smile touched Mum's mouth. "That's because I'm an eloquent speaker. In reality, dependence is one of the hardest disciplines, but it can be learned. With time and diligent practice, you can learn to wait upon the Lord with confident expectation and discern His heavenly promptings."

Before Clara could respond, something tapped her boot. An automaton stork chick flapped and flailed on the ground, half a porcelain shell stuck upon its head. Noting a trail of porcelain shards a few paces away, she picked up the distressed device. A leather tube was strapped to its back of molded bronze down. She removed the eggshell from the chick's head, and the freed chick craned its neck toward the sky, brass beak opening and closing with pitiful metallic squeaks as though it expected to be fed. The automaton would have no peace until reunited with Grand's watch.

Clara cast a sideways glance at the Canopy of Stars, where Mr. Arthur leaned against the hotel's half-timber wall, watching over the street vigilantly. What was she to say to him? "What if he won't forgive me?"

"He will." Mum rotated her to face Mr. Arthur and whispered against her ear. "Just apologize and give the boy a smile. His cheeks flush red as a robin's breast when you smile."

"Mother—"

A gentle push sent Clara staggering toward the hotel.

The tinkling melody of Grand's pocket watch coaxed Clara closer despite her trepidation. Mr. Arthur's face remained unmoving at her approach. She rested against the wall next to him, gaze fixated on the stork chick in her palm. If she met his eyes, she might never manage to string two words together.

Mr. Arthur touched the pocket watch to the chick's beak, alleviating the automaton's hunger and silencing both devices. "Has Mrs. S. sent you to reconcile?"

She kicked a stray pebble, sending it skittering into the river with a plop. "Yes."

"Will this imposed apology be sincere?"

"Quite."

"Right-oh, then." Mr. Arthur positioned himself in front of her and waved a hand. "You may proceed, Miss Stanton."

Clara clutched the sleeping automaton chick to her chest. Why did apologies have to be so hard? Wetting her lips, she pushed the words out before she lost all gumption. "I am truly sorry, Mr. Arthur. I never meant to shove you like that. It's just . . . you see . . . I have more experience with pickpockets than gallant knights, so I tend to see pickpockets under every bush and react with this reflexive protectiveness of my family that isn't always necessary or expedient or . . . coordinated. That's not an excuse, mind. Just a fact. A reason, rather. When one has been taken advantage of by a pickpocket, one doesn't trust naturally. Nor does one expect gallant knights to render aid. Or even believe in them, really. Thus, when one's mother is kicked off a roof by an angry stork, one assumes she won't be rescued unless one is the one to perform said rescue . . . oneself."

Perspiration slicked down her neck. *Bring this ramble to a point, Clara.* "In conclusion, I reacted in haste, and I'm sorry. I shall try not to push aside gallant knights in the future." And heaven help her, she would try not to push away God's saving hand either.

When Mr. Arthur gave no response, she lifted her gaze. He just stared at her with intense eyes of green. No trace of emotion, for good or ill, evident on his features. Had she said too much? Too little? Perhaps . . . perhaps she ought to test Mum's theory.

Clara smiled hesitantly. "Am I forgiven?"

A reddish tint flushed beneath Mr. Arthur's blond beard, and his countenance relaxed. "Since about five minutes ago,

Miss Stanton." Tucking his hands into his overcoat, he short-ened the distance between them, eyes agleam. "So . . . you think me gallant, aye?"

Stars, had she said that? She put on an air of nonchalance, hoping to conceal the sentiment her words betrayed. "Why, sir? Don't you?"

Like a bucket of water over a fire, the question doused the gleam in Mr. Arthur's eyes. He favored his crutch. "You know, this isn't the first time I've been attacked by the fairer sex."

In the spirit of reconciliation, she ignored his abrupt change of subject. "By whom were you accosted?"

"A rather striking young woman in London who blud-geoned my nose and dragged me into an alley."

Was his use of *striking* a play on words or a compliment?

"You look very like her, I think. Although she didn't pos-sess your bloom."

Warmth washed over Clara's cheeks. If her complexion lacked color before, it certainly didn't now. Time for her to change the subject before she said something stupid. She held out the automaton. "Would you care to read Grand's stork?"

Like that.

Mr. Arthur accepted the device with a grin. "It would be an honor."

Clara clasped her hands as her blush turned scalding. Idiot. She was a blathering, blushing idiot. Why was she a blather-ing, blushing idiot? The hobgoblin was merely teasing so he might watch her squirm. That was all.

Mr. Arthur retrieved a tiny note from within the satchel on the chick's back. "'Dear Little Stargazer, no amount of study can make us all-knowing. There will always be some fact we've yet to learn. Some location we've never found on a map or explored in a book. Today I want to take you to such a place. A square on the Grand Île where the inventor who made this note possible is honored. Don't fret about not knowing the way, my girl. Sometimes getting lost is half the fun. Your devoted, Grand.'"

Why did people tell other people not to fret? Didn't they realize such a command only made one fret all the more? She took the note from Mr. Arthur, pulling her lip between her teeth. Odd. Instead of Grand's familiar penmanship, the words on this note had been printed. *A square on the Grande Île where the inventor who made this note possible is honored.* What might that indicate? To her recollection, none of her travel guides had named such a square.

"I wonder, Miss Stanton. What if Drosselmeyer's clue is a reference to Gutenberg, the inventor of the printing press? In my school days, I read a book about the lives of famous inventors, and I believe it mentioned something about Gutenberg living in Strasbourg for a time."

"That would explain why Grand chose to have this note printed, but there was no mention of Gutenberg or a square honoring him in *Touring the Idiosyncratic Alsace.* It might be anywhere on the Grand Île! I wouldn't even know where to begin looking."

"I do believe that was the point. To venture into the unknown like explorers of yore. Unencumbered by preconceived notions. Unsure where we're bound or how to get there or what we'll find when we arrive at last." Mr. Arthur offered the use of his arm and a lopsided grin. "Care to get lost with me, Miss Stanton?"

Clara stared at his outstretched arm, every fiber of her being immediately hesitant. Every thought in her mind immediately wary of letting down her guard. She pursed her lips. *Lord, please help me to heed your peace more than my fear.* She took a breath and accepted Mr. Arthur's arm.

Triumphant ovation disrupted the relative quiet and drew all eyes to the Stork and Spoon, where Mum applauded, a beaming audience of one, jumping on the cobbles.

Engulfed in mortification, Clara used her bonnet to obscure strangers gawking on the street. "Do lead on, Mr. Arthur. I should very much like to get lost now."

"Congratulations, Mr. Arthur, we're lost." Clara crossed her arms, having withdrawn from Mr. Arthur's approximately two hours and thirty-six minutes ago. "You do realize my earlier remark was made in jest? I'd hate to think my refined sarcasm has dulled."

"If your sarcasm ever dulls, it shan't be from lack of use." Mr. Arthur walked beside her on yet another cobbled street she could not name. Or rather she walked and he sauntered. Buoyant and leisurely. One hand lounging in his overcoat while the other used his crutch as though it were a cane. "Come now, Miss Stanton. Relax and enjoy the beautiful scenery."

Being told to relax was even worse than being told not to fret, for it had an immediate effect upon the body. Muscles tensed. Nerves twitched. The jaw clenched so tight as to recreate the distinctive squeak of a rusted hinge upon movement. In short, it was most unpleasant. "I have enjoyed the beautiful scenery." *For two hours and thirty-six minutes.* "Now I'm quite ready to reach our destination."

Glancing over her shoulder, Clara discovered that Mum had stopped to make the acquaintance of yet another stray dog. Hopefully, fleas weren't taking part in the exchange of pleasantries. She tugged on the sleeve of Mr. Arthur's coat and rolled her eyes in Mum's direction. Mr. Arthur's mouth quirked in amusement, and he leaned against the half-timbered exterior of a haberdashery. Proceeding to wait, with an ever-patient countenance, for Mum to finish conversing with her new canine friend.

Clara tilted her head in observation. "Your propensity for perpetual relaxation can be quite irritating, Mr. Arthur."

"Ah, that's only because you've never been schooled in the science of relaxation, Miss Stanton. Here. Allow me to give you a rudimentary lesson. It is not so complex. First, one must unwind." Mr. Arthur unwound her arms from their tightly cinched knot, placing them at her sides. "Second, one must loosen up." Grasping her hands, he flapped her arms like a pair of ribbons fluttering in the wind.

A balding fellow in the haberdashery raised a critical brow.

Clara averted her gaze from the window, cheeks flaming as Mr. Arthur continued to flail her arms. "This is stupid."

"Exactly." He waggled fair brows. "The third step in relaxation is to accept one's own stupidity. This eliminates the stress of caring what people think and the frustration of never meeting their expectations." He stopped flapping her arms, which now felt quite wobbly, but maintained his hold of her hands. "The fourth and final step is to breathe."

"I am breathing."

"Nay, you only *think* you're breathing. In actuality, you're only using a fraction of your lung capacity. What you need to do is inhale until your chest feels fit to burst and then exhale every last ounce of oxygen. Really expand those nostrils. Like this."

When Mr. Arthur's nostrils flared like a horse's, it took all of Clara's restraint not to laugh.

"Right-oh, Miss Stanton. Your turn."

This was a foolish exercise. Impractical, nonsensical, and . . . very much like playing pretend. A smile tugged at the corner of her mouth. Inhaling until she could hold no more, she locked eyes with the balding fellow and exhaled, flaring her nose like a thoroughbred crossing the finish line at Ascot.

Mr. Balding's jaw fell upon his necktie, and Clara laughed without inhibition.

"See, is that not better, Miss Stanton?"

Much. A fact Clara found quite alarming, especially in conjunction with the sudden awareness of Mr. Arthur's near-ness and the way his calloused fingers grazed the top of her bare wrists. She withdrew her bandaged hands and cleared her throat. "What would truly make me feel better is to ac-quire a map of the Grande Île." Maps she could control and understand. Unlike the odd fluttery sensation unsettling her stomach.

"I've always found the inhabitants of a given place to be more reliable than a scrap of paper. They know all the local landmarks and shortcuts and are often eager to help a bloke out." Mr. Arthur surveyed the street. "Here. Let me show you. Come along, Mrs. S. Dawdling is for snails and slugs, as you say."

Mr. Arthur led them to a shop abloom with flowers, which dear gardening Granny would've adored. Baskets of daisies hung from the eaves and boxes of petunias sat in windows, their petals of white and purple contrasting beautifully against the celadon walls cut with timber.

A workbench had been rolled outside, and there stood a woman of middling years. With a stiffened scowl and skin gray as her frock, she appeared a veritable coffin surrounded by bouquets of condolence. Toiling as though flowers were her bane, she clipped away soil-laden roots and grouped the posies into bunches, which she bound with twine and placed in a nearby cart. The only greeting extended them was the ominous snipping of her shears.

Clara gulped. This woman didn't look eager to help a bloke out. She looked eager to put a bloke in the ground.

Mr. Arthur sauntered up to the workbench with unwar-ranted optimism, and after taking note of the shop sign in French, he addressed the dour woman in that language. "*Bon-jour, madame.* These beautiful ladies and I are in dire need of directions, if you would be so kind as to lend us your exper-tise. Where, pray tell, is Gutenberg Square?"

Slivers of stems took to the air, fleeing the woman's shears as she responded in clipped French. "I don't know. Where is it?"

Mum huffed. "Feathers and figs, if we knew where it was, we wouldn't be asking you, now would we?"

"Industrious workers rarely stray from the grindstone, Mrs. S. I'm sure this diligent lady doesn't wish to fritter her time away with sightseeing. One square's much the same as the next, you know." Propping an elbow on the workbench, Mr. Arthur plied the woman with a lopsided grin. "All the same, I'd wager you overhear the wagging tongues of many an idle sightseer. Perhaps even one that's been to Gutenberg Square. An intelligent woman such as yourself—"

The woman's shears snipped a breath from Mr. Arthur's nose. "Silence your silver tongue, or I'll silence it for you. I don't have time to waste on tourists with nothing to spend but flattery. I have a store to run and a landlord breathing down my neck for twenty francs I haven't got." The woman resumed her task. "I must be seeing to my own needs. Lord knows no one else will." The metallic snip-snip-snipping failed to conceal a slight waver in her brusque voice. "Now be gone. All of you."

Clara knew that waver all too well. Some man had left this woman alone and aggrieved, and she'd obviously rather be hanged than help one. She tugged on Mr. Arthur's sleeve but not quickly enough to still his tongue.

"Right-oh, madame. I apologize for troubling you. As recompense for your precious time, I'd like to purchase three of the purple irises in your shop window."

Dark glower unrelenting, the woman retreated into the shop. When she returned, she held the irises back and shoved an empty palm forward for payment.

Mr. Arthur withdrew a golden franc from his pocket and folded the woman's fingers around the coin as though to assure her it wouldn't be taken away.

Clara's eyebrows vaulted. The twenty-franc piece far exceeded the value of three irises. Was he . . . could he seriously be trying to pay the woman's rent? Out of his own pocket?

The woman's eyes narrowed. "That's not—"

"Correct change? I know." Mr. Arthur patted his overcoat. "But I'm afraid it's my last franc. Do me a favor and keep it, will you? I'm rather tired of lugging old Napoleon III's face around."

The woman's mouth fell agape.

Taking the irises, Mr. Arthur bestowed one on Mum and one on Clara, and the third he presented back to the grim florist. "For you, madame."

She accepted it without a word, and they took their leave.

Clara twirled the purple iris in her fingers. "Know all the landmarks, he said. Eager to help, he said." She chuckled, shaking her head. "Mr. Arthur, how did you manage to find the surliest woman in Strasbourg?"

Mr. Arthur shrugged as they followed a curve in the cobbled path. "Perhaps I'm not the one who found her. Perhaps . . . we were never lost."

The narrow street opened into a square, and there in its center stood a statue.

It was Gutenberg, or rather a bronze likeness elevated on a towering granite base. Relief panels on the four sides of the base depicted the invention of the printing press, while above, Gutenberg held the fruit of his labor. A piece of paper on which was printed, *Et la lumiere fut.*

And there was light.

Beside the monument, a steam-driven carousel awash with giggling children twirled to the joyous tune of a calliope. Clara shook her head. All this time, Gutenberg Square had been just around the bend in the road. A map would've made that clear from the start, but it also might have caused her to select a faster route. One that bypassed a certain flower shop.

Perhaps Mr. Arthur was right. Perhaps they'd never been lost. Perhaps they'd been nudged along a path of God's own choosing so a woman could cease fretting about her rent. Cease feeling forgotten because no one ever thought to give flowers to a florist.

The carousel slowed, and Clara's gaze drifted to her iris. How many years had the woman lived unaware of the beauty just around the bend? Too embittered to hear the music. Too consumed with striving to meet her needs alone. An ache tugged at her chest. She didn't want that to be her story.

She wanted to join the music.

Clara tucked the iris into her bonnet, hoisted her skirts, and ran toward the waiting carousel's promise of merriment. "Last one on the carousel has to carry the others back to the hotel!"

A blur of fuchsia whooshed by Clara and assumed the lead. Mum leapt upon the carousel, climbed to the top of its second deck, and mounted a wooden stallion with a mane of white. Leaning over the golden railing, Mum beamed a smile. "I win."

Clara ascended the lower deck and was immediately drawn to a piebald horse, harnessed to a small cart, that resembled a favorite childhood toy Grand had made her one Christmas. She mounted the horse and looked over her shoulder. "Aha, you're last, Mr. Arthur. You shall have to carry Mum and I back to the hotel."

Panting, Mr. Arthur hefted himself onto the carousel and collapsed in the cart. "I'm not sure I've the strength, Miss Stanton."

"Do you dare insinuate that we are heavy?"

"And risk you shoving me to the ground again? Never!" He tossed her a wink and then clutched the knee above his mechanical prosthetic.

Clara's brows drew taut. Perhaps a race had been an ill-conceived notion. Lugging a metal boot around must be strenuous enough without her instigating a mad dash. Was there any way Mr. Arthur's pain might be eased? Before she could voice this inquiry, the carousel lurched.

Calliope music floated through the air, and the ride began its first rotation. Parents standing on the cobbles waved to children who squealed with delight. As the carousel picked up speed, the breeze invited the ribbons of Clara's bonnet to dance. Her heart swelled, and she lifted her face toward the azure sky. When they found Grand, she must thank him for this day. Ask him how many times he'd ridden the carousel round and round.

As they continued to twirl, the familiar chiming of Grand's pocket watch lilted over Clara's shoulder, and the wooden horse beneath her whinnied. She blinked. Her gaze fell to the piebald. Was it her imagination or did the patches of black and white look less like painted wood and more like . . . metal?

As if hearing her thoughts, the horse nickered and leapt off the carousel.

When Clara found her grandfather, she was going to box the old man's ears.

The automaton horse galloped down the street at a breakneck pace. Each clanking hoofbeat rattled her bones and threatened to bumpity-bump her out of the saddle. She leaned forward and grasped a mane of yarn. *Don't fret, my foot!* Grand might've given a more helpful instruction, such as "ride astride if you value your life." Even blithe Mum would've given her that much warning. She gasped a mouthful of mane.

Mum!

Where was Mum?

Spitting yarn like a frazzled feline, Clara looked over her shoulder. Mr. Arthur remained in the cart, gripping the sides as it bounced over countless cobbles. Behind him, parents gawked, children cheered, and on the carousel's second tier, Mum waved a handkerchief in farewell, shrinking from view until she was naught but a miniature figure on a windup toy.

A wave of dizziness upset Clara's equilibrium. She latched on to the horse's cold neck and willed her head to stop spinning. She had to turn this machine around. She couldn't let Mum slip out of reach.

Straightening into a semblance of proper form, Clara pulled the reins. The horse didn't react, let alone slow down. She pulled the reins again. Still no reaction. She was completely out of control. Half-timber buildings whooshed in her peripheral. People on the street exclaimed in German and French, but she couldn't grasp what they said any more than she could control the story they were sure to tell their families. Their neighbors.

Their newspaper.

She leaned into the piebald's soft mane, clutching the useless reins to her chest. Resigning herself to travel the unknown course charted by the flights of Grand's fancy.

Eventually, the horse slowed from a gallop to a canter. A canter to a trot. A trot to a blessed stop. Dismounting before the piebald could change its mind, Clara clung to the withers for balance and took stock of their surroundings. The automaton steed had conveyed them to another historic landmark, the grandiose Palais Rohan. The horse had positioned their cart to provide an optimum view of the palace's riverside façade, shaded beneath the boughs of a majestic tree.

Mr. Arthur bounded to her side, blond hair tousled and curling at the ends. "That was amazing!"

More like terrifying. "How did you manage to place Grand's watch on the horse and deactivate the automaton without taking a horrible spill?"

"That's just the thing—I didn't! The automaton stopped of its own volition." Scratching his head, Mr. Arthur surveyed the machine with wide eyes. "I don't know how he did it, but somehow he did. Somehow, Drosselmeyer designed the horse with a mechanical instinct that draws it to this location and compels it to stop here without requiring contact with the watch's unique mechanism. It's a wonder."

Indeed, a conspicuous wonder. She glanced at the street, where a smattering of people traveled in opposite directions. "We need to hide the machine somehow." And get back to Mum posthaste.

"If we haven't attracted a crowd by now, I think we're safe enough." Mr. Arthur leaned against the automaton horse, which didn't budge under his weight. "Besides, no amount of brute strength is going to move this machine. 'Tis far too heavy and far too large."

"Then what are we to do? People are bound to notice an automaton standing in a public square."

"Not necessarily. People rarely pay attention to things outside their direct line of sight." Mr. Arthur helped her into the cart and climbed in alongside. "If we act as though this is a real horse and cart, people will see a real horse and cart. We're just a couple of tourists out for a drive, so enjoy the view, Miss Stanton. Trust that Drosselmeyer has planned this day with your best in mind. I've a feeling when next the pocket watch chimes, our faithful steed will return to his stall and reunite us with a certain stork expert."

Clara worried her hands. She certainly hoped he was right. For there seemed nothing else to be done. Shifting in the cart, stiff and uneasy, she surveyed the Baroque edifice before them. Designed symmetrically around an *avant-corps* of four Corinthian columns, the palace's rear wall was comprised of windows upon windows, overlooking the glistening River Île. A triangular pediment adorned the sandstone façade with the House of Rohan's coat of arms, but its grandeur was overshadowed by the Gothic spire of Strasbourg's famed cathedral, which lorded over it from the sky. It was as though the palace architect wished to remind passersby that all were subject to the sovereignty of God.

She exhaled a pent-up breath. *Lord, I believe you are both sovereign and good. Please watch over Mum in my stead.*

Two members of the Garde Impériale walked the length of the palace, heads erect, eyes vigilant, and strides purposeful as they monitored the perimeter, defending the property of the French state from those who would wish to do it harm.

"If only people cared for one another so well." Clara flattened her lips, regretting the utterance of her private musing.

Mr. Arthur angled toward her in the cart, placing an arm on the low-backed seat. "Such lament. Whatever does it mean?"

Her gaze drifted to the cobbles paving the street, dust strewn and worn down from years of constant use. "Merely that not all people are treated as palaces, admired by travelers and protected by armed guard. Some of us are treated as a cobbled road, trod upon and soon forgotten. That's just the way of things."

A gentle touch on Clara's chin drew her face to Mr. Arthur. Concern furrowed his brow and tenderness gleamed in his eyes of jade. "Oh, Miss Stanton. Whatever did that cad Forrester do to you?"

Withdrawing from Mr. Arthur's touch, Clara settled her gaze on her bandaged hands. What harm could there be in telling him now? Her well-meaning family had probably blabbed much of the sorry tale already, and with Mr. Forrester now pursuing them across Europe, Mr. Arthur would do well to know the sort of man they were dealing with.

"If I am to tell you what transpired with Mr. Forrester, you must first understand that his coldness of heart was not always so plain. I was raised to expect kindness and sincerity from everyone. To believe that when a boy smiles at you, he is in earnest. Thus, when we became acquainted with Mr. Forrester through our fathers' textile trades . . . well . . . suffice to say he was then fifteen, and I, a girl of twelve, was blinded by naïveté and infatuation."

Heat singed her cheeks, but a merciful spring breeze prompted her to continue. "When our families socialized, Mr. Forrester would seek me out in the library, and we'd play pretend with my maps and travel guides. Years later, when everything fell apart, I realized our adventures were but a joke to him. *I* was but a joke to him. I was just too starry-eyed to perceive the brittle edge of mockery in his smile. In any case, I believed us to be friends. For he was a constant companion, my Buccaneer Bill. That is . . . until his father died.

"When Mr. Forrester inherited Forrester Freight, I finally began to perceive signs of his true nature. Only then I called them grief. The darkness in his gaze and severity of his tone. The thinly veiled insults directed at me and my family." A shudder disturbed Clara's lips, and she could only hope her bonnet concealed it from Mr. Arthur.

"Then, one day, Mr. Forrester was seemingly himself again. Smiling, attentive, and complimentary. When he proposed to me a fortnight later, I was taken aback. But Granny was gone by then, and I was tired of trying to see to the family's needs alone. When Mr. Forrester promised to take care of us . . . to take care of *me* . . . why, it was enough to win me over. To make me hope the companionship we'd shared might be revived and inspire deeper affections. Thankfully, I discovered the truth of things before we married."

"And what was the truth, Miss Stanton?"

"That our engagement was an entrapment. A cruel means to an end." Clara clasped the compass on her chatelaine, squeezing it tightly. "Everything came out the night of our engagement party. Papa wished to make a toast, but Mr. Forrester had disappeared. I sought him in the library, thinking he'd retreated there, as the revelry had become quite boisterous."

"I'd wager Mrs. S. had something to do with the rumpus."

A weak smile tilted her mouth. "She was singing a romantic

Irish ballad while Papa accompanied her on violin and our canine quartet improvised harmonies."

Mr. Arthur's laugh was like the first ray of sunlight after a storm. "I should like to take in an encore of that performance."

Clara's smile strengthened. That she did not doubt. For unlike Mr. Forrester, Mr. Arthur treated her family with respect and kindness and . . . *love.* Genuine and unconditional.

"Forgive my interruption, Miss Stanton. Do go on."

She fortified herself with a deep breath. "At the library door, I overheard a heated conversation between Mr. Forrester and another man. From their argument, I gathered that Mr. Forrester had inherited gambling debts from his father. Instead of coming into a thriving business, his back was laid bare to the leeching creditor in the library who wouldn't be shaken until he was bled dry. Only there was nothing left to bleed."

She sighed deeply. If Mr. Forrester had only been honest, Papa would've readily helped the son of his old friendly rival. "The creditor refused to leave without collecting the vast sum he was owed, so to pry the leech from his back, Mr. Forrester offered my inheritance as collateral."

A shiver crept along her spine. She could still hear Mr. Forrester's voice, calculated and callous. *"Once I have legal control of her stocks in Stanton Shipping, you'll have your money with interest. Why else do you think I'm fettering myself to this idiotic family?"*

The tears could not be prevented from sliding down her cheeks. "Instead of protecting me from his precarious circumstances, Mr. Forrester chose to ensnare me in them unawares. I, on the other hand, determined to shield my family from his fraudulence. Once the creditor left, I broke off the engagement. Mr. Forrester tried to persuade me that I'd misunderstood. To keep me from walking away, he grabbed hold of this . . ." She traced a finger over the compass's dented brass.

"So you see, Mr. Arthur, if I'd known that I'm just a cobbled road, I would've expected to be treated as such and seen through Mr. Forrester's alleged affections. Perhaps then I might've spared my family the havoc he has wrought. The gossip, derision, and social cuts. The constant threat of Mr. Forrester's spies deceiving their way into our home to steal the letter informing Grand of his son's death in an asylum. Of Mr. Forrester using that letter as leverage to blackmail me into becoming his wife to keep Grand out of Bedlam. The heartache of having our greatest pain exposed and twisted into cruel rumors of hereditary insanity. As it is . . . I can only endeavor to shield them from the perilous chaos I unleashed."

Having reached her story's conclusion, Clara exhaled a long breath and settled into silence. She expected Mr. Arthur to make some rejoinder, but he said not a word. The man merely stared at her with illegible intensity, brows stitched together so tightly it looked as though his forehead might bust a seam. Since when was the hobgoblin speechless?

"I believe this is the part of the conversation where you're meant to say something reassuring. You know, offer a poignant tonic that puts my tattered past into perspective and alters the course of my life."

Mr. Arthur pursed his lips, then took her hand in his two. "That was a load of rubbish."

Squinting, she waited for him to finish his sentence. Surely that was not all? "If that was my poignant tonic, sir, I should like a refund and to file a complaint with management. Here I've exposed the most embarrassing, painful, and intimate details of my life, and you respond with 'rubbish.' Is that what my feelings are to you? *Rubbish?*"

"Rusted cogs, I never meant that!" Mr. Arthur blustered. "The last bit you said was rubbish, not the first bit."

"And exactly which bit of the 'last bit' was the 'rubbish' bit?"

"The bit concluding you were to blame for that cad's actions. That was the rubbish. What Forrester did—what Forrester has done—is not your fault."

She swallowed, hard. "But if I had been more astute . . . if I had been stronger—"

"For such a selfless person, you say 'I' a great deal." Mr. Arthur cupped a hand to her cheek. "Listen well, Miss Stanton. Forrester was the one who blundered. Not you. Forrester was the one who failed. Not you. Forrester was the rat who chose to scamper through the gutter of deceit and back alleys of treachery rather than ask for help. Forrester was the clod who threw away a chance at a family without guile and a woman beyond compare. Just because one malevolent man trods on you, don't for a second think you deserved it. Heaven knows you're precious and worth protecting even when men don't, and heaven will defend you even when men fail."

Warmth washed over Clara from bonnet to boots. If she wasn't on her guard, she could easily fall in love with this man.

Pocket watch chimes stilled her dangerous train of thought, and a swat from a yarn tail severed her connection with Mr. Arthur. As the music flitted through the air on metallic wings, they turned to the automaton. The horse flicked its tail as if to ward away flies, and the movement caused something to thud against its metal buttocks. Something hidden amongst the abundance of black threads. Clara blinked. Was that one of the cylindrical satchels Grand used to shelter his notes?

Lifting the horse's tail, with no small amount of awkwardness, Clara found a leather container tied to the extremity. She freed the rounded satchel and, scrunching her nose, viewed it with incredulity. "Of all places, why would Grand hide it there?"

Mr. Arthur smirked. "Because that's the one part of a horse's anatomy no one cares to examine."

With a snort of billowing steam, the horse took off at a canter and conveyed them through the Grande Île's winding streets, retracing their previous course. When Gutenberg Square came into view, the number of people around the carousel had doubled, and adults outnumbered the children. Clara pursed her lips. This did not bode well. Huddled around the carousel, people talked over one another in loud voices and pointed at the empty spot where the automaton horse had once stood. A pair of gentlemen in bowler hats appeared to be jotting in notebooks as they conversed with a lady in a fuchsia dress.

Mum!

As the automaton horse and cart neared the carousel, all eyes turned toward them. Children squealed, and murmurs amongst the adults increased in volume as a cacophony of languages collided in midair. Unable to make sense of German, Clara's mind latched on to the phrases in English and French.

"Is it related to the clockwork owl?"

"Marvel of marvels!"

"Do you think that chap's the inventor?"

The horse accelerated to a gallop, and the throng scattered, evading its path with gasps and shouts. As the machine's intentions became clear, the hair on Clara's neck raised. Muscles seizing, she braced herself against the cart and Mr. Arthur's arm. The horse leapt through the air and landed on the carousel platform with a clatter before trotting back to its original location and resuming its deep and dreamless slumber.

The pocket watch fell silent.

For a moment, all was still.

Then the crowd erupted in a gaggle of questions, and the

reporters fumbled with their notebooks, desperate to capture every detail on paper.

Clara's stomach clenched. They might've given Mr. Forrester the slip, but he'd know exactly where to find them once tomorrow's paper hit the pavement.

Muscles taut as an overwound clock spring, Theodore rowed their rented boat across the lake, his attention riveted on the grounds of Orangerie Park. His gaze examined the trees hedging the shoreline, which afforded shade for them and possibly concealment for others.

Had he done enough to keep the Stantons safe?

As they'd fled the carousel, he'd lost the reporters by employing the old dodge-and-switch through the winding streets. After retrieving the animals and luggage from the Canopy of Stars, he'd located a new hotel, where they'd regrouped later that evening. The clue Drosselmeyer left on the horse had directed them to Orangerie Park—still in Strasbourg but, thankfully, off the Grande Île. They lay low the following day to avoid the newspaper men, and then under the cover of night, he'd escorted the ladies to an inn near the park.

Today, he'd insisted Mrs. S. and the animals stay at the Plucky Orange Peel rather than venture into the park. He'd wanted Miss Stanton to stay behind as well. Let him assume the risk of locating the next clue. But the woman's stubbornness and logic had prevailed. Strength and security are found in numbers, she'd said.

Still, he couldn't shake the nagging thought that all their precautions were for naught. That Forrester was already in Strasbourg. Lurking. Hunting. Every newspaper in Europe had already given them away, printing the story of Drosselmeyer's runaway carousel horse, so it was only a matter of time before the rat showed his yellow teeth. Somehow, he had to keep the scoundrel away from the Stantons.

After hearing Miss Stanton relate the whole of Forrester's treachery, he now understood her valid suspicions upon their first meeting. He also understood why the slippery thief in Drosselmeyer's apartment hadn't purloined the money box or other valuables. Forrester had sent the boy after that letter, and the letter only. Dastardly fiend. The nerve of him threatening Drosselmeyer. Blackmailing Miss Stanton. It was enough to make his blood boil!

Water splashed against Theodore's cheek and seemed to sizzle, snapping his attention to the rowboat.

Miss Stanton used a handkerchief to dry her bare hand. "I apologize, but I'd called your name numerous times without effect, so drastic measures seemed warranted." She slipped on her brown glove. "Are you aware that you've been rowing us in circles?"

The allure of her smile rendered Theodore dumbstruck. "Was I?"

"Indeed, and you were beginning to look like the hero of a gothic novel, which is completely unacceptable. I cannot abide any form of brooding."

Neither could he. That's why he endeavored to keep his tormented thoughts under control. Theodore reflexively swept the evidence of his foreboding into the mental clock casing, already stuffed full of nightmares and shadows. Gah, but it was becoming hard to shut the door again. And keep it shut.

He forced a chuckle, hoping it sounded more sincere than it felt. "Off with your oblique flattery, Miss Stanton. I'm no hero. Though I might wish to be the gallant knight who saves the day astride a white charger, 'tis my lot to be the peg-legged, blundering squire."

Miss Stanton's dark brows knit together. "When was the last time you slept?"

His grin wobbled. "At night. That's usually when people sleep, so I'm told. Why do you ask?"

"Because you've the look of a mouse that's been taunted by the cat all night. And because I've heard your cries through the hotel wall betwixt our rooms. You're having nightmares again, aren't you?"

So much for hiding his torment. The chiming of Drosselmeyer's pocket watch offered a well-timed distraction. Shading his eyes, Theodore surveyed the lake. "I'd wager Drosselmeyer's fashioned an automaton waterfowl this time. Perhaps another stork or a mallard duck or a regal swan. Think I spotted a few of the latter nesting near the lake. See anything, Miss Stanton?"

"Just a man drowning in a sea of denial."

Despite the lack of waves, the boat seemed to rock. He slipped, almost losing an oar to the lake. Pulling the wooden paddles out of the water, he tucked them into the bottom of the boat beside his crutch. The pocket watch's metallic notes faded into silence, revoking his excuse to avoid Miss Stanton's gaze.

The woman observed him from the bow, gray eyes void of disparagement. Black ringlets swaying in the warm, languid breeze. Defined contours of her face softened by a rosy bloom. The pretty little grump, having retired her murder of ravens, was now all beauty and kindness. Each night since the carousel incident, she'd had a poultice sent to his room to soothe his injured leg, and each night when it arrived, he nearly came undone. For she had seen him—the pain, the tears, the brokenness—and she had not thrown him away.

"You know, Mr. Arthur, since all of London believes my bloodline to be riddled with madness, I'm the perfect person to entrust with the keeping of secrets. For even if I should give up my honor and betray a confidence, not a soul would ever take me at my word."

Theodore slouched forward, propping an elbow on either knee. "It is not your honor I question, but mine."

"People are often poor judges of their own character, esteeming themselves either too highly or too little. Why don't you tell me what's really bothering you—who you really are—and let me determine whether your estimation of yourself is accurate? If my honor isn't in question, then I should be able to come to a fair verdict, for good or ill."

She made an excellent case. One he'd not the strength or inclination to argue. Perhaps if he finally spoke of the past . . . of the nightmares . . . they might lose their power over him. In any case, after she'd found the courage to entrust him with her history, how could he refuse to share his own?

Theodore ran a hand over his beard. "I admit, Judge Stanton, I don't quite know where to begin."

"Begin at the beginning and conclude at the conclusion. I've nowhere else to be, so by all means, take your time."

He sighed. "My name isn't Arthur."

"I'm all astonishment." She smirked, but a gleam of tenderness in her eyes softened the expression.

Like the turning of a silver key, those eyes unlocked the hidden crypt wherein Theodore had buried himself alive. For that was truly what his carefully constructed mental encasement had become. A crypt bearing a false name. One that could no longer conceal the pain and brokenness within. At least not from one pair of perceptive silver eyes. Dare he let Miss Stanton see the whole of him—the faulty pieces as well as the humor and smiles? Dare he resurrect his former life?

If he didn't do so now, he never would.

He cleared his throat and slowly opened the door long shut to his past. "Theodore was the name given me by the mother who didn't survive my birth. From the father who resented my existence, I received daily reassurance that I could never be worthy of it."

Miss Stanton's lips parted. "Your father . . . he's the person in your nightmares? The one you beg for mercy?"

Theodore shifted his gaze to the lake's dark green water. "Throughout my childhood, Father's disdain of me festered. He disapproved of my interest in clocks and preoccupation with tinkering. Compared me to my seven elder brothers, who—unlike me—met his every expectation. I was admonished to be like them. To keep my hands clean by pursuing academia instead of a trade. Achieve high marks. Adhere to tradition." Live up to the esteemed Kingsley lineage.

"Father instructed our tutor to use the switch if I fidgeted, daydreamed, or made a mess. That's what he called my disassembling clocks to figure out how they worked . . . making a mess." He tugged at his constricting shirt collar, finger grazing a raised scar on his chest. "To avoid the switch, I learned to hide my mess. To shove the unacceptable parts of myself deep inside and lock them away so no one could see. And I pulled it off for years. Until one day Father discovered I'd been secretly learning from an estate clock-winder, and for the first time, struck me with his own hand."

He ground his teeth, still feeling the heat of that slap biting across his cheek. Splitting his lip. The nightmares wouldn't let him forget.

Miss Stanton's voice reached out gingerly. "Is that what you relive in the dreams?"

He sucked in a breath. "In part. The rest involves the consequences of the decision I made that night. When Father hit me, I determined to adhere to tradition and join the army. I thought if I could prove myself heroic on a field of battle, I might finally garner his respect. Make myself worthy of my mother's name. Make myself good enough to be called his son."

His gaze drifted to the crutch lying beside his metal boot, carved from handle to tip with name upon name. "But on October 25, 1854, Father was proven right once and for all."

Silence joined them in the boat, a heavy companion that weighed their tiny vessel.

At last Miss Stanton spoke, her whisper half reverence, half horror. "You were there . . . at the Light Brigade's charge?"

"Aye." Theodore ground his jaw. No longer seeing the crutch. No longer feeling the breeze. "I was the dispatch sent to relay Lord Raglan's order to 'advance rapidly to the front' and 'prevent the enemy from carrying away the guns.' I'm the one who was uncertain as to which guns his order referred. I was the one who sent the Light Brigade galloping through batteries of shell and shot into the Valley of Death. Because of my ineptitude, two hundred and sixty men were killed or gravely wounded. Good men—brave men—slain. And I had the audacity to survive.

"A friend of Father's, a Colonel Chicanery, found me unconscious amid the carnage. Knowing I'd bungled Lord Raglan's order and suspecting the battle would become infamous once word got back to London, the colonel had me transported to my father in secret."

For as long as he lived, he'd never forget the moment he awoke in a guest room in the little-used east wing of Kingsley Court. Father at his bedside, laying a damp cloth on his brow. For the first time in his life, he thought Father might actually care for him. Why else would he roll up his crisp white sleeves and tend to his wounds personally? Spoon-feed him broth. Bathe and dress him without the aid of a servant. For the span of three months, Theodore thought he'd finally earned his father's love.

"But the colonel's secrecy was to afford Father the opportunity to prevent our family name from being sullied in the quagmire of my shame. Father made good use of that opportunity. He nursed me back to health, all the while keeping my survival and my presence unknown to the household. A fact I discovered upon my recovery.

"'If you were going to besmirch the family honor so spectacularly, you could've at least had the decency to die.' Those were his words to me the day I was finally well enough to hobble from my bed. Once again, I had disappointed him . . . by failing to die." A tear wetted his cheek, and he turned his face away. "I was then informed that my death had already been announced, my funeral attended, and a headstone engraved with my name. The stipend I was to inherit legally divided amongst my brothers. Only Father and Colonel Chicanery knew I yet lived, and the latter had been compensated into forgetfulness. Theodore was effectively no more, and I was ordered to make certain he stayed that way. To leave through a back door under the cover of night . . . never to return."

The force of Miss Stanton's indignant gasp shook the boat. "That brute! He would disown his flesh and blood?"

He shrugged. "I tried to convince Father to reverse his pronouncement. Demanded to know if he thought my mother would be pleased by what he'd done. It was the one time I dared question Father about anything." Not that it had done any good. Theodore removed the broken gear from his pocket, turning it in his fingers.

"What did your father say to that?"

"'I'd trade your life in a second if it would restore the life of my Theodora. But as a trade cannot be arranged, I'll settle for your dismissal. Be gone by first light. I've no use for broken pieces.'" Theodore clenched the gear, letting the teeth bite his flesh. "Those were the last words my father said to me. The same words that toy with my mind whenever sleep does chance to come. I've come to accept the nightmares as penance for my part in the Charge . . . along with the fact that I can never find a place where this faulty gear belongs."

Silence threatened to sink them in the depths of the lake.

Tucking the gear back into his overcoat, Theodore cleared his throat and straightened to meet Miss Stanton's blanched expression. He shouldn't have overwhelmed her with details, so gritty and grim. "I apologize for the conclusion to my tale, Miss Stanton. I should've come up with a better story for you. Spun some epic legend of a gallant knight named Arthur with a fancy for circular furniture and a talent for getting cutlery dislodged from boulders."

Miss Stanton opened her mouth, but her words were preempted by the chiming of Drosselmeyer's pocket watch.

Had he truly wasted an hour on his sorry tale? Theodore retrieved the oars and placed the blades in the water. They must get back to searching for Drosselmeyer's clockwork clue. If they didn't find it soon, he would need to convey Miss Stanton back to the inn for refresh—

"Honk, honk."

On the far side of the lake, a pair of white swans glided with the air of a king and queen, trailed by a devoted court of downy gray cygnets. The royal couple led their graceful procession toward an arched tunnel at the base of a stone terrace constructed at the water's edge, beneath the fluttering branches of a willow. As the watch continued to chime, one of the cygnets veered from the flock and swam toward the boat. Sunlight glinted off the cygnet's back, revealing its downy feathers to be made of molded pewter.

A smile eased the tension in Theodore's face. His grip on

the oars relaxed, and he waited for the automaton cygnet to come to them, drawn across the shining water by clockwork instinct. As it neared the boat, the cygnet trumpeted for joy with the smooth note of a brass horn. The feathered royals glanced back at the sound, and one of them swam to retrieve their wayward child.

Miss Stanton's eyes widened. "Oh dear . . . we've a cranky cob at two o'clock. Better make haste with those oars. We need to retrieve Grand's device before the cob carries it under the terrace."

"Right-oh." Theodore rowed them toward the automaton, on the double.

Leaning against the edge of the boat, Miss Stanton stretched her arm to its full length, gloved fingers straining for the cygnet.

Honking and beating its wings, the cob swam to intercept.

"Faster!" Miss Stanton rose from her seat, increasing her reach.

The boat tilted, and Miss Stanton's sleeve touched the top of the lake.

Theodore scooted to the edge of his seat, trying to provide a counterbalance as he rowed. "Careful or you'll capsize the boat."

"Oh, don't be such a negative newton. I've al . . . most . . . got—"

Splash!

C lara was sinking toward the bottom of an idyllic lake.
And the timing was most inconvenient.

Bubbles floated from her nose, escaping to the sunshine with ease. She tried to follow them—arms flapping, legs kicking—but waterlogged garments dragged her downward. Ever downward. The dress must come off. This instant!

Propriety could drown in her stead.

Reaching behind, she floundered to find the ties of her skirt. Her heart thrashed like a fish out of water. Her lungs ached with envy of the beached fish and its death by air. Oh, for a drink of blessed air! Wrenching her shoulders, she clawed at her waistband. Why must her fingers be so awkward?

She gazed upward, skyward, heavenward.

Help!

A pathetic prayer, but the only one she could manage. Yet no sooner had the plea formed than a shadowed silhouette dove into the lake. Mr. Arthur, plunging toward her at a fast clip. Extending his crutch as a lifeline.

She seized the wooden handle, and Mr. Arthur pulled her up. Crushed her against his chest. Mr. Arthur held her in one arm and reached for the light with the other, holding the crutch. Going through the motions of swimming as though they weren't sinking at a faster clip. As though they weren't weighted down by petticoats and bronze.

As though they had a chance.

Percussive pops resounded through the water, followed by a whoosh of bubbles.

Sun? How were they traveling toward the sun?

And why was Mr. Arthur upside down?

Clara burst through the lake's surface and gasped for air with desperate gulps. She hadn't drowned. They hadn't drowned. How in the name of heaven and earth had they managed that? She sought the gaze of Mr. Arthur, the human buoy she'd clung to for dear life—and absolutely no other reason. *Ahem.*

Cheeks aflame, she coughed and sputtered. "B-by what magic are we afloat?"

"Not magic. Ingenuity." With a lopsided grin, he pointed the crutch toward his feet.

The mechanical boot, which had sent Mr. Arthur plunging through the water, was now encased in what appeared to be a red balloon, floating on the surface of the lake. Somehow, Grand had turned his apprentice into a literal human buoy.

Another cough rattled water in her lungs. "While I should like an explanation, my curiosity is far surpassed by my new-found disdain for this lake. Let's head for solid ground."

"Right-oh. Take hold of the flotation device, and I'll dog-paddle us to shore faster than a Labrador."

Clara smirked. "You're beginning to sound like my mother."

"I'll take that as a compliment." He raised a brow humorously. "I think."

Once transported to the lakeside, Clara collapsed in a sodden heap on the grass and wiped her hands over her face. Her *empty* hands. "Crumbled biscuits, I lost the cygnet! I had it in my hand just before I went over and now . . . it's gone. There's no telling how long it will take us to find it again." Her shoulders slumped, hands falling to her lap. "We almost drowned for naught."

"Don't be such a negative Nelly." Mr. Arthur planted his crutch on the shore and rose from the lake. With his free hand, he retrieved Grand's pocket watch and held the precious timepiece to his ear. "Drosselmeyer's watch still ticks, so there's hope of our tracking down the automaton yet. Especially now that we know what we're looking for."

He hobbled in her direction, taking care not to rupture the flotation device's inflatable, and lowered beside her on the luxuriant blades of grass. Dripping blond locks obscured his eyes and most of his bearded face.

How had the brawny man in the lake emerged from it a winsome whelp? "I know you wished to be a Labrador, but I believe a shaggy briard would be closer to the truth."

"Is that so? Perhaps I should spruce up then, eh?" Mr. Arthur gave his head an energetic shake and sent droplets flying in all directions.

Shielding her face, Clara fell back on the grass with a hearty laugh.

Mr. Arthur reclined on an elbow, resting his head atop a fist, tousled waves now combed back with a carefree air. His gaze shone down on her with palpable warmth. "I should've listened when you told me to shove off at the London docks. Taking a dive in the Thames would've been worth it to hear your laugh."

Clara swallowed, suddenly finding it difficult to breathe.

Only now she couldn't blame the lake. "Y-you were supposed to explain about the flotation device once we got to shore. How does it work?" Perhaps if he jabbered about engineering and gadgetry, her lungs would remember how to function.

"I haven't the foggiest. My supposition would be a controlled release of hydrogen gas triggered by submersion in wat—"

"You assisted Grand in the creation of the prosthetic, did you not?"

"I offered a few ideas to increase the knee joint's range of motion, but Drosselmeyer carried out the bulk of the construction alone as I was sent off to bathe before attaching the prosthetic. He's quite the genius, your grandfather. He's not limited by the obvious or the logical. Not intimidated by the achievements of others or bound by his own limitations. He just imagines and creates. I only wish he'd informed me of this inflatable safety measure. As it is, I'm at a loss—"

"Informed?" She propped herself on an elbow, mirroring Mr. Arthur on the grass. "Are you saying you had no knowledge of being outfitted with a flotation device when you dove into that lake?"

"That's correct."

"And you dove after me anyway . . . with a veritable anchor strapped to your person?"

He chuckled. "Well, I didn't exactly have time to remove the prosthetic, now did I?"

Her jaw slackened. Mr. Arthur hadn't known, and yet he dove off the boat without a second thought. The very same Mr. Arthur who thought he was a useless failure. A faulty piece. No, not Arthur. Theodore. The man who believed himself unworthy of his true name. The man who was not only a jovial soul, but a brave one who'd endured trauma and survived horrors that, for all their ill, had shaped him into a

caring protector. A daring hero willing to risk the high prob-
ability of drowning to save her.

No other possible gain, monetary or otherwise.

Just . . . *her*.

Clara's heart swelled as she stared into Mr. Theodore's eyes
of jade. The ones looking back at her now, with a gleam of
sincere tenderness, as though she were worth being rescued.
"Your father was wrong about you. Woefully and deplorably
wrong." With a smile, tentative and small, she placed her
hand on the patch of grass between them. "I hope you know
. . . I no longer wish you to shove off and out of our lives. You
belong in the shop, Mr. Theodore. Our family keeps better
time with you in it."

His throat bobbed. "I can't remember the last time I was
called by that name."

"It's what you should be called. What I should like to call
you from now on . . . unless you object. I could keep the name
between us, if you'd prefer."

His mouth quirked. "You may keep and use the name as
you like, Miss Stanton."

"What of your surname? Is that to remain a mystery?"

"I think it had better. If I told you my surname, I should
want you to keep it too." Cheeks reddening, Mr. Theodore's
gaze fell to her lips.

Clara's stomach rolled into the lake with a plop. She inched
backward, but Mr. Theodore clasped her hand upon the grass.
Quieting any thoughts of running away. Quieting every
thought but one. Mr. Theodore was going to—

"Honk, hooonk!"

Mr. Theodore's eyes widened, and a shriek tore from his
lips.

Clara bolted upright. Their old friend the cob loomed over
Mr. Theodore's posterior, wings raised and slender neck
arched in a menacing hook. "Stars, did it bite you?"

The swan answered for Mr. Theodore by snapping at the red inflatable on his boot. The balloon popped, and the resulting noise sent the swan into a frantic, flapping retreat.

Mr. Theodore grabbed her hand, pulling her onto her feet. "We must flee before the winged demon strikes again." He retrieved his crutch and thrust it into her keeping. "Let us make haste, Miss Stanton!"

Hand in hand, they sprinted away from the lake as the outraged cob gave chase, honking and flapping. Honking and pecking. Honking and drawing the attention of every soul in Orangerie Park. Sophisticated couples promenading the neat trails. Dignified families picnicking beneath silk parasols. All eyed them with bewilderment, and all were deftly dodged by the sodden pair darting across the grass, Mr. Theodore clutching the torn fabric of his trousers and Clara laughing without fear of what the onlookers might say.

Drosselmeyer's invention had evaded them for too long. Every day spent scouring Orangerie Park for the automaton cygnet afforded Forrester another day in his search for the Stantons. Theodore hadn't been too concerned at first, but now he could almost hear the hands of time ticking away the wasted minutes. Each tick and tock echoing through his mind like approaching footfalls. Forrester must be in Strasbourg by now. The question was, how long would it take the scoundrel to figure out they'd left the Grand Île?

An April breeze chased a sinewy cloud across the blue expanse above Orangerie Park, and Theodore shifted on the blanket they'd spread upon the grass. On the opposite side of the blanket, Miss Stanton and Mrs. S. enjoyed a picnic luncheon prepared by the accommodating cook at the Plucky Orange Peel inn. Every instinct in his marrow wanted to shepherd the ladies to another location, but they couldn't leave that evasive automaton behind. It was their only means of finding Drosselmeyer. And it could not be allowed to fall into Forrester's hands.

Theodore's gaze scanned the lake for the glint of pewter feathers in the sunlight, then combed through the surrounding trees for the figure of a man in a yellow waistcoat. Nothing, and . . . nothing. For now.

He sighed through clenched teeth. If only he'd rowed faster, Miss Stanton might've caught the cygnet that first day instead of catching a chill. That topple into the lake had cost them a day of waiting at the inn for his and Miss Stanton's clothes to dry. The next day, he'd searched the park alone while the ladies had remained in their room, Miss Stanton to recover from her chill and Mrs. S. to nurse it away. This morning, a recovered Miss Stanton and giddy Mrs. S. had been anxious to be out of doors, so after breaking their fast, they'd traipsed to the park together. If they didn't find the automaton today, he didn't know what—

A metallic melody reverberated in his waistcoat pocket. "Eyes up, Stantons. Time for cygnet patrol."

The ladies straightened to attention, and collectively, they inspected the lake and surrounding shore for any telltale signs of an automaton cygnet. A rustle among the reeds. A ripple on the placid waters. A faint trumpeting of a metal beak. Yet, once again, the pocket watch tolled the hour and fell silent. Once again, it was time to move out.

The search party took to their feet.

Miss Stanton gave the blanket a good shake, scattering crumbs and fallen petals into the air, and then retrieved the white basket containing the leftovers from their picnic. "Be sure all the children are accounted for this time, Mum. I'd rather not have to double back."

Mrs. S. peered inside the wicker basket she carried. "Oh dear . . . Phileas has scampered off again." In a trice, the woman was on all fours, peering through an ornamental hedgerow. "Phileas Vulpini, you come back here this instant!"

A grin tugged Theodore's mouth. Phileas could make himself scarce faster than a confirmed bachelor in a ballroom aflutter with debutantes. Hmmm . . . Bachelors hid away in places debs weren't likely to go. Smoke room. Billiard room. Dark corner of a library with a flask of scotch. What might be the fox equivalent? Mrs. S. continued to trim the hedges with shears of scolding, while Miss Stanton searched nearer the lake, both focused on the ground.

I wonder . . . Theodore looked up.

In a nearby magnolia tree, among clusters of pink blossoms, a pair of blue eyes implored not to be given away. Theodore grinned. *Sorry, chap, but I can't let you worry Mrs. S. after she's taken us in with such kindness.* "At ease, ladies. He's over here."

Removing Phileas from the low-hanging branch, Theodore returned the kit to the wicker basket. Fred, who'd appointed himself surrogate father, gave Phileas a gentle nip of chastisement while brother Todd and sister Honorine welcomed their sibling with enthusiastic sniffing. The kits' fur was beginning to molt from brown into a reddish hue, and their snouts were more pointed. At the rate they were growing, he'd soon need a better way of toting them around.

Theodore scratched Phileas' ears, now doubled in size. "We're going to have to keep a sharp eye on this one, Mrs. S. He seems to have inherited your talent for tree climbing."

"Come along, you two." Miss Stanton smiled over her shoulder. "If we don't dally, we might have time for another round of Clever Cumulus. Who knows, perhaps Mr. Theodore can finally manage to win a match." Her dark brow arched, taunting and tantalizing, then she was off, sauntering around the rim of the lake with an alluring sway of her bell-shaped skirt.

The match he longed to win might as well be in the clouds, so far was it from reach.

As they walked to the next quadrant of the lake, Theodore leaned heavily on his crutch and allowed Mrs. S. to form a human barrier between him and her daughter. He wouldn't take any chances with Miss Stanton's honor. Not after that near disaster three days ago. *"If I told you my surname, I should want you to keep it too."* What kind of addlebrained rot was that?

The besotted kind, that's what.

Rusted cogs, he'd gone and gotten besotted!

With a swing of his metal boot, Theodore kicked a twig into the lake. Just because Miss Stanton had finally accepted him as Drosselmeyer's apprentice, just because she'd finally come to trust him with her family, didn't give him the right to hope for more.

Beneath a classical gazebo with white columns, the ladies set up camp. Miss Stanton unfurled the blanket upon the base of marble. "Isn't it a beautiful prospect?"

Following her line of sight, Theodore took in Orangerie Park anew. Here, a fount concealed within the lake created a water willow as it rained back to earth. A variety of trees clustered about the shoreline, many crowned with a prized stork nest. Like guardians, the stately birds watched over the park, reporting to one another in their bill-clattering code.

"Beautiful, yes." Mrs. S. lowered in a billow of bright fabric and set the basket of furry ones at her side. "And quite romantic too, with the scent of orange and magnolia blossoms drifting on the breeze and the stork's portent of fertility blessing young lovers below." She cast an oblique glance at her daughter before lobbing a wink at Theodore.

Which somehow set his beard afire.

Tugging at his sweltering collar, Theodore turned his face

toward the sky. "Let's play another round of Clever Cumulus. I'll start. Erm . . . that cloud looks like a flea-bitten rat. Your turn, Miss Stanton."

Forty minutes later, Mrs. S. claimed another win at the game of her making with a cloud in the shape of a platypus—whatever that was—and Drosselmeyer's watch began to chime. Theodore stood with the aid of his crutch as a faint trumpet resounded from the lake. He released a sigh of relief. Finally!

Miss Stanton rushed to the edge of the gazebo. "I see the cygnet! It's swimming this way. Come, Mr. Theodore, let's fetch it from the lake."

"Oh-ho-ho, no. I'm not getting any closer to that water than I have to. Here." Unfastening the fob from his waistcoat, he placed the timepiece in Miss Stanton's gloved palm. "This will be sufficient assistance. You don't need me."

A teasing smile lifted the corner of Miss Stanton's rosy lips. "If you're afraid, Mr. Theodore, all you had to do was say so. It's quite understandable. After all, swans are most fearsome creatures." Twirling about in a manner most dizzying, she raced toward the water.

Suddenly self-conscious of the patch sewn on the back of his trousers, Theodore's smoldering cheeks relit the kindling of his beard. Perhaps another dip in the lake would be wise.

Mrs. S. appeared in his peripheral. "I'd like to thank you, lad."

"For what?"

"For making my ducky laugh again." Mrs. Stanton turned a smile on him, warm and reassuring. "You've done her good, lad, and I'm grateful. The day God led you to Drosselmeyer and Son was a blessed one. We're glad as a gaggle of geese to have you in the family. In whatever capacity you choose."

Did he even have a beard anymore? With his face engulfed in roaring flames, any whiskers that remained must be composed of ash and soot. Theodore tightened his grip on his crutch and leaned against a nearby column, welcoming the marble's coolness. *Keep a level head, man.* He had to be strong. Put Miss Stanton's welfare above his own feelings.

"Please . . . don't tempt me, Mrs. S. I've nothing to offer your daughter but myself, and that's simply not good enough. You need to cease this matchmaking scheme."

"She told me everything, you know. About the other day. About you."

Not surprising. He dug a nail into the groove of a name carved on his crutch. "So you understand, then?"

"I understand that Clara talks about you more often and more fondly than she realizes. I understand that you make her smile and have reacquainted her with the joys of life, which she had long forgotten. I understand that you take care of my girl, Theodore. You love her, and she loves you right back. Though you're both too afraid to admit as much."

Theodore tried to swallow her words but couldn't. "She deserves better than the likes of me."

"Don't confuse the character of your heavenly Father with the voice of your earthly one." Mrs. S. placed a hand on his rigid shoulder. "Depend on Him, and I have no doubt that my girl will be able to depend on you."

Theodore turned the crutch in his hand. Might that be true? Might God be willing to welcome him home? Free him from a life of nightmares and anguish? Give him a life of peace?

A life with Clara? It seemed such an impossibility, but for the first time in years, a flicker of hope burned in his soul.

"I got it!" Miss Stanton held the automaton cygnet aloft and beamed a triumphant smile.

With a jubilant hurrah, Mrs. S. leapt from the marble gazebo to the lush grass and hastened to join her daughter at the lake's edge. As the pair chattered and laughed and admired Drosselmeyer's latest marvel, Theodore couldn't help but smile.

Until a movement in his peripheral triggered alarm.

His head snapped to the right. Senses heightened and every nerve on edge. *There.* A flash of yellow on the other side of the lake, beneath the shadow of a gnarled oak tree.

Forrester had found them.

Dear Little Stargazer,

About the next stop on our merry scavenger hunt, I shall speak plainly. I wish you to visit Strasbourg Cathedral, and let your gaze see beyond the ornate architecture crafted by man. Let your heart seek the One who crafted you. Let your mind contemplate the following notion: If Jesus, the very Son of God, had to walk this earth in complete dependence upon the Father, how can our finite souls shoulder on without Him?

Even the strongest youths grow weary, my girl. Oh, you can get by on might and main for a time. Until something goes wrong. Until the pieces of your carefully crafted, precariously held life fall apart and leave you in grief-stricken disbelief because it wasn't supposed to be this way. My son wasn't supposed to die before me. Your fiancé wasn't supposed to betray your trust. Our beloved Norma wasn't supposed to leave us so soon. Yet these things happened, and they've left us with a choice. Will we still depend on our Lord?

Throughout this journey, I've wrestled with this question: How are we to depend on One who feels so far removed? How are we to worship when we're standing by a grave?

I wanted answers. I wanted to see God's promises fulfilled according to my desires and expectations, but while navigating the vast skies, I realized God has never been one to do the expected. Just as His power isn't limited by human laws of science or logic, His promises aren't limited to earthly laws of time or space. With His sovereign power and eternal perspective, God turns expectation on its head. A virgin isn't supposed to conceive, but she gives birth. The Messiah isn't supposed to die, but He breathes His last upon a cross. Sealed tombs aren't supposed to be empty, but with one word from God, a centuries-old promise is fulfilled and death ceases to be the end.

God may not answer our prayers the way we want or fulfill His promises the way we expect—but He never fails to keep His word. Whether it's on earth or in heaven, we can rest assured that we will see the goodness of the Lord in the land of the living. For that reason, I have chosen to trust. I will worship my Savior as I stand by the grave because I know the latter is empty, just as He said. Though He may feel removed, I know Emmanuel is with me still, just as He promised. He is with you too, my girl. Constant and caring. Don't be afraid to trust the Lord's sovereignty and depend on His goodness. His is a love that can be trusted.

His is a love that we both need.

Your devoted,
Grand

God's love might be trustworthy, but human affections—especially those of a romantic nature—had proven themselves unreliable. A fact Clara reiterated to her traitorous stomach every time a glance from Mr. Theodore caused it to turn a somersault.

As they strolled along the streets of Strasbourg, bound for its famed gothic cathedral, Clara secured Mum's right hand, grateful for the maternal buffer. Why must things become awkward between she and Mr. Theodore? She'd just begun to feel at ease around him, to feel secure in his presence instead of continually poised on a fraying tightrope of dread. Perhaps that was the problem. They'd grown too comfortable, too familiar. A dangerous combination that too easily led to fondness.

Endearment.

Yearning.

Mr. Theodore's glance snagged on her stare. He flashed a lopsided grin, and her stomach turned a new manner of flip. Dash that charming smile! Dash both strapping shoulders! Dash those mesmerizing eyes and that enticing grin! Oh, she'd already dashed that one. Repeatedly. Night and day, she had dashed it to pieces with logic and reason. Yet, still, to that smile her mind kept wandering. Recalling that day in the park when Mr. Theodore had seemed intent on kissing her . . . but hadn't.

Why hadn't he?

And dash her own turncoat stomach, why did she care?

Clara bit the inside of her cheek to punish it for blushing. That day didn't matter. No matter what happened or didn't happen, no matter what her renegade emotions felt or didn't feel, it simply did not matter. Just as Mum's presence served as a buffer, so too must the formality of Mr. remain a fixed safeguard between her and the man who'd let her keep his name to use as she liked. She and *Mr.* Theodore were— and would remain—friends. Nothing more. Friendship was fenced in with societal expectations and rules of etiquette. It was the utterance of "I love you" that swung the gate wide open for pain and loss.

She had no intention of opening that door again.

Especially not now, when she needed to be on guard more than ever.

"*We're being watched.*" The memory of Mr. Theodore's hushed warning provoked a chill along Clara's neck, and she shuddered, glancing over her shoulder to examine the people on the street. She didn't know what was more terrifying—Mr. Forrester's persistence or his stealth. To think, he'd been just a few stone skips across the lake yesterday. Watching. Waiting.

When Mr. Theodore calmly spirited them out of the park, it had required all her self-control not to look back for the dark eyes she knew were on them. After recovering their bags at the Plucky Orange Peel and paying their bill, Mr. Theodore had taken every precaution to throw her ex-fiancé off their scent. Planted false trails. Utilized circuitous routes. Moved them to a new hotel under cover of night. But the fact remained. Mr. Forrester was in Strasbourg and might even now have them in his sights.

"Are you familiar with this structure, ducky?"

Clara startled and then released a shaky breath. She placed a hand to her bodice, willing her frantic heart to beat normally. "I'm s-sorry, which structure?"

Mum's sloping shoulders seemed quite bare without Fred, but considering where they were bound, leaving him to watch the kits at the Grande Île Hotel was for the best. She gave Clara's hand an understanding squeeze and pointed to a towering medieval residence situated on a corner of the Place de la Cathédrale. "I was curious as to the purpose of that pulley on the fifth floor and thought perhaps the home might've been mentioned in one of your books."

A myriad of windows paned with bottle-bottom glass made the home in question distinctive. Rust-hued walls and dark woodwork carved with intricate motifs created a stark contrast against the adjoining buildings' plain cream and white façades. Like a Black Forest sire flanked by Boulonnais stallions. How could such a structure not have been mentioned in her travel guides?

Clara's hand slipped into her pocket, grasping the journal and pen. Perhaps later she might attempt to describe it herself. "This building isn't mentioned in my books, I'm afraid, but the pulley might be used to hoist supplies directly to the uppermost floors. Would save one from carrying heavy loads up all those stairs."

As they continued down the cobbled street, Mum tucked her hands in either pocket, swishing her skirt enthusiastically. Evidently, Clara wasn't alone in her excitement for the next stop on Grand's scavenger hunt, a historic wonder she'd not allow Mr. Forrester to overshadow with fear. For she'd dreamed of seeing it for far too long.

Cathédrale Notre-Dame de Strasbourg, the city's crowning glory.

Placing a hand on her bonnet, Clara tilted her head, desiring to take in every facet of the elaborate edifice, knowing such a thing couldn't be achieved by the eye's limited scope. The April sun kissed her face, evoking recollection of another spring day when she and Grand had visited this place in the realm of imagination. Even now, she could hear him reading from *A Rambling Rector's Guide to the Cathedrals of the Old World.*

"'Like an ancient fossil, the western façade of Strasbourg's Cathedral has petrified the transition from Romanesque to Gothic architecture in rosy sandstone. The cathedral features the tallest pyramidal tower from medieval times and is lavishly carved with hundreds of biblical figures. The main doorway features scenes of Christ's Passion, from Palm Sunday to His Ascension. In this way, worshipers must come to the Father by way of the Gospel.'"

Clara at last permitted her overawed eyes to blink. Pity, that in all his ramblings, the rector had neglected the rose window above the main door. It was like delicate lace braided from stone. Might the interior be filled with stained glass? She hastened to investigate, trailed by a familiar duo of foot-steps. Clip-clap-clip. Clank-tap-clank. Before she could open the emerald green door, Mr. Theodore performed the task.

With a word of thanks, Clara entered the candlelit nave. Clip-clap-clip-clap. She halted. Where was clank-tap? She glanced at the open cathedral door, where sunshine backlit a masculine silhouette hesitating to step beyond the thresh-old. Just as he'd done at the chapel in Prague. Only now, she understood why. An ache constrained her heart. *Oh, Theodore.* She approached the man clinging to the doorway's shadow and held out her hand. "Come with us."

Mr. Theodore's throat bobbed as he favored his crutch. "Can't."

With a sigh, Clara let her hand fall unaccepted. "The story engraved above your head says otherwise. I can only pray you'll let yourself believe it one day." She rejoined Mum alone, and they proceeded down the great vaulted hall.

Sunlight filtered through several stained-glass windows, including the lace rose, and bathed the cathedral in lumi-nescent color. A handful of tourists milled about the nave, each face dour and grave, as though they toured a cemetery. How could people look so miserable while surrounded by such splendor?

A whack to her skirt prevented further reverie. To her left, Mum stood with hands in pockets, flouncing her skirts with a mirthfulness contradicted by a furrowed brow. Odd behavior, even for Mum. "Is something amiss?"

"Amiss?" The word pitched Mum's voice to a squeak. "Why would you think something's amiss, silly ducky dilly?"

"Furrowed brow, conspicuous pocket fiddling, gratuitous additions to my nickname, and you *hit* me."

"Such an outlandish accusation! And of your own mother,

who birthed and fed and clothed you as a wet, wriggling tad-pole of a babe. I'm mortified. Absolutely mortified you could think me capable of such senseless violence as hitting my own daughter. Blood of my blood, flesh of my flesh, mole of my mole."

Clara rolled her eyes. "Do cut the dramatics, mother! You're being ridiculous. Besides, I don't even have your mole."

"Actually you do, Miss Stanton."

Mr. Theodore clank-tapped toward them, and Clara's heart swelled. Coming alongside, he pointed at the back of his neck. "The mole's about here. Just below your right ear."

"You're not serious? Of all the genetic inheritances, have I truly become heir to the Drosselmeyer mole? Grand's has three gray hairs now. Three!" Clara's hand flew to her neck, gloved fingers desperate to conceal the alleged mole.

"I assure you, Miss Stanton, your handsome mole is quite hairless."

Clara stilled. "That, sir, was the most disturbing compli-ment ever constructed by man. Exactly how much study have you given to my handsome mole?"

That lopsided grin improved Mr. Theodore's face as he drew closer. "When you're irritated, your gray eyes seem to strike together like flint and steel, creating the most delight-ful sparks. Did you know that?"

Clara's treacherous stomach somersaulted backward and out the door. *Just friends.* Resisting the pull of that dashed smile, she looked away, only to discover they were quite alone. Where was her maternal buffer? Escaping down the nave, Clara headed for a bright fuchsia bonnet. Mum had joined a cluster of tourists admiring the collection of tapestries hanging from each of the pointed arches in the cathedral's arcade. Shaking her head, she hastened to retrieve her wayward chaperone.

Until a scream threatened to shatter the stained glass.

Beneath one of the tapestries, a middling woman twirled

about in frenzied circles, beating her skirts with lace hand-kerchief and shrieking with the power of ten lungs. "Raaat! Heaven save me, I'm being defiled by disgusting little claws. I shall die of the plaaague!" The Englishwoman flailed into the arms of her male companion. "Get it out, Reginald. Get. It. Out!"

Mr. Theodore materialized at her stunned side. "What the deuce? How did a rat get in the cathedral?"

Clara gulped. "I've a sinking feeling it's not a rat."

A furry blot scurried up the nave, and right behind it bobbed a fuchsia bonnet.

Mr. Theodore guffawed. "She didn't!"

Heat singed the top of Clara's ears. "Oh yes, she did."

In a blink, the ball of fuzz leapt over Clara's shoulder, landed on a nearby chair, and met her gaze with deceptively innocent eyes of blue. She sighed. "Hello, Phileas."

Phileas took off with a yip.

Seconds later, Mum whizzed by in a flurry of skirts hoisted well above the ankle. "No time to explain, ducky. Rescue mission in progress. Help Todd."

Stars, had Mum brought all three of the kits? Clara whirled around, wincing as the other woman's screams of travail continued to echo through the cathedral. "Where is he?"

Cutting a deft right, Mum pursued Phileas as he jumped across the immaculate rows of chairs. "Caught in the screech owl's crinoline. Make haste before she squishes the poor dear!"

"What about Hon—"

A piercing screech sent Clara's hands flying to shield her ears. A fox kit lodged in crinoline, another on the run, and a third missing. In a cathedral. How was she supposed to take care of this unmitigated disaster?

Mr. Theodore placed a hand on her shoulder, strong and steady. "I'll find Honorine while you help Todd." He commenced searching under chairs.

Clara exhaled and ran toward the pandemonium. All the

other tourists had since fled, leaving the screech owl to carry on without an audience. Not that anyone had told her. With theatrical hysteria, the woman wept and flapped and whirled, begging God to spare her life from demonic rodents. All the while her rotund husband played the role of useless stump. A sight that increased Clara's gratitude for the man now coaxing a fox kit down from a gilded organ.

Clara summoned her calmest of tones. "Ma'am, if I am to render aid, you must stand still."

The woman threw herself into a chair and screeched all the louder.

Very well. They would do this the hard way. Clara leveled a glower on the stump. "Secure your wife's shoulders and hold her still. Unless you'd rather go deaf."

The man did as he was told. Something, she'd a feeling, he did often.

Relieving the screech owl of her handkerchief, Clara shoved it in the woman's open beak. Blessed silence returned to the cathedral. Much better. "Breathe through your nose, ma'am. There you are. Just so. Now stay still and calm, and we might yet remedy this situation with a modicum of propriety. For what I must do, I beg your pardon." Lowering to the floor, she disappeared beneath the woman's colossal hoop skirt.

A wide-eyed Todd met her gaze. Wedged between two rings of spring steel wire, the plump kit strove in vain to wriggle out of the contraption on his own.

Clara set to the work of liberation. "Peace, little one. This will be over soon."

"Miss Stanton, be quick! The police have been summoned!"

CHAPTER

28

If someone had told Clara she'd one day find herself fleeing Strasbourg Cathedral with a juvenile fox while being pursued by policemen wielding batons and an irate priest armed with brimstone, she would've chuckled. Nervously.

For in her world, such bizarre occurrences weren't wholly improbable.

With Todd in hand, Clara ran toward Mum and the main doorway on the west side, trying to elude the policemen now entering from the south. The clacking of their boots echoed through the vaulted cathedral, combating the policemen's shouts. A bead of sweat trailed her brow. Would the police pursue them beyond the cathedral doors? And where on earth was Mr. Theodore?

Up ahead, Mum burst through the double doors and was transformed by brilliant light into a blackened silhouette. The petite shadow veered right and disappeared. Clara slipped through the closing doors, sights set on a fuchsia flutter in the distance.

Boots battered the ground behind her, punishing the pavers for aiding her escape. "*Arrêter, mademoiselle!*"

Apparently, the authorities *did* intend to give chase beyond the cathedral. A cold lump lodged in Clara's throat. What might be the punishment for sneaking fox kits into a place of worship? A fine? Time in prison? Hung, drawn, and quartered by an incensed priest?

The fuchsia speck took a left on the next street, and she hastened to follow suit. Cheeks burning from exertion, stomach roiling at the thought of being apprehended, she took the turn.

A hand plucked Clara from the street, and she fell backward against someone crouched behind an apple cart. A rock-solid male someone. *Mr. Forrester?* Little Todd whimpered in her left hand, and every fiber of her maternal instinct bristled. She dug claws into the strong arm wrapped about her waist and prepared to ram the back of her head into the stranger's nose.

"It's me, Miss Stanton."

Mr. Theodore. She heaved a sigh of relief and jammed an elbow in the hobgoblin's gut.

He released her with a grunt. "Liver and onions, woman! What was that for?"

Clara pinned the hobgoblin with a glare. "Pardon me, sir, for not realizing you must be informed of my unusual aversion to being grabbed from behind and thrown to the ground."

"Don't be melodramatic, ducky." Mum peeked over Mr. Theodore's shoulder, along with Phileas and Honorine. "The lad was only trying to prevent you from becoming separated from our merry band of fugitives."

"We're not fugiti—" Oh, who was she kidding? The lot of them were crouched behind an apple cart, as though they were trying to outwit the Sheriff of Nottingham. "Fine. I'll concede to fugitives, but we're not merry. We're in trouble."

Even now the stomping of boots drew closer, and the voices of those searching for them grew more exasperated. Clara peered around the cart's spoked wheel. Gulped. Four scowling policemen stood mere paces away at the corner of the street, looking this way and that, planning their next move. Ducking behind the cart, she nuzzled her chin betwixt Todd's soft ears. "They're almost on us. What are we to do?"

Mr. Theodore rubbed a hand over his beard. "Mrs. S., can you manage the kits on your own? Take them back to the hotel and stay put until we join you?"

"Aye, lad. I'll not be so foolish as to trust the little scamps in my pockets a second time. The tattered holes they chewed will be the dickens to repair. Best to keep them in my sights and postpone their baptism until we return to London." Mum placed Phileas and Honorine inside the deep crown of her bonnet and reached for Todd.

Clara relinquished the fluffy fox reluctantly. "This is imprudent. The police will spot her straightaway."

Mr. Arthur took up his crutch. "Not if we create a diversion."

Something about the inflection of his voice made her apprehensive. "What sort of a diversion?"

"The sort with live bait." Seizing her hand, Mr. Theodore relocated them to the middle of the street.

The policemen's gazes swung their way.

Clara's heart stopped. When this was over, she was going to kill the hobgoblin.

As if perceiving her murderous intent, Mr. Theodore gasped in a theatrical manner. "The authorities have spotted us! Let us flee!" He bolted *toward* the uniformed men, dragging her along like a flightless kite skittering across the ground.

At their direct charge, the policemen staggered back.

Mr. Theodore and Clara darted between them. In the next

moment, the men gave chase with shouted commands to halt. *Immédiatement!* She pinched her lips as Mr. Theodore led them back toward the cathedral. Far away from Mum. Too far.

Everything in her wanted to glance over her shoulder—reassure herself that Mum had gotten away—but that would only disclose Mum's presence. As they ran past the cathedral, people cheered at the spectacle they were making of themselves. Her cheeks flamed. Their distraction was working all too well. How exactly was the live bait to avoid being devoured?

Just ahead, the rust house with the bottle-bottom windows offered the reassurance of a familiar face. The rope had been lowered and hooked to a huge wooden crate surrounded by barrels waiting to be loaded. Mr. Theodore skidded to a stop beside the crate, and Clara crashed into his side. "Ooof! What are you—"

"Afraid of heights, Miss Stanton?"

She glanced at the fast-approaching police. "Not as much as imprisonment."

"Right-oh, that's the spirit." Mr. Theodore handed his crutch to her and hefted her into the wooden crate. He hopped in alongside, grabbed one of the two ropes strung through the pulley attached to the attic, and started pulling, hand over hand.

The crate rose from the ground and tilted. Clara's stomach lurched as she careened forward, slamming face-first into Mr. Theodore's broad chest. Her right arm shot around his torso and squeezed. Tight. Was it possible to be seasick in midair?

With one final lurch, the crate reached the top of the pulley on the fifth floor, and the air erupted with applause. Clara hazarded a glance over the side of the crate. Policemen waved batons at the sky amidst the crowd of smiling faces below.

Far, far below.

Suddenly Mum's fear of heights didn't seem so irrational. Clara latched her gaze to Mr. Theodore's overcoat. "We've scaled the castle walls. What now?"

"Not sure. I, erm . . . hadn't thought that far."

Of course he hadn't. That would be too convenient, and in real life, things were never so convenient as they were in ballads of swashbuckling outlaws in Lincoln green. The attic window flung open, and a stout fellow dressed in brown greeted them with a jovial smile. Clara gaped at his bearded face and shiny scalp. "Friar Tuck?"

The man chuckled and addressed her in English with a distinct German accent. "Grocer Kammerzell. Are you the crazy tourists who took a pack of wild foxes into the cathedral?"

Clara winced. "That would be us."

Leaning out the window, Mr. Kammerzell secured the ropes with a brawny hand. "The police are at my door, demanding to search the house. You'd best come in and quickly."

He didn't have to bid her twice. Clara slid the crutch through the window with a thud. Then, holding on to Mr. Theodore for balance, she climbed into the attic, stepping down onto a floor of wooden planks. Sturdy and solid. Never had a musty old attic been so beautiful.

Mr. Theodore slipped through the window next and shook the grocer's hand before retrieving his crutch. "Much obliged, Mr. Kammerzell. Are you certain you want to lend us aid? I wouldn't want to get you in a scrape."

"Who am I to turn away Maid Marian and Robin Hood?" Tossing Clara a jolly wink, Mr. Kammerzell latched the window. "Come, Providence has already supplied your means of escape by redeeming the consequence of human folly."

Mr. Kammerzell ushered them across the attic stocked with barrels of flour, sugar, and other dry goods. At the far wall, more barrels had been arranged one atop the other, four across and three high. Bracing against these, Mr. Kammerzell slid the barrels down the length of the wall with remarkable ease, revealing the barricade to be a façade that concealed a jagged hole in the wall. Beyond this opening lay another attic with exposed beams illumined by a single window.

Clara's jaw hit the floor. A conveniently located secret passage. Perhaps they were living in a ballad of yore. "We will find longbows and arrows in the rafters, I suppose?"

A hearty laugh shook Mr. Kammerzell's rotund frame. "*Nein*, but you might stumble across one of the Ludwig children. Upon buying the seven adjoining homes, the Ludwig brothers connected their attics so the children might visit their cousins at will. Only our families know of this, for the brothers, carpenters by trade, didn't wish it to be known they knocked through my wall by mistake."

Shouts reverberated through the floorboards.

"It seems my wife can stall the police no longer." Lolloping to the other side of the barricade, Mr. Kammerzell readied to push the barrels back into place. "Hurry. Follow the chain of attics to its end and make your escape through the home of Clive Ludwig. He'll help you for my sake while the police search my home."

If ever Friar Tuck existed, this man was surely him. Clara placed a kiss on the grocer's ruddy cheek and stepped into the other attic, followed closely by Mr. Theodore. The stacked barrels slid across the opening without a sound, concealing them at once in a completely different residence. When Mr. Kammerzell assured the police there were no crazy tourists under his roof, it would be no falsehood.

Aside from the single window, this attic housed an ornate wardrobe and two doors—one of which was carved with the words *Onkel Peter*. Crossing the musty space, Clara opened the door and discovered another attic, which they promptly entered. Upon closing the door, she noted the reverse was carved with the name *Onkel Edmund*. The Ludwig brothers must be very close indeed to thread their homes together in such a way.

As they proceeded into the home of Onkel Digory, a pang tugged at Clara's heart. How she would love at the end of this eventful day to rest her cheek against a tweed jacket and revel in the soothing scent of peppermints. A sigh deflated her chest.

"How are we to retrieve Grand's clue from the cathedral now? After today's memorable escape, the police are sure to be watching for us, and even if we manage to slip by them, that furious priest is likely to escort us straight to the gates of Sheol. Assuming Mr. Forrester doesn't get to us first."

Mr. Theodore assumed the lead, opening the doors of Onkels Kirke, Eustace, and Clarence in turn. "Shame we don't have any of Robin Hood's masterful disguises."

Disguises . . . or costumes? Clara stilled in the doorway to Onkel Clive's attic, a peculiar plan beginning to form. "You've given me an idea, Mr. Theodore, and it just might work too. It would employ our individual talents and involve a great deal of absurdity. Are you willing to give it a go?"

Placing a hand on the doorframe behind her shoulder, Mr. Theodore leaned toward her so that his lopsided grin was but a breath away. "My dear Miss Stanton, I'd much rather be absurd with you than normal with anyone else."

Whenever Clara had envisioned growing old with someone, she'd assumed Mr. Forrester would be the one at her side as the years whittled wrinkles along their features. Never would she have thought it possible to grow old with Mr. Theodore in the course of one hour.

Backstage at the Opéra de Strasbourg, Clara sat before a dressing table, transfixed by the elderly woman staring back at her in its oval mirror. She stared in wonder at the crow's feet roosting along her eyes, the laugh lines around her mouth, the tinge of gray in her hair. She touched the lace collar around her neck, the only adornment on her borrowed day dress of white cotton printed with a simple design of tiny lilac blossoms. A sheer lace bonnet adorned with a sprig of lilac completed the disguise. Though twenty years out of fashion, the unassuming ensemble was most becoming and, more importantly, quite transformative.

When she'd recalled reading about the Grande Île's Opéra de Strasbourg, Clara had been hopeful that Mr. Theodore's amiable way with people might persuade someone at the theater to lend them some costumes, but she'd never imagined they'd happen upon a veritable illusionist in the form of a doe-eyed actress on her way to work.

Clara grasped the hands that had masterfully made her up with powder and paint and deftly altered her figure with padding and pins. "*Merci beaucoup* for lending us your talents, Miss Laurent."

"Call me Jacqueline, and the pleasure was all mine." With a flourish, Jacqueline flicked luxuriant chestnut curls over the shoulder of her dressing gown and curtseyed low. "After all my years on the stage, taking part in your delightful *opéra comique* is perhaps my greatest theatrical accomplishment. For who has seen such a show? Carousel horses come to life. Feral foxes romping through a cathedral. Each scene is rife with surprises."

Was that what she was living in, an opéra comique? Here she'd always thought it a comedy of errors. "How did you know the carousel horse was us?"

Jacqueline arched a sophisticated brow. "Please, *ma cherie*. I've seen many peculiar people come through this city, but your troupe has broken the mold for the eccentric."

"And without a single regret." An elderly man strode toward them in an old-fashioned walking suit composed of dove gray frock coat and checked black trousers. He wore one black oxford and one metal prosthetic boot, which had been disguised with a coat of black shoe polish. His graying beard was trimmed and stately. A monocle dignified his face, its silk cord draping to a button on his waistcoat, and a top hat crowned his head.

My, but he'd aged well. Clara removed a fan from her pocket and put it to use. "Have you upheld our end of the bargain, Mr. Theodore?" The one he'd effortlessly arranged.

Mr. Theodore gave a gold-topped cane a jaunty twirl. "Every chore's been ticked off my list. Wobbly costume rack unwobbled. Rusted hinges on the prop trunks replaced with shining brass. Every timepiece in the place wound, oiled, and polished, and I've outfitted your dressing room with a new lock, Miss Laurent, so you'll not be troubled by unsolicited theater patrons."

A smile bloomed on Jacqueline's rosy lips. "*Excellente!* Now, you best be off before the managers arrive and catch us at our fun. They're not as obliging as I am. I'll keep your things in my dressing room, and when your performance is concluded, you may come back for them and return the costumes. I'll be waiting to let you in the theater's back door."

"Right-oh. Until then, we bid you *adieu*, Miss Laurent." Turning from Jacqueline's rouge-enhanced blush, Mr. Theodore placed Clara's arm in the crook of his elbow and together they departed the opera house, exiting stage right.

A gossamer curtain of indigo clouds lowered over the city, drawing the day's final act to an end. Shopkeepers latched doors and pedestrians dwindled in number as a lamplighter made his rounds along the winding streets. Arm in arm, Clara and Mr. Theodore assumed a leisurely pace. Reveling in their role of an old married couple, they reminisced about an imagined courtship and laughed over the antics of twelve fictionalized children. Engaged in their pretend world, she could almost forget the lingering threat of Mr. Forrester's pursuit.

Almost forget to be afraid.

As they approached the cathedral, the sun's fading hues of amber, coral, and crimson illuminated the silhouette of its gothic spire. To think, if the day had gone according to plan, she might never have beheld this unique wonderment. Might never have experienced such pleasant company and delightfully absurd conversation.

"My dear Miss Stanton, I'd much rather be absurd with you than normal with anyone else." Never had a sentence made her glow with such ridiculous pleasure. Never had a remark embraced her with such warmth of camaraderie. Never had someone, beyond the framework of immediate family, known her so well and accepted her so completely. Clara peered up at the man on her arm. Dear Mr. Theodore, how had she ever got on without his friendship?

A pair of uniformed figures flanked either side of the cathedral's main doors. Gooseflesh pricked Clara's arms beneath the fitted sleeves of her borrowed dress. Would their disguises prove effective? Mr. Theodore tipped his top hat in a silent greeting. The policemen responded with a cordial nod and allowed them to pass unhindered.

Mr. Theodore opened one of the cathedral's double doors and bowed at the waist. "After you, my dear."

As Clara preceded him into the cathedral, her discarded arm suddenly felt quite cold and forlorn. She hastened into the candlelit nave, boots clacking a stern reprimand. *Just friends. Just friends. Just . . . no use.* Despite her best attempts, she could no longer deny her burgeoning feelings toward Theodore. So she wouldn't.

I have feelings for Theodore.

There. Her feelings had been acknowledged and could now be expelled.

For feelings, she'd learned, were naught but drunken guests with skewed judgment and boisterous laughter that made merry at your expense and left a disastrous mess come the sobriety of dawn. The only way to deal with them was to admit their presence, escort them to the street, and bar the door. Firmly. Now that she'd done so, she could resume enjoying *Mr.* Theodore's company without fear of succumbing to romantic inebriation.

Clara made her way to the right transept. This was agreed to be the most logical place to search for Grand's next clue. For what better place to hide an automaton in Strasbourg Cathedral than near an astronomical clock inhabited by numerous automated figures?

Before the collective craftsmanship of painters and technicians, clockmakers and sculptors, Clara was struck breathless. Moonlight streamed through a stained-glass window behind the clock's turret, towering sixty feet above her, whilst flickering light from surrounding candelabras glinted off the lavish gold leaf. To the right, a spiral staircase accessed the clock's various levels. The orrery. The twelve-hour clock flanked by cherubs. The twenty-four-hour calendar dial. Yet the clock's defining feature lay at its base, behind a pair of glass panels labeled in golden lettering. *Comput ecclesiastique. Equations solaires & lunaires.*

Mr. Theodore drew nigh with a clank and an awed gasp. "Is that—"

"Schwilgué's perpetual mechanical Gregorian computes." Clara couldn't help but smirk at the childlike glee of the septuagenarian at her side. "I thought that might attract your gaze." She couldn't imagine the unique mechanism's display of turning gears and whirring thingamajigs failing to captivate anyone, least of all a tinker-heart like Mr. Theodore.

"How well you know me, madam." Mr. Theodore fixed his jade eyes upon her alone, his jaw working as though he was struggling to arrange his thoughts into satisfactory words. "We make a great team, you and I. It has made me wonder if I might—if you might . . ." He cleared his throat. "When all this is over . . . when we return to London . . . may I call on you?"

Clara's heart gave way to palpitations. Surely he didn't mean that how it sounded. "Of course we shall see each other for dinner every Sunday and luncheon on Wednesdays, just as before. None of us would have it otherwise, and if you attempted to renege, Mum would have a fit of the vapors. At this juncture, you are thoroughly stuck with us."

"That is a fate I've no desire to oppose." Mr. Theodore's gaze fell to his cane as a ruddy flush overtook his graying whiskers. "What I meant—what I was clumsily trying to inquire—was if I might call on you. Yourself. Alone. I mean, chaperoned, of course. But perhaps not . . . so . . . closely? So that we might feel alone. The both of us." His gaze sought hers. "Together."

Together.

The word spread brilliant warmth across Clara cheeks, turning her stomach in the most delightful and dreadful way that inspired those troublesome feelings to climb in through an unguarded window. "I . . . I think that would be—"

Watch chimes signaled a new hour, echoing through the cathedral as a distinct mechanical melody rang out in answer. Clara retreated from Mr. Theodore. Never had she been so grateful to hear that little watch chime. Without another word, they began to search for Grand's device. Hasty discovery was imperative. The devices must be rejoined and silenced before their chimes gave them away to the police outside.

Mr. Theodore veered left while she went right. There. Something stirred by the statue of a griffin. Dashing up the spiral staircase, she reached the griffin figure and found an automaton bear cub climbing down the clock casing as though it were a tree trunk. She leaned forward and, with the tips of her fingers, grasped the bear by the back paw.

"*Arrête, voleur!*"

The command rattled Clara as she raced down the stairs, clutching the little bear to her chest. The familiar pounding of police boots grew louder. Drew closer.

Leaping from the final step, Clara reached for Mr. Theodore's outstretched hand.

CHAPTER 29

Tell me, ducky. Did growing old alongside a strapping, amiable, charming man ring any notions of wedding bells?" Mum raised a sixth cup of tea to her lips, arching a puckish brow over the porcelain. "Ding-dong, ding-dong." The clangor drowned in a slurp of equal subtlety.

Ding-dong was an apt description of Mum when she was giddy on caffeine. Clara shot a glare at the overcast sky, which tilted a lacy parasol of clouds over the sun's face and denied her a scapegoat for her reddened cheeks. That traitorous blush proved irrefutably that the feelings she'd tried to evict had never truly left. "I enjoyed our little adventure, but that's all, Mother. No bells. No ringing." Except for his terrifying question still pealing in her ears.

The one she'd never answered.

Mum lowered her cup and saucer to the table with an emphatic clatter. "Do you mean to tell me you were out until two o'clock in the morning, and you didn't even kiss the boy?"

"Mother!" The blush burst into flames, scorching Clara from the tips of her ears to the nape of her neck. She glanced at the people strolling by their table outside the Gingerbread Gnome Inn. Was this private discussion to be shared with all of Strasbourg? "I told you. After retrieving Grand's device from the cathedral, we had to outrun the policemen, return the costumes to the opera house, have Jacqueline assist us in ridding our faces of all that paint, and walk back to the hotel to fetch you before switching locations to keep a certain prowler off our tail. It took time."

"Time spent alone with a strapping, amiable, charming man." Mum sighed. "Time wasted, so it seems."

"Would you have preferred that I ruined myself like some trollop?"

A childish pout scrunched Mum's mouth. "Of course not, but you might've at least heard a few bells."

"Do you want to be rid of me so badly?"

Mum cupped a gloved hand to Clara's face. "I want to see my daughter freed from the belief that her father, mother, and grandfather are children she must look after. You should feel free to build a life, a family of your own."

A tremor unsettled Clara's jaw. "What if that's not what I want?"

"In that case, I'll gladly keep you till my ears are shot and wrinkles outnumber the hairs on my head." Mum held up the broken compass dangling from Clara's chatelaine. "But please, child, don't let your life be navigated by fear."

The door of the half-timbered inn opened, unleashing the warm aroma of ginger and cinnamon as Mr. Theodore stepped outside, flaxen hair still wavy and rumpled from slumber. Broad shoulders filling out every stitch of his patched overcoat. Clara's heart stumbled a few beats. Snatching the fan on her chatelaine, she created a breeze before her face, which must surely match the color of the gingerbread on her plate—little hearts dipped in red icing. Perhaps she shouldn't have let Mum select the biscuits.

Mr. Theodore took a seat beside her, propping his crutch against the table. "Top of the afternoon, ladies. Is this to be our last day in Strasbourg?"

Considering the fantastical renown they'd garnered in the city, that might be for the best. "I thought we ought to wait for you and make that discovery together." Clara patted the journal in her pocket, where Grand's clue remained unread.

Mr. Theodore unfurled a smile. "You did, eh?"

"It seemed the polite thing." Clara evaded his mesmerizing eyes only to be confronted with a knowing look from Mum. She flicked her fan closed and passed the inn's menu to Mr. Theodore. "Do order yourself a biscuit, sir. I recommend the gnome in the green cap. The hearts, I'm afraid, have far too much icing."

Mr. Theodore requested another pot of tea and, against her advice, a plate of the soft ginger hearts. For, as it so happened, he was in favor of superfluous icing. As their party reveled in the practice of afternoon tea, they discussed the rapid growth of their three dear kits, hypothesized about where Grand's scavenger hunt might lead them next, and squabbled with Mum over how many cups of tea constituted an insalubrious caffeine dependency.

In the midst of this debate, a wheat stalk of a man strolled up the cobbled road, pushing a dingy pram, as an accordion bounced upon his slight back. Stopping before the inn, he deposited his cap on the ground.

Mum clapped eagerly. "A musical performance! How delightful! Perhaps I ought to fetch the children?"

And risk someone identifying them as the crazy tourists featured in today's paper? Clara shook her head. "You're not to take those naughty children anywhere until we have them fitted with leashes."

A passing couple speared her with looks of horror and quickened their pace.

Clara bit her tongue. They understood English. *Perfect.*

Rising from her chair, Mum crept toward the inn at a snail's pace, as though slowness might render her unseen.

Mr. Theodore obstructed her path. "Now, now, Mrs. S. You know the kits are safer in your room under Fred's attentive care, so just sit yourself down. Right-oh, just so. I'm sure the little nippers will be able to enjoy the music well enough from their window. Besides, what if this musician has a dancing monkey in that pram? Why, it might cause a territorial tiff and result in injury to one of the furry youngsters. You wouldn't want that, eh?"

Mum rotated sulkily in her seat to take in the forthcoming concert. "I hope the music man does have a monkey, providing it's well cared for and treated as an equal business partner."

Clara bit back a laugh. Mr. Theodore did the same, a fist pressed to his mouth.

She offered a grateful smile, which he answered with a wink. My, how the man's green eyes could dazzle. Quickly, Clara averted her gaze, lest her complexion catch fire.

The lanky musician swung his accordion around to the front of his chest and proceeded to tune the instrument, subjecting them to a dissonance of sweet and sour notes. Once satisfied, he reached into the pram and pulled out a turtle.

Clara blinked. Yet the bizarre sight did not alter. Not as the man placed the turtle on the ground beside his cap. Nor when he began to play a mournful dirge. The accordion wheezed as it contracted and expanded, each bellowing movement a woeful cry for help. All the while, the turtle stared straight ahead, unblinking. Resigned to its pitiful lot in life.

Mr. Theodore whispered in her ear. "I've a feeling that poor bloke wasn't hugged as a child."

"I've a feeling that poor turtle isn't an equal business partner."

As the accordion continued its inconsolable lament, pedestrians hastened to escape the sound of melancholy, dashing by without dropping a single coin in the musician's forlorn cap. Mum's slackened jaw began to quiver, as though she might take to weeping. The funerary song concluded at last, only to be proceeded by the sorrowful opening notes of Thomas Moore's "The Last Rose of Summer."

"No wonder the chap's thin as a sixpence. He hasn't a clue how to sing for his supper." Mr. Theodore sprung from his seat, leaving his crutch idle at the table. When he approached the musician, the accordion's heart-wrenching ballad ended in time to spare the rose's lovely companions from fading.

After a brief conversation between the two, the musician began to play quite a different tune, the ever-popular "Sir Roger de Coverley." As the notes of the sprightly jig pranced through the air, Mr. Theodore offered encouragement by clapping in time and tapping his metal boot on the cobbles.

A young couple strolled toward the inn. Grabbing the lady's hand, Mr. Theodore gave her a twirl and sent her spinning into the arms of her beau. The couple laughed, and the beau dropped a coin in the musician's cap before sweeping his lady off her feet into a merry dance. One by one, passersby slowed and lingered. Danced and laughed. Coins fell from every hand, clinking into the cap. Mr. Theodore even directed a group of children to link hands and skip rings around the lonesome turtle.

Clara smiled. Never had she known anyone to rush toward a problem and find a solution with such ease. A man so eager to help everyone he could without ulterior motives. His fingers wouldn't pinch so much as a single coin from that cap. Not one. For Mr. Theodore was not only strapping, amiable, and charming. He was also kind, selfless, and noble.

Why would such a fine man ever bother with her?

As if hearing her thoughts, Mr. Theodore met her gaze. Raising a mischievous brow, he dispensed with the distance between them and drew her toward the merriment on the street.

Twirling her three times over, he took Clara into his arms and broke into a spirited dance. She struggled to follow his lead, bumping into him one moment, turning the wrong way the next, but when that lopsided grin shone her way, her missteps hardly seemed to matter. Mr. Theodore simply drew her back when she strayed. Held on when she faltered. She didn't have to keep time. She didn't have to fret about where they were going or manage the manner in which they arrived. All she had to do was follow Mr. Theodore, and somehow, that made the sun seem brighter. The music jauntier. The dance twice as exhilarating.

Clara stumbled over a raised cobble and trod on Mr. Theodore's leather boot.

He winced. "Now who's stepping on toes, Miss Stanton?"

She chuckled. "I ought to have warned you. I'm a dreadful dancer."

"Indubitably, but frank self-assessment is fair compensation for lack of grace."

She punched the hobgoblin's shoulder. "The impudence!"

"Exclaims the woman who leaves questions unanswered and carries on as though they were never asked."

The accordion concluded "Sir Roger de Coverley" with a flourish, and cheerful applause broke out on the street. Mr. Theodore brought their dance to an end, knocking Clara off-kilter with the sudden stillness that intensified the effects of their proximity. The warmth of the hand holding her right glove. The strength of the arm encircling her waist. Neither of which seemed inclined to let go. "You never did answer my inquiry last night, Miss Stanton."

Utterly breathless, Clara grasped for words. "In my defense, I was rather busy evading the police and an irate priest spewing hellfire. Safety is a lady's priority in such situations."

The accordion struck up a romantic French folk song with a narrative of gallant knights defending damsels fair. Mr. Theodore drew Clara even closer, swaying back and forth as the music flitted on a spring breeze. He pressed his cheek to hers. "You're safe now."

Clara's heart swelled. Indeed, she'd not felt this safe in a very long time. Yet could it last? Mr. Theodore might be the very best of men, but he was still a man and love still fraught with the risk of being hurt.

"May I, Clara? May I call on you when we return to London?"

Oh, Theodore. She pursed her lips. How was she to respond when her heart and mind were so conflicted? As they swayed to the music, her gaze wandered the street, searching for an answer amid the cobbles. A flash of yellow in the distance raised gooseflesh.

"You're trembling." Mr. Theodore held her at arm's length and searched her face, brows drawn. "What's wrong?"

He was back. Why did the man keep coming back? Clara swallowed but was unable to dislodge the dread constricting her throat. Unable to voice her former fiancé's name, she made a discreet gesture toward the garish yellow waistcoat lurking beneath a lamppost on the street corner. Toward the man watching them with unnerving intent.

Mr. Theodore's fingers tightened around her arms. His voice edged the closest it had ever come to fierce. "This ends now." He bolted down the street, and in turn, Rupert Forrester fled like the yellow-bellied coward she knew him to be.

Clara grasped the dented compass on her chatelaine. Why couldn't Mr. Forrester just leave her be? Hadn't he done enough damage? Caused enough heartache? *God, I cannot bear any more heartache.*

Mum.

She must take Mum to their room and lock the door.

Turning on a heel, Clara faced Mum just as a mammoth man broke a teapot over her head. Stunned by the violent commotion, the accordion player fainted dead away.

As Mum crumpled to the ground, a canvas bag slammed over Clara's head, muffling the sound of her cries.

Where had that yellow-toothed rat skittered off to? Theodore skidded to a halt at an intersection, keen to pounce on any flash of yellow. One that was not to be found. Rust and rot.

His fingers curled into fists, knuckles cracking. *I know vengeance belongs to you, Lord, but this once, couldn't you have used me as your willing vessel? Did you have to let the vermin escape?*

Better question: Why did Rupert the Rat Forrester have to appear at that precise moment? Right when Miss Stanton was comfortably nestled in his arms, considering his plea to remain with him forever. All right, so he hadn't mentioned *forever* exactly. That was going to be a secondary conversation, assuming his request of courtship was accepted. But it was what he wanted. More than anything, he wanted to marry Miss Stanton and give her the life she deserved. In that precise moment, when she'd looked at him with gleaming silver eyes—as if he were worthy of that honor—he'd begun to believe such a thing might be possible.

That she just might have him.

Unclenching his fists, Theodore turned back the way he'd come. He needed to ensure the Stantons' safety. The rat's extermination would have to wait. For now.

As Theodore neared the Gingerbread Gnome, an unearthly stillness pervaded the atmosphere. Gone was the music. Gone was the laughter. Turning the corner, he found the inn's outdoor dining area deserted and the street vacated. Except for the lone figure of a woman slumped on the ground, clutching a turtle to her chest.

Mrs. S.

Theodore rushed through overturned tables and scattered chairs. Kicking aside trampled gingerbread and shards of porcelain, he knelt by the dear woman who felt more like a mother every day. The woman whose crushed bonnet hung from her neck by limp ribbons. Whose hair was now matted with blood. *What the deuce happened in my absence?* Where was Clara?

He took a breath. One thing at a time. Assess the wounded. Then gather information about Miss Stanton's whereabouts.

He placed a hand on Mrs. Stanton's shoulder. "Are you able to stand?"

Unblinking, Mrs. S. remained still as death. "He just ran. They all just ran . . . ran away . . . and left us."

Theodore's heart caved in on itself. *Oh, God, what have I done?* His hand retreated. Raked through his hair. He should've taken more precautions when that rat scuttled out from the gutter. Confirmed the women were safe before giving chase. A blackened coal of regret clogged his throat, reducing his words to ashes. "I'm sorry, Mrs. S. I never should've left you alone."

"Alone." A shudder disturbed Mrs. Stanton's petite frame. "What sort of monster abandons their turtle in the street?"

Exactly how severe was her head wound? He inspected

the injury on the back of Mrs. Stanton's cranium, but dark hair matted with blood obscured his view. He withdrew a clean handkerchief from a pocket and searched for water. After locating a pitcher on the table farthest from Mrs. S., he returned to attend his patient. She remained silent as he wiped away the mess of sticky scarlet, but every now and then, she'd stroke the turtle's shell and shudder.

Once her scalp was clean, Theodore resumed his examination. The wound was shorter than the pad of his thumb. A jagged abrasion. Thankfully, no deeper than the edge of his fingernail. The broken china surrounding Mrs. S. made sense now. She'd been hit over the head, but by whom? And why?

Might the same brute have taken Clara?

Theodore laid aside the pitcher and soiled handkerchief. He needed to get Mrs. S. out of the street and squared away in her bed. That's what Miss Stanton would wish him to do above all else. Take care of her mum. Now, how to get Mrs. S. to her feet without exacerbating her state of shock? "Does your turtle friend have a name?"

Not a word. Not a flicker of recognition.

God, help me get through to her. "I bet the timid fellow would be more inclined to peer out of his shell if he felt safe. Why don't we convey him to your room, let him take shelter there?"

The dazed expression dissipated from her eyes as she met his gaze at last. "Excellent idea, my boy. I'm sure the little dear would feel much safer in the chamber pot. The porcelain appeared quite solid. 'Twas twice fired, I believe. Chamber pots that've been twice fired are less prone to cracks, you know."

A smile eased the tension gripping his face. "That is most reassuring."

Theodore provided her a steady arm as they ascended the inn's narrow stairwell. Once secure in her room, Mrs. S. placed the timid turtle in the perfectly clean, twice-fired chamber pot. He settled her in bed, propped with many a pillow, and placed the chamber pot on a bedside table so the turtle was in her sights. Fred and the kits leapt on the bed, nestling around Mrs. S. tenderly, as if sensing she was unwell.

Pledging to return swiftly, Theodore raced downstairs to the kitchens. His abrupt entry startled two women he presumed to be cook and maid. From them he procured a cold compress and poultice, but unfortunately, no answers. Neither had witnessed the attack, and according to the ruddy cook, those who had were likely long gone or scared silent, but the soft-spoken maid reassured him there was no need to worry as the police were even now being summoned.

He only hoped said police were inclined to forgive the fox debacle in light of Miss Stanton's disappearance. Surely they'd agree her safety was all that mattered now.

After treating Mrs. S. with the poultice and placing the cold compress upon her head, Theodore sat at her bedside, leather boot tapping wooden planks as he awaited the police. With each passing second, Miss Stanton's absence—abduction, more likely—grew more worrisome. For what else could prevent Miss Clara Marie Stanton from tending her wounded mother? Nothing, that's what. Some brute had to have dragged her off, and that brute had to be connected to Forrester. The timing of the two events was too coincidental. Too perfect.

Too planned.

He restrained his fist from flying into the wall. Gah, he was the densest of idiots! That yellow-toothed, flea-bitten, scurvy-scummed rat was the distraction! The bait in a primed trap. One he'd gobbled up like a blind dormouse.

A hand gripped his arm like a vice.

Mrs. Stanton's eyes latched on to him with wild desperation. "You'll find her, won't you, lad? Promise me. Promise you'll bring Clara back to me unharmed?"

That was a promise he couldn't make. No matter how much

he wished otherwise. But he *could* scour the streets for Miss Stanton instead of waiting idly for help that was long in coming.

"I won't stop searching until I find your girl, Mrs. S. On *that* you have my word." Prying Mrs. Stanton's blanched fingers from his arm, Theodore placed a kiss on her hand. "Wait here with the little ones until I return . . . and pray for me. Pray for Clara."

Back on the street, Theodore found the inn's elderly proprietor surveying the toppled furniture and debris as he anticipated the return of his grandson with the authorities. Theodore paid for the damages, dipping into the savings concealed in the lining of his overcoat, and requested that a maid be sent to look after Mrs. S. in his absence.

Eyes welling with tears, the innkeeper clapped him on the back and assured him Mrs. S. would want for nothing. Then the man handed Theodore his crutch and the answers to his most pressing questions—there'd been two attackers, and the one who'd taken Miss Stanton fled westward.

Waiting be hanged!

The police could follow his lead.

Theodore raced toward the setting sun, searching for signs of a trail. Something that didn't fit in the surroundings. Something like . . . the glint of metal on a dull stone street. He bent down to investigate. It was a silver vial of smelling salts.

Smeared with blood.

Was this from Miss Stanton's chatelaine? Tucking the object into a pocket, he proceeded along the street. Forty paces ahead, another glint of silver caught his eye. A small pair of scissors. Farther down the road, another glint. A dented compass. His pulse quickened. That brilliant, beautiful woman!

Theodore ran with renewed vigor, following the glinting reflections of hope. *I'm bringing back our girl, Mrs. S. I'm bringing her home.*

CHAPTER

31

Of all the creepy-crawly criminals in the world, she would be abducted by one who reeked of putrid onions and had no sense of direction. Stifled by a sack secured around her neck with firmly knotted ropes, Clara's lungs ached for fresh air. Blood pounded in her ears due to hanging upside down over her abductor's shoulder like a bag of, well . . . putrid onions.

Clara clutched her head, trying to massage her temples through the grating burlap. "For the fifth time, sir. If you'd simply disclose where you wish to convey me—against my will—I could, perhaps, provide you with concise directions to get us there faster." Anything to get her feet back on the ground and her face far, far away from this ogre's stinky personage.

Her body swung from side to side. *Oh bother, here we go again.*

The ogre turned this way, then that way, groaning with indecision. His thick accent gave him away as a cockney, born under the sound of Bow Bells in London's East End. "The boss is gonna murder me, for sure and certain. But I told 'im! I told 'im not to take this job. Plain and straight, I said, 'Boss, there ain't no way I'll recall me way 'round these foreign parts.' But did 'e listen? Not on your life. Just tosses the bag in me face and barks 'is orders. 'Grab the skirt, run fast, and bring the skirt back 'ere.' So I grabbed and I ran and now I'm lost just like I said. 'Ow can I bring the skirt back 'ere when I can't recall where 'ere is?"

If Clara's olfactory senses weren't dying an agonizing death, she *might* feel a smidge of compassion for the stupid ogre, but said smidge would quickly be quashed by the fact that his accomplice had struck her mother. Her stomach roiled. She needed to get back to Mum. Now.

Once more, she attempted to pry herself from the ogre's grasp, pushing against his meaty arm and kicking his chest, but to no avail. Her might was no match for his brawn.

With a sigh, Clara let her body hang limp. What else could she do? She'd screamed until her throat was parched. No one seemed to hear. No one came to her aid. Perhaps the lightheadedness was getting to her, but helping the ogre seemed her only recourse. Topsy-turvy though it might be. "Did your boss give you a map of the city, perchance? Some written directions to your lair of iniquity?"

"Not on your life." The ogre stomped a boot. "I told the boss 'e ought. I told 'im, 'Boss, I'd like to 'ave me a map for when I can't recall me way.' But did 'e listen? Not—"

"On your life. Right." Clara bit her lip even as it trembled. The breadcrumbs she'd dropped for Mr. Theodore were going to prove utterly useless after all the ogre's wandering. She reached for her chatelaine, reexamining the end of each chain with fingers worn raw from tearing off gadgets blindly. None remained. She'd used every blessed crumb. Even if she could guide the ogre to his destination, she'd nothing left to correct Mr. Theodore's course. How would he find her now?

The clip-clopping of hooves and clatter of rolling wheels

stilled Clara's heart. Someone was coming their way. Perhaps a rescue was still possible. The horse and cart grew louder. Drawing ever closer. She wet her lips, readying a scream.

"Chester, where in blazes 'ave ya been?"

The recognition in the man's voice froze the scream in Clara's lungs.

"I don't rightly know, boss. That's the problem of it." The ogre shrugged, jostling her stomach. "Told you I'd get lost. All these streets look the same, and I can't make out any of them signs."

The horse and cart went silent. Boots smacked the ground. "I'll 'ear none of your excuses." A slap rent the air.

The ogre yipped like a whipped dog, and his arm withdrew from her waist.

Clara slipped from his shoulder and hit the ground. Hard. The wind was knocked from her lungs, and pain exploded in her left shoulder. She gasped, rolling onto her back with a moan. Up. She needed to get—

"Now ya gone and done it, Chester. 'Ow do ya expect to collect our pay if she's damaged?"

Clara was yanked to her feet and clutched against the rotund body of the ogre overlord, who smelt of pipe tobacco and cheap wine. She willed her body to cease throbbing. Her head to stop spinning. *You are not to faint, Clara Marie. You will fight.* Dredging the last of her strength, she dug her nails into a coarse shirt and rammed her knee upward.

A high-pitched whimper proved she'd struck true.

"That was for Mum, you cowardly cur." Shoving the sniveling overlord aside, she staggered off in the dark, clawing at the burlap sack's knotted ropes.

The overlord's groans blackened to a growl. "Idiot! She was 'posed to be out cold."

"I told you, boss. I said, 'Boss, 'tain't right to use chloryfoam on a skirt.' But did you listen? Not on your—"

"Bring 'er back!"

Run. Clara shoved her hands in front of her, breaking into a haphazard dash.

Arms clamped around her waist, hefting her off the ground.

No, no, no! Screaming with all her might, Clara thrashed and kicked and clawed, but the arms only squeezed all the tighter. She wasn't fast enough. Wasn't strong enough.

"Get over 'ere quick, so I can shut 'er up."

The burlap sack smashed into Clara's face, drenching her senses in a sweet aroma that weakened her knees. Doused her will to fight.

Overpowered, overwhelmed, overcome, she sank into the darkness.

Clara awoke to blessed air caressing her face. Air cool, fresh, and perfumed with orange blossoms. Perhaps she might pick a few flowers to tuck in her bonnet. She strained to lift her head. Why was it so heavy? Her eyes fluttered open, lashes catching on long locks. Why was her coif in disarray? She tried to brush aside the hair tickling her nose, but her arms were sore and . . . restrained. Her spine stiffened as gooseflesh prickled her skin.

She was bound to a chair.

And her favorite bonnet was gone!

With a huff, she blew a curl out of her eyes. Oh, those odious ogres would pay for this. Although, from the sound of things, someone was already giving them a tongue-lashing.

No doubt the very someone whose name sent shivers up her spine.

Don't so much as think his name, Clara. Not yet. Not until you've gotten your bearings. Blinking, she took in her surroundings. A single lantern glowed upon a rustic wooden table littered with dirt, clay pots, and a gardening trowel. She appeared to be in a potting shed, windowless and cobwebbed with neglect. Faint silver moonlight crept through gaps in the wooden boards, so evening must have fallen long ago. An assumption confirmed by an empty pang in her stomach.

On the other side of the shed door, male voices exchanged volatile whispers.

"A deal's a deal! We're 'posed to stay with ya until the machine's back in London."

The ogre overlord. The one who'd struck Mum. Clara grimaced. She hoped the coward wouldn't sit right for a month.

"Aye, Grimes told you, 'You can 'as an extension if and only if the boys tag along. There and back.' There and back, 'e said!"

And there was the ogre with half an onion for a brain.

"We would've been there and back already if it weren't for you bumbling idiots slowing me down at every turn!"

Mr. Forrester. Even in thought, the name left a bitter taste on Clara's tongue. She tried to swallow, but her mouth was too dry. Part of her had known he was in league with the ogres, but oh, how she'd wanted to be wrong.

"I'll not have another day wasted because of you lot. I'm done! Go back to London and tell Grimes he'll have his money as we agreed, but from here on out, I'm doing this my way. Alone." The latch turned, and Mr. Forrester stepped into the potting shed, the pair of ogres fast on his heels.

"Oi, ya can't be ordering us about!"

"Not on your life!"

As Mr. Forrester started to close the door, one of the ogres attempted to shove his way into the shed. Mr. Forrester whipped out a pistol and fired. The bullet burrowed into the doorjamb and scattered splinters as the ogres bolted into the night, spewing curses.

"Next time I won't miss!" Mr. Forrester slammed the door with a frustrated growl. He faced her then, dark eyes rimmed with shadows. His countenance was haggard, shoulders taut and slumped, as if he carried a heavy load. Wrinkles creased his ostentatious suit, the crown of his bowler hat had been dented, and his hair and chin whiskers were devoid of their usual gleam of pomade. But the most startling change in his appearance was the pistol in his hand.

"I'm sorry it has come to this, Clara, but you left me with no alternative." Raking a trembling hand through his hair, Mr. Forrester lowered his gaze to the ground, as if pained by the sight of her. "I hope those brutes didn't rough you up too much, and I . . . I apologize for how forcefully they handled your mum. That wasn't part of the plan, I assure you. But they're gone now. So . . . so things will be different. From now on, things will be handled on *my* terms. And if you and your mum cooperate, I promise no one else will get hurt."

The condition on that promise rendered it of little comfort. Clenching her muscles, Clara willed the tremors coursing through her veins not to give themselves away. "When did you start carrying a pistol?"

He took note of the gun in his hand, now hanging lax at his side, and heaved a ragged sigh. "When I found myself forced to travel with half-witted henchmen."

Henchmen who worked for Mr. Grimes, the unscrupulous creditor he'd brought into her home under false pretense. "Was it wise to send them back to London? I can't imagine your creditor will be—"

"Grimes was *Father's* creditor, not mine. The debt was Father's shame, not mine! I'm not the weak-willed louse who couldn't keep away from the card tables. I'm not the sorry excuse of a man who had to rely on his frail wife and young child to work his way out of debtor's prison. I'm not the one who looked his son in the eye and swore on his wife's grave to quit placing bets, only to skulk back to the gaming house. The burden of debt might've landed on my shoulders, but I'll not be held responsible for its making. And I'll not go back to that rat-infested prison where she died!"

Clara's shallow breath caught in her throat. In all the years she'd known him, Mr. Forrester had never once mentioned his dead mother, and she'd never once suspected the poor woman had perished in debtor's prison. "Why did you never tell me any of this?"

"And have you pity me? I think not."

"What shame is there in pity? There's no disgrace in sharing your pain with another and receiving their sympathy and comfort."

"You want to hear my painful story, Clara?" Returning the weapon to the inside of his tailored jacket, Mr. Forrester crossed his arms as if to brace himself. "My father inherited Forrester Freight from my grandfather. The business was established and profitable. All my father had to do was maintain what he'd been given, and we'd have enjoyed a prosperous, comfortable life. But my father was an ungrateful, selfish man with a secret addiction to placing bets. When father's gambling debts accrued to a sum beyond his ability to pay, his creditor had him thrown in debtor's prison."

Mr. Forrester's tone dripped with caustic derision. "Since you're so fortunate as to know nothing of that institution, Miss Stanton, I'll explain how it works. People sent to debtor's prison are incarcerated until such time as they can pay their debt or reach a new agreement with their creditor. But paying said debt is made more difficult by the requirement for inmates to pay the prison for their keep—or what constitutes as keep in those places." The slightest of trembles unsettled his rigid frame. "Many inmates don't survive the dampness, the vermin and squalor."

Clearing his throat, Mr. Forrester took to pacing the shed's limited confines. "Father's creditor refused a more lenient agreement. Father's acquaintances, having lost all respect for him, refused to give him a shilling. And despite my mother's pleas, Father refused to sell some of our ships to pay the debt.

He was determined to retain the company's physical assets so he'd have a means of starting over once he 'got back on his feet.' Therefore, the burden of debt fell on me and my mother to shoulder. I was but five years old. At night, we resided in the prison with Father, and during the day, we were forced to take up grueling forms of employment to work off the debt. A feat we eventually accomplished . . . though Mother did not live to see us walk out the prison doors for the last time."

Clara's jaw hung slack. No wonder he'd been such a serious lad when they'd first met. At fifteen, her Buccaneer Bill had already lived through a lifetime of suffering.

Pausing before the wooden table, Mr. Forrester clenched his fists. The lantern's meager flame haunted his face with shifting shadows. "The worst part of my story is that my father learnt nothing from his mistakes and the pain they caused. After we worked so hard to rebuild our lives, he went right back to his addiction and his lies and destroyed everything all over again. And once again, it's left to me to shoulder the consequences. Only this time, I must do it alone."

A pang for the young boy of five ached in Clara's chest, wrestling with the anger she felt toward the man who even now held her captive. "Oh, Rupert . . . why didn't you tell me all this from the first? Papa might've helped you."

"You always were naïve. The consequence of a sheltered childhood, I suppose." Mr. Forrester sighed and faced her, shaking his head as though despairing of her utter ignorance. "Allow me to educate you once again on the way of the world, Miss Stanton. Depending on someone else—anyone else—is insane. A man has to help himself. To keep the skin on his back by any means necessary."

Any means necessary? A chill crept down her spine, raising gooseflesh. "Why have you brought me here?"

Mr. Forrester's voice was eerily matter-of-fact. "To bait an owl trap."

O f all the low-life criminals in the world, Miss Stanton would get snatched by one who was skilled at evasive maneuvers and possessed a keen sense of direction.

Sweat matted hair to Theodore's brow, now taut and furrowed. His good foot ached, and his stump of a knee chafed against his automaton prosthetic. Yet he trudged forward. On the quiet streets of Strasbourg, he trudged and begrudged the sun for giving up on the day. He trudged and begrudged the people in the shops for barring their doors and settling down for a peaceful night's slumber. But mostly, he begrudged his own stupid self for losing Miss Stanton's trail.

Hours upon hours ago, the search had commenced with promise. Theodore had been joined by uniformed officers within the first fifteen minutes. A few had recognized him from the fox incident, but they'd reassured him the matter wouldn't be pursued further as the priests had elected not to press charges. Miss Stanton's safe return was their sole priority. Heartened by the metal breadcrumbs he'd found, the

policemen had rallied to his aid. Banging on doors. Questioning possible witnesses. Scrutinizing the cobbles for glints of
metal in the waning light.

Theodore dug his nails into his crutch. They'd been so close!
He'd felt it in his marrow. Then, without reason or rhyme, the
metal breadcrumbs had started to twist and turn until the
trail had gone cold. The braggart who'd taken Miss Stanton
must know the city like the warts on his face. When night had
descended like a candlesnuffer, the uniformed brotherhood
had remained undaunted. With lanterns alight and torches
ablaze, the police had continued their search, advancing farther and farther ahead of him on legs hale and hearty.

Now Theodore trudged alone. Unable to keep up but determined to keep his word. *"I won't stop searching until I find
your girl, Mrs. S."*

You shouldn't have lost her in the first place.

He ground his teeth. If only he'd thought the situation
through . . . if only he hadn't fallen for Forrester's baited trap,
none of this would've happened. Mrs. S. wouldn't have been
hurt. Miss Stanton wouldn't have been abducted by some
dirty-handed miscreant.

You're the one with dirty hands.

Slumping against a glowing lamppost, Theodore stared at
his work-worn hands. At the names carved into his crutch.
How had he started to believe that he was good enough for
Clara? He didn't deserve such a blessing. After all, he was
dead. What could he possibly offer her? He couldn't even
manage to rescue her. A lump clogged his throat. No, he must
keep trying. Keep searching. For he'd not return to the inn
and tell Mrs. S. that he'd failed.

Again.

Theodore shifted his weight to the crutch and forced himself to trudge along. In the distance, the moon outlined the
city's great cathedral. He never should've stepped foot in that

hallowed place. No matter how the Stanton women tried to persuade him otherwise, he knew. God could never—would never—welcome him home.

The crutch lodged in the cobbles and jerked with a sickening snap. He lurched forward, unable to stop the momentum, and cold stone punched the breath from his lungs. His breath returned in a gasp that became a moan. With great effort, he sat up and examined himself for serious injuries. A scrape here. A scuff there. No broken bones, but there would be aches and bruises for days. Weeks.

Too exhausted to stand, he crawled out of the street, dragging his crutch along. He crumpled against the cathedral's northern wall and glared at the crutch. The wood was nearly cracked in half. Broken and useless.

Like him.

Theodore tightened his grasp on the shattered crutch until splinters dug into his palm. Why did he always have to muck things up? Why couldn't he just do what was expected of him? Perform like he was expected to perform. Protect who he was supposed to protect. Why did everything he touch have to die?

"I'd trade your life in a second if it would restore the life of my Theodora."

"Shut up!" The shout pried itself through clenched teeth. Theodore pressed his head against the wall of sandstone, long since cooled by the dark of night, and willed the cold to numb him through. His heavy eyelids closed. Just for a moment. Only a moment.

And he was back on the battlefield.

And it was far too quiet. Unnaturally dark too. As though the sun, moon, and stars had never existed, and light had never been experienced by man. By him. What did sunlight feel like? He couldn't remember.

"Mr. Theodore, where are you?"

Flickering candle in hand, Clara searched for him among the fallen. Theodore wanted to run to her but refrained. He needed to stay far away and protect her from what was coming. Anyone close to him would die.

Clara spotted him and smiled. "There you are, Mr. Theodore. Come. Share my candle."

Theodore staggered back as she drew near. "Get out of here, Clara. It's not safe."

"You'll protect me. I believe in you."

How he wanted her to be right. Theodore grasped for her hand as a cannon blast snuffed the candle's flame. Darkness snatched Clara from him. Flailing, he crumpled into the mire. Crippled once again. The pain he remembered all too well coursed through his stub of a knee, but this time, it seemed numb compared to the gut punch of loss.

No, no. He couldn't lose her too. Not his Clara. He had to get her back. He had to find her! Theodore floundered through the mud, his useless stump trailing behind as he clawed, grasped, searched. He laid hold of her candle and clutched it, despite the hot wax searing his hand. This proved Clara was nearby. She just had to be.

Theodore dragged himself forward and slipped headlong into a pit. Landed on Turkish carpet.

He was back at Kingsley Court.

A fire crackled in the hearth, but Theodore couldn't feel its warmth. Sprawled on the floor, bloodied and encrusted in mud, all he could feel was the weight of shame gripping the back of his neck. Holding his face down to the plush carpet. Smothering him with the sight of the stains he'd left on the intricate pattern of crimson vines and golden birds.

A pair of polished shoes came into view, reflecting the firelight. Theodore gritted his jaw, attempting to squelch the tremors writhing through him body and soul. Father was going to be so angry. He shut his eyes, unable to bear the disappointment, the disgust that was sure to come. Not again.

"Lift your head, dear boy."

Theodore's eyes flashed open, still an inch from the dirtied carpet. That voice—those words—could not belong to his father. Who was with him now? Wearing Father's shoes?

"Son, I can't tend your wounds if you won't meet my gaze." The man knelt, resting his pressed trousers in the muck that dripped from Theodore's hair. Fingers warm and calloused took his chin and tapped three times. "All will be well. Just lift your head."

Theodore pushed against the carpet, against the weight, to sit upright. The broken crutch lay across his lap just above his tattered uniform and bloodied knee. Though he wished to meet the man's gaze, he could only stare at the pristine trousers kneeling in the mess of his making. "I'm s-sorry."

"Why?"

"For tracking in all this filth."

There was a smile in the man's voice. "Anything that can be made filthy can be made clean again." He produced a bowl of water and a rag and proceeded to bathe what was left of Theodore's leg.

How could this man bear to touch him? To look at him?

Once he'd been thoroughly cleansed, the man bound his wounded leg with gauze and pointed toward the crutch. "You don't need that anymore."

"But it is mine to carry."

"Who told you it was yours to carry? I didn't. I would never burden you with something so heavy and useless. Give it to me, and I'll give you something in exchange."

Who would offer to trade for something ugly and useless? Not an ordinary man.

At last, Theodore met the man's eyes, which seemed to be composed of every possible color, aglow with the most impossible light. Yet the radiance was not blinding. It was inviting. Loving.

A tear slicked down Theodore's cheek, and he placed the crutch in the man's outstretched hand. When the shattered wood came to rest in his weathered palm, the crutch was set aflame and glowed like a burning coal.

Theodore blinked, and the glow dimmed.

The crutch vanished.

In its place sat a golden crown fitted with bloodred rubies.

Raising the crown aloft, the man waited with a smile that beckoned Theodore to draw closer. "Come, son. Let me put it on you."

Theodore shook his head. "I'm not worthy of such a gift."

"I didn't ask you to be worthy. I asked you to *come*."

Theodore bowed his head, shedding tears as the crown settled upon his brow.

Lifting Theodore's chin, the man looked on him without disgust. "Never let anything keep you from coming to Me. I will always claim you as My child. I will always love you. You can depend on that. You can depend on Me."

Theodore awoke to the gentle warmth of morning light.

A yawn stretched his lips as he arched his back. He rubbed his palm across his eyes, which felt oddly . . . rested. Clear. The sun crested the rooftops, gracing Strasbourg with another day. He reveled in a deep cleansing breath. He couldn't remember the last time he'd awakened like this—without the skittering spider legs of terror crawling along his skin. Without unshakable cobwebs of fatigue clinging to his mind. To awaken well rested in the arms of peace . . . was a miracle.

You can depend on Me.

The words echoed in Theodore's spirit, vibrating with the power of a solemn promise. Tears welled in his eyes even as a smile unburdened his face.

Depend on Me.

The words were a promise to lean on and a command to obey.

One he could no longer deny or ignore.

Wiping away the haze of tears, Theodore grabbed the crutch and strode toward the cathedral, steps sure and determined in what must be done. No one barred his way as he entered the main doors—confirmation he was on the right course. He proceeded down the nave to the cathedral's crossing, climbed a set of stone stairs, and stopped at the apse.

Here, Theodore knelt and laid his broken crutch at the foot of a towering wooden cross. "From now on, I pledge to lean on you and nothing else. I'll follow where you lead. Help me to keep my oath. And please . . . help me find Clara. What would you have me do?"

"A prayer so humble is sure to be heard."

Theodore found himself joined by a graying priest with a kindly countenance.

The priest smiled, creasing gentle lines around his eyes and mouth. "What is your name, my son?"

Rising to his feet, Theodore left the crutch on the ground. Left it behind, for good this time.

"Name's Kingsley. Theodore Kingsley."

Clara measured her breath, deliberate and defiant, in an effort to keep panic at bay. Remaining calm—remaining in control—was the only way she'd get through this night. The only way to protect her family from Mr. Forrester's latest plot.

"You've left me with no choice, Clara. But because I'm a reasonable man, I'm going to graciously give you two: become my wife or give me the owl machine. Either option will provide me with the means to free myself from the creditors and save my business. Then we can put all this ugliness behind us and live in peace, together or separately. The choice is yours."

The vein along Clara's right eye twitched. She blinked hard, willing it to be still. To let her think. Any choice offered by this indubitably *unreasonable* man was no choice at all.

Marriage to Mr. Forrester was an unthinkable existence, and allowing him to claim the owl as his own invention would only put her family in greater danger when the lie threatened to unravel. What was to stop Mr. Forrester from blackmailing them again to maintain his ruse? Were they to spend the rest of their lives looking over their shoulders, under constant threat?

No. She had to escape. She had to find some way out of here. Something she had yet to try.

Once again, Clara surveyed the potting shed, having adjusted to the darkness what felt like hours ago. The lantern Mr. Forrester had extinguished remained on the table. The door he'd shut and now guarded bodily remained the only point of entry. Liberating herself from the ropes had already proven useless. Her efforts only caused the ropes to burn her arms and stockinged ankles. She'd tried to reach the gardening trowel, hoping to cut through the ropes, but to no avail. Screaming had increased her thirst and summoned no aid.

A pang of emptiness gnawed her stomach. That was the long and short of it, then. All her resources had been considered and exhausted. There was nothing more to do. She couldn't break free, she couldn't escape, and her failure was putting her family in unknown peril.

"I don't want to hurt your family, but know this—if you thwart my plans again, I will do whatever I feel is necessary in order to survive. So please . . . don't try my patience. Don't make me do something I'll regret."

Tremors coursed through Clara's restrained hands. She dug her nails into the chair's wooden arms. No! She refused to accept that Mr. Forrester had won. Her hands might be tied, but she had one unaccounted-for resource. The man who'd outsmarted a pickpocket to retrieve Mum's purse. The man who'd dived into a lake to save her from drowning. Theodore wouldn't give up because night had fallen. He wouldn't give up when her breadcrumbs led in circles. He would come for her. She could depend on that. She *would* depend on him.

"Depending on someone else—anyone else—is insane."

Sudden doubt squeezed her heart. What if Mr. Theodore didn't arrive in time?

Her breaths shortened. Fragmented into shards that snagged in her chest. What if Mr. Forrester shot at Grand the way he'd shot at the creditor's henchmen? Shivers skittered up and down her arms. Her neck. Her spine. She couldn't live with that loss. She couldn't bear it.

Nor could she wait a moment longer.

Planting her boots on the floor, Clara hefted the chair upon her hunched back, straining against the ropes with all her might and bashing the chair against the table with all her main. Willing something to work. Something to break. Something to—

She lost her balance and fell on her side with a clatter.

A derisive sigh on the other side of the door mocked her pain. "Pitiful."

Mr. Forrester was right. She was pitiful. For now she was not only bound, she was exhausted and winded and lying prone on the dirt-strewn floor. Rough wood grated against her cheek. She sighed, skittering clumps of soil across the planks to collect against the wall at the left of the door. She stared at the shadowy pile of dirt. Body aching. Eyelids heavy.

Until a glint of light caught her attention.

Clara lifted her gaze, and a silvery glimmer winked at her through a knothole in the lower portion of the wall. Maiden Moonlight must be in her full splendor. Perhaps with the comfort of her company, she might not feel so woefully alone. She maneuvered closer to the wall, ignoring the pain in her limbs as she dragged the chair along, and peered into the knothole as though it were the eyepiece of a telescope.

A sob caught in her throat. Maiden Moonlight had brought along an old friend. The North Star. Ever shining, ever steadfast, Polaris illuminated the heavenly expanse with its inextinguishable promise, the one she'd clung to in childhood and tossed aside once grown. Even on the darkest of nights, even on the most perilous of journeys, there was a sovereign Lord who would lead her home—if she would only rely on the guidance of His light.

Dependence wasn't insanity. It was the posture of faith.

Clara blinked away a mist of tears. "Lord, forgive my stubbornness. I . . . I can't do this alone. I need help. I need you." The tears broke free then, unbidden and unseen in the darkness, as she clung to that pinprick of moonlight. *I need you.* The three little words unlocked a forgotten memory—or rather, a melody. One that had been sung to her on dark nights long ago when she could not sleep by a lilting voice both comforting and dearly missed. *Granny.* What were the words to her favorite song?

She licked her dry lips and tried to find them. "'I need Thy p-presence . . . every passing hour. What but Thy grace can f-foil the tempter's . . . power? Who, like Thyself, my guide and s-strength can be? Through cloud and sunshine, Lord, abide with . . . me.'"

"Abide with Me." That was the song. Clara attempted to clear her throat and started the hymn from the beginning, her voice weak and tremulous. "'Abide with me; fast falls the eventide; The darkness deepens; Lord with me abide. When other helpers fail and comforts flee, Help of the helpless, O abide with me.'"

As the song poured from her soul, Clara could almost hear Granny's harmonies and feel the warmth of her touch on her brow. Shooing away terrors, wiping away tears. Humble, wrinkled hands ministering with the love of holy, scarred ones. "'Thou on my head in early youth didst smile, And though rebellious and perverse meanwhile, Thou hast not left me, oft as I left Thee. On to the close, O Lord, abide with me.'"

Though her body remained physically weary, each verse infused her heart with new strength. Though her hands remained bound, a thin veil of unexplainable peace enveloped her mind. Though no one was nigh, a blessed assurance that she was not alone settled in her spirit. "'I fear no foe, with Thee at hand to bless; Ills have no weight, and tears no bitterness. Where is death's sting? Where, grave, thy victory? I triumph still, if Thou abide with me.'"

Clara gazed at the stars twinkling through the knothole as tears washed the grit from her face. "'Hold Thou Thy cross before my closing eyes; Shine through the gloom and point me to the skies. Heaven's morning breaks, and earth's vain shadows flee; In life, in death, O Lord—'"

The door whooshed open and slammed against the wall.

Illuminated by moonlight, Mr. Forrester's boots stomped into Clara's line of vision, and she froze. Grabbing the back of the chair, he hoisted her upward and righted the chair legs on the floor with a jarring thud. Backlit by silver, Mr. Forrester was but a shadowed silhouette, menacing and unreadable. She held her breath. What was he going to do?

"I'll untie your bonds if you'll stop singing. D-deal?" His voice broke as if unnerved.

She nodded. "Deal."

As Mr. Forrester moved to loosen the bonds, Clara detected a tremor in his hands as he fumbled with the ropes in the dark. Was he shaken by the song's meaning, or by the memory of the woman who'd treated him like a grandson? The ropes around her arms fell, and she gingerly moved her stiff limbs, rubbing feeling back into her fingers as they pricked and tingled.

After untying the ropes around her legs, Mr. Forrester rose and stood in the shed doorway. "There's water in that can under the table. I'll bring you something to eat in the morning. But you must stay silent and stay put." With that, he left and shut out the moon's light.

Clara heaved a ragged sigh. *Thank you, merciful Lord.* Sinking from the chair onto the floor, she felt about in the shadows and found the tin watering can and drank her fill. Her limbs were weak, stiff, and sore. Though she wished to flee, she couldn't overpower an armed man and make a run for it in this state. Nor was she confident she could navigate her surroundings in the dark of night. It seemed wisest to stay put and silent as she was bid. At least long enough for her to recover her strength.

Pouring some of the cool water on her hands, Clara splashed it on her face, washing away tears and dust. She reached for the extra handkerchief in her pocket, and her fingers brushed against the journal from Grand. After drying her face, she returned the handkerchief to her pocket and pulled out the journal. She made her way back to the knothole and, slumping against the wall, held Grand's last clue up to the moonlight.

Dear Little Stargazer,

As our journey draws to an end, there are a few things remaining to be said.

I know you fear losing control of your family and the flurry of circumstances that ever swirl about us, but heed my words, dear heart. You cannot lose what you never had. Control has been, and always will be, the sole property of our sovereign God. It is impossible for Him to lose it, and it can never be stolen from Him. He is now and forever more in control of our lives, and we are now and forever more held in His scarred hands, utterly dependent on His endless grace and matchless love.

Rest assured that the weight of the world is not on your shoulders, but on His. God is in control of the flurry of circumstances around us, and though you may not see evidence of it yet, He is surely working all things together for our ultimate good. He is our strength and a faithful refuge, a very present and well-proved help in trouble. He delivers in His time. He heals in His way. And not a single one of His good promises fails.

Before we make our way home, it is my prayer that you will release all white-knuckled illusions of being in control and revel in the freedom Jesus came to give you. May you rest assured that Emmanuel is God, so you don't have to be.

Bear with me as we make one fiNal stop in a place where the memory of young lOve lingers and laughteR bubbles forth like a Marvelous fountAin.

Your devoted,
Grand

Slowly, the pieces of Grand's clue came together in her mind, and Clara smiled at the utter perfection of the last location of their merry scavenger hunt. She tucked the note into her pocket and hugged the journal to her heart. *Abide with me tonight, Lord. Help me to sleep. And take care of them for me, will you? Papa, Mum, Grand . . . and Theodore. Reunite us in your way and time. Deliver me by your might and main.*

Knots unwound in Clara's shoulders as she rolled against the wall and drifted to sleep.

Now Theodore remembered why talking to God was so dashed frustrating—the Almighty had a penchant for answering him with a particularly profane four-letter word.

Wait.

The word bristled over Theodore's skin like a rough woolen blanket, each letter a prickly fiber woven into a heavy encumbrance that itched and irritated and warmed at all once. Why God would answer his prayer for a course of action with a directive to be still, he couldn't fathom. But he'd returned to the inn all the same. It was not his place to understand, but to obey. This time, things would be done His way.

Even if that four-letter word made him break out in hives.

With a haggard sigh, Theodore bolted the lock, wincing as the metal clanked into place. A glance over his shoulder reassured Mrs. S. still slept despite the disturbance. That was a mercy. The longer she slept, the longer he could avoid having to explain why he'd returned without her daughter.

He checked the compress on her head wound. The one he'd applied had been exchanged for a different cloth containing some sort of poultice. He must thank the innkeeper for tending to Mrs. S. as he'd promised. There were decent people in the world yet. Like his new friends in the Strasbourg police, who even now carried on with the search for Miss Stanton and stood guard at the inn's front door.

Curled about Mrs. Stanton's hands, Fred lifted his head and squeaked in greeting. Theodore gave the faithful ermine a scratch between the ears, shaking his head at the shy turtle still tucked in the chamber pot on the bedside table. He then sought out the fox cubs, confirming that none of the scamps had slipped out as he entered. Todd slept under the bed, Honorine slept in an open drawer, and wide-eyed Phileas dangled from a curtain rod overhead.

"Thanks for keeping watch in my absence," Theodore whispered, then he grabbed the room's lone chair and positioned it before the locked entry. He removed his leather boot and bronze prosthetic before leaning back to rest his head against the door. No rat was getting past him this time. Heaving a sigh, he closed his eyes. Now to follow His orders and wait.

Guttural snorts disturbed the morning stillness. By jove, but Mrs. S. could snore with the best of them. The noise was practically reverberating through his skull. Snort, snort, snooooor—

"Scoot, bonny boar! Root for truffles elsewhere."

A thwunk to Theodore's leg woke him with a start. Sunshine overwhelmed his eyes with brilliant white. He blinked as his eyes focused on the slight form of Mrs. S. positioned with a hand on either hip. Dark tresses streaked with gray tumbled about her shoulders. She quirked a smile. "My, lad, but you can snore with the best of them."

His huff of indignation gave way to a yawn. "I don't . . . snore."

"And I'm a chimney sweep from Liverpool." Mrs. Stanton's smile faltered and, with a wobble, fell. "Any news?"

The frailty in those small words gored the very heart of him. "We never did catch up to them last night. I . . . I returned to the inn about two hours ago, but the police assured me they'd continue to scour the city's every cobble."

Mrs. S. secured his hand and squeezed it three times. "It's a new day, son."

That it was. Theodore's jaw unclenched as he accepted the grace offered him. For today he'd not be leaning on a support carved by his own hand. *Strengthen us, Lord. Strengthen me.*

Squaring her shoulders, Mrs. S. swatted his leg. "Boots on and move out, my boy. You're keeping me from my breakfast, which is hazardous for all concerned."

"Breakfast?" Emptiness clawed at his stomach. A painful reminder he'd not eaten since afternoon tea *yesterday*. He prayed Miss Stanton wasn't as hungry as he this morn. He slipped on his boot, reattached the prosthetic to his knee, and stood with a groan. Aches stiffened his neck into a rusted axle that creaked upon rotation. Unjust punishment for his protective stance by the door. Wait . . . was someone knocking?

With him out of the way, Mrs. S. moved to open the door, but his quick hand stilled hers upon the knob. She raised a dark brow. "You stand upon a crumbling cliff ledge, son. I'm not a good Christian woman until after my tea and toast."

"Understood. Just let me verify that tea and toast are the only chaps behind this door before you go charging through it. Miss Stanton would want me to do as much."

Mrs. Stanton's bottom lip quivered, but she nodded.

Theodore pressed his ear to the door. "Identify yourself."

"It's just me, sir." A familiar voice, accented by German, came through the door. "Gretel from the kitchen, with victuals and a fresh poultice for the lady."

Cracking open the door, he confirmed the young woman was alone in the corridor.

Gretel brought in a tray of food and set it on the chest of drawers. "*Guten morgen*, Mrs. Stanton. Let's have a look at that wound." Apparently, the woman had grown accustomed to the menagerie her employer graciously chose to overlook, for she didn't bat an eye at the curious kits scampering about her feet. She just set to work.

She pulled back the bed's rumpled quilt, with its rows of hand-stitched gnomes, then fluffed the red pillows and settled them behind Mrs. S., tucking her in snugly. She then examined the back of Mrs. Stanton's head. "Bleeding stopped, and the swelling down. *Gut.* I believe you're on the mend."

After applying a fresh poultice and compress to the wound, Gretel placed the tray of food on Mrs. Stanton's lap and produced a piece of paper from her apron. "This message was left for you, *gnädige frau*."

Gooseflesh pricked Theodore's neck. Who'd know to direct a message for Mrs. Stanton to the Gingerbread Gnome in Strasbourg, France? "I'd like to see that, if I may." After getting a nod from Mrs. S., Gretel handed him the message. It was an unremarkable piece of paper, folded in half and marked with the initials *R. F.*

His muscles tightened. "Who delivered this? How did they get past the police?"

"An errand boy dropped it off, sir. Little Raoul. And as I already explained to the policemen, he is no stranger here. He brings our regular order of groceries from the market every day just before dawn, and on occasion, he delivers messages for us. Raoul said this note was to be delivered to Mrs. Stanton and no response was required. Will that be all?"

Theodore nodded, and after seeing Gretel to the door, he locked it firmly behind her. A cherub-cheeked boy known to the inn's staff made for a perfect Trojan horse. No wonder

Officers Firmin and Armand had let him through without suspicion.

Mrs. Stanton's voice wavered. "Is it from that man?"

Sitting on the end of the bed, he nodded grimly and unfolded the paper and read aloud. "'Mrs. Stanton, be advised that I have your daughter, and she is unharmed. To facilitate her swift return, please follow the subsequent instructions exactly. Any deviations or attempt to involve the police further will only make things more difficult for all concerned. Locate your father and instruct him to bring the owl machine to me in exchange for Miss Stanton. This exchange will take place in one week's time on April 28 at Port de Strasbourg on the Rhine River. I'll be waiting with Miss Stanton at a warehouse marked Alsatian Freight. Drosselmeyer is to land the owl on the warehouse roof at the stroke of midnight— alone and unarmed. If you follow these instructions, all will be well. If you try me, we will both have regrets. I'm sorry it has come to this. R. F.'"

Like acrid smoke wafting from a fired cannon, Forrester's subtle threats lingered in the air, noxious and nebulous. Theodore's hand balled into a fist, strangling the man's slanted scrawl in lieu of his ratty neck yet out of reach. Seven days. He expected them to leave Miss Stanton in his keeping for seven days? To locate Drosselmeyer in seven days? To trust the word of a known prowler and abductor to hold true for seven wretched days? *God, you cannot mean me to wait that long?*

Mrs. S. shook her head. "I don't like it."

"Neither do I."

The demand for an exchange felt suspect. There had to be another way to get Miss Stanton back. A way that didn't involve sending Drosselmeyer into a dark rathole. Theodore propped his brow on the fist still crushing the menacing message. *Lord, what would you have me do? Should I abide by these instructions or attempt to locate Clara?* He steadied himself with a deep breath that smelt of toast and a hint of citrus.

His gaze latched on to Mrs. Stanton's tray of food. Steaming teapot, matching cup, plate of toast. "You don't have any oranges."

"Keen observation, hawkeye. Why? Do you have a hankering?"

No, just a fragrant hunch his prayers had been answered. Theodore sniffed the crumpled paper. Not oranges, but the blossoms. The scent was faint but definitely present, along with a whiff of—

He recoiled. Gah, something not nearly as pleasant. He held the note up to the sunlight. On the back of the paper, there was a distinct white smudge. Or rather, a *splat.*

He grinned. "Stork excrement."

"Oranges and stork excrement, hmm?" Mrs. S. grimaced and shook her head. "I'll stick with my tea and toast, thanks." Her eyebrows raised. "Wait. Are you thinking—"

"He's holding Miss Stanton in Orangerie Park. Somewhere off the beaten path. Somewhere the tourists don't frequent, and the groundskeepers have neglected or abandoned." He consulted Drosselmeyer's watch. If he and the police made haste, they could search a good portion of the park before nightfall. *What say you, Lord?*

A sense of peace imbued Theodore with renewed confidence and hope. Right-oh! Now it was time to take action. Crushing the note, he tossed it to the foxes, who batted it across the floor. "I believe Miss Stanton has been away from us long enough. Wouldn't you agree?"

Mrs. Stanton nudged the tray toward him. "You'd best have some toast, dear. A gallant knight should never rescue a damsel on an empty stomach."

If a lady must endure captivity, she oughtn't have to do so on an empty stomach. While the yellow-bellied dragon guarding her dungeon door had snored the night away, Clara had tossed and turned, dreaming of teapots steaming with Darjeeling and plates towering with chocolate éclairs.

After dawn, she'd awoken to her stomach growling its discontent. Thankfully, a loaf of bread and wedge of cheese had been left on the table, and she'd found the watering can refilled. Mr. Forrester had apparently entered the shed during her dream about cream puffs.

The food, though not éclairs or cream puffs, had done much to revive Clara. After breakfast, she'd taken up pacing the confines of the potting shed, stretching out her sore limbs. The exercise kept her body from growing restless and her mind from running down trails of thought overgrown with thorny vines of anxiety. Vain imaginations must not be entertained. No matter how eerie the silence. No matter how the light, prying through the slatted walls, waned before the coming of another night. She must ignore the lies whispered by solitude and cling to the truth she'd found.

Slipping a hand in her pocket, Clara clasped her journal. *Abide with me, Lord. Take care of me and mine.* She halted before the door still locked fast and inhaled a deep breath sweetened by the fragrance of orange blossoms. Hours ago, she'd deduced that they were in Orangerie Park. For what else could be assumed after she'd awoken to the bill-clattering of storks and the park's distinct floral perfume? The question was, how long did Mr. Forrester intend to keep her here? What was the next step in his plan?

Dropping to her knees, Clara peered through the knothole in the wall. Mr. Forrester was still standing guard in front of the door. Just as he had been all day. If she was going to have any chance of escaping, she needed to get him to leave. "Mr. Forrester . . . I need more food."

A frustrated sigh seeped through the boards of the shed. "All I have left is my day's ration, and I'll not be sharing. What I gave you was enough to last till the morrow. You should've eaten more sparingly."

Clara pursed her lips. *Lord, give me wisdom to outwit this dragon.* She softened her tone to one of meek submission. "Please, Rupert. I'm of no use to you if I starve to death."

There was a minute of silence, followed by a monotone reply. "Fine. If it'll keep you from pestering me all night."

Were her ears hoodwinked by hope, or was Mr. Forrester actually leaving? She dropped to look through the knothole again. Mr. Forrester was indeed stomping away from the potting shed. This could be her chance! Ten seconds ticked by. Mr. Forrester disappeared from her limited line of sight. Twenty seconds. Her heart raced, urging her feet to do the same with every beat, but she needed to be certain he was well out of hearing. She glanced at the tantalizingly unguarded door. Forty seconds. One minute. That would have to do.

Clara snatched the rusted gardening trowel from the nearby table and thrust the blade into the doorjamb, stabbing downward upon the latch and willing the old mechanism to break. As she bore down, the blade snapped off the trowel. Botheration!

Palms chafing, she tossed aside the rough wooden handle. She took a step back and steeled herself to use her shoulder as a battering ram. *One, two, slam.* Pain burst through her shoulder, but the door remained unmoved. Come on. She twisted the latch and steeled herself to ram into the door again. *One, two, slam.*

Stars, that hurt! And the pain was for nothing. The door held fast.

No amount of striving was going to set her free. Clara sighed. Had she not learned as much last night when she'd been unable to break her bonds? Yet, here she was once again, trying to do everything by her own might and main. Though she'd determined to cling to the truth she'd found, she'd let it slip right through her fingers.

Backing away from the door, she came to rest upon the chair. *It's not up to me to deliver myself. It's not up to me to protect my family. Our help comes from the Lord, just like Grand said. He is our strength and a faithful refuge, a very present and well-proved help in trouble.*

Humming the tune to Granny's hymn, Clara transferred her focus from the confines of the shed to the place where her help came from—the One who abided with her. Peace tucked itself within her spirit. Like a hot brick placed at the end of her bed in winter, it warmed with a soothing comfort she never wished to leave. She closed her eyes and imagined the night sky, wishing she could chart every aspect of the Creator who'd fashioned it with words, simultaneously disappointed and delighted that such a feat was beyond her capabilities. Her pen could never convey the height, depth, and breadth of the Omnipotent One any more than the four corners of a page could contain Him. Yet she suddenly longed to try. Not to prove her skills, but to come to know Him through the use of them. The God who held the globe in the palm of His scarred hand couldn't be mapped, but He could be known. More amazing still, God—in all His splendor—wanted to be known by her. In all her smallness. In all her need.

Now, that was insane.

Clara laughed, fully cognizant of how odd it made her look, but caring not a whit. Whenever she was freed from this potting shed, she wanted nothing more than to spend the rest of her life exploring the world for glimpses of its Maker and seeking encounters with His presence.

The rattle of a doorknob severed her reverie.

Had Mr. Forrester returned so soon? Clara moved to peer through the knothole and spotted a pair of boots in the grass. One fashioned of leather and the other of metal.

CHAPTER

35

Impossible. Clara blinked away what was surely a hallucination and peered again through the knothole in the wall. One leather boot and one metal boot remained before the door, plain as day. It had to be him, and yet . . . it couldn't be. Her trail of tools spiraled the Grande Île. How could Theodore have known to leave the island and search the park?

He delivers in His time. The words from Grand's final clue reverberated through Clara's weary soul, shooing disbelief and stoking her waning hope. "Theodore?"

"Thank God!" Mr. Theodore's exclamation sent her giddy heart staggering into her ribs. "Stand clear, Clara. I'm going to break down the door."

She took refuge at the back of the shed. "All clear."

A bronze boot crashed through the door amid a hail of splinters. A second kick propelled the door inward, and Mr. Theodore strode over the debris-strewn threshold, muscles taut and fists primed to slay the yellow-bellied dragon. His brow furrowed as though he feared he'd come too late, but the moment their eyes connected, the creases vanished and that dear lopsided grin softened his utterly masculine profile.

Clara's heart skipped a beat and tripped over three more. For years she'd thought it necessary to save herself, lest her family be burdened, but being found, being rescued awakened an exhilaration beyond reckoning. She wanted to leap, to dance, to fly, but all she could muster was a wave, equal parts timid and awkward.

Mr. Theodore closed the distance between them in two strides and ever so gently swept a loose tendril from her face, his calloused fingers brushing across her temple. His deep voice wavered. "Did he hurt you?"

She leaned into the warmth of his palm. "No. I am well, truly." But that could change if Mr. Forrester happened upon them. She seized Mr. Theodore's hand and pulled him out of the potting shed and into the amber glow of evening. "We must be away from here. Mr. Forrester might return at any moment."

"Good." Mr. Theodore's grin sparked a gleam in his eyes. "I'm looking forward to having a lively chat with the scoundrel."

"I think that's a chat we'd best forgo, seeing as the scoundrel is armed with a pistol."

All jest evaporated from Mr. Theodore's countenance. "Let's continue this reunion elsewhere, shall we?" He took off at a sprint, and she followed suit, running a few paces behind as he led the way. Head pivoting back and forth, he appeared to survey the surrounding trees as though looking for someone. "The men will be so relieved to see you."

The men? What was he—

Something slammed Clara from behind, and she hit the ground with great force. She gasped, sprawled facedown in the grass. Pinned down by something heavy.

"I warned you, Clara." Mr. Forrester's voice was hot against her ear, his words blackened with rage and despair. "I warned you not to try me."

Her lungs forgot how to breathe. *God above, don't leave me now.*

The weight lifted, and Clara was hoisted to her feet. Mr. Forrester's arms clamped around her waist in a vicelike grip as he dragged her back to the shed. Up ahead, Mr. Theodore ran on, unaware he ran alone. *No!*

Regaining her breath, she let out a scream and swung her elbow backward, striking Mr. Forrester in the face. He cursed and retracted his hold.

Clara broke into a run, gaze fixed on Mr. Theodore, who now ran to meet her.

A hand snatched at her skirt, and she fell headlong as fabric rent. Mr. Forrester landed beside her in the grass, seething and clutching what had once been her pocket. She tried to get to her feet, but he lunged for her, hands grasping at her ankles. Her skirt. Her waist. She landed a few kicks, but she couldn't break away.

"Unhand her!"

Suddenly, Mr. Forrester was removed, and Clara freed. She rolled over and witnessed Mr. Theodore landing a punch to her ex-fiancé's jaw. Reeling backward, Mr. Forrester landed in the waiting arms of two policemen, backed by nearly a dozen other uniformed men.

Back at her side in a flash, Mr. Theodore helped Clara to her feet and held her steady with a hand on either shoulder. "Are you hurt?"

"I . . . I'm just glad it's over."

"This is far from over, Clara! Do you hear me?"

A shudder provoked a wave of nausea, but Clara leaned into Mr. Theodore's support and faced Mr. Forrester boldly. Blood trailed from his nose as he strained against the policemen's grasp. Dark eyes seared her with hatred, glowing like embers on the verge of bursting into flame.

As the policemen hauled him away, Mr. Forrester clutched the torn pieces of her pocket in fisted hands, determined to never let go. "Mark my words, Clara. You will see me again."

CHAPTER

36

When masculinity donned the gleaming armor of protector and came to one's defense, my but was it beautiful. And stars above, how it made one blush! Clara sat before a looking glass, hours after being conveyed on horseback to the Gingerbread Gnome, and her cheeks were still flushed as though permanently stained. She had always considered herself a genteel woman with refined sensibilities. Never would she have thought herself capable of deriving girlish glee from a knuckle-cracking uppercut!

"Porcupine quills."

Clara passed a few hairpins over her shoulder, eyes fixed on Mum's dear reflection and heart overcome with gratitude. God had taken care of them all, and her shoulders had never felt so light. Mum handed the pins to Fred, who clasped them between his pointy teeth, holding them at the ready. She then proceeded to gather Clara's hair into a low bun.

"Do continue, ducky. This story gets better with each telling, and this part is my favorite."

"And here I thought your favorite part was when I fell into your arms and promptly burst into tears." As any grown woman would upon being reunited with her mum after a traumatic interlude.

"I enjoyed that part too, of course. But . . . I do so love fisticuffs! Tell me again how our Mr. Kingsley walloped that man."

Mr. Theodore Kingsley. How well the name suited him. How taken aback she'd been to hear him reclaim it as the police escorted them to the Grande Île in a triumphal procession. *"If I told you my surname, I should want you to keep it too."* The hue of Clara's cheeks deepened from rosy pink to crimson. At some point, she was going to have to reckon with this blush and the feelings it betrayed, but not yet.

At present, she just wanted to revel in the joy of this moment. "You should've seen Mr. Kingsley, Mum. He hauled Mr. Forrester off me as though he were nothing and then—thwack!—his fist struck with the force of a lightning bolt and felled Mr. Forrester like an oak."

The pair laughed as Clara lowered her gaze to her skirt, and Mum secured the underside of her coif with more pins. Thankfully, Mr. Kingsley had recovered all the metal breadcrumbs she'd dropped, including her silver needle case with spare thread and tiny sewing shears, which Mum had then used to make quick work of mending the rips her traveling dress had incurred. With her reassembled chatelaine gleaming atop the brown corded silk, it looked good as new until compared with the pristine fabric of her reserve pair of cream-colored gloves.

She twirled the silver pen between her fingers. "Last night's rescue would make for an exciting addition to a book, for it had all the makings of a swashbuckling adventure. When the police rallied around Mr. Kingsley, clapping him on the back like a band of brothers, he was the very image of a gallant knight of yore."

"I don't doubt it, ducky. I shall ever be grateful to our gallant knight and the Strasbourg police for rescuing my girl and bringing that man to justice."

As would she.

"That man should be grateful *I* wasn't among your rescuers. If I had been, he would've suffered a worse fate than incarceration." Mum stabbed pins into Clara's hair with increased violence. "No, indeed. Instead of confiscating his pistol, I'd have put it to use. To think you could've been—"

"But I wasn't." Clara secured Mum's shaking hand and met her eyes in the glass, noting the shadows beneath them. The tinges of red haunting the inner corners that evidenced an empty well of tears and a heart brimming with love. Clara prayed her words would douse any remaining cinders of fear. "I was never alone."

A quiver unsettled Mum's chin, and she nodded as if she'd known as much but was relieved to be told all the same. "Nor was I, ducky. Nor was I."

Clara squeezed Mum's hand three times. *I love you.*

Four squeezes countered affectionately. *I love you more.*

A nudge from a tiny whiskered nose settled the dispute irrefutably.

After deeming Clara's coif satisfactory, Mum fetched Clara's newly polished boots and a buttonhook. She perched on the edge of the bed, and the fox kits leapt from the floor— one, two, three—to nestle alongside her. Mum gestured for Clara to produce her unshod foot. "While I'll always admire Strasbourg for its hospitality to the noble stork, I must admit I'm quite ready to resume our travels."

On that front, they were all in agreement. They would set out on the first available train. Clara placed a stockinged foot in Mum's lap. Upon their return at the break of dawn, the thought of arranging the next leg of their journey had overwhelmed her already spent emotional and physical resources, but before she could confess as much, Mr. Kingsley had assured her he'd take care of everything. And true to character, he had. Right down to the smallest detail.

As soon as Mr. Kingsley had placed her sobbing form into Mum's care, he'd set to work. While she'd bathed, he'd obtained a hearty breakfast and settled with the innkeeper. While she'd eaten, he'd procured collars and leashes for the fox cubs, who would travel as "puppies," allowing the turtle Mum had adopted in her absence to travel in their old wicker basket. As she'd sat to have her hair brushed, Mr. Kingsley had dashed off to purchase their train tickets to . . .

Clara straightened. "Where? How?"

"Ooooh! What are questions asked by mourners at a funeral?" A smile brightened Mum's countenance as her deft hands threaded the buttons of Clara's boot. "Great idea, ducky. I do love a game of word association."

"I'm not playing—"

"Of course you aren't. It's my turn now. Rutabaga. Parsnip."

Apparently this game would be played with or without her participation. "What are root vegetables?"

"Pshaw! The answer is 'vegetables only rabbits should eat.' Honestly, dearest, I gave that one to you on a platter, what with you being abducted and all. Are you sure you feel all right?"

"I'm fine. Merely confused. Mr. Kingsley has gone to acquire train tickets, but *how* does he know *where* we are bound? He had the automaton, but I had Grand's clue. What with being kidnapped, held captive, and rescued, I never had a chance to tell Mr. Kingsley our final destination. How did he figure it out?"

With a knowing smile, Mum finished buttoning Clara's boot and set it on the floor. "There was a second clue."

"A second clue?"

"Aye, ducky." Mum set aside the buttonhook and reached

into the nearby gadget bag, retrieving the automaton Grand had hidden at the cathedral with his last note. A bear cub with twinkling eyes of glass and scruffy bronze fur. The automaton *was* a clue within itself, confirming beyond doubt the meaning of the final clue in Grand's merry scavenger hunt. The combined clues of paper and metal directed them to Bern, Switzerland, where the memory of Granny and Grand's young love lingered at the inn where they'd honeymooned and marveled at a fountain.

Clara gently took the automaton into her arms as tears sprung to her eyes. Stars . . . this wasn't just a bear cub. This was *the* bear cub. "*Norma nearly jumped out of her skin when one of the bear cubs came to life and began dancing around its bronze mother's claws. My, how she laughed.*"

Oh, Grand. How had she not seen it before? All this time, he'd been leading her to the place where the story had unfolded so that he might tell it once again . . . so they might finally remove the black mourning bands from their hearts and tell Uncle and Granny good-bye.

A tear broke free as she looked up. "Will we arrive in time?"

Mum's blue eyes glistened. "Our train will arrive in Bern on the very day."

Hugging the cub to her chest, Clara grinned even as tears flowed. She was going to see Grand! Finally, they would reunite, on the very day he and Granny had said "I do." She chuckled. Grand always did have perfect timing.

"I must show you Grand's final clue. It was so terribly clever."

Bear with me as we make one fiNal stop in a place where the memory of young lOve lingers and laughteR bubbles forth like a Marvelous fountAin.

The capitalized letters spelled Granny's name—Norma— the one whose contagious laughter bubbled forth nearly every day of her life.

Passing the bear cub to Mum, Clara removed the journal from her pocket and found the spot where she'd tucked all the scavenger hunt clues between the pages. Her brow furrowed. "It . . . it's not here."

"Perhaps you tucked it in a different page?"

Clara thumbed through the journal backward and forward. The clue directing them to Bern was nowhere to be found. "It has to be here. I read it in the potting shed, and then I put it in my . . . pocket." *Not* in the journal. Her heart faltered. *Oh, Lord, what have I done?*

Reaching into the pocket where the journal had been stored, Clara turned it inside out. Empty. Like the hollow sensation carving out her stomach. For her other pocket—and Grand's clue—were long gone.

Ripped away by the desperate man who'd warned her not to try his patience. Clutched tight by the furious man who'd screamed her name like a curse.

"This is far from over, Clara!"

Indeed it was not. Not even close.

He'd figure out the clue. He'd get out of prison. And he'd follow them to Bern, resolved to seize the owl at any cost. After all he'd endured and survived—after he'd come so far and risked so much—Clara knew full well he'd stop at nothing now to make good on his parting oath.

"Mark my words, Clara. You will see me again."

The bandages on Theodore's hand were worth it in this moment, when, on April the twenty-third, Miss Stanton alighted from the train in Bern and accepted his proffered arm without hesitation. She simply rested her glove upon the crook of his elbow and favored him with a smile. Ever since he'd popped that rat on the snout, she'd taken to smiling at him with an air of familiarity that beckoned him to come closer. Close enough to awaken hope, which was a treasure that far exceeded the discomfort of a few scraped knuckles.

Relieved of its passengers, the locomotive heaved a sigh of exhaust. Steam drifted along the platform, swirling amid the swishing skirts and flapping overcoats of countless travelers who made their way through the low-hanging clouds. Just ahead of them, Mrs. S. forged their path through the crowd, ermine "stole" around her neck, basket of "lunch" in her hand, and trio of "puppies" scampering before her on their leashes. He scrutinized the haze of tourists pressing in on every side. It would be all too easy for a bloke to sneak up on someone in such a throng.

Adjusting the lapel of his coat, Theodore reassured himself that the weight pressing against his ribs—the pearl-handled pistol from his new friends in the Strasbourg police force—was still secured in an inner pocket. *"To protect those you love,* mon frère. *May you never have need of it."*

While the gift had been bestowed with the best of intentions, the gun's cold barrel prodded at his failure on the Grande Île, revealing his inadequacy like dirty fingerprints on gleaming steel. Forrester never should've gotten so close. Never should've gotten his hands on Clara and the all-important clue in her pocket. He eyed the train cars warily, any number of which Forrester might've gained passage on without his notice.

"You look as though you're trying to repair a clock with a mallet." Miss Stanton nudged his ribs with an elbow. "What is causing you such consternation?"

Theodore followed Mrs. S. in skirting a stack of unclaimed trunks. He didn't need to distress Miss Stanton by bringing up that louse. *Avert and—*

"Don't you even think of changing the subject, Mr. Kingsley, or I shall be forced to employ a secret weapon, sharp and deft in the art of extracting information."

He chuckled. "You'd sick Mrs. S. on me? I'm both honored and terrified."

"As well you should be. Now, speak. Before the matter troubling you does irrevocable damage to your handsome face."

Handsome, eh? He grinned, tucking that compliment away to be addressed at a more opportune moment. "The matter troubling me is no more than a lingering sense of regret." And none too little guilt. "I should've seen through Forrester's trap. I should've kept you safe. I should've kept the man from walking off with the motive and means to continue his pursuit."

There was a moment of silence. Then Miss Stanton tightened her hold on his arm, drawing him closer, securing their bond. "Your hands aren't the ones that keep me, Mr. Kingsley. But they fought for me, and for that, I shall ever be grateful."

Theodore exhaled a breath he'd been holding. Miss Stanton was right, of course. Ultimately, the protection of those he loved fell under God's purview, and the Lord of angel armies would not—indeed, could not—be thwarted. Not by any blunder of his, and not by the likes of Forrester. That was an assurance of greater weight than any pistol.

Switzerland's capital city welcomed them with a brisk breeze, a sky of brilliant blue, and the clip-clop-clatter of horse-drawn carriages. Mrs. S. marched toward a queue of carriages. "Rest your webbed feet, duckies," she called over her shoulder. "I'll find us a driver who's affable to animals."

Theodore gaped. "Have I just been distinguished with the endearment of *ducky*?"

"Indeed you have. Apparently Mum thinks you're worthy of the honor."

"Really, now." He lowered his face toward Miss Stanton, still snug on his arm. "Does she also think I've a handsome face, or is that just you?"

Miss Stanton's fair complexion reddened like a rose, and she shifted her gaze to the street, attempting to conceal the enchanting blush. A maneuver that failed miserably without the aid of her favorite bonnet. "Which way ought we to go, I wonder?"

Changing the subject, was she? Now the woman was pilfering his tricks along with his heart. How annoyingly clever. Well. Two could play that game as well as one. "I do believe, my dear Miss Stanton, I left that choice up to you when last we danced."

Dancing in Mr. Kingsley's arms felt more akin to a dream than a memory. One Clara would gladly resume here and now if the man saw fit to waltz her down the streets of Bern. At the moment, however, Mr. Kingsley searched her face for an answer to the question he'd asked days ago. The one she'd yet to answer.

He pulled her even closer to his side, near enough to feel his heart beating through his overcoat. Through her glove. "Have you decided which way we should go, or are you still uncertain?"

Oh, she was quite certain.

Certain that Theodore was the truest friend she'd ever known.

That he was one of the finest men she'd ever met.

That if he were to kiss her now, she'd come undone in the best way, and if he were to break her heart, she'd come undone in the worst.

God help her, she loved this man! She loved Theodore Kingsley with all her heart, but was she brave enough to say as much and accept his suit? Of that, she was not certain. Not yet. She needed more time to sift her emotions with prayer. If she'd done as much the first time . . . if she'd sought the Lord's guidance before accepting Mr. Forrester's proposal . . . how much pain might have been avoided? How much pain was *still* caused by the likelihood of Mr. Forrester following them to Bern? By the fear of what desperation might drive him to next?

No, she mustn't act in haste. For both their sakes, she must know the door to the past was firmly barred and the door to her future clearly marked by Providence. "Mr. Kingsley—"

"We've a carriage, duckies! Let's make haste."

Dear sweet Mum to the rescue.

Mr. Kingsley sighed in resignation and trained a smile on Mum. "Right-oh, Mrs. S."

In quick order, the bags were loaded and their party situated. Somehow, Mum had convinced the driver to let her ride topside with her basket, which left Clara and Mr. Kingsley to manage the three foxes inside the jostling hackney. Silence sat betwixt them, obvious and awkward, like a chaperone of substantial girth. Clara worried Honorine's leash as the kit slept in her lap, blissfully unaware. Mr. Kingsley looked out the window vigilantly, leashes firm in hand, as Phileas and Todd played tug-of-war at his feet with the hem of his overcoat. If they sat any farther apart, they'd go tumbling out the respective carriage doors.

"Please don't be cross with me."

The appearance of Mr. Kingsley's lopsided grin set her at ease. "I could never be that, Miss Stanton. Disappointed, yes. Pining for you, most earnestly. But never cross."

She took a breath, hoping it would cool her warming cheeks. "Rest assured, I am very interested in accepting your suit. My hesitation stems from fear of making another impulsive decision without sufficient consideration and fear of my last rash decision haunting me forever. I need to know I'm truly safe from Mr. Forrester—that I'm free of him for good and all—before I can contemplate a life with someone else. I need God to direct me before I can move on. I need Him to grant me peace and the courage to follow where He leads. Will you . . . will you pray for me in all this, Mr. Kingsley?"

Eliminating the distance between them, Mr. Kingsley pressed a kiss to her glove. "I pray for you every day, Miss Stanton. For not a single day goes by that you are not in my thoughts. Even if the Lord sees fit to have us part ways entirely, I shall pray for you daily still. You are fixed in my heart, an intrinsic gear amongst its windings, never to be removed."

Clara could hardly wait for the hackney to stop. Indeed, only the fox in her lap and the tether of Mr. Kingsley's hand prevented her from leaping out in an uncouth somersault. She could see it, just beyond the open window. The Lolloping Bear Inn from Grand's favorite story. It was just as he'd described.

Situated on the fringes of Bern's Old Town, the inn was hemmed in by the aquamarine waters of the Aare River and presented a breathtaking view of the Alps, crested with sparkling snow. The reality of it surpassed the loveliest pictures she'd painted on the canvas of imagination. Next time Grand offered to take her somewhere, there would be no hesitation. She'd have a bag packed within the hour!

Finally, the carriage rolled to a halt. The sandstone building featured a medieval arcade, and a sign in the shape of a bear's paw swung over the door. Tables and chairs clustered near the river's edge for alfresco dining, and in the very midst of them stood a Renaissance fountain. Clara's heart swelled, for she recognized the colorful figure of a mother bear. Standing on her hind legs, the bear reached toward the sky as a stream of water sprung from her snout and two bronze cubs frolicked in the spray.

At one of the tables, there sat a man in a tweed jacket, his white hair haloed by a flutter of glinting butterflies. It was dear Grand, at last. Safe and sound, and oh so near.

Honorine was lifted from Clara's lap, and the fox's leash unwound from her fingers. Mr. Kingsley, holding all three squirming kits, nodded to the door as a lopsided grin quirked his blond whiskers. "Away with you, woman, before you spontaneously combust."

She promptly burst from the carriage, and the moment her boots hit the cobbles, she took off at a run void of decorum, hoisting her skirt well above her ankles as tendrils broke free from pins to fly in the spring breeze. If people gawked in her direction, she did not see them. Nor did she care. For her sights were fixed on Grand. She almost shouted in greeting, but something made her refrain. She slowed to a stop behind his tweed-clad back, maintaining a respectful distance. A reverent silence.

For Grand, it seemed, was not alone.

Admiring sunset's first brushstrokes of orange and gold and pink, Grand sat at a table set for two. The plate before him was strewn with crumbs, while the second plate sat untouched. His wineglass contained naught but dregs while the adjacent glass was filled with merlot. Grand emptied his drink and took the second glass for a walk to the water's edge. Reaching into his waistcoat, he removed an envelope with a familiar black seal. It was the devasting letter he'd held on to all these years. A son's final words held near a father's broken heart.

The envelope trembled as Grand pressed a kiss to the black-edged paper and released it, allowing the breeze to lay the letter to rest in the peaceful River Aare. There was a moment of stillness. Of hushed remembrance. Then he raised the wineglass to the setting sun, toasting she who was no longer there to sip it across from him, and with a shaking hand, poured every last drop into the river. Crimson tears for love known and love lost.

For love that remained even in the face of death.

Clara's breath stilled as an ache pulsed through her heart. *I want to love like that. To be loved like that. God, is such a thing possible?*

The ambient sound of water, spraying heavenward from the nearby fount and pattering upon the bear figures as gentle rain nurtured the seed of a memory long buried in the soil of time. Granny's laughter blossomed, drifting through her mind like magnolia petals dancing on a spring breeze. *"Love is much like a flower, child. You can't guarantee it'll grow or endure a bitter winter to bloom again. All you can do is plant what you're given, tend it faithfully, and rely on the God who cares for the lilies of the field as much as He cares for our hearts."*

The forgotten words took root in Clara's soul, grounding her with peace that weeded up thorny fears too long permitted to choke her hopes. It was time to truly put her trust in the One who arrayed the lilies in splendor. It was time to plant something new. With Theodore.

Of that, she was now assuredly certain.

Grand set the empty glass on the table and at last met her gaze with love-drenched eyes. "Right on time, right on time. I can always count on my Little Stargazer to be punctual."

In a heartbeat, she was in Grand's arms, face nestled against his jacket as she reveled in the scent of peppermints and the warm embrace of home. "Happy anniversary, Grand."

He kissed the top of her head and held her at arm's length. "Eyes bright. Countenance light. Does this mean you've unburdened your shoulders?"

"I have. Although I may have to do so again in the morning."

Grand smiled as his kaleidoscope of clockwork butterflies flitted about his head. "That is what mornings are for, dear girl." He glanced over her shoulder. "Where are my daughter and apprentice?"

"Securing our accommodations in the Lolloping Bear, I expect. They probably thought it prudent to allow me a few moments of your precious company before I was forced to share you."

"Prudent, indeed. Prudent, indeed. I take it you were able to restrain yourself from flinging my apprentice off the first available clock tower?"

She lowered her brows in mock gravity. "It required every ounce of my better judgment and fear of imprisonment to resist the temptation, especially those first few days when he was such an impertinent hobgoblin."

Grand chuckled. "And what do you think ought to be done with the hobgoblin now?"

"I should like to keep him."

"My, my, that is a surprise. You don't still wish me to dismiss him?"

"Stars, no. I might have to reconsider accepting his suit if he's no longer gainfully employed."

"Well, then I shall keep him on. We don't want to go breaking the lad's heart, now do we?" Something behind Clara caught Grand's eye, dousing his smile with confusion. "I say. What are you—"

A swift arm hooked Clara's waist and yanked her against a solid figure. Before she could scream, a second hand snaked around and held a knife to her throat. She stiffened, her breath severed in gasps. The blade smelt of chicken. A glance toward the table, the only movement she dared though her arms remained at liberty, confirmed the set of silver was bereft of one knife. Grand had gone ashen, but his coloring returned in a rush of red. His fists clenched, and he took a step forward.

"Stay back, old man!"

Spittle seared Clara's ear, and her stomach roiled. *Mr. Forrester.* She swallowed, and the blade scraped against her skin. *God, preserve us.*

Hot breath steamed her neck. "Give me the letter, and I'll release her."

The wrinkles along Grand's brow furrowed. "If you mean the letter about my son's fate, you've come too late. Its tidings of sorrow have been laid to rest in the river. Washed away, washed away."

A curse shattered into a rumbling growl in Mr. Forrester's chest. His arm cinched tighter around Clara's waist. "Fine. Then I'll be keeping a hold of Miss Stanton while you lead us to wherever you've hidden the owl."

Grand's eyes widened. "Why do you want—"

"Take me to it. Now!" Mr. Forrester's shout reverberated through her skull. "I'm not leaving without that machine. I have to have it!"

Trembling from hairpins to boots, Clara begged Grand with her eyes not to comply. Nothing good could come of acquiescing to Mr. Forrester's demands and removing themselves to wherever Grand had secreted the owl. It was sure to be far away from prying eyes and any hope of aid. They needed to stay here, in plain view of the inn. She needed to distract Mr. Forrester until Theodore came outside. *Help me, Lord.*

"Rupert . . . how did you get away? What happened to the men guarding you in Strasbourg?"

"I . . . It was an accident. I never meant to hit him so hard. I never meant for any of this." The fiery rage in Mr. Forrester's voice crumbled to ashes of regret. Slowly, the blade fell away from her neck to her chest, hovering near enough to menace but far enough to reveal the shaking in his hands. "I was just trying to survive another day. Just doing what I had to do to keep from going back to debtor's prison. To keep from . . ."

To keep from dying there, just like his mum.

A sob wrenched itself from Mr. Forrester's chest and racked his whole body.

Clara ached for the little boy she'd never known. For the young man she'd once adored with the whole of her naïve heart. *Lord, help me get through to him.* "What happened to your mother was a tragic injustice. I can't fathom how—"

"Of course you can't!" He lashed out. "You, born into privilege and security. You, with your fine house and enough food to waste on vermin. You've never known what it is to go without." Mr. Forrester sneered. "You know nothing of loss."

Clara bit her tongue. Apparently the deaths of Uncle Fritz and Granny Drosselmeyer were of no account.

"I know what it is to lose a mother." Mr. Theodore appeared on the cobbles, pistol drawn and aimed at Mr. Forrester.

Dragging in a breath, Mr. Forrester stoked the coals of his anguish. "Do you know what it is to have her die in your arms?"

"Nay, but I know what it is to be the one who caused her death. That is its own pain." One cautious step at a time, Mr. Theodore approached them, speaking in a soothing cadence, as though to calm a skittish colt. "I also know what it is to spend your days striving to outrun a past that's shackled to your feet like a ball and chain. No matter how you try to ignore the cold weight slicing into your flesh at every turn, the blasted thing can't be shaken. But it can be unlocked by the One who holds the key. I know what it is to finally have that ball and chain removed. To be given a second chance. You can have that same chance now, Forrester. Just put down the knife and release Clara."

Shaking his head, Mr. Forrester wiped what must be tears against Clara's hair. "No. Nothing ever comes to me so easy. I was born out of chances." The knife, though quivering with hesitation, remained clutched in his white-knuckled grasp. An unrelenting threat.

He wasn't going to surrender. Clara could see that now as clearly as she saw Theodore's determined green eyes. She held the gaze of the man she loved and mouthed two words. *Be ready.* With the slightest of nods, Theodore communicated his understanding. His willingness to fight alongside her for however many days God saw fit to give them.

Help us, Lord.

Slowly, Clara reached for her chatelaine and found her sewing shears. Drawing from strength not her own, she fisted the handle and slammed the blades into Mr. Forrester's thigh.

With a horrible yell, he recoiled hand and blade. Slipping through his lax arms, she dove out of the way, and a shot rent the air.

Mr. Forrester screamed, and the knife flew from his hand.

Ears ringing, Clara hurried to secure the weapon, but Mr. Forrester lunged for it with a desperate roar. She landed a kick to the handle and sent the blade skittering across the cobbles, out of his reach. Mr. Forrester turned on her with unhinged fury and charged. As Clara flailed a retreat, Theodore swooped in, seized her attacker, and landed a cracking punch.

Mr. Forrester fell to his knees and slumped upon the cobbles.

Standing over Mr. Forrester warily, Mr. Kingsley seemed to assure himself the man was knocked out cold and then knelt to examine Mr. Forrester's wounded hand. The shot had gone clean through. Clara stood and gave Mr. Kingsley the handkerchief in her pocket, which he promptly used to bind the wound tight and staunch the bleeding. Grabbing a clean cloth napkin from the nearby table, he then bound up the stab wound on Mr. Forrester's thigh.

"Well done, my boy. Well done." Grand appeared beside Clara, unharmed, and she latched on to his tweed jacket. *Thank you, God.*

"That, sirs, is the villain who took my girl. On the hooves of justice, I beseech thee to chaaarge!" Mum raced across the road, leading a cavalry of Swiss police. She reached them first, and with the level of violence only a frightened mother can achieve, yanked Clara unto her bosom and unleashed a torrent of tears upon her head.

Blinded by the bounty of said bosom, Clara squeezed Mum tight and then painstakingly extricated her face from the wellspring of maternal love, lest she suffocate. "I'm fine, Mum."

Mum took Clara's face in hand. "Are you sure, ducky? If he hurt one feather of your being, I'll order Mr. Kingsley to aim low, shoot true, and end his chances at reproducing."

"That won't be necessary, *gnädige frau.* We will take it from here." A pair of uniformed policemen hefted Mr. Forrester off the ground as their commanding officer, a fellow with the thinnest of mustaches on the edge of his upper lip, addressed Clara. "Do you know this man?"

While Mum clung to her side, Clara assessed Mr. Forrester. Bereft of his bowler hat, his once well-groomed hair and whiskers were overgrown, disheveled, and unwashed. His once immaculate attire was now stained, rumpled, and torn. The garish canary waistcoat had flown from his rib cage. Like a weather-beaten scarecrow, he hung limply from the policemen's arms as blood soaked the makeshift bandages tied about his hand and leg. Her throat closed. No. She could say in all honesty that she had never known this man.

"His name is Rupert Forrester." Mr. Kingsley stepped in

to provide the answers she could not voice. "He's an obsessive harasser who's followed us from London, tracking our movements for weeks and inciting fear at our every turn. When we were in Strasbourg, he went so far as to abduct Miss Stanton, hold her against her will, and profess a plot to rob her grandfather in order to pay off his substantial debts."

A gasp disturbed Grand's whiskers. "He did what?"

"With the aid of the Grande Île police, Miss Stanton was recovered, and Mr. Forrester promptly arrested. Last time I saw him, he was secured behind bars. I'm loath to think what became of the prison guard assigned to his cell, for it is now apparent that Mr. Forrester is capable of violence. He's accosted Miss Stanton a second time and scored her throat with this knife." Mr. Kingsley kicked the fallen blade toward the policeman's boots.

Picking up the knife, the policeman reviewed the shallow slash along Clara's neck. "When the man comes round, we shall see what he has to say before the magistrate." Clearing his throat, the policeman acknowledged each of them in turn. "You need fear this man no longer. I imagine he'll soon be receiving a lengthy prison sentence. Every precaution will be taken to ensure he remains in custody and behind bars, where he can do no more harm." With that, the policemen hauled Mr. Forrester away.

As the setting sun transformed the rustic cobbles into rose quartz, Clara heaved a long sigh and took hold of Mr. Kingsley's hand.

With a scratch of his head, Grand sent clockwork butterflies flitting in all directions. "Well, well . . . that wasn't part of the plan, but good riddance and justice served, I say." He retrieved a bottle of merlot from the table and held it aloft as a butterfly came to rest on the cork. "Anyone fancy a glass of wine and a little stargazing?"

CHAPTER

39

I can't believe my machine caused such a hullabaloo." Grand laid aside the day's paper on their table outside the Lolloping Bear Inn. The automata butterflies nestled in his hair glinted in the jubilant sun, and a May breeze fluttered his wispy mustache as he poured himself another cup of tea. "I don't understand it. Not a whit, not a whit. Surely Prague's Orloj or the Zytglogge clock tower we toured yesterday is more impressive than my giant wind-up toy."

Clara smiled at Grand—or rather, her existing smile broadened. In the two blissful weeks since their eventful reunion, the outward expression of joy had become a permanent fixture of her face, one she could neither control nor contain. "You don't give your achievements the credit they're due, Grand." She gestured toward the paper, with its headline story of "the entire field of journalism flocking to Zürich," where the great owl had last been sighted. "This hullabaloo is more than warranted. Your creativity is a gift, and your inventions are veritable marvels."

"Hear, hear." Mr. Kingsley clanked his teacup against

Grand's as though it were a stein of ale. "The owl is an innovation without equal, Drosselmeyer. Is it any wonder the public's enchanted and the prince is keen to become your patron?"

Mum beamed at Grand as Fred nuzzled under her chin. "My father, Inventor to the Crown. Oh, I'm so proud I could prance like a pony all the way to London."

Grand gawped at the paper. "I just don't understand it. Not a whit, not a whit." A distinct and familiar melody lilted through the air on metallic wings. Leaning back in his chair, he consulted the watch Mr. Kingsley had returned to him as it struck four o'clock. "As much as I delight in your company, children, I do think the time has come for a respite."

After today's adventure, they might all do well to take a nap. Circumnavigating the peninsula on which Old Town was built had made for a long, albeit delightful excursion. If she closed her eyes, she could yet hear the sails of their boat flapping in the wind as they cruised down the River Aare, taking in the scenic beauty of Bern. Granny would've loved it so. The thought tugged at her heart as the flexing of a scar might pull at the taut and rigid skin, but the wound no longer bled. No longer gaped. Time might not heal all wounds, but the Lord surely healed a surrendered heart in due time.

Clara squeezed Grand's weathered hand. "I suppose I can endure your absence for a few hours, but you had best appear at my side come time for dinner."

Gripping the arms of his chair, Grand creaked to his feet. "That's a promise, Little Stargazer." He pressed a kiss to her crown, still woefully hatless, and made for the inn.

"I'd best be off as well, duckies." Mum rose, spurring Mr. Kingsley to do likewise, as she placed her napkin on the table. "The kits will be getting restless for their afternoon walk, and I've an errand to run in town. I assume I can trust the pair of you not to do anything scandalous whilst unchaperoned?" Her dark brows waggled as though goading Clara to break that trust.

Raising her porcelain saucer, Clara attempted to blame the steam wafting from the freshly brewed Ceylon for her flushed complexion. "If you send another telegram to Papa, do give him my love, will you?"

"Ah, that's my ducky. More love to give than a church has bells to ring." With a flamboyant swishing of skirts, she set off with a song in her step. "Ding-dong, ding-dong."

Dear Mum, subtle as ever.

"Alone at long last." Mr. Kingsley claimed the vacated seat beside her and drew close enough to steal a sip of her tea. To steal her very breath. "As much as I respect Mrs. S., I'm afraid I can't abide by her wishes in this case. For quite some time now I've longed to do something scandalous. Something I can resist no longer. Will you indulge me, Miss Stanton?"

Her blush intensified. "My good sir, whatever are you suggesting?"

Mr. Kingsley's mouth parted in a grin. "I'm suggesting, my dear lady, that we order another round of dessert and thoroughly spoil our appetites for dinner."

Clara raised a brow over the rim of her cup. Why, that cheeky hobgoblin. She attempted to bite back a smirk and failed miserably. "Those chocolate truffles were rather delectable."

"Sinfully."

She slanted a saucy look toward Mr. Kingsley. "If we're going to ruin ourselves, we might as well do it properly."

"Right-oh." Mr. Kingsley summoned a waiter, and minutes later, their table was laden with a fresh pot of Darjeeling and a profusion of confectionary delights.

As the feast progressed, conversation veered once again to the subject of their youth. On their second day in Bern, Mr. Kingsley had revealed to them his noble ancestry and grim life at Kingsley Court. Yet even now, she struggled to comprehend the utter cruelty of his father, Lord Edgewood. Struggled to reconcile that the unassuming man before her was, in fact, the eighth son of an earl. For in her mind, he would always be Mr. Kingsley.

Her Theodore.

The incredibly patient man whose question she was finally ready to answer.

Clara lowered her teacup. It was time to trust God with the final piece of her heart still clutched in her grasp. "Theodore, I—"

Jade eyes connected with her own, and the resulting blush melted Clara's senses. Botheration, she couldn't speak to the man if he insisted on looking at her in such a way. Tenderly and intimately, as though she were the only thing he wished to look upon for the rest of his days. It accentuated the handsomeness of his features and breadth of his shoulders to the point of distraction. There was only one thing to be done.

She shut her eyes. "Yes."

"Yes . . . what?" Confusion skewed Mr. Kingsley's tone.

Was he quite serious? Clara's eyes flashed open, and at the sight of the hobgoblin's smirk, she swatted him soundly. "Yes, I accept your suit, Mr. Theodore Kingsley. When we return to London, you may call upon me as often as you wish. For I would like nothing better than to wake up every day and know you'll be a part of it."

A gleam illuminated Mr. Kingsley's eyes, and he interlaced their fingers upon his knee. "My days are yours, Miss Clara Marie Stanton. Come storm or fair weather."

Her heart swelled, and she rested her head against his shoulder as they watched the aquamarine river ribbon around the shoreline.

Mr. Kingsley's chin nestled atop her head. "I suddenly find myself quite eager to set foot on English soil. To go home for good and all."

Since he'd opened the door, she might as well broach the

subject now. "How would you feel about escorting Mum back to London unaccompanied?"

"Unaccompanied? Where are you going to be, I should wonder?"

"Oh, I'd be nearby." She smiled. "Grand said I could fly the owl back to London."

With a melodramatic huff, Mr. Kingsley eyed her warily. "I see how it is, you crafty minx. I pledge you my days, and then you soar off amongst the clouds, leaving me behind to wrangle your mother's ever-growing menagerie."

"Growing? Stars, what sort of creature has Mum rescued now?"

"A one-eyed kitten. She found the scrawny thing begging outside the inn yesterday."

Clara shook her head with a chuckle. "Serves me right for having the audacity to take a nap. Where has she hidden the little stray?"

"Mrs. S. stowed the furry bag o' bones in mine and Drosselmeyer's room. A temporary arrangement, I was told, until she could find the opportune moment to tell you. I could hardly sleep last night for the mewing."

"You poor man." Clara cupped his face, tracing a gloved thumb along his temple. "Don't worry. I'll speak to Mum straightaway and tell her to leave the kitten in your room. The furry bag o' bones should train you well for the time you'll spend bedding down with three raucous fox kits and a snoring ermine." Before he could protest, she rose and flounced toward the inn.

"Wait just one confounded minute." A clanking against the cobbles signaled Mr. Kingsley's anticipated pursuit. "I'll follow you round the world happily and escort Mrs. S. with pride, but couldn't you take a few members of her traveling zoo?"

Twirling about with a flourish, Clara grinned at her automaton suiter. "Right-oh. Since you asked nicely, I'll take the turtle."

CHAPTER

40

Just a few months ago, if Mum had attempted to board a steaming locomotive with Fred, three fox kits, and a one-eyed kitten, Clara Marie Stanton would've had a proper conniption. Today, when Mum and her menagerie boarded the train with Mr. Kingsley and chugged out of sight, Clara had a good laugh with Grand in between bites of apple strudel.

Well, half an apple strudel. Donatello the turtle, who'd finally emerged from his shell, had proven to be quite a voracious eater.

Having bid their farewells at the station and fortified their bodies with a breakfast of strudel and tea, Clara and Grand set out to reunite with the great owl machine. Together, they headed for the countryside, trekking over the Swiss Plateau's rolling hills and dales. Grand, carrying his knapsack and her carpetbag. She, holding the wicker basket wherein Donny was tucked snuggly in the purple shell sweater Mum had knit for him during their stay in Old City.

When a farmer returning from market offered them a lift in his horse-drawn cart, they gladly accepted and purchased from his unsold wares the largest wheel of cheese they could carry. Dotted with marble-size holes distinctive to the region, the pale-yellow cheese was tangy, nutty, and, in Clara's mind, better than gold!

Upon reaching their destination, which seemed the very definition of the middle of nowhere, the farmer eyed them quizzically. "Certain this is where you wish to part, *mein freund*? There's nothing here but the ruins of the old Spyri farm."

Grand nodded, setting his kaleidoscope of butterflies to dancing. "Precisely, precisely. This is the place. Always stop to explore the ruins, I say. You never know what astonishing wonders might be hiding amid the dusty memories of yesterday."

The farmer guffawed dubiously. "Only thing you'll find hiding in there is a barn owl."

Clara snorted and arched a brow at Grand in question. *Should we tell him?*

A twinkle in Grand's eyes offered a silent reply. *And spoil the surprise? Never.*

With a word of thanks, she and Grand climbed down from the cart. The farmer tipped his hat and continued his journey along the winding road.

A companionable silence enveloped her and Grand as they faced the land that once upon a time had been Granny's childhood home.

Lush grass no longer kept short by grazing cows swayed in the breeze around an abandoned farmhouse and a huge barn. Like an elderly couple relaxing on their front porch in a pair of rocking chairs, the gray-haired buildings reminisced about the good old days when a little girl named Norma had milked the cows with her father, churned butter with her mother, and frolicked through meadows of daffodils with a nanny goat.

Clara indulged in a wistful sigh. She could understand why Granny had missed this place so dearly. How heartbroken little Norma must've been when they'd been forced to immigrate to England. She shook her head in reproach. "It looks so forlorn. Whoever bought the land off Great-grandfather Spyri certainly hasn't done much with the place."

"That they haven't, but who knows, Little Stargazer? Their lack of appreciation for the land might compel them to sell and thus restore it to Spyri descendants." Grand nudged her with an elbow. "An alpine farmhouse would make a lovely summer home for a pair of turtle doves looking to start a family."

Clara blushed to her ears. The idea certainly had its merits, but she didn't exactly wish to discuss them with her grandfather. "You're as incorrigible as Mum."

"I should hope so, seeing as I taught the girl everything she knows. But I won't press the matter just now." He whispered confidentially, "I'll wait till we're up in the clouds and you've no place to hide." With a mischievous grin, Grand led her toward the barn.

Though long-neglected and forgotten, the old gray barn had aged well. The roof had lost a few shingles but hadn't gone completely bald. That it remained structurally sound was a testament to Great-grandfather Spyri's workmanship. Clara ran a glove over the barn door, wiping away years of dust that had settled into a carving above the latch: a stylized interlocking S and P—no doubt the family farm's brand. A mark of ownership and legacy. She smiled. Skilled craftsmanship ran on both sides of Mum's family, it seemed.

Together, she and Grand opened the barn's double doors, their hinges creaking with age and dereliction. Afternoon sun flooded the barn, and a refreshing breeze encouraged dormant specks of dust and hay to take to the air in a lively folk dance. Clara wandered into the expansive space, peering into the numerous stalls that, according to Granny's stories, had once housed a herd of prized dairy cows, beloved pet goats, and a draught horse. Now, according to Grand, it housed but one whimsical inhabitant.

One that, oddly enough, she couldn't find. The barn appeared as empty as the neighboring farmers believed it to be.

"Grand, where is the machine?"

"Look up, Little Stargazer. Up!"

Far above her head, Grand stood in a massive loft, the carpetbag and knapsack at his feet and a mound of hay at his back. "How did you get way up there?"

"The mechanical butterflies hoisted me by my whiskers."

Placing a hand to her chest, Clara assumed an expression of mock alarm. "My stars, what a terribly painful means of travel! I'm surprised you've any whiskers left."

"As am I, as am I," assented Grand in the gravest of tones, gingerly floofing his injured mustache. "It would've been so much easier to use that handy ladder there." As he gestured to his left, a smile ended their absurd pretense, and he tossed her a wink. "Come on up, then. Quick as you like."

He didn't have to ask her twice. Holding Donatello's basket firmly against her bodice, she ascended the ladder and joined Grand in the loft. A gleam of brass, not visible from the ground level, peeked over the haystack.

"How did you manage this by yourself?"

Grand placed her basket by their luggage. "Oh, 'twas nothing. The owl's talons did the heavy lifting. Once I'd flown the lot up here, all I had to do was arrange the stack with one of these." He retrieved a pair of pitchforks, passed one to her, and began tossing musty hay over the edge of the loft. "Give us a hand, then."

Together, they dismantled the haystack. When this task

was completed, they paused to let Grand catch his breath and allow Clara a moment to get reacquainted with the old friend who'd been concealed by straw and shadow.

The great owl machine.

It roosted in a nest of stale hay, with broad wings folded against its sides, long legs tucked under its barrel-shaped body, and ear tufts nearly touching the vaulted wooden ceiling. Brass feathers, individually and intricately hammered, reflected the sun's warmth onto the world with an intensified radiance. The owl's circular eyes of amber glass regarded her unblinkingly with the gentle gaze of a loved one that can be held indefinitely without discomfiture.

Grand presented a skeleton key to her with a ceremonious air. "You do the honors, Little Stargazer."

Clara accepted the key and approached the owl, a delightful thrill coursing through her veins. Locating a feather that was almost imperceptibly raised above the others on the owl's chest, she swiveled this escutcheon aside and turned the key in a secret keyhole beneath.

A metallic clank activated an unseen mechanism, which languidly whirred and hummed like a person rolling over in bed, vacillating between slumber and awareness. The owl's great head lethargically rotated to the left, and as it did so, the feathered abdomen opened a sliding pocket door to reveal a cylindrical lift. When the head completed a two-hundred-and-seventy-degree rotation, the mechanism drifted back to sleep.

After fetching their baggage and wicker basket, Clara and Grand stepped into the owl. Inside the machine, a second aperture awaited the skeleton key. She reunited the pair, and with a resounding clank that echoed all around them, the mechanism reactivated. The sliding door reemerged from its pocket, sheltering them within the owl's plumage. Overhead, an amber glow kept darkness at bay. When the door clanged shut, the hydraulic-powered lift began to rise, elevating them up . . . up . . . up the owl's spine. The cylindrical wall fell away as they ascended into an open space, bright and wonderful and homey.

Here, inside the owl's extraordinary head, the lift stopped. The torpid hum of machinery waned as the listless owl fell asleep once again.

A pair of leather chairs was situated before the owl's round eyes. These windows to the soul were the pilots' windows to the world. Though the glass was amber-tinted, a means of ocular protection from the sun, the view through them remained unaffected and true to color. Clara and Grand gravitated toward their respective seats—he on the left and she on the right. The well-worn leather was as comfortable as she remembered. A modified ship wheel stood in front of each chair, fixed upon a wooden panel littered with levers, knobs, and buttons. Amongst these controls were a central compass and a keyhole. Balancing the basket on her lap, she inserted the skeleton key in the hole but didn't turn it just yet.

Instead, she lifted the basket lid and peeked at Donatello. The sweater-clad turtle raised his head and opened his mouth as though to ask for more strudel. She smiled. "Don't worry, Donny. Snacks will be distributed once we reach a safe flying altitude."

"Quite right, quite right. But first we must safely stow our luggage in the underfoot compartment." Grand pressed a button on the floor with his boot. A section of the metal floor whooshed open, revealing a cubbyhole wherein he placed his knapsack and Clara's carpetbag. Then he strapped on his chair's safety harness, which resembled a gentleman's suspenders, and reached for the wicker basket. "It is a truth universally acknowledged that you can't very well fly an owl with a turtle in your lap."

Clara chuckled as she passed off Donny. "Reading *Pride and Prejudice* again?"

"I had to have something to keep me company while I waited for a certain Little Stargazer to follow my trail of clues." A glimmer of jest sparked in Grand's eyes. "Truth be told, she's a rather slow mover, that one."

"Is she, now?"

"Donatello moves faster."

She gasped. "Well, that hardly seems a fair assessment. Little Stargazer was unexpectedly waylaid, if you'll recall."

"I recall." All humor fled Grand's voice, and the mechanical butterflies sank into his wispy white hair as if weighted by the abrupt solemnity. "That certainly was unexpected."

The change in tone and allusion to her abduction raised gooseflesh on Clara's skin, and she found herself looking over her shoulder reflexively.

The time they'd spent in Bern's Old City had been so idyllic, so peaceful. A holiday from reality. But now their holiday was coming to an end, and they were going home to resume their everyday lives. The prospect shone light on a cobweb of dread that yet lingered in the corner of Clara's mind, sticky and hard to shake, no matter how vigorously she tried. Could she really move forward and stop looking over her shoulder for haunting specters? Mr. Forrester was incarcerated, yes, but he'd escaped a prison once before. Was it so unreasonable to fear he might do so again?

"What's wrong, child?"

Clara's gaze fell to her lap, where she'd unconsciously been wringing her gloved hands. "Do you think it's over, Grand? Is Mr. Forrester truly out of our lives for good?"

Placing a hand on her knee, Grand gave it a squeeze. "Yes, love, it's over. For good and all. I had the magistrate's personal assurance that young Forrester *will* serve time for his crimes. When he's released in the years to come, London is the last place he'll want to go. His creditors will have seized what remains of his assets and would likely kill him if he ever stepped foot on English soil again. Nay, I don't think he'd be so foolhardy as to try and reclaim his former life. 'Tis much more likely that he'll make a fresh start for himself someplace far, far away. Perhaps, when his fever of desperation breaks, he'll realize imprisonment has in fact set him free from the dire circumstances of his father's making and come to regret what he has done. But even if he never repents, one thing is certain, my girl. You needn't fear that man anymore."

The logic of Grand's words dusted away the cobwebs, freeing Clara's mind from their sticky grasp. She needn't look over her shoulder any longer. It was over. Truly, blessedly over.

A single butterfly alighted from Grand's hair and kissed her cheek with its wings.

Clara smiled. And now it was time to fly. "Where are my goggles?"

"Right where you left them, dear."

Ah, that they were. Hanging from one of the handles of Clara's steering wheel were her old goggles and fingerless leather gloves. She replaced her cotton gloves with the leather pair, and after strapping herself into the safety harness, donned her goggles. Grabbing a lever between the two steering wheels, she pulled it to the right, giving her control of the machine. Giddy anticipation fluttered in her stomach. "Hold on!"

Turning the skeleton key, Clara brought the owl to life.

This time, the machine didn't merely hum in a drowsy stupor. It awoke with a wide-eyed alertness—clockwork heart tick-tick-tocking with an exhilarating vitality that pulsated through the machine's body. Stirring Clara's blood. Awakening her desire to soar!

With a boot, she flipped a lever on the floor, and the owl rose on taloned feet. She pulled another lever on the control panel, feeling the clicking together of unseen gears. Unfurling its wings, the owl hopped from the loft and landed on the straw-covered barn floor. Grand cheered, and Clara laughed, even as her stomach tried to recall where God had originally placed it. Taking hold of two smaller levers, she flicked them back and forth. The owl walked with an awkward bouncing gait out of the barn and across the Spyri farm's sprawling fields of green.

The smiling sun embraced them, and a cloudless sky beckoned the owl to explore its boundless blue expanse. Clara turned a brass knob on the control panel, and as the owl raised its wings, she pressed a button. The machine leaned forward and sprang from the ground, alighting on the wind. Mighty wings outstretched to their full span; it flew silently as she directed from the helm of the great airship. With a turn of the wheel, the owl glided over the Spyri farmstead, bidding it a fond farewell. *Auf wiedersehen. Adieu!*

Consulting the compass, Clara set their course toward England and home. The owl followed the winding road that ribboned along the ground below and soared over a neighboring farmstead. Like miniatures in a toy shop, two figures sat on the porch of a quaint farmhouse. Could it be? Following an impish whim, she lowered their cruising altitude. Ah yes, it was their farmer friend who'd given them a ride!

"Get ready to wave, Grand."

Clara carefully decreased their elevation another few degrees and then banked to the left. In a wide arch, the owl glided in front of the farmhouse, where the farmer and a woman—presumably his wife—shot to their feet, slack-jawed and wide-eyed. Framed in the eyes of the owl, she and Grand waved in unison. The farmer gave a shout and fainted into his wife's arms. The impish pilots erupted in laughter as the owl completed its circle of the farmhouse and soared away, mounting to new heights.

Clara could not stop grinning. Not since her childhood had she felt so elated and carefree. Wonderstruck by anything and everything around her, from the dear old man at her side to the snowcapped Alps below, laced with meadows of edelweiss blossoms. This feeling, this flight, was only the beginning. For back in London, entombed in an attic, was a trunk full of maps waiting to be unpacked and unfurled.

Each one wrapped in a delightfully foolish dream.

Each one replete with the possibility of another merry adventure.

"How would you fancy a trip to Brussels for your birthday, Grand? According to *A Confectioner's Guide to European Sweets*, Belgian chocolate is a life-changing experience."

THE TIMES
LONDON, TUESDAY, JUNE 30, 1860

*Buckingham Palace Takes a Flight of Fancy under Its Wing!
    Last night, C. E. Drosselmeyer was welcomed at Buckingham Palace by Queen Victoria and Prince Albert amid
a dazzling spectacle of pomp and circumstance. In the presence
of the peerage and a select group of technological innovators, Mr.
Drosselmeyer was honored with the newly established title of Inventor to the Crown and awarded a special patronage from Prince
Albert. Invitations to the royal presentation and subsequent ball
were highly coveted, and rightly so, for never has the Season concluded with such an extraordinary finale!*

*   Mr. Drosselmeyer, once a simple clockmaker, came to fame three
months ago when his mystifying owl machine soared across Europe, enchanting the populace and capturing the imagination of
royalty. Now, with support of the prince, Mr. Drosselmeyer has
acquired a vast studio in which to continue his revolutionary work.
Mr. Drosselmeyer has endowed his humble clock shop to a former*

apprentice, one Mr. Theodore Kingsley, who is said to be courting his only grandchild, Miss Clara Marie Stanton. Miss Stanton is rumored to have recently purchased a ramshackle farm in the Swiss Plateau for reasons unknown. If these two hearts keep ticking in time, we may soon have news to report of a matrimonial nature.

Meanwhile, the Inventor to the Crown's daughter is ruffling feathers. Mrs. Heidi Stanton, an avowed animal advocate, recently collected a hefty purse from a private club taking bets on the identity of the Great Owl's pilot. Members of the club cried foul, claiming the wager she placed via telegram was invalid due to her knowledge of her father's exploits. However, at last night's ball, Mrs. Stanton expressed her intent to use the prize monies to construct two orphanages in the city—one for foundling children and one for disabled animals. By sunrise, public opinion swung like a clock's pendulum in her favor and prevented the matter from going to court. Plans for the orphanages are underway and ground-breaking is to begin next summer.

Until then, London waits with rapt anticipation to see what sensations and scandals Mr. Drosselmeyer and the Stantons create next!

THE FIFTH DAY OF CHRISTMAS
DECEMBER 29, 1860

In the capable hands of God, one's worst nightmare could transform into a fantastical dream that surpassed the scope of one's wildest imagination.

Nowadays, the Stanton family's eccentricities were oft front-page news, printed in bold black and white, and yet one and all of them were safe and well. Deliriously happy, no less. The Lord had taken care of everything. The glory was His and His alone.

Which suited Clara like a steaming cup of tea.

"Thought I might find you here."

Mr. Kingsley filled the library with his smile as the strains of holiday cheer skipped up the stairs from the ballroom in the Stantons' London home. Clara's stomach turned a somersault as warmth flooded her cheeks. My, but he looked fine tonight in his polished evening suit of black, offset with white pleated shirtwaist and gloves. Blond hair ever so slightly tamed with pomade. Chiseled face clean-shaven but for a neat frame of side whiskers. Demeanor confident and comfortable.

"Tired of dancing with me so soon, Miss Stanton?" Mr. Kingsley feigned dejection.

"So soon?" Clara scoffed from her place on the sofa. "Why, I have danced with you seven times tonight. *Seven*, my good sir. Plus, twice with Grand, three times with Papa, and once with Prince Albert himself. All while trying to evade frolicking foxes, cavorting cats, and a goat intent on eating the flowers in my hair." She waved a gloved hand to the red roses situated in her carefully arranged tresses. "Do you have any notion how exhausting it is to exude grace whilst a bucktoothed goat is nipping at you from behind?"

Mr. Kingsley chuckled. "Hardly."

"Well, let me tell you, I deserve a medal, and my feet deserve a rest. Which is precisely why I hid away to join Beatrix here." She patted the wee hedgehog rolled into a prickled pillow beside her voluminous skirt of shining red taffeta.

"While you're certainly entitled to a respite, my dear, you are missed, nonetheless. Mr. Wyld, in particular, has been asking for you. The man's quite keen to see your finished manuscript." Mr. Kingsley glanced at the open journal upon her lap. "How goes the writing?"

"I've made it to Bern at last." She used her silver pen to mark her place in the journal before setting it on an adjacent table. "*An Adventurous Lady's Guide to Travel* will be completed by the first of February, as agreed upon with my publisher. If the good gentlemen at Barton Books can wait until then, my cartographer will have to content himself in like fashion."

A smile touched her face. How odd those words sounded together! *My* publisher. *My* cartographer. Though she'd signed the contract months ago, Clara's mind still reeled at the incredible manner in which her dreams were coming true. When Mr. Wyld—creator of Wyld's Great Globe and Geographer to the Queen—had approached Barton Books with an offer to design custom maps for each of the locations in her book, she'd fainted for the first time in her life. Mr. Wyld's increasing enthusiasm for the project was a daily source of amazement.

As Papa's violin commenced with another jig, she reclined once more against the plush sofa cushions. "Is that why you've sought me out, Mr. Kingsley? To restore my company to the party for Mr. Wyld's benefit?"

"I'm loath to admit my motives are without altruism. Rather, I was hoping to claim a moment of your company for myself."

Her heart gave way to palpitations. Was it her imagination, or did the man's eyes attain a deeper shade of green when illumined by gaslight? "Why, then, do you linger at the door, sir?" She inclined her head toward the section of the sofa occupied by the perpetually napping hedgehog. "Come stake your claim."

Grinning at her invitation, Mr. Kingsley removed the prickled hog-cushion to a nearby chair and took possession of the seat beside Clara, drawing her weary feet into his lap. He removed her silken slippers and proceeded to massage her swollen soles without remarking upon how her stockings must reek.

Oh, how she loved this man!

"How goes the party? Mum has things well in hand, I trust." Since their return to London, Mum had proven herself quite the hostess. Her spirited soirees had evolved from a curiosity to "the thing" seemingly overnight. Many families had chosen to stay in town, despite the end of the Season, in the hopes they might receive an invitation to the Stanton abode for a taste of Mrs. Stanton's signature vegetarian cuisine and a peek at her renowned menagerie.

"She does, indeed. Just before I ventured upstairs, Mrs. S. remarked to your father that the house was a merry beehive, buzzing with life and joviality. Then she partnered off with Dudley the Dane for the next dance. As I made my leave, the dwarf and giant were eliciting raised brows from first-time guests and knowing smiles from regular visitors."

She would have it no other way. "And what of Grand? Is he still holding up beneath the crush of recognition?"

"Last I saw, Drosselmeyer and His Royal Highness were tucked in a corner of the parlor, examining clockwork butterflies and discussing aerodynamics." Mr. Kingsley nodded toward the table's pile of gold-gilded envelopes with elaborate wax seals. "More invitations?"

"Dozens. With more arriving every day." All of London's most well-to-do families wished to host the Inventor to the Crown and his family at their country estates or townhomes. If they wished it, their social calendars could be booked through next Season. Grand, of course, cared not a whit. His head was too occupied with whimsical notions to spare a thought for his new standing in society.

Clara pursed her lips, noting the pinched lines along Mr. Kingsley's brow. Poor Theodore. Every missive on that table must cut with the painful reminder that he'd yet to receive a single one from Kingsley Court. Not a letter. Not even a telegram. Just silence, dismissive and resounding. She laid a gloved hand upon his sleeve. "Have you had a reply today?"

The question put an end to her foot massage. "No, and I don't expect I will. Never did, really. My father is a mountain, stone cold and immovable, once his mind has been decided, and he carved my brothers in his image from birth. Their allegiance to him and remembrance of my mother didn't exactly cultivate affection toward me."

A deep breath loosened his clenched jaw. "It's not in my power to change them. Nor was it my intention. When I posted that letter to Kingsley Court, I did so because the Lord asked it of me. I extended forgiveness where it was unlikely to be received—not in the hopes of gaining acceptance in return, but as an act of obedience. Reply or no reply, I am a child of God, and that is an inheritance no man can revoke."

Just when she thought she couldn't possibly love this man to a greater degree, he went and astounded her all over again. "I love you, Theodore Kingsley."

A lopsided grin relaxed his countenance. "I love you back, Clara Marie Stanton. Which reminds me . . ." Mr. Kingsley withdrew a rectangular box from his pocket. "This is for you."

A foot massage and a present? How had she become so thoroughly blessed? Clara snatched the box with a squeal, tore off the ribbon, and threw back the lid. A shining gold chatelaine rested on a bed of red velvet. The medallion was fashioned into the head of an owl, and from it dangled three chains, each attached to a unique treasure. Her mouth fell agape. Completely bereft of words.

"Drosselmeyer helped me with the detailing." Mr. Kingsley's complexion reddened, lending his smile an endearing nervousness. "I wanted you to have the essential gadgets for travel and no other burden. Just a pocket watch for catching every train and ship on time, a compass for navigating cities unknown, and a retractable telescope so you can always find your way home by the North Star."

If her heart swelled any more, it would burst. "It's perfect." Alighting from the sofa, Clara dashed across the library's thick carpet with the strains of Papa's violin fast on her heels. "Let's try the telescope."

As she pushed aside the curtain and opened the door to the balcony, a December wind rushed in, raising gooseflesh on her exposed skin. The marble balcony was frigid beneath her stockinged feet, but she was too excited to be bothered with shoes and shawls. If she froze in this happy state, all the better.

The night sky was clear and the stars bright, as though London's smog knew better than to interfere with the Magi's journey. With upturned gaze, she looked through the telescope. "Oh . . . Polaris is quite pleased with himself this night. Come, look."

"I don't need to, Clara. I found my North Star months ago."

The violin turned sentimental, beckoning her with heart-stirring notes. Clara turned slowly and found Mr. Kingsley kneeling on the balcony. Stars . . . was he about to—

"God has been too good to me already, but I've asked Him for one more blessing I don't deserve. The privilege of calling you my wife."

Her breath caught, and the strains from the violin seemed to draw closer, building with emotion.

Mr. Kingsley produced a small velvet box and revealed a gold ring. "You have given me the home I've always dreamed of calling mine and the loving family I've always prayed would call me theirs. Because of you, I no longer have to wander. I can finally build a life for myself, and I want to build it with you." The violin soared on a series of notes, reaching for the heavens. "I want to wake up every day and know you'll be a part of it. Miss Clara Marie Stanton, will you marry me?"

Clara cupped a hand to his cheek. "My days are yours, Mr. Theodore Kingsley. Come storm or fair weather."

The violin screeched to a halt. "Does that poetic falderal mean yes or no?"

Papa? Her head whipped about in time to catch the curtains rustle.

A masculine grunt indicated that a feminine swat had found its mark in a rotund stomach. "Quiet, George. You're going to ruin our duckling's romantic moment."

"Am not. I serenaded them, didn't I?"

An aged timbre gave a firm shush. "Don't squabble, don't squabble. You'll give away our position."

Clara bit back a smile, heat engulfing her face despite the frosty presence of winter. Theodore stood, and she draped her arms about his neck, whispering in his ear. "One last chance to revoke your proposal and make your escape. Are you absolutely certain you wish to marry into the absurdity that is my family? For the lovable trio behind the curtain are included in my dowry."

Another masculine grunt signaled Mum's ire. "Told you they could hear us."

Clara laughed as strong arms encircled her waist and drew her nearer still, whisking the breath from her lungs.

Theodore's jade eyes locked onto hers, gleaming with a love beyond the descriptive powers of even the finest poetic falderal. "Dearest Clara, I would rather be absurd with you than normal with anyone else."

"Then let the adventure begin."

Clara kissed him then, well and true, amid triumphant violin accompaniment and uproarious applause from the owners of three pairs of shoes peeking beneath the curtain.

Author's Note

James Wyld

James Wyld (1812–1887) was a renowned geographer and cartographer, as was his father James Wyld Sr. James Wyld Jr. became the owner of the family mapmaking business after the death of his father in 1836. Over the course of his career, he was elected as a fellow of the Royal Geographical Society, gained the title of Geographer to the Queen and HRH Prince Albert, and became a member of Parliament.

Wyld's Great Globe

(Also known as Wyld's Globe or Wyld's Monster Globe)

Wyld's Great Globe was a one-of-a-kind attraction located in London's Leicester Square from 1851–1861. Within the domed hall was a hollow globe, measuring sixty feet in diameter. For the price of a shilling, visitors could climb raised platforms and admire plaster models of the world's continents, oceans, rivers, and mountains on the globe's incurved surface. Galleries throughout the globe advertised Wyld's business with displays of his surveying equipment alongside maps and globes he'd designed.

Geographer James Wyld Jr. initially submitted the globe for inclusion in the Great Exhibition with the hopes of it being constructed within the Crystal Palace, but his proposal was denied due to the globe's substantial size and his desire to use it to promote his trade. Instead, Wyld persuaded the owners of Leicester Square to give him a ten-year lease, and the globe was built there. In 1851, the same year as the Great Exhibition, the Great Globe opened to much success. However, once the exhibition ended and the vast crowds dwindled, interest in the globe waned. By 1852, the novelty had been mostly forgotten by the public. When Wyld's lease expired, the globe was demolished and sold for scrap. An engraving of Wyld's Monster Globe can be viewed on the Victoria and Albert Museum's website.

BIBLIOGRAPHY

Bly, Nellie. *Around the World in Seventy-Two Days*. New York City: Pictorial Weeklies Company, 1890.

Bly, Nellie. *Ten Days in a Mad-House*. New York City: Ian L. Munro, 1887.

Dumas, Alexandre. *The Nutcracker*. 1845.

Hoffmann, E. T. A. *The Nutcracker and the Mouse King*. Berlin: In der Realschulbuchhandlung, 1816.

Verne, Jules. *Around the World in Eighty Days*. Paris: Pierre-Jules Hetzel & Cie, 1873.

ACKNOWLEDGMENTS

Dianne, my best friend and beloved Mama. As much as this book is my accomplishment, it is also your accomplishment. You were the one who fostered my imagination and creativity. You were the one who lovingly praised the drivel I called poetry and that first "book" with its illustrations in scented marker. You were the one who instilled in me a love of history and story. When I started to dream of becoming an author, you were the one who immediately sought out writing resources, classes, and conferences. Over the years, you've supported me with unconditional love, unrelenting encouragement, and an unwavering belief that one day my dream would come true. When I'd resigned myself to the likelihood of that never happening, you were the one who dared to keep dreaming big. I'll forever be grateful that we get to experience this dream-come-true together. Thank you, Mama. For everything. I love you more!

Jeremiah, Tabitha, and Ashley Lynn, the best siblings a big sister could ask for! If "home is your people," as Drosselmeyer says, then y'all are my home. I'm so proud of each one of you and so grateful to have all three of you in my life. Thank you for celebrating every single milestone in my writing journey—from the minuscule to the monumental—with boisterous enthusiasm! Thank you for being there on the dark days and encouraging me to keep going when I wanted to quit. I wouldn't be here without your steadfast love and support.

Norma Jean, my dearly missed Granny and fellow voracious reader, who always believed in this dream of mine and told me never to give up. I'll always treasure your books and the last letter you sent. I wish you were here so I could give you a hug and a signed copy of a book with my name on the cover. I know you'd be tickled pink!

Teri Dawn Smith, my writing teacher and mentor. Meeting you was a pivotal moment in my writing journey! You gave me a foundation in the craft of writing, introduced me to the Christian fiction community, and encouraged me to believe that becoming a published author when I grew up was a dream worth pursuing, despite the difficulty and the odds. I wouldn't be here without your influence, and for that, I thank you! I'm so grateful for your continued support.

Chawna Schroeder, my bosom friend and kindred spirit. When I was a painfully shy teenager, tucked away in my room with a stack of books for company, I used to pray for God to give me a friend. Just one friend who would be my Diana Barry. My Samwise Gamgee. I'm so glad He gave me you! I cannot adequately express how much your friendship has impacted my life for the better. Thank you for the countless pep talks, critiques, prayers, check-in texts, movie nights, brainstorming sessions, and lengthy phone calls!

Amanda Luedeke, my incredible agent, who worked so hard to make this dream-come-true possible! Thank you for taking a chance on a young writer who was still figuring out who she was as a storyteller. Thank you for sticking with me through health crises, unexpected delays, and countless rejections. Thank you for believing in me and this unconventional story when no one else did! Your guidance, expertise, and determination have been indispensable.

Michelle Griep, Amanda Barratt, and Sharon Hinck, wonderful writers and dear friends. Thank you for giving your time to thoughtfully critique this book and make it stronger! Thank you for cheering me on and praying me through. Your friendship and support are a blessing!

The amazing team at Bethany House! Special shout-out to Rachael Betz, Anne Van Solkema, Raela Schoenherr, and my editors Jessica Sharpe, Jennifer Veilleux, and Hannah Ahlfield. Thank you for making my biggest dream come true, for making this novel of my heart stronger, and for being so unbelievably encouraging and excited about this story!

Lastly, I must give all praise and honor to God. I abso-bloomin-lutely could not have written this book without Him! Thank you, Emmanuel, for being ever patient and always gracious when this tense-shouldered, white-knuckled girl of yours tries to hang on to what you've mercifully promised to carry. *Soli Deo gloria.*

Angela Bell is a twenty-first-century lady with nineteenth-century sensibilities. She resides in Texas with her charming pup, Mr. Bingley Crosby. One might categorize her books as historical romance, but Angela likes to describe them as "a cuppa Victorian whimsy" because it sounds so much more poetical. Whenever you need a respite from the modern-day hustle, you're welcome to visit her parlor at AuthorAngelaBell .com, where she can be found waiting with a pot of tea and a great book.

Sign Up for Angela's Newsletter

Keep up to date with Angela's latest news on book releases and events by signing up for her email list at the link below.

AuthorAngelaBell.com

FOLLOW ANGELA ON SOCIAL MEDIA

Author Angela Bell   @AuthorAngelaBell